BLUE

BLUE

Walter Jones

Spellbound Pictures Ltd USA LLC
Spellbound Pictures Ltd Books
Los Angeles, California

Spellbound Pictures Ltd Books

Dedication

BLUE is dedicated to the memory
of my loving parents,
Mary Louise and Russell Donald Jones

Acknowledgements

First, I thank God for this incredible journey and education.

A special thanks to Pamela Edwards McClafferty
Without Pamela, the story of Blue would never have come to fruition. She is my friend, my mentor, my editor, my advocate, and my publisher. She has worked tirelessly for years. In return for her labor, she only asked that I do the same for another unknown author whose voice must be heard. She is a guardian of the arts and of those things that inspire and enlighten humanity. She is rare and precious.

I am thankful for the support, patience, and love of
My wife, Lesa Jones
My sisters and brothers, Dorothy Jones Connie,
    Rebecca Jones Randall, Russell Jones,
    Kenneth Jones, and Gerald Jones
My children, Walter "Boo," Nicole, Jason, Kenneth,
    Eteria, and Marcus
My best friend, Keith Spencer
My cousin/brother, Urie (Rick) Clark
My mother- and father-in-law, Margaret and
    Carnell Drummer
The late Clemine and Richard Derrick
Joan Derrick
Mark McClafferty
Clint Smith
Dennis Irvin
Christopher Benson
Kay Benson
Melody Rosales
The late Gloria Michaels

Mary Anderson
Debra Thomas
Lisa Orloff
Marilyn Graham
Pinkie Harris
Natalie Stigger
Carol and James Fujimoto
Walter Jones
January 2014

Family Tree

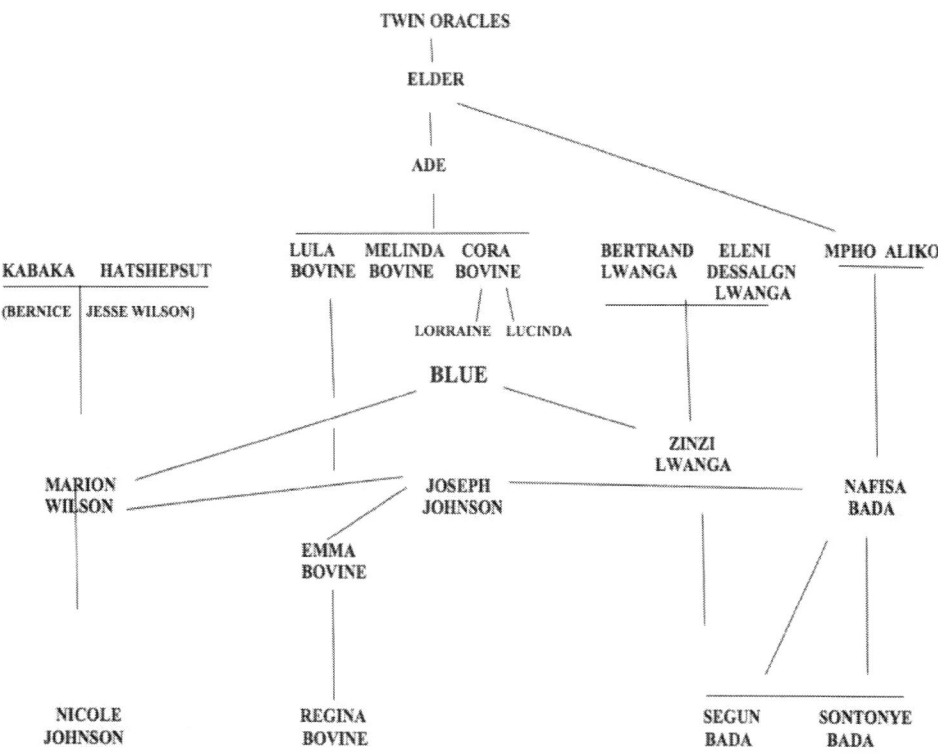

Table of Contents

Part I
Ancient Prophets proclaimed:
The children of Africa are the people of
yesterday and the day after tomorrow.
The day after tomorrow begins the
moment BLUE ends.

Nicole and Regina

1990, Chicago, New Orleans

Chapter 1

On this unusually hot Chicago summer's day in 1990, Nicole Johnson stood first in line at the bus stop. Fumbling through her purse, she searched for her bus pass. Her best friend, Regina, constantly warned her about opening her purse on the city streets. That warning was far from her mind as the old Number 4 slowly lumbered toward her up Cottage Grove, swaying from side to side, its tires trying to avoid the sting of the steamy pavement. *Where did I put that thing?* she thought. It dawned on her as the bus came to an abrupt halt and its doors swung open. She reached into her skirt pocket and pulled out the pass.

Nicole's delicate profile and high cheekbones were reminiscent of eastern Ethiopian royalty. Heads turned as she maneuvered her stunning five-foot-eight-inch frame through the crowded bus. The air conditioning was obviously out. Perspiration gathered on her mahogany brow. Her full, well-formed lips parted slightly, trying to drink in the stifling air. She let out a sigh as she found a seat toward the back of the bus. Taking a tissue from her pocket, Nicole arched her regal neck and dabbed her forehead. In this sweltering heat, the twenty-minute ride from 71st to 49th Street would feel like an eternity.

Nicole's large raven eyes reflected a confidence to the world. One could almost get lost looking into them, and only then would one notice a hint of melancholy deep in their recesses. That sadness was more pronounced today as she sat back and looked around the bus at the traveling sideshow.

Before her in the crowded aisle, a woman stood providing rush-hour bump thrills for every pervert on board while teenagers blasted their boom boxes and an elderly woman fussed at her invisible husband. A drunk babbled about women being nothing more than low-down whores. A young mother, holding an infant in her arms, started screaming at her toddler seated beside her. Nicole shook her head and stared out the window, but the show outside was even less tolerable.

In days gone by, Cottage Grove had been one of the most prestigious avenues in Chicago. Lined with theaters and ballrooms, its breathtaking architecture was second to none. Now, it was nothing more than miles of urban blight.

Her parents had scrimped and saved for years to move her, their only child, away from all of this to give her a better life and education. Nicole loved them for their sacrifice, but she had felt out of place in the predominately white middle-class community where they had lived and she was known as the little colored girl, Nicole. Often, she wondered how she would have survived on these streets.

Teenagers stood on the street corners flashing gang signs, selling drugs, cursing, and disrespecting themselves and everyone around them. Sixteen-year-old drug dealers in their Mercedes cruised down side streets laden with broken glass and debris. The homeless rummaged through trash cans. Paper-thin women with bloodshot eyes, women who might be twenty but looked fifty, sold their bodies for one more fix. The mentally ill hid amongst the boarded-up buildings. In spite of all of this, Nicole knew that somehow the purpose to her life was here.

At the peak of the civil rights movement, her only marching was down the aisle at her kindergarten graduation. Even then, she remembered the pride and the purpose enveloping the African American community. It had inspired her and stayed with her as she grew up, and her purpose ultimately became clear. She graduated from Howard University in Washington, DC, where she earned her MBA. Then she returned to the city to work.

The greatest pain of her life came on her twenty-third birthday with her parents' untimely death. On Interstate 94, a semi-trailer smashed Marion and Joseph Johnson's car into the wall under the 11th Street Viaduct. She missed them more than she could say. Often she talked to them, and today was no exception.

I know I've asked you this a thousand times, Daddy, but how did the '60s' hope transform into the '90s' despair? Why did it happen? Someone should write a book about the Invisible Master.

Nicole shifted irritably on the seat. That brutal *Invisible Master* worked undetected and downsized the old slaves' progeny. It was such an insidious creature. Nicole wondered if it might annihilate her whole race as history recorded it as the self-destructive tendency of Black Americans. *Oh Momma! If I had the power, I would stop all of this by any means necessary, but I don't. Not yet.*

Suddenly there was a loud screech. The bus driver slammed on the brakes to avoid a car that was jumping lanes. All of the passengers in the aisle tumbled. Nicole's shoulder smashed against the seat in front of her. Moans and groans were heard.

"Let me off this damn bus!" the young mother yelled, carrying her infant and dragging the toddler behind her.

The bus driver pulled closer to the curb at 63rd Street and released the rear exit door. The young woman stepped off the bus with the infant. The toddler was left to climb down by himself. Afraid of falling, he wouldn't move.

"If you don't get your stupid ass off that bus, I'm gonna beat the shit out of you!" the mother yelled.

The toddler froze in place. Hastily the woman laid the infant on the sidewalk and snatched the boy from the step.

Nicole watched the woman slap her son across the face, and a rage passed through Nicole like a flame through a wind tunnel. She jumped to her feet.

"Stop it! You hear me? Stop it!" she yelled, banging on the window.

"Mind your own damn business!" the mother ranted.

Nicole's interference further enraged the woman. Slaps turned into punches. The child fell to the ground and covered his head.

I've got to stop this, Nicole thought to herself. She rushed toward the rear door.

Without warning, the sunny sky blackened. The wind gusted so violently that it rocked the bus. Just as Nicole reached the exit, the door slammed shut. She banged her fist on the glass and yelled at the driver.

"Open this door!"

"I'm trying to, lady. The release handle is jammed."

Sirens pierced the air. Flashing blue lights reflected in the bus windows. A police officer rushed to the aid of the child. Two other officers tried to subdue the mother. She kicked, clawed, and bit the officers until one of them wrestled her arms behind her back and cuffed her. Once she realized she was overpowered, the mother glared at the bus and spit toward the exit door window where Nicole stood.

"Come out here and I'll kick your ass too!" screamed the mother as a powerful blast of wind swept a trashcan high off the ground.

Paper and broken bottles flew through the air. The handcuffs rendered the young woman helpless. A broken wine bottle catapulted toward her and smashed into her brow. A jagged piece of glass lodged in her forehead. The police had covered their faces, unaware of the blood gushing from her puncture. In seconds, it covered her face. Her chest heaved. Her body jerked spastically. Her trembling legs caused her knees to buckle. She couldn't break her fall, and her face hit the concrete with such a tremendous impact it forced the embedded bottle through the top of her head.

Nicole covered her mouth and gagged.

A crowd gathered. The police worked frantically to remove her handcuffs.

Nicole saw the baby crying in the squad car and the toddler being restrained by a police officer.

"Mommy, Mommy!" the toddler yelled.

Everyone on the bus was in shock. Even the drunk in the back was sobered. Nicole pulled the exit cord, but the driver ignored her signal and laid on the horn, breaking up the gapers before hurriedly pulling out into the heavy traffic.

Back in her seat, Nicole was shaking. She placed her head in her hands to calm down. *At the next stop, I will get off and walk back.* A few moments had passed when she noticed a hollow silence. She raised her head.

Everyone was gone. Through the windows, she only saw the star-filled sky. She got up, went to the exit door, and pulled the emergency release cord. Neither the front nor rear doors opened.

"I'm sorry, but you cannot exit the bus at this time," a deep baritone voice echoed.

She looked around the bus and saw no one. Stepping down to the front exit door, she peered outside the window. No one was there either.

"Who said that? What's going on?"

"For your own safety, please step away from the exit door," the voice said.

Nicole backed up the steps into the aisle. "Just get me out of here. The Transit Authority is going to compensate me for this!"

"The door will open in a moment. I strongly advise you to look carefully before attempting to exit."

The doors parted slightly. Nicole peered out. There were no buildings, no people, no trees, nothing. She held onto the bar, looking down. There were only stars beneath the bus. It was as if they were suspended in outer space.

"Where's the ground?"

"Nicole, do not be alarmed," the voice said as the interior lights popped on.

She backed up the steps, unzipped her purse, and clutched her mace. "Enough with the games. Where are you? Show yourself."

"As you wish."

Below her, the front doors of the bus opened wider. "I know all of this is disconcerting," the deep baritone voice said more clearly, yet still coming from outside. "I must talk to you, Nicole. I am coming aboard."

Nicole backed down the aisle. "If you come near me, you'll regret it."

"Then I will make sure not to come too near."

The voice was colored by an intriguing, melodious accent and fit the stature of the tall stranger in his early fifties ascending the steps. His complexion was flawless. His features were East African with eyes of the deepest ebony she had ever seen. His full lips framed a smile of perfect white teeth. From his finely tailored midnight-blue suit to his perfectly manicured fingernails, he projected an air of sophistication. Still, Nicole did not let his appearance disarm her.

"Who are you? How do you know my name?"

"I am truly sorry. I didn't mean to be rude. My name is Bertrand Lwanga. And I know much more about you than your name, Nicole Johnson."

He stepped toward her.

"I told you. Don't come near." Nicole raised her mace. "I'm not playing, damn it!"

The man stopped. "I know you think you are having a bizarre dream. What you are experiencing is outside of your personal acceptance. From your parapsychology in college, I know you are familiar with the concepts of telepathy and psychokinesis."

"How do you know so much about me?"

"At this very moment, you are riding the bus home," he said, ignoring her. "In less than three minutes, you will be at your stop. At the same time, you are here with me. Using an ancient method of telekinesis, I have summoned you here. You have a mission that must be accomplished one year from today. Powers have been bequeathed to you. I will teach you to use them."

Nicole kept her eyes on him while she grabbed the back of the nearest seat for support.

"You are perfectly sane," he continued as he walked toward her. "Our time together is almost over, but understand that your powers have already been unleashed. Today you controlled the elements with your rage. You do not know the hidden powers you possess."

Nicole sprang back as he stopped in front of her, but not before he dropped a business card into her purse. Looking into his ebony eyes, she wanted to refute what he was saying, but could not collect her thoughts.

"Go home and rest, Nicole. I'll see you tonight. We will celebrate. Tomorrow is your thirtieth birthday and the beginning of your magnificent new life."

With those words, he retraced his steps to the exit. When the doors opened, rays of brilliant blue light flashed. The beams were so startling that Nicole had to cover her eyes.

When she had uncovered them, Bertrand was gone, and once again she was on the crowded bus only a block from her stop. She pulled the cord and hurried to the exit door.

Once on 49th Street, she stood momentarily in the middle of the sidewalk. Taking a deep breath, she postured herself. Then, as Black women had done for centuries, she walked forward as if nothing had happened. This grin-and-bear-it legacy made it easier to nullify her experience.

***

"Hello, house. I'm home! Lord knows I'm happy to be here!" she exclaimed, opening the door to her noble old brownstone.

Her home lifted her spirits. Reigning on Drexel Street, on the borderline of the exclusive Hyde Park and the decaying Grand Boulevard communities, the brownstone epitomized her personal declaration of independence. Except for the major electrical, carpentry, and plumbing work, it was entirely her labor of love. She had stripped and stained the oak wood. Walls and ceilings were replastered and painted. The kitchen and bathrooms were retiled and wallpapered. Decorating the home, she had combined European antiques with African designs. From tapestries to bathroom fixtures, the home was picture perfect.

Nicole picked up her mail and climbed the stairs, gliding her hand over the oak banister. This staircase was the masterpiece of her home, curving gently from the foyer to the second floor. At the top of the stairs, she glanced back.

With the help of a local architect, she had designed the staircase to give the illusion of ivory piano keys suspended in midair. She loved this view and always looked back to admire it.

Most of her associates were in awe of her home but never understood why a single woman would want to be burdened with the responsibility and upkeep of such a large residence. She didn't care what any of them thought. She had acquired her home for a third of the price of a similar dwelling in Hyde Park. It was her money and her life, and this was her castle. She entered her room, dropped the mail on her bed, and took off her clothes.

For the last few years, she had slept alone. The bond between her parents had set a high standard. Marion and Joseph Johnson had enjoyed good times and had always shown each other deep and loving respect. She wanted to share that quality of love in her own life, so she poured her energy into her work until that special someone came along.

In the bath, she turned on the shower and stepped in, still thinking about her parents. Every summer, Marion and Joseph had held company picnics for their construction company employees. Inevitably, her father played basketball with the younger men. From the picnic bench, her mother would call out for him to be careful.

With a sly grin and an upturned eyebrow, her father would laugh. "I've got to stay in shape to keep up with you, baby!"

"If that's the case," Marion Johnson would call out, "you need to save that energy for later!"

This was always Joseph's cue to stop playing with his younger teammates. "I've got to go now, fellas. My woman needs me."

Nicole smiled as she dried off. Would she ever have a relationship like theirs?

She put on her summer nightgown, an extra-large man's T-shirt, and flopped across her king-size bed. For over twenty minutes, she scanned the TV channels. Although it wasn't a heavy news day, there was no coverage on the horrific accident. Obviously, life on the streets wasn't newsworthy. Maybe it was just as well. That was all that was needed, another story about an abusive Black mother gone berserk.

Nicole sat up on her bed, turned off the TV, and sorted the bills and junk mail. *What's this?* She examined a tattered old envelope that looked as if it had been stuck for years in the crack of some loading dock. Originally it was addressed to Nicole Johnson, Howard University, Washington DC. The address had been changed and forwarded several times. The postmark was July 12, 1983. *That was eight years ago,* she thought.

Although this mysterious letter intrigued her, Nicole was apprehensive. She carefully opened the seal. On the outside of the greeting card was a picture of a beautiful African princess with features identical to Nicole's. On the inside panel was inscribed:

> *To our precious daughter. Happy Birthday!*
> *You have always been the Princess in our lives.*

> *Dear Nicole,*

10

Your father spotted this card in a little shop downtown. He said it reminded him so much of his baby girl, he had to buy it. After he brought it home, we started talking about how we have always spent your birthdays together. We know how busy you are working to complete your master's thesis, so we've decided to fly to DC for your birthday. Your father wanted to surprise you. He doesn't know I've slipped this note in the card. He hasn't accepted you've grown up yet. So I thought I'd warn you in case you had planned some other overnight visitor.

We'll see you on the fifteenth.

Love, Momma

At first, she thought receiving this communiqué was a miracle. Then the tears began to flow. She grabbed her pillow and hugged it tightly.

"They died coming to see me. Lord, no!" Nicole lay back, paralyzed.

The day's emotional rollercoaster ride crashed down on her, shutting down her mind. She spiraled into a coma-like sleep.

***

Brrring, brrring, brrring, brrring.

The telephone awakened Nicole and she reached for it.

"Nicole? Nicole? Are you there, girl?"

"I'm here, Gina! I'm just turning on the light."

"Were you sleeping?"

"I was trying to forget about today! I'm so happy to hear your voice!

"What happened?"

Nicole recapped the events of the afternoon.

"No wonder you passed out. I'll be right over."

"No, Gina. I think I'm going back to sleep."

"Are you sure? You might be fooling me. You're really getting ready for your date with Birdsong Mugamba. Didn't he say he was seeing you tonight?"

"Very funny. Bertrand Lwanga was a figment of my imagination—just a dream. I know it sounds strange, but that's all there is to it. I'm fine, Gina, really."

"Then we'll have to get a psychiatrist to analyze that dream! Don't forget we're going out for your birthday."

"I won't forget. Eight o'clock." Then, before her best friend could ask, Nicole answered Regina's question. "Really, I'm fine. I'll see you tomorrow."

Nicole snuggled under the covers, thinking of Regina. They had met in 1984 while waiting to be interviewed for jobs at the Brummel Advertising Agency. Nicole was vying for an executive position. Regina was looking for a secretarial job. Before their separate interviews, they spoke briefly. Nicole was astounded when Regina quoted Joseph Johnson.

"People always ask why one goes into business. I've never heard a better answer than 'for the continuance of the business.'"

"That's my father's quote!" Nicole had exclaimed. "Where did you hear it?"

"At the Palmer House Hotel here in Chicago in 1981. It was my twenty-first birthday! Joseph Johnston was speaking. Were you there too?"

Maybe Nicole and Regina would always have become fast friends, but Joseph's quote cemented their bond. Regina was hired. Nicole was not. Months later, Regina telephoned Nicole about an opening for an ad executive. Brummel was under pressure to hire a female minority. Nicole's credentials were impressive, and she was hired to head the department that developed campaigns for Brummel's clients to attract minority audiences.

Within a few months, Nicole was able to transfer Regina to her department. Nicole's advanced technical skills paired with Regina's natural creativity made their department one of the top producers in the agency. Both women were graduates of difficult schools, Howard University with honors for Nicole and the Dusable High School of Hard Knocks with honors for Regina.

By 1988, they had signed several major clients and amassed a small fortune for Brummel. They reassessed their position and decided to found their own agency, Fresh, Inc. Moving into a building across from the old South Shore Country Club on 71st Street, they saved several months' rent by renovating their own offices.

When word hit the street that they had gone independent, several companies contacted them. One such company was Futrob International, Inc., the third-largest multinational technology and consulting corporation in the world.

Just before she left the office today, Nicole had set up a teleconference with Futrob. Fresh, Inc. was vying for the advertising account for one of Futrob's mysterious international subsidiaries based in Botswana. Nicole smiled as she drifted off to sleep. Capturing this account would ensure their success. Regina would be very pleased.

Chapter 2

Sleep once again spun its concentric circles. No sooner had her eyes closed than Nicole found herself floating in a pale blue sky filled with billowing clouds. Her arms spread out like wings. In total peace, she glided through the heavens. At last, she decided to come back down to Earth. Turning over on her back, she slowly descended toward a field of beautiful African violets. A gentle breeze lowered her onto a blanket of lavender and gold. As the flower petals tickled her face and caressed her body, she heard a distant voice.

"Awaken, beautiful one, awaken. It is time to go."

Nicole opened her eyes. Bertrand Lwanga stood at the side of her bed smiling down at her. "What are you doing in my home!" She grabbed the phone and frantically dialed 9-1-1.

"Chicago Police Department, how may I help you?"

Nicole gave the intruder the *you're-in-trouble-now* look. "A man has broken into my home! Please send help!"

"Yes, I know. Bertrand Lwanga has come to pick you up."

She dropped the phone.

"Nicole, dear, calm yourself. I have only come to take you to your birthday celebration. If you continue to toss and turn, you will ruin the beautiful garment the flowers have woven for you. You cannot fully appreciate how beautiful you are lying down. Come look at yourself in the mirror."

Nicole stared at her reflection. Deep hues of blue and magenta were interlaced with streams of gold in the spectacular African gown that clung to her slender, tall frame. Her hair was adorned with a delicate diamond tiara accented by a blue sapphire necklace and bracelet trimmed in miniature diamonds.

Lwanga stood behind Nicole, staring at her reflection. "As I gaze upon you, Nicole, I see perfection personified. Nefertiti would have bowed to your beauty."

Nicole turned around to face Lwanga. "What's happening? Is this a dream, or are you an apparition determined to haunt me?"

"Nicole, dear, your beauty is only surpassed by your intelligence. I mean you no harm. That should be obvious to you by now."

"Nothing is obvious, and I have no reason to trust you."

"Let's see what you think after this evening."

"A hallucination has just offered me a challenge? Well, Mr. Bernard Lwanga—what is it you do?"

"I am a Philanthropist, Nicole."

"Well, Mr. Philanthropist, let's finish this dream, so I can be rid of you."

"As you wish, mademoiselle." Lwanga opened Nicole's bedroom door and bowed as she exited.

The moment Nicole stepped out of her front door, she noticed the streetlights seemed dimmer than usual and the landscape in her yard was entirely different. Homes had replaced vacant lots across the street. The buildings looked new and were made of beautiful bricks. Even in the night shadows, every lawn appeared full, green, and freshly manicured. The parkway was aligned with towering elm and maple trees. The half-ravaged block now had the appearance of a quaint hamlet. Shiny new classic-model cars were parked on the street, including a 1960 powder-blue Thunderbird convertible with a white interior.

Lwanga hurried ahead of Nicole to open the passenger door. Once inside himself, he started the T-Bird while Nicole reached over her shoulder and came up short.

"Where is the seat belt?"

"Most automobiles don't have them yet."

"What do you mean?"

"Today is July 14, 1960. I thought you would enjoy celebrating your birthday on the day of your actual birth. We have another twenty-seven minutes. 12:12 a.m. was when you were born. By then, we will have reached our destination."

He turned off Michigan Avenue onto Congress Parkway and drove the T-Bird up to the entrance of the Congress Hotel. Two doormen bowed and opened their car doors.

15

"Good evening, Your Highness."
"Is everything prepared as I ordered?"
"Yes, Your Highness!"

Nicole was treated like royalty. Although flattering, it seemed decadent and unfitting. She sensed the Black doormen were only painting on a guise of respect. In this year of 1960, they seemed insulted that they had to show any consideration to her and Bertrand. Lwanga was unaffected. He spoke to the doormen as mere underlings. Nicole reflected on her people and all they had to learn about each other in 1960.

The light from the chandeliers reflected off of every stone in Nicole's tiara and gave the appearance of a halo. When she and Bertrand passed through the crowd, people stared in open amazement at their regal finery. She had to remind herself again that this was 1960. Even though a few employees bowed as they passed, Blacks, or Negroes in the vernacular, weren't openly welcomed guests at restaurants and hotels on Chicago's Gold Coast, even if mistaken for African royalty.

Like unswerving ebony pillars, two Zulu sentries stood guard outside the Gold Room. Without a doubt, no uninvited guest could forge past them into the main ballroom, but the guards swung open the gold ballroom doors for Nicole and Bertrand.

Each guest paid homage to them with bows and broad smiles as Nicole and Bertrand strolled down the hundred-foot red Persian carpet bordered in gold.

Am I having a hallucination within a hallucination? Nicole thought in amazement. *George Washington Carver is standing there, wearing his shabby lab coat with a bow tie and a starched white collar! And there is Mary McLeod Bethune, Bessie Smith, Dinah Washington, Frederick Douglass, Martin Luther King Jr., James Baldwin, Malcolm X, Gandhi, Medgar Evers, Mary White Ovington, Charles Latimer, and Albert Einstein. I know that isn't Nat King Cole over in the corner at the grand piano!*

Everyone Nicole had ever revered was present. Many of the greatest minds and talents that ever existed on this planet were assembled in this magnificent ballroom, transcending time. Nicole felt the adrenaline rush so feverishly through her veins that she couldn't feel the floor beneath her. She floated to the stage on Bertrand Lwanga's arm and faced the audience of admirers. A deafening silence fell over the hall.

"We are all privileged to be here tonight," Bertrand said, "to celebrate and pay tribute to Nicole on her thirtieth birthday. This woman-child's birth consecrated the beginning of the end of The Freedom Code. Let us pay tribute to DOM anew!"

The crowd stood. "DOM Nicole! DOM Nicole!" they chanted.

Bertrand Lwanga motioned the crowd to silence. When he and Nicole were seated, Nicole turned to Lwanga and touched his shoulder.

He smiled with pleasure. "What is it, my princess?"

"Why were these people chanting 'DOM Nicole'? What does it mean? And what is The Freedom Code?"

"The answers will come. Tonight, this celebration is in your honor. I have another surprise for you."

Bertrand took Nicole's hand. They stood in a spotlight as the houselights dimmed and an enormous cake, lit with flaring candles, was rolled to a stop in front of them.

"Happy birthday to you! Happy birthday to you!" the crowd sang.

"Happy birthday, baby girl!" rang out above them all.

Nicole clutched her chest. "Momma! Where are you, Momma?"

The lights brightened. There, next to the cake, stood Marion Johnson.

Nicole rushed into her mother's open arms, reverting to that beautiful primal state of security one can only feel in a mother's bosom. Marion rested her cheek on top of Nicole's head and rubbed her daughter's back.

"Momma loves you so, my baby girl."

"Oh, Momma, I never had the chance to tell you how much I love you! I never thanked you. I didn't even have a chance to say goodbye. Momma, I..." Tears choked her words.

Marion gently tilted her daughter's head until their eyes met. "Our love is not limited to our lives on earth. We are always together. Please, promise me you will never forget that I am always with you."

"I won't forget, Momma."

"Excuse me, ladies," Bertrand interrupted. "May I escort you to the table of honor?"

Nicole turned and hugged Bertrand. "I don't know how you did this. Thank you so much. This is the most wonderful gift I have ever received."

Nicole placed one arm through her mother's and the other through Lwanga's. The three paraded down the runway.

"Finally, it is as it should be!" Lwanga exclaimed.

The crowd cheered. "*DOM Nicole! DOM Nicole!*"

Once the trio was seated, the waiters brought forth a bountiful array of delicacies. The lavish feast tempted every epicurean desire. Nicole couldn't remember ever tasting salad this crisp, fruit and meat this tender, or wine so full bodied.

If this is all a dream, how can I taste this cuisine and eat so much?

Nicole glanced at Lwanga. He sat erect, confidant, even regal. Suddenly a chill came over her. He smiled victoriously at her stoic mother.

Nicole was startled to see Marion's eyes filled with deep-seated hatred. It was as if her mother were painfully yearning for her chance of restitution. And Bertrand? His maniacal smile deepened, sending a clear warning to her mother. Like a hopeless prisoner, Nicole watched Marion succumb and bow her head in shame.

What is happening? Nicole thought wildly.

She stared transfixed at an eerie, cold azure light surrounding Bertrand. For a split second, a hideous vision flashed before her eyes. It was so quick, she couldn't hold onto it, but it frightened her. She grabbed her mother's arm. Marion held Nicole's hand protectively. They were inches apart. In the excitement, Nicole had not noticed that her mother had aged.

How can this be? Nicole thought. *She died eight years ago. Why does she look so much older?*

"What's wrong, baby?" Marion asked.

"Momma, I know this can't be real. But it feels so real."

"I am here with you, Nicole, in a reality that you have never experienced." Marion stared into her daughter's eyes, trying desperately to send her a message. "Give me your hand, Nicole."

Marion forced a small object into Nicole's palm, rolled her daughter's hand into a fist around it, and held it tightly until Nicole's fingers throbbed. With a look, Marion cautioned Nicole not to react or respond.

"Is something wrong?" Lwanga asked.

"Nothing at all," Nicole answered, trying not to grimace. "I am still trying to take all of this in."

Nicole looked from Bertrand back to her mother and then out to the audience. A strange aura suddenly appeared over the gathering. Nicole felt a chill. It was as if the guests were held captive or were under the control of Bertrand Lwanga. Only one person in her life had always made her feel safe. She called out to him.

"Where is my father?"

"He is here," Bertrand Lwanga answered. "You simply do not recognize him."

Nicole sprang to her feet. "My father is here? Daddy, Daddy Joe, where are you?" She tried to free her hand from her mother's to go into the crowd, but her mother would not release her.

Enraged by Nicole's outburst, Lwanga met her eyes with bitter disgust. "No SOS will be allowed here. You are the daughter of a master, not a slave!"

What does SOS mean? Nicole thought wildly, *SOS* echoing in her mind.

The odor of burning meat attacked her senses. A vision came to her mind's eye of seething, smoldering flesh burning into scars shaping the letters *SOS* into a man's back. Nicole was outraged. Unafraid, she confronted Lwanga.

"Where is my father? What have you done with him! "

When Lwanga didn't respond, Nicole snatched her hand from her mother's to confront him. With the gesture, her fingers opened and an old rusty key clattered onto the table. Silence fell as all eyes focused on the key.

"What is the meaning of this? I warned you not to interfere, Marion. You will suffer for your disobedience!"

Marion rose to her feet. "I am not your slave and you'll never have my child. I'll destroy you first!"

"Ha! It is you who will be destroyed, ignoble wench! I am your true master."

As Lwanga tried to strike Marion, Nicole felt the rage she had felt on the bus. It erupted from the core of her being, and she powerfully blocked his arm.

"Stay away from my mother!" she commanded.

The strength of her voice hit Lwanga with such force that he stumbled backwards, knocking over tables and chairs. The crowd scattered.

"Be gone, all of you, be gone!" Lwanga yelled at the crowd.

"No, *you* be gone!" Nicole demanded.

With her words came a violent tremor. Everything in the room began to shake. Chandeliers crashed to the floor. Walls crumbled. In seconds, the entire room was in shambles. All of the guests had disappeared, leaving only Nicole, Marion and Bertrand Lwanga.

Suddenly, Nicole saw an image forming. She strained to see it. It was a sword, a beautiful sword that had materialized as if to protect her. She grabbed her mother's arm.

"Come on, Momma! We've got to get out of here."

They hurried down the runner to the door while the sword detained Lwanga.

"You're wasting your time, Nicole," Marion said. "There's no way out."

"We've got to try, Momma!"

The sword traveled with them, guarding Nicole's back as she pulled open the door and ran right into a wall.

Swiftly, Nicole turned around. The sword was poised and ready in the air between her and the approaching Lwanga. It defended her and her mother on its own, piercing Bertrand's eyes. His pupils expanded. His retinas burst. Molten bile spewed from his empty sockets. Lwanga screamed out as his body was engulfed in burning lava.

Within seconds, Lwanga was reduced to a heap of smoldering volcanic ash. Nicole stared at the remains in disbelief as the sword disappeared.

Where her mother had stood, a ghost-like image of Marion emerged in a worn dress chained and shackled at the neck, wrist, and ankles. Fighting the weight of her chains, Marion tried to reach out to her daughter. Her lips moved, but her words went unheard.

Nicole's tears blurred her vision. She strained to reach Marion, but the doors of the ballroom flew open. A rapidly approaching funnel cloud swept Marion into its vacuum. In a flash, the storm and the image of Marion vanished.

Nicole cried out like a lost, frightened child. "Momma, I am coming, Momma! She leaped into the darkness after her momma and found herself spiraling down into a bottomless cavity.

Chapter 3

*D*ing, ding, dong, dong, ding, ding, dong, dong.
Huh, what? Nicole struggled to open her eyes.
Again, the doorbell chimed.
"Nicole, are you in there?"

Nicole rolled over in her bed and opened her eyes. She had been sleeping with her face pressed against her balled-up fist. She felt a tingling pain in her hand as she tried to get her bearings. Pushing herself out of bed, she walked over to her second-story bedroom window.

Regina stood below at her front door ringing the bell. The summer sun had warmed Regina's skin to a lovely hue of honey gold. She wore her light brown hair brushed back in a ponytail, leaving her enchanting face open to showcase her stunning hazel eyes.

Nicole tapped on the windowpane to get her attention. When Regina looked up, Nicole signaled she was coming down.

"Happy birthday, thirty-year-old," Regina sang as Nicole opened the door.

Regina could always bring a smile to Nicole's lips. "Get in here, girl, before you tell the whole neighborhood my age."

"Wait just a second. I've got something in the car. It is so cool," Regina said, making animated hand gestures.

She dashed back to her car and returned pushing a dolly supporting a five-foot-cubed, beautifully wrapped gift.

"Gina, you are a complete nut! Do you need some help? What is this?"

"No, girl. Just open the other door. I'm on a roll."

Nicole pulled the latch bolt at the bottom of the double door right before Regina came barreling through. In the middle of the foyer, Regina extended her hands to showcase her artwork.

"Best friend, best gift."

Nicole wrapped her arms around Regina. "Thank you. I never thought I'd have a friend like you."

"What's the matter?"

"Gina, I think I'm having a nervous breakdown."

Regina closed the double doors. "I doubt that. Let's go in the kitchen. I'll brew us up some tea."

"What about my gift?" Nicole asked.

"It will be here after we finish our tea."

Once the kettle was on, Nicole and Regina sat at the table. As Nicole recounted the events that had occurred after their telephone conversation, she noticed Regina starting to fidget. Suddenly, the kettle whistle blew and Regina jumped up and rushed to the stove.

"What do you make of all this, Gina? Am I losing it?" Nicole asked.

Regina made the tea, but her hands trembled so much she had to set down the cups and saucers to prevent them from clanking together.

"What's wrong?" Nicole asked, rushing to her in concern.

"Would you please pour the tea, Nicole?" Regina sat down again. "Then I'll explain."

Nicole hurriedly did as Regina asked, placing the cups of tea on the table. "Now tell me," Nicole said, sitting again beside her.

"You aren't the only one who had a nightmare last night. I think we dreamed about the same terrifying man! Nicole, he forced me to kneel in front of him. I was afraid—and you know I'm never afraid—but I was afraid and I was trembling as I am now. I didn't have a clue who he was, why he was there or what he wanted with me. He made me feel as if I'd done something wrong, so I asked him if I had."

"What did he say?" Nicole asked, almost in a whisper.

"Oh Nicole! It was so degrading. He said he was my true master and he called me a sub-human slave. He said, I quote, 'Your crimes are against me and you must die!'

"I didn't have time to think. He took out his dagger and drew it back to kill me! I just remember screaming and the next thing I knew I was sitting straight up in bed, soaked with perspiration."

"I can't believe this, Gina. He does sound like Bertrand Lwanga—the man at my birthday party. Lwanga called my mother a slave! Who is he, Regina? How is he linked to us both? Why are we both dreaming about this monster?" Nicole extended her palms. "Oh Gina, what did he do with my momma?"

Regina grabbed her wrist. "Nicole, what is this?"

They both stared at the impression of a key perfectly recessed in Nicole's right palm.

"I don't know," Nicole whispered.

"It's not a burn. It's not ink. Nicole, how is it visible on your palm?"

"I don't know."

"It's nothing I've ever seen before. You've traveled somewhere and brought back proof, but where have you been?"

"Gina, get the pad and pen from the telephone table. Sit here. Write down these letters as I read them to you. Doowyam (space) knab (space) tsrif. Second line: tisoped (space) efas. Third line: 8011." Nicole stopped reading.

"Why did you stop?"

"I was reading the words backwards as I called them out. The key impression says: First Bank of Maywood, Safe deposit, 1108. I remember going to this bank when I was a child. The key must be to my parents' safety deposit box."

Regina got up. "I don't know if I'm more curious or scared. Let's go find out."

Nicole rushed upstairs to dress. As she slipped into jeans and a shirt, she heard Regina call up from the entry.

"Hurry up, Nicole, before I lose my nerve!"

"Calm down. I'm going as fast as I can!"

Within five minutes, Nicole returned to the entry, barely having had time to put a comb through her hair.

"I haven't even opened my birthday gift."

"It will be here when we get back," Regina said, pushing Nicole out the door.

***

Within fifteen minutes, they were driving down Interstate 290 in Regina's twelve-year-old Chevy Cavalier headed to Maywood, a small western suburb of Chicago.

"This is the route my parents took to the Brookfield Zoo when I was a little girl," Nicole said. "I will never forget the way my mother communicated with the animals. The wildest and most ferocious of them were tame in her presence. Right after we left the zoo, my mother would ask my father if we could stop by a bank. There it is! That's the bank!"

***

THIS BUILDING IS SCHEDULED FOR DEMOLITION ON AUGUST 1st. THE LAST DAY OF OFFICIAL BUSINESS FOR THE BANK OF MAYWOOD IS JULY 15th. THE DOORS WILL BE PERMANENTLY CLOSED AT 1:00 P.M.

Nicole and Regina entered the lobby and looked around at the furnishings, circa 1930s, and the wallpaper and carpeting predating World War I.

"This is a grand old place, isn't it?" Nicole said, admiring the crown molding.

The vault door was directly behind the tellers' counter and built into the wall in clear sight of anyone entering the bank. At the midpoint of three small tellers' booths stood a lone silver-haired lady. As they approached, she didn't glance up. Her nameplate read "Alice Plunkett."

"Almost didn't make it, did you?" she said, completing her business. "You're lucky. I was going to leave at twelve thirty, but I got sidetracked."

"We're very sorry," Nicole said. "We had no idea the bank was closing."

Nicole watched the woman freeze and drop her pen as if she were seeing a ghost.

"Marion, is that you? It can't be you!"

"No, no, I am Nicole, Marion's daughter."

"Lord, child, you almost gave me a heart attack. I'll tell you one thing, you are the mirror image of your mother. I was just clearing the last file left in the bank." Alice placed the file folder on the counter. "Look at those names—Marion and Joseph Johnson. I was going to take this file with me and try to contact the next of kin." The teller paused a second and wrinkled her brow. "You said your name was Nicole, didn't you, darlin'?"

"Yes, ma'am."

"That's what I thought you said. I know I saw an envelope in here with your name on it." She thumbed through the file. "Here it is, marked confidential for Nicole Johnson."

Nicole extended her hand to take the letter.

"I know who you are, darlin'," the teller said, holding onto the letter, "but I've got to see two pieces of identification before I can release this communiqué."

"Of course. I have all you need."

The teller examined Nicole's identification. "I guess you are surprised, getting a communication from the past."

"Actually, ma'am, the last two days have been full of nothing but surprises."

"Do you have your key?"

"Why, no."

"I just can't believe two people as lovely as your momma and daddy came to such a tragic end. Your mother must have put it somewhere."

Nicole held the envelope and ran her finger over her full name. This told Nicole that the contents were very important. She broke the seal and unfolded the neatly creased sheet of stationery. Taped inside was the key to the safety deposit box 1108. At the top of the sheet was a single sentence of instruction:

Nicole,
Open the security box. The parcel
inside is private.
Love, Momma

Alice led them through the heavy doors to the bank vault and the safe deposit boxes. She unlocked the cage gate and pointed.

"There it is, dear. It's the only box still locked. Your mother paid thirty-five years in advance. Legally the bank couldn't touch that box. Of course, I told them they would be in a lot of trouble if they tried!"

Nicole opened the box and removed a rectangular package. Placing the package under her arm, she walked back to the cage door.

"I'll never forget," Alice said. "It was about thirty years ago when your mother came in here so upset her hands were trembling. She didn't even answer me when I asked how the new baby was. In less than a minute, she removed that exact parcel from that safety deposit box and fled out of here like a thief in the night. I didn't see her for several months. When she brought that box back, she was happy as a lark. So, darlin', I have no idea what's in there, but I guarantee it's very important."

The teller was about to lock the gate, but stopped in mid swing.

"I've spent the last forty years of my life in this bank. Your parents and those customers like them were my favorites. They sacrificed to ensure a legacy for their children. I've always looked at my job as being a guardian of people's trust and dreams. I don't think a computer can do that." Alice sighed. A slight mist filled her eyes.

"We know exactly how you must feel," Nicole said, filled with empathy. "Regina and I have talked about it so many times."

"I know it's the natural order of things for the young to replace the old, but I'd just hate to see the future of the world determined by something without a heart, soul, conscience, or imagination. I suppose it's up to your generation."

"We're working on it," Nicole said.

"Amen to that," Regina said.

Back at the teller's counter, Alice grabbed the file and handed it to Nicole. Then she swooped up a rubber tree plant, deposited it in Regina's arms, brushed the dust from her hands, and took one last look around the lobby.

"Well, that's that."

They gathered outside the locked building. "I'm really thankful you two were here," Alice said. "I don't think I could have done it without you."

"It was our pleasure," Regina replied. "By the way, I'm Regina Bovine, but everyone calls me Gina."

"Nice to meet you, Gina. I'm Alice Plunkett."

"I know I speak for both of us," Nicole said, "when I say I'm really grateful there are people like you in this world, Alice." Nicole reached into her purse. "Here are our business cards. Our office and home numbers are on them. I want you to promise that you'll keep in touch."

Alice kissed the girls and tried to take the rubber tree from Regina.

"Oh no, Alice, I can carry this to your car or wherever you need to go."

"Don't worry, Gina. See that little green house with the brown shutters, right across the street? That's where I live."

A minute later, they watched the elderly lady unlock her door.

"Don't forget to call us," Nicole called out.

Alice waved before entering her home.

As Regina drove her back to her brownstone, Nicole sat pensively resting both of her hands on the package in her lap. She appreciated Regina more than ever. Her best friend knew this was not the time for small talk. When Regina pulled up in front of her home, Nicole looked at her watch. It was 2:00 p.m.

"Oh, Gina, I'm sorry. I forgot all about your family reunion. I know how nervous Momma Emma is about flying for the first time."

"I've got an idea. You and I still have a date for tonight, birthday girl, but why don't you come with me? Momma would love to see you."

"No, I want to open my parents' package. Tell Momma Emma I love her, and I'll see her tomorrow when I take you to the airport."

"I'm not sure whether I should leave you alone."

"If anything strange happens, I know your phone number."

"I'll be back by four thirty with food."

"That sounds great. Don't worry, I won't open my present until you return."

***

Still clutching the box under her arm, Nicole entered the living room and sat on the sofa. She placed the package in front of her on the cocktail table. Several times, she reached for it but drew back. Finally she convinced herself that nothing from her mother would hurt her. In a surge of emotional strength, she lifted the package.

Under the butcher paper, Nicole found an old El Producto cigar box, taped shut. She carefully removed the tape and raised the lid. Inside, she discovered an envelope and a faded brown pouch with a tightly tied drawstring. On the front of the envelope was written "To my Baby girl." Nicole opened the envelope and read the letter.

My dearest Nicole,

Young America's Foundation: *Protecting and preserving Ronald Reagan's Ranch home for 20 years*

"...Are we doing a good enough job teaching our children what America is and what she represents in the long history of the world?"

~ Ronald Reagan

BLUE

If you are reading this letter, it means your father and I are no longer of this earth. Nicole, do not be saddened by our physical departure. Our spirits and our love will always be with you.

There are so many things I need to explain. Hopefully, I will have that opportunity long before you read this letter. Although every parent thinks his or her child is special, you truly are. Every aspect of your existence (from your conception to this very moment) is part of a plan that will direct or alter the future of our world.

For some mystical reason that is beyond my comprehension, I was chosen to be that tabernacle of your life. My entire purpose for existence was to have the privilege of giving birth to you. Nicole, what I'm telling you is not maternal sentiment. It is predestined and etched in the universal configuration. I know what you're reading might sound like the babbling of a mind bordering on psychosis. But believe me, I am of sound mind.

I also need to tell you, your father was truly an angel on earth. I have loved him as far back as I can remember. His love for you is pure and unconditional. He is my soul mate and our saving hero, for more reasons than I can explain in this letter. When he called you 'his little princess,' he meant it more than just as a term of endearment.

My time is growing short, so I will explain the contents of the pouch. Inside of this minute sack, you will find wealth beyond your wildest imagination. The smallest gems are of great value.

This inheritance is not to be squandered. It is the legacy of every future generation in our bloodline. In your entire life, I sold only one of these gems. You may do with them as you desire. Use them to finance a dream, if you wish. I have complete confidence in your wisdom and decision-making.

Nicole, there is one rule you cannot forget or break. You must never part with the mammoth blue stone. Without it, you are vulnerable to the most formidable of evils. Guard it with your life. I must go now. Never forget I am always with you.

Love, Momma

Momma, Nicole thought sadly, *is this what you were trying to say last night before you disappeared? Please come back. Oh my, I must be losing my mind!*

29

Nicole placed one of her mother's doilies on the cocktail table, loosened the drawstring, and slowly poured out its contents. Brilliant white and blue prism lights radiated from the doily, refracting sunrays at thousands of acute and obtuse angles. The intensity was so pervasive it blurred her vision.

The diamonds were flawless, at least twenty in number. Each was cut to perfection, from an impeccable white two-karat stone to the superlative mammoth blue diamond her mother had written she should cherish forever. Nicole could not believe she was now the proprietor of such unfathomable riches. She held the majestic blue diamond for a few moments, examining its perfect form, color, and stunning beauty. Then she noticed a business card.

Breck & Breck, Purveyors of precious gems since 1892
7 North State Street, Chicago, Illinois

Her mother had thought of everything. Nicole put the card in her pocket before carefully returning all but one stone to the pouch and then the cigar box. She marveled at the two-karat diamond left shining brilliantly on the doily. Tomorrow she would take this diamond to Breck & Breck.

Up to this point, Fresh, Inc. had been underfinanced. With this new capital, she and Regina could turn Fresh, Inc. into the company of their dreams. She gazed at her diamond and vowed she would only use this single one.

Quickly she carried the cigar box to the basement, unscrewed an air vent, taped the cigar box about a foot and a half from the vent opening, and screwed the vent back into place. The diamonds would remain safely tucked away for her descendants.

Although Nicole was confused about the events of the last few days, she knew these diamonds were real and no one other than her mother had the mystical powers to send her a gift from the other side.

***

Nicole always depended on Regina's punctuality. At 4:27 p.m., Nicole opened her front door. There was Regina walking up to the house, carrying two bags.

"How did you know I was here?"

Nicole took one of the bags from her. "Gina, they set Big Ben by you."

Nicole smelled the aroma of her favorite food. In the kitchen, she started to unpack one of the bags. Regina lightly slapped her hands and ordered her to wait in the living room.

"Go find yourself some business. I'll call you when I'm ready."

Nicole was amused by her dismissal. "Well, I never."

"How do you keep your complexion so clear, if you never?"

Nicole laughed on her way out of the kitchen. "You keep your mind in the gutter and that's where it's going to stay!"

In less than five minutes, Regina summoned her back.

"This is beautiful!"

The artistic Regina had displayed the dinner on colorful china dishes.

"Cantonese! I knew it! And the cake!"

A beautiful birthday cake was ablaze with thirty candles. A rainbow of flowers covered the cake's rim.

"Happy birthday to you!" Regina crooned. "Happy birthday to you! You're thirty years old. Boo hoo, hoo, hoo, hoo!"

"I'm still three months younger than you, Regina Bovine!"

"Blow out the candles, dear, if you still have the breath," Regina said, wanting the last word.

Nicole laughed, and blew out every candle. "Can we eat now, Gina, or do you need to take a little nap? I know a woman your age must be plum tuckered out after putting together this lovely buffet."

"All right, you got me. I give."

The two friends sat down and enjoyed their meal.

"My mother's over fifty years old," Regina said, "and you know her last trip was on a Greyhound bus from New Orleans to Chicago when she was pregnant with me."

"It's difficult to believe…"

"She never seemed as though she should have been living in the projects and working as a hotel maid, but she would never talked about her life. Our conversations were always turned back to me. My momma was a mystery. Thank goodness Auntie Melinda sent me airline tickets and Momma didn't mind me traveling to New Orleans, even though she refused to go herself."

"I just thought she had to work, Gina. Why didn't she go?"

"You know Auntie raised Momma after Grandma died."

"Of course."

"But I never told you the deep dark secret that sent my momma packing."

"I'm waiting, girl!" Nicole said, narrowing her eyes.

"Momma thought she had broken Auntie's heart when she got pregnant with me, so she left New Orleans. Auntie told me all about it. Momma's spent the last thirty years of her life paying penance for being an unwed mother."

"That's terrible, Gina! I love your momma like my own. I can't believe she's carried this with her all these years! Did you talk to her about it?"

"Yes, that's why she's finally agreed to fly home with me to New Orleans."

"You should have shared this with me, Gina."

"Remember when I told you that I didn't know who my father was?"

"Yes."

"You should have seen the look on your face, Nicole. You took it very hard. Maybe it was because your parents hadn't been gone long. I decided I'd tell you about my momma later. You had enough on your mind."

Nicole watched Regina's beautiful hazel eyes soften. Her best friend had tried to protect her. Now Nicole wanted to do the same. She sensed Gina needed to talk about her momma.

"I remember," Nicole said, "your stories about your momma's struggling between two jobs."

Nicole smiled inwardly when Regina took over. "She would wake me up at five thirty every morning, feed me, and take me next door to Miss Greensley's apartment. Then around six o'clock, she'd be home and we'd eat dinner together. Afterwards, we would watch our old used television with the two stations or draw in coloring books and play with paper dolls. By eight o'clock, I had my bath and Momma would take me next door to sleep on Miss Greensley's sofa.

"When I woke up the next morning, I was always in my own bed. Momma had come home after all those hours of work to take me back to our apartment. I used to think that grownups never slept," Regina said as she finished her meal.

"What your mother had to do to survive, Gina!"

"Your momma's life was the exception for the Black mother, Nicole, where my momma's life was the norm." Regina smiled. "Listen to me go on. Returning to New Orleans with Momma has me reflecting on the past, where I never go."

"Sometimes," Nicole said finally, "we have to live with the decisions we make or the decisions others make that affect us. Maybe our future and part of our past is simply our destiny. I know that since we met many things have happened that link us together." Nicole hugged Regina. "We might not know where we're going, but we know we'll be together, and we will take care of Momma Emma along the way." Nicole stood. "There's something I want to show you. Come with me."

They sat down in the living room at the table in front of the doily. Regina loved intrigue, and Nicole played it to the hilt.

"We've been worrying about how we are going to really compete with the large ad agencies," Nicole said dramatically. "We have the talent, but we haven't had the working capital to cover travel, presentation materials, and overhead. Well, my dear partner, our worries are over."

In a grand gesture, Nicole unfolded the doily to reveal the diamond.

"Lord, that is the most gorgeous diamond I have ever seen!" Regina exclaimed.

"It takes your breath away, doesn't it?"

Regina leaned over to examine the gem closer. "A diamond this perfect must be worth a small fortune." She glanced at Nicole. "This was in the safety deposit box! Nicole, you can't use your inheritance to finance our business. I'm sure this stone has been in your family for generations!"

"My mother's instructions were explicit. I am to use this diamond to finance my dream. She even left the jeweler's card for me." Nicole took the card from her pocket and handed it to Regina.

"It's not fair for you to use your money. We're partners. I won't take a free ride."

Nicole folded the ends of the doily back over the diamond. Then she looked Regina in the eye. "Regina Melinda Bovine, if it weren't for you, I wouldn't have had an opportunity to work for a major advertising firm. You have shared your ideas, your knowledge, your wisdom, and most importantly your friendship. You've never said I owed you. But truth be known, I do. It's my turn. If you think for one minute you are going to deny me this privilege, you are out of your cotton-pickin' mind. You were my partner yesterday. You are my partner today. And you will be my partner in the future, and that's that. You got it?" Nicole glared at Regina until she answered.

"I got it."

"Good, now let's go open my present!" Nicole rushed to the foyer. With the excitement of a child on Christmas Day, she unwrapped the gift.

"After you finish destroying my beautiful wrapping, open the box from the side, not the top."

Nicole did as ordered. Inside of the carton was a crystal ball perched on an antique wooden tripod.

"I know how you love the unique and mysterious. So I decided this would be perfect for you. You need an eye catcher here in the foyer. It's the Horus Crystal Ball, and it has the power to protect, to heal, to show personal vision, and to warn of evil and danger."

"Oh, Gina, this is gorgeous. Thank you so much. You're the best." Nicole hugged her. "This should be the first thing guests see when they walk in the front door. Help me put it over next to the staircase."

They placed the Horus Crystal Ball and its tripod at the base of the stairway in front of the fern plant. Then they stood back to view the effect.

"Doesn't it have a real dramatic look, Gina?"

"It really does, girl. The wood on the table stand matches the wood on the banister."

"You know what? I am going to rub it for good luck each time I leave the house."

"Well, with the gift you got from your parents, it looks like your good luck has already started." Regina looked at her watch. "I'd better get going. I need to pack a few things for the trip. I can't believe I actually talked Momma into flying tomorrow!"

"Since I'm borrowing your car and driving you to the airport anyway, why don't I help you pack at your place, and then we'll come back here and you can spend the night? That way we'll only have to make one stop in the morning to pick up Momma Emma."

"Good idea, Nicole!"

"I'll just put the diamond away."

Nicole was back upstairs and ready within a few minutes. Regina was already walking out the door.

"Wait, Gina," Nicole called from the foyer. "You didn't rub the crystal."

Regina joined her and placed her hand next to Nicole's on the Crystal Ball.

"Oh Crystal Ball, tell us what the future brings," Nicole chanted.

When Horus didn't react, Regina asked, "Are you happy now?"

"Yes, I am. Thank you very much."

"Let's get out of here before Horus answers. I definitely couldn't handle that today!"

As they walked to the car, the tiles on the foyer floor began to vibrate from the intense humming emanating from the Horus Crystal Ball. Floating in the haze of the Horus Crystal were the words *You are not the future DOM, but he will think you are.* In seconds, the message faded and Horus cleared, and the humming ceased.

***

It was around 8:45 p.m. when the two returned from Regina's tiny apartment in Calumet City. Nicole put fresh sheets on the bed while Regina showered. They were both ready to call it a night.

"Sleep tight, Gina. I set the clock for six a.m. Thanks again for the happy birthday. I love Horus. Where in the world did you find it?"

"It's my Aunt Melinda's. She was a fortuneteller. So was her grandmother. Auntie still has a shop in the French Quarter, but she stopped telling fortunes a few years ago. My cousin, Lorraine, runs the shop now. She's always been afraid of the Horus Crystal. I was always fascinated with it even as a kid, but you know how superstitious the folks are on the bayou."

"How could you give me such a valuable family heirloom, Gina?"

"Because you are my family and you are the only person I know who would appreciate it the way it should be appreciated." Regina yawned.

"Well, I feel privileged. Thank you again. Goodnight."

"Goodnight, kiddo. Happy birthday."

At 6:00 a.m., the clock radio blasted. "It's WJPI RADIO, good Sunday morning. I'm going to start your Sunday with a musical passage from the *Book of Wonder*."

The pulsating beat jarred Nicole completely out of her sleep. She stumbled to Regina's room and knocked on her door. "Gina, time to rock and roll."

"Morning," Regina answered from downstairs.

Nicole looked over the handrail.

"I've been up for an hour. Breakfast will be ready in ten minutes!"

By 6:30 a.m., they were ready to go. Regina had already packed the car and stood impatiently in the open front door.

"You're forgetting the Horace Crystal again," Nicole said.

This time, Nicole asked Horus to make sure Regina and Momma Emma had a safe trip.

Regina smirked. "And Horus, make sure Nicole behaves herself while Momma and I are gone."

As Nicole drove them down the street, the Horus Crystal once more released a message:

Welcome home, Emma.

Chapter 4

If her mother hadn't been facing one of the greatest fears of her life, Regina might have found it amusing that Emma was holding onto her arm with her eyes clamped shut.

It was about two hours after takeoff that Emma found the courage to look at her surroundings. She was about to close her eyes again when she glanced at Regina and saw the clouds beyond the window.

"Just think, Momma," Regina said, trying to distract her, "it's been almost thirty-one years since you left New Orleans. I'll bet you can't wait to see the family again. Auntie Melinda will be asking a million questions."

Hearing Melinda's name was the spark Emma needed to talk. "I was only seven years old when my mother died, and neither Aunt Cora nor her daughters had time for me. Melinda took me under her wing and raised me as her daughter. She has always been a part of my heart. Fortunately, she had the power. The spirits walked with her and she would call upon them. No one crossed Aunt Melinda."

"Momma, you don't believe in all that Voodoo, do you?"

"I'm a Christian, but I have seen things in my life that cannot be explained. As a child, I remember Ade, a strange old African woman, who would come to visit Auntie. She lived in the swamp with the gators. Children made fun of her. Some would even throw rocks at her. Whenever she visited with Auntie, everyone in the shop would go to the back room and draw the curtain.

"I would sneak a peek. The two of them would sit on either side of this three-legged table with the Horus Crystal Ball and chant.

"Not Negroid, not Mongoloid, not Caucasoid.
It is Blue that must be destroyed.

"As soon as they completed the chant, images of a sword and a shield would appear over the Crystal Ball. The moment the images disappeared, the African woman would nod and leave.

"Some people are given a second sight, Gina. In our family, one person is given *the power* every other generation. My grandmother and her first cousins didn't have it. Neither did I or any of my first cousins, but my great-grandmother and Aunt Melinda were given the power."

"Momma, the sword you saw appear over the Horus Crystal… was the handle studded with diamonds?"

"Yes, it was. How did you know that, Gina?"

Regina didn't feel it was time to reveal the phenomenal series of events of the last few days. "I don't know, Momma. I guess that's how I pictured the sword in my mind. What is that chant again, Momma? '*Not Negroid, not Mongoloid, not Caucasoid. It is Blue that must be destroyed.*' Who is Blue?

"I don't know. We'll have to ask Melinda."

Regina knew Emma sensed that she was holding back, but she and Nicole had to figure this out on their own. She didn't want to unduly worry her mother, especially when Emma was finally returning home after all these years.

***

Emma allowed Regina her private thoughts. Lord knew she had her own! How had she gotten herself into this pickle?

For years Emma had wanted to tell Regina who her father was, but Emma was ashamed of her past. What would Regina think of her, knowing she had a one-night affair with a man whose heart she knew belonged to another?

When Emma had finally mustered the courage, Nicole entered their lives. She felt this was a sign. How could she tell the girls that they were actually half-sisters? For Joseph Johnson, Nicole's father, was also Regina's.

Regina's life was much more modest than the life Nicole had shared with Joseph and Marion in the suburbs. Living at the Robert Taylor Housing Project, Emma and Regina had to identify themselves using the number twenty-seven to gain safe passage through gang territory to their building, 4527. Emma had to admit to herself she was afraid Regina would blame her for keeping her from a better life. The thought of her own daughter rejecting her was too much to bear.

"Nicole always looks out for us," Emma said suddenly. "I am so happy you are close."

"Like sisters, Momma, and she always tells me you are like her second mother... Momma, why do you look so sad?"

Before Emma was able to think of a plausible answer, the pilot announced that they were about to land. Emma didn't even have time to brace herself and close her eyes before the jet bumped onto the runway.

***

Cousins Lorraine and Lucinda stepped aside to reveal Aunt Melinda in a wheelchair. "Welcome home, Emma Helen Bovine!" Melinda declared with open arms.

The moment Emma was in Melinda's embrace, tears of joy poured from her eyes, washing away thirty years of anxiety.

"My baby has come back to me," Melinda said.

Until this moment, Regina had never fully understood the life her mother had given up.

***

It was 1990 and the parishes of Louisiana were still filled with excitement, mystery, and historic grandeur, just as they had been when Emma left for Chicago thirty years ago. From Lake Pontchartrain's floating bridges to Bourbon Street's jazz, from the bayou's gators to the sugar cane factories, from the plantation ghosts to the French Quarter and Armstrong Park, the grand and mystical held the heart and soul of New Orleans. It was unlike any other city in the States.

Like the landmarks, Melinda Bovine was a New Orleans icon. For over fifty years, Madame Bovine's House of Mystery had been one of Bourbon Street's main attractions. As Madam Bovine, spiritual advisor, Melinda was loved and respected by all New Orleans's residents.

She owned a spacious colonial home on Basin Street where Emma grew up and Regina spent many summers during her youth. Melinda, Emma, and Regina loved this house. It was boarded up now. When Melinda had a stroke, Lorraine and Lucinda had moved her to their home in Slidell.

As children, Lorraine and Lucinda had looked down on Emma and had shunned their Aunt Melinda. Now Lorraine and Lucinda tolerated her because she helped them financially.

For Melinda's part, she knew her nieces' sentiments, but they were family. She only wished the girls had let her live on her beloved Basin Street. Melinda desperately wanted to return to her home.

An hour after they left the airport, they arrived in Slidell. The trip had really exhausted Melinda.

"This is the first time Melinda has taken a ride anywhere in years," Lucinda said. "It looks like your visit has given her a new lease on life, Emma."

"I'm flattered, Auntie," Emma said to Melinda.

Once in bed, Melinda took Emma's hand, kissed it and placed it against her cheek. Emma sat down in the chair next to the bed. They both were asleep within minutes of the door closing.

An hour or so later, Emma opened her eyes.

"Did you rest well, baby?" Melinda asked with a smile.

Emma stretched. "I surely did, Auntie, but I had no intention of falling asleep."

"Well, it looks like your body had different intentions and won." They caught each other's eyes. "We used to laugh a lot, didn't we, baby?" Melinda asked.

"We did, Auntie. I never thought I'd see you again."

"Well, here you are. And since you're back home, you might as well stay."

"What in the world are you talking about? I've lived in Chicago for over thirty years. It's where I raised Regina. I have my apartment there. I'm due back at work on Tuesday morning."

"That all may be true," Melinda said, with a smile of wisdom. "I grant you, you have a job and an apartment in Chicago, but I can see you aren't happy. Can you tell me that you don't struggle to exist?"

"It's not that simple. New Orleans was the place of my childhood. I am no longer a child, Auntie. I don't belong here anymore."

"Emma, just as your life has changed, so has mine. Baby, those people we thought we were are gone. Thirty years ago, I was strong. Now you are strong, and I pray you will be my strength. My health, my home, my business, my life's savings and work are deteriorating right before my very eyes. You're the only one with the know-how and guts to save them. Lord knows I've missed you, but now, I need you."

Emma was speechless.

"Long ago, I lost your mother, my beloved sister, but you and I— we had each other. You were the daughter I prayed for. You have brought me so much joy! I didn't want you to leave when you did. I've missed you, Emma. All I ask is that you think about my offer. You've lived a life you never should have lived."

Emma tried to speak. Melinda kissed her on the forehead. "Don't answer me now. Go check on my great-niece and get ready for the reunion."

***

Regina had just awakened from her nap when her mother came into the room.

"Feeling better, sleepyhead?"

"Actually, I am, Momma."

Emma sat on the bed. "I've got to ask your opinion about something."

"What, Momma?"

Emma told her about the conversation with Melinda.

"Momma, there has to be a reason why you got up the nerve to come to this reunion. To be honest, there is nothing holding you in Chicago unless you are counting on an overcrowded, dangerous housing project and a minimum-wage job. I am thirty years old. If you feel like you have to be responsible for someone's care, it should be Aunt Melinda's and your own."

"Did you and Auntie plan this, Gina?"

"No, but it does make sense. Not to change the subject, but I have a little surprise for you."

Regina unzipped the garment bag. "Last week, Nicole and I were window shopping on North Michigan Avenue, and we both spotted something we couldn't pass up. Take a look at this."

She removed a peach chiffon designer dress. The garment had striking lines with a delicate bodice gathered at the waist, accenting a free-flowing skirt.

"Oh, Gina, that is gorgeous. You'll knock them dead tonight."

Regina laid the dress across Emma's lap. "No, I won't. This dress is for you."

"Gina, I can't accept this. It is much too expensive."

"You can and you will," Regina said defiantly, "along with these shoes and accessories." Regina handed her mother two additional bags. "Before I took a nap, I made a three o'clock appointment for us at the beauty parlor. Lorraine will be dropping us off in forty minutes." Regina paused. "I almost forgot. There is a card in the shoe box you should read."

Emma opened the shoebox and removed the card. On the outside was a picture of a single yellow rose. On the inside was written:

You'll be the bell of the ball tonight.
Love, your daughters. Regina and Nicole.

Tears came to Emma's eye. "I haven't blubbered this much in thirty years. Just wait until I get my hands on that Nicole."

"Nicole said you'd say that."
***
That evening, a radiant Emma descended the stairs. Regina always knew her mother was attractive, but she had had no idea how truly stunning she was. At fifty-two, she had not lost her petite hourglass figure. Her raven eyes, glowing skin, and high cheekbones automatically brought attention to her perfectly sculpted features.

Sitting in her wheelchair at the base of the stairs, Melinda was the first to speak. "Now, that's my Emma, Queen of the cotillion. Baby, you're beautiful."

"Momma, you're a knock out!" Regina exclaimed.

Even Lucinda and Lorraine had to admit Emma was a vision. Emma humbly thanked them all.
***
The reception started at 8:00 p.m. at Big El's Night Club on Bourbon Street. Emma was the center of attention. Friends and family crowded around her. Women bent her ear with thirty years of news. Men glided her around the dance floor. No one was more pleased with this turn of events than Melinda. Although she hadn't been up this late in the last few years, she wouldn't have missed this reunion for the world. She was glowing with pride.

42

Around 9:00 p.m., Big El Hunt, the famous trumpeter and owner of the club, arrived through the back entrance. He was a towering, powerful figure, obviously just back from a sunny climate—his white skin was tanned to a golden brown. When he took center stage, the crowd hushed.

"It is my privilege and an honor to host the reunion of one of the most prominent families in our beloved N'awlins. It is particularly gratifying to be blessed with the presence of the matriarch of the Bovine family. She has loved and guided us all through life's mysteries. My sweet Melinda, Madame Bovine, welcome and God bless, Miss Melinda."

The crowd burst into applause. All eyes turned to Melinda.

"Would someone please escort Madame Bovine to the stage? We would all love to hear any words of wisdom she would care to bestow on us."

The crowd parted like the Red Sea. The doorman stepped behind the wheelchair to push her forward. Melinda was greeted with cheers and applause. At the foot of the stage, the doorman turned Melinda to face the audience. El presented her with a beautiful bundle of red roses.

"Miss Melinda, these three dozen roses express the triple love, respect, and admiration we hold for you in our hearts."

The trumpeter gave Melinda a kiss on the cheek and held the microphone for her to speak. She pulled the trumpeter close.

"You were always such a kindhearted, loving boy. That's why God blessed you with Gabriel's gift."

The gray-bearded trumpeter was reduced to a schoolboy. "Aww, thank you, Miss Melinda."

"Nearly five score years ago, in a makeshift cabin behind a sugar cane field," Melinda said to the crowd, "I was born. The century and I share the same birthday, January 1, 1900. Now, I'd love to end this century, since I started it. But I truly doubt that I will."

A voice from crowd interrupted. "You'll live forever, darlin'."

"Thank you, baby," Melinda called back. "But I've learned the length of your life doesn't have as much meaning as the time it takes you to fulfill the reason you've been placed on this earth. Some have many tasks; others have only a few. Time changes, but people really don't. They just simply react to the world as it is presented to them. They adapt to their individual realities. My children, when faced with the challenges of your individual life circumstances, I implore you to remember this one truth. Reality can only be one of two things. It is what you accept or it is what you create."

Melinda paused for the crowd to quiet. "My family and friends, I want to thank all of you for sharing this special evening with me. My great-niece, Regina, and my beautiful daughter, Emma, are home, and I'm the happiest woman in the world. God bless you all. Now I have made my appearance. You all know I am expecting you to have a beautiful evening and I will be thinking of you as I return home to bed."

Melinda received an extended standing ovation. Big El fell to one knee beside her. Melinda could feel the vibrations of his trembling hand as he held the arm of the wheelchair.

His voice cracked. "Emma is here?"

Melinda only smiled as Emma placed a hand on his shoulder. "Hello, Elbert."

In one motion, El stood up, turned around and swept Emma completely off the floor. "My little Emma! You've finally come home. Lord, I've missed you so much!"

"I've missed you too, Elbert!" Emma laughed.

El eventually allowed Emma's feet to touch the ground, but neither released the other. They had been best friends for as long as they could remember. Regina joined them.

"Look, Gina, my two children are back together again. Say hello to your Uncle Elbert," Melinda said.

"Sugarplum, I'm so happy to see you!"

"Uncle Elbert. Do you like your surprise?"

"I couldn't be happier." The three stood in front of Melinda, with their arms around each other's waists. "Now, this is what I call a family reunion," El said.

"It sure is, baby. It sure is. I am ready for home now," Melinda said to Regina.

"Yes ma'am," Regina replied.

"Darlin'," Melinda said to El, "would you make sure the rest of my girls get home safely?"

"It would be my privilege, Miss Melinda." The trumpeter directed one of his male staff to escort Regina to the van.

***

Regina washed her fragile aunt and put her to bed.

"Is there anything else you need, Auntie?" Regina asked as she dimmed the lights.

"Yes there is, baby. Come over and sit next to me."

Regina did as her aunt instructed.

"What I am about to tell you is for your ears only. In a very short time, you will travel to another part of the world. In this foreign land, you will face the greatest challenge of your life. Regretfully, I don't know the outcome, but I do know that in the cosmic configuration, your role was written many centuries ago. You are the heir to the Elders' legacy. When I leave this earth, you will have the power of the spirits. Everything that has happened in your life has been part of the Elders' plan. You are the Shield, a Protector like your Grandma Lula and you are one of the Blessed Children.

"The reason your mother has returned home is clear. She is the Deliverer. You are thirty and her job is complete. She is free to live her life, and you are ready to meet your fate."

Gina was startled.

"I know you want to share some recent experiences with me, Gina, but that would be extremely dangerous. As a medium, I can pass information to you from supernatural channels, but the reverse is also true. The Demon Blue can access anything you tell me. I already know you are aware of him through Nicole. Yes, he calls himself Bertrand Lwanga, but as Nicole learned, he is not! You also met him in your nightmare. I will say no more.

"As the Deliverer from the Motherland, Ade brought a child with her for my sisters and me to protect from Blue…"

"Ade? Is she the African Lady that the children used to make fun of?"

"Yes, the cruel little monsters!"

"And who is Blue, Auntie? And who was the child Ade brought to you to protect?"

"You must learn this from others. I may not interfere. After my beloved friend, Ade, was murdered, the Horus Crystal's light vanished and the Demon Blue placed her heart on my doorstep. It was 1959, the year of your conception. Blue couldn't penetrate my door because of this medallion."

Melinda lifted the chain over her head, revealing a golden shield medallion that had been hidden in her bosom. Melinda placed the necklace around Regina's neck.

"You, as one of the Protectors, have been delivered as the Bearer of the Shield. What was secretly written will now be revealed. The Horus Crystal Ball will guide you. With you as its new master, it will unite you with the Bearer of the Sword." Melinda took Regina's hands in hers and instructed her to repeat after her the next incantation.

"Not Negroid, not Mongoloid, not Caucasoid.
It is Blue that must be destroyed."

Once Regina had repeated the words, Melinda told her to raise her arm, and the vision of a shield appeared in her hand.

Regina stared in awe at the magnificent shield, which was light to the touch. She could almost hear it speak to her with assurances that it would protect her and her loved ones all of her life.

How can this be, that it tells me I'm safe? Regina asked herself.

"Auntie, what is happening?"

"You will call on this shield if the Demon Blue tries to harm you," Melinda proclaimed. The image lingered for a moment, then Melinda told Regina to lower her arm, and the shield vanished.

Regina felt the shield around her, although it was no longer visible.

"It is done," Melinda said. "I wish there were more to tell you, Gina. What you saw was real. The reasons are written in your destiny. Now I must stay out of your spiritual world."

"But I have so many questions…"

"And I cannot answer them. It is for your own safety. Just remember these three rules," Melinda said. "Rule number one. If you remove the necklace, you must remain in the house with it. Travel nowhere without it. It guards you from this day forward. Rule number two. If you reveal the medallion to anyone, they become part of its destiny. Rule number three. You must always remember you are the

Shield and not the Sword. The battles and the final confrontation are not yours."

"Auntie, I don't understand."

The cathartic ritual had completely exhausted Melinda. "You will with time, Gina," she said, and then she fell into a heavy slumber.

Regina kissed Melinda on her forehead, turned off the light, and left the bedroom. Upstairs, she entered the guestroom. Without turning on the light, she walked over to the window and opened the blinds just enough to allow a glimmer of moonlight into the room. There she pulled the medallion from the inside of her blouse, held it in her hands, and stared at it.

Nicole said a sword had protected her in her nightmare against the monster Auntie called "Blue." Auntie said what we saw was real. That impression of a key in Nicole's hand certainly was! Didn't Auntie say she had needed this medallion to protect herself from Blue? What would happen to Auntie without it? And what did Auntie called me? One of "the Protectors"—the Bearer of the Shield? A Blessed Child? Why is Blue impersonating Bertrand Lwanga?

I thought I was coming to a reunion, but now I'm caught up in something I don't understand! Why couldn't Auntie tell me more about this Blue? How is he able to listen to my conversations? I need some kind of sign that this is real or I'm throwing this medallion into the Mississippi.

At that moment, a golden light beamed from the medallion and guided her to raise her arm. A shield appeared. She was overwhelmed by its power. Safe and secure, she wished it would last forever. Then, in the blink of an eye, the golden light had engulfed her entire body, reversed, and traveled back into the medallion. Regina lowered her arm. The shield disappeared, and she stood at peace. Carefully, she walked from the window to the bed. When she collapsed across it, she fell into a deep sleep.

***

At 6:00 the following morning, Regina heard a voice.

"Gina, wake up."

In a moment of regression, Regina reacted. "I don't wanna go to school today."

"That must be some dream you're having," Emma laughed. "I want you to take me somewhere before everyone else wakes up."

Emma went into the washroom and wet a washcloth. She handed it to Regina.

"Momma, what is the big rush?" Gina asked, wiping her face.

"Freshen up. I'll explain along the way."

***

The two tiptoed downstairs. Emma peeked into Melinda's room. She appeared to be asleep, but when Regina glanced in, Melinda opened her eyes and gave her a mischievous grin and a wink. Regina smiled. On their way out of the door, Emma liberated Lorraine's key ring from the telephone table. Regina still had the keys to the van in her pocket. Emma drove them toward town.

"It would be very helpful if you told me where we're going," Regina said.

"We're going to the shop."

"Okay, Momma, why are we going to the shop?"

"The way Lorraine rushed me in and out of there last night made me think something fishy was going on. I've got to know if it's true."

By 6:55, Emma and Regina were in Aunt Melinda's office. The first sign that something was awry was when they found the door unlocked. Emma put her hands on her hips. The office was in total disarray. She sat at the desk and thumbed through the volumes of paper strewn all over.

"I can't believe it. This ledger hasn't been filled in for months. The register tapes aren't in order. There are no daily income reports—no employee time sheets." Emma walked to the safe. "I wonder…" She bent over and started to turn the dial. Emma pushed down the handle; the safe door sprang open. "They haven't changed the combination in thirty years!"

"Momma, I can't believe you remembered the combination."

Emma was so preoccupied she didn't hear Regina. She pulled a handful of deposit envelopes out of the safe and showed them to Regina.

"How can they explain this? They haven't made a bank deposit in three weeks. There's money in every envelope, but none of them are sealed. Worse than that, there's nothing written on them to balance against the register tape. Anyone could be robbing Auntie blind. I managed this store better than this when I was sixteen years old. Let's go, Gina."

Gina drove to the end of the French Quarter and made a left on Basin Street. After traveling some blocks, they were approaching Melinda's old colonial home.

Emma pointed. "Over there, Gina. Please park the car."

Regina pulled into the driveway of the stately old homestead. "I bet Lorraine's got a key to Auntie's house on this ring," Emma said as she pulled the key ring from her purse. Everything was exactly as Melinda had left it. Lucinda and Lorraine hadn't even covered the furniture. It was dusty. The odor of mildew was pervasive.

"You know, Gina, with a little cosmetic facelift, this old house could be a show place. Although I never cared for the color schemes," Emma laughed.

"Momma, I'm gonna tell Auntie."

Emma stuck out her tongue at Regina. "See if I care."

Regina had never known her mother to joke around. Since arriving in New Orleans, she had transformed into a vibrant, relaxed, talkative, aggressive person. It warmed Regina's heart.

"Gina, I've made up my mind. I'm going to stay. Maybe not forever, but at least long enough to put Auntie's affairs in order. She needs my help. I don't have a choice."

"It's the way it should be, Momma. It's time to lay down your burdens."

Chapter 5

Nicole arrived at her office at 7:55 a.m. Mr. Oliver from the Futrob International Corporation had called from Botswana at 3:00 a.m. and left a message that Fresh, Inc. had been selected as one of the three finalists for the advertising and marketing contract with their Botswana subsidiary, Q.P.S. Mr. Oliver wanted Nicole to be prepared to receive an international conference call that afternoon.

Nicole laughed. "This is the way to start a Monday morning!"

Nicole worked on answers to questions that might be asked during the conference call. She drafted a brief synopsis of Fresh, Inc.'s track record and compiled a list of client references. By 9:30, she had covered all the bases. She left the office for her first appointment.

***

At 10:00 a.m., she was pulling into the parking lot on LaSalle Street. It was a short walk to State Street. In five minutes, she was entering Breck & Breck Jewelers.

"Good morning, may I help you?" the receptionist asked.

"I have a ten o'clock appointment for an appraisal. My name is Nicole Johnson."

"Yes, one of our associates has been waiting for you."

A man in his late twenties appeared in the doorway and extended his hand. "Hello, Miss Johnson. I am Reginald Breck. I understand that you would like an appraisal. Please, follow me."

When they entered the viewing room, Reginald offered Nicole a seat and a cup of coffee.

"You know, Miss Johnson, Breck and Breck has a rather exclusive clientele. We normally appraise with the intention of purchasing. We only deal with the rarest of gems. I am only telling you this because our appraisal fee is somewhat costly for the average consumer."

"I appreciate your candor, Reginald, but without knowing me, don't you think that it is rather presumptuous of you to suggest that I am average in any form or fashion?"

"I apologize, Miss Johnson."

"Apology accepted. I am on a very tight schedule. Please, avert your eyes for a moment."

Reginald reluctantly complied. Nicole removed the cloth sack from her inner clothing and cleared Reginald to look. She placed the diamond on the jeweler's cloth to be examined. At his first sight of the gem, Reginald lowered the light, popped in his magnifying eyepiece, and scrutinized the diamond from every possible angle. Then he lost any semblance of sophistication.

"Gramps, Gramps!" he yelled. "Come here and look at this."

Obviously perturbed by this outburst, an elderly gentleman hastily entered the room and demanded an explanation. Reginald handed his eyepiece to the elder Breck.

"Just look at this diamond, Gramps."

The senior Breck didn't even glance at Nicole as he sat down to examine the stone.

"My word, I haven't seen a diamond this perfect in thirty years. Back then, it was a flawless one-karat white diamond, exquisitely cut, with the same D coloring. This one is a full two karats. The chances of procuring a diamond this perfect are about one in twenty-five million. I never thought I would see such a diamond again in my lifetime."

The elder Breck couldn't take his eyes off the diamond. He was oblivious to anyone else in the room.

"I'll never forget the day I saw the first diamond. A very attractive Negro woman came to the store for an appraisal. You know how gullible those people can be. I thought she probably had a rhinestone. I didn't feel like humoring her, but the woman was tenacious and very articulate. It was clear that she was one of those educated Negroes. I finally gave in and let her into the office. What was her name, Jones? No, it was Johnson, Marion Johnson. Her gem was perfect, just like this one. I thought it might be stolen or smuggled in on a slave ship, but she read my mind and told me it was an heirloom."

Reginald feigned a cough to alert his grandfather to Nicole's presence. The elderly man ignored him and continued to look at the diamond as he spoke.

"I knew it was an African diamond. It must have been extracted from the Kimberlite Pipes in South Africa and cut in Eastern Africa. I paid her fifty thousand dollars for that stone. Two years later, I sold it for over a hundred thousand."

"Grandfather, we would love to hear more, but Miss Johnson is on a tight schedule."

"Miss Johnson?" The elder Breck raised his head and met Nicole's eyes. "My God, you haven't aged a day in thirty years."

"You obviously have me confused with my mother. But I will take that as a compliment. My mother was very beautiful. I am Nicole Johnson, Marion Johnson's daughter."

Reginald reacted with a hard swallow.

Nicole realized that she was in a position of power and she intended to take total advantage of it. The Brecks were salivating over the diamond, like two vultures hovering over a prospector who was about to take his last breath.

Nicole began to speak in a very impatient and hurried tone. "I have an international teleconference scheduled for noon at my office. You have examined the diamond. I will give you a check for your services as soon as you write up the appraisal. Then I will be on my way."

"I can appreciate your busy schedule, Miss Johnson," said the elder Breck. "I'd like you to know I am very interested in acquiring your diamond. I am willing to make a sizeable offer. If we can come to an agreement for purposes of expedience, I will have a bank courier hand deliver a certified check to you in this office in less than fifteen minutes."

"This all would be very interesting if the diamond were for sale, but it is not. Now, do I need to go elsewhere for a simple appraisal?" Nicole asked, wrapping up the diamond.

Nicole was savvy. She knew Breck was aware of this, yet he had no intention of giving up the diamond. She watched him pull a pad from his suit coat pocket and write down a dollar figure.

Nicole scanned the offer and laughed. Then she lied through her teeth. "I already know the value of my diamond. You must not have been listening when I said this is the second appraisal. You clearly have no respect for me or my time." Nicole stood up.

Breck handed her a pad and pen. "If the stone was for sale, what would be a fair price in your estimation?"

Nicole scribbled a number and handed it back to Breck.

He looked Nicole in the eye. "Your cashier's check will be here in fifteen minutes. Is it a deal?"

Nicole nodded her head and the two shook hands.

Breck summoned an assistant. "Call the bank right now. In sixteen minutes, Miss Johnson will walk out of here with her diamond. And that is not going to happen."

***

At 11:10 a.m., Nicole was driving out of the parking lot in Regina's rusting, twelve-year-old Cavalier station wagon.

Well, Momma, there's nothing like reciprocity, even if it takes thirty years.

Back at the office, Nicole refined her notes for the Futrob teleconference. At exactly 12:00 noon, the call came through. Mr. Rolls, Executive Vice President of Futrob, and Mr. Ray Oliver, Futrob's Liaison Manager, bombarded Nicole with questions. For two hours, Nicole showed her business acumen, her creativity, her spontaneity, and her ability to remain cool under pressure. The Futrob executives were impressed. They asked their last question.

"Although you and your partner have a stellar track record, Fresh, Inc. is a new company. Do you have the financial resources to compete with the more established firms?"

She stared at the check on her desk. "Fresh, Inc. is prepared to absorb its own expenses. If necessary, we will disclose a complete financial statement."

"Congratulations, Miss Johnson. I would like to extend an invitation to your agency to compete with a select few advertising agencies to represent our subsidiary Q.P.S. Off the record, I would like to compliment you on your clear perspective. For the record, I wish you the best of luck on your bid. As you know, Ray Oliver is Futrob's Liaison Manager, and he will meet you at the airport in Gaborone on August 5th."

Nicole accepted Mr. Rolls's invitation and thanked him for the opportunity.

She wished that Regina were here to share in the moment. She closed the office early to run a few errands before she picked up Regina at the airport. Her first stop was Seaside Bank, where she deposited three hundred thousand dollars into the corporate account and twenty-five thousand into her personal account. Then she stopped and purchased an ice bucket and a bottle of 1960 Dom Pérignon champagne, in honor of the year she and Regina were born. By 5 p.m., Nicole was on her way home.

Chapter 6

Emma sat on the edge of the bed and watched her daughter pack the last few articles of clothing in her suitcase. When Regina had finished, Emma gestured for her to sit next to her.

"Gina," Emma said, putting her arm around her daughter, "I've been thinking about how my staying in New Orleans is going to affect us. We've never lived more than an hour apart, with the exception of your summer vacations down here as a child. I am going to miss you so much."

"I'm going to miss you too, Momma. I'll just think of it as your turn to be on vacation at Aunt Melinda's."

They both smiled and gave each other a hug.

"Gina, I need you to take care of some business for me this week. First, I'll send you a list of my clothing and personal items I want shipped here. Then there's the business of our bank account."

"Our bank account?"

"Every week over the last ten years, I have religiously deposited thirty dollars into a savings account in both our names. The balance is fifteen thousand, six hundred dollars. That might not be a fortune to some people, but it is my life savings. I'll be sending you my new account number. I want you to transfer ten thousand dollars to the new account. Leave the rest in the bank there, in case you have an emergency and need to get your hands on some cash quickly. Will you do that for me, baby?"

"Of course I will, Momma! I'm so impressed with you!" She hugged her mother.

"Well, Gina, I never told you, but I received an associate's degree in business when I lived here."

"What?" Regina was astounded.

"In Chicago, I applied for many management positions, but every time I handed prospective employers my resume, they handed me back a mop and a bucket. Finally, I got the hint."

"Oh, Momma!"

In the last few days, Regina had seen Emma in an entirely new light. Whether it was new maturity that allowed her to see her parent as a human being or merely that Emma was free to be herself, Regina was so happy to see her mother transforming into this multifaceted, talented, and personable woman.

"I love you and respect you so, Momma," Regina said, hugging Emma.

Emma blushed. "Go on now. Say your goodbyes to your auntie."

Regina ran to Melinda's room. The two hugged and kissed.

"Remember. When I come to you, the power will be yours," Melinda whispered in Regina's ear. "Until then, you must promise me that you will follow all my instructions."

Regina felt the shield medallion dangling in her blouse and pondered over its clandestine powers. "I promise, Auntie."

Melinda stared into Regina's eyes. "Go now, child."

Chapter 7

Nicole prepared dinner for Regina. She was putting a plastic container of vegetables in the refrigerator when the telephone rang.

"Hello, Nicole. This is Alice Plunkett."

"Hi, Alice! How are you?"

"Just fine, dear. How are you, and how's Gina?"

"I'm doing great. Gina is flying in from New Orleans tonight."

"I just wanted to ask my newly found daughters to dinner Friday night."

"Wonderful! Gina and I make it a practice never to pass up home cooking, especially when it's made by someone we like so much."

"Well, I know what to make for dessert—crunch cake."

"If you make crunch cake, Gina will bring her own utensils and probably wash dishes too."

"Well, crunch cake it is, then. Seven o'clock?"

"Perfect. Goodnight."

"Goodnight, dear."

Nicole hung up the phone and walked to the foyer. She laid her hand on the Horus Crystal. "That Alice sure is a sweetheart. Isn't she, Horus?"

Nicole left the house and got into the car.

The Horus Crystal did not vibrate. The sphere filled with black smoke. The first words to appear were *No longer will you be Guardian of Trust and Dreams.* When those words disappeared, others appeared. *Bless your soul, Alice Plunkett.* And the foyer went dark.

Nicole saw the lights go out and in an instant come back on. It was probably one of those power surges that happened in the summer when too many people used their air conditioners. She had to hurry or she'd be late to pick up the punctual Regina from the airport.

***

In the quiet of her front room, Alice sat resting on her overstuffed sofa, looking through a photo album. Almost every photo in the album was in some way related to the bank. Alice had never married, had no children or living relatives. Her coworkers and her customers were her family. Pictures of picnics, Christmas parties, annual dinner meetings, children's Halloween parties, and Easter egg hunts filled the album. Coworkers had even taken pictures of Alice.

Alice found comfort in this old album. For some reason, tonight, she had a profound need to revisit her life. She flipped the pages back to 1949, the year she had started working at the First Bank of Maywood.

***

Nicole spotted Regina coming out of sliding glass doors. She assumed Emma wasn't far behind. Regina threw her bags in the car and closed the passenger door.

"Nicole! Did you hear from Alice today?"

"How did you know?"

"The Horus Crystal sent me a message just as I landed."

"What?"

Auntie Melinda had not prepared her for the new overwhelming power which linked her thoughts to the Horus Crystal. It was like she had a secret friend whispering in her ear or showing her visions. It took some getting used to. She was still a bit disoriented when the voice or vision came to her as she tried to stay part of the real world.

She told Nicole about it and added, "Without any warning at all, I saw the words 'Bless your soul, Alice Plunkett' flash before my eyes. It was eerie. Is she all right?"

"We're all having dinner Friday night."

"Thank goodness. We'd better go, Nicole, I don't want another parking ticket and a boot on my tire!"

"Where is Momma Emma?"

"She stayed in New Orleans."

"You've got to be kidding! Momma Emma is staying in New Orleans and Horus is now your best friend! I'd say you have plenty to tell me."

***

Alice had reached the year 1960 in her photo chronicles. As she turned the pages, she came across a picture that made her speak out loud. "Well, I'll be switched. I'd forgotten all about this picture."

It was a black-and-white photograph of Alice at her teller station. Marion and Joseph Johnson flanked her. *Nicole won't believe this,* Alice thought. *She should be back from the airport by now. I'll call her. What was that number?*

Alice carried the photo album into the bedroom and spotted Nicole's and Regina's business cards on the nightstand. She picked one up before laying the open photo album on the bed. She didn't notice the rustling movement behind her as she dialed Nicole's phone number.

Regina's business card flipped off the neat stack, exposing a card that read "Bertrand Lwanga Peace Foundation." The card dropped to the bed and slithered across the bedspread to the open page of the photo album. It positioned itself over the picture of Alice, Marion, and Joseph. Once settled, the card began to slowly pulsate.

When no one answered at Nicole's, Alice hung up and turned her attention to the cards in disarray. Gathering them up, she set the cards on the nightstand beside the photo album, but stopped short when she noticed Lwanga's card pulsating on the open page.

She peered at it closely. Low and behold, the card was slowly expanding and contracting. When she touched the card, it radiated a heat so intense that it singed her fingertips. Alice was dumbfounded.

Before she could react to the burn, the card ignited into a ball of fire. Alice ran into the adjoining bathroom and snatched a towel from the rack. No water came out of the faucet. She scurried back to the bedroom, where she found the photo album engulfed in flames. Frantically, she swatted the fire. With the first blow, the ball of flames rocketed upward, propelling itself to a different part of the floor. Upon impact, the flaming ball ricocheted from one surface to another. Within seconds, the fire had engulfed the room. Alice dropped the towel and grabbed the phone. The line was dead. She tried the front door. It was sealed shut. She yanked the door and screamed, "Fire, fire! Somebody please help me. I'm trapped!"

A fireball catapulted towards her. She jumped out of the way and the fireball crashed into the door. The smoke was thickening. The windows wouldn't open. She grabbed a brass candelabra from the china cabinet to break the window. Again, the ball of fire barreled toward her. She fell to the floor, and it crashed into the china cabinet.

Alice strained to catch her breath as she struggled into the kitchen and slammed the door shut. Her mind raced feverishly trying to figure out what kind of demon had invaded her home. She knew it had something to do with Marion and Joseph. That card had burned their page vengefully.

Alice had to destroy the fireball. The stove was in the direct path of the kitchen door. It was an old-fashioned stove, with one of those ovens that had to be lit with a match each time you turned on the gas. Alice stood up and took the frying pan from the top of the stove and gripped it with both hands. Then, she bent over and positioned her head directly in front of the open oven.

"Come and get me, you devil!"

In the split second it took for Alice to step back and stand erect, the flaming ball came crashing through the kitchen door and headed straight for the open oven. Alice drew back the frying pan at the exact instant the flaming globe crossed her path. Swinging the pan, she batted the fireball straight into the oven, slammed the oven door, and barricaded it with her body as she turned on the gas full throttle.

The flaming ball frantically banged against the walls and doors of the oven, trying to escape. With every ounce of strength in her body, Alice held the door closed.

"You thought you were going to destroy me and harm my girls, you evil demon! You will leave this earth with me!"

As the inferno came within inches of Alice, she calmly prayed. "Thy kingdom come. Thy will be done."

At that moment, Alice's house exploded, hurling the roof and flames six stories into the air. The fury of the holocaust could be seen miles away.

***

Traffic on the Eisenhower Expressway came to an abrupt halt as travelers, including Nicole and Regina, watched the shooting flames.

"My God, what type of fire could cause an explosion like that?" Nicole asked, looking out the front windshield. "Now we know why the traffic has been so heavy."

Several police cars entered the expressway. Their sirens punctured the air.

The extra time in the car gave Regina an opportunity to tell Nicole about her trip. Nicole was thrilled to hear about Emma's rebirth, the reunion, the old house, the store, and Emma's amazing business acumen, but Regina said nothing about the medallion.

"It doesn't surprise me at all about Momma Emma," Nicole said. "Our mothers taught us more by example than I think we ever realized."

"Now that you mention it," Regina said, watching the police move the gapers along, "it's as though they trained us to finish a mission they began."

"I'm looking forward to it," Nicole said with a smile.

"Me too, Nicole."

As the traffic picked up, they both felt the baton of womanhood being passed to them, and they accepted it with open strong arms.

Chapter 8

An hour later, Nicole and Regina entered Nicole's brownstone, carrying Regina's luggage and takeout food from Soul Queen.

"Leave your luggage in the entry. Let's eat. I'm starving," Nicole said, heading for the kitchen.

Regina set up snack trays in the living room in front of the television. Within ten minutes, they were watching the evening news, eating their favorite soul food.

"I almost forgot. Here, look at this," Nicole said, handing Regina a receipt.

"What's this?" Regina asked.

"I deposited most of the proceeds from the sale of one diamond in our corporate account. That's the deposit slip."

Regina's eyes nearly popped out of her head. "You have got to be kidding me. This can't be real. This is three hundred thousand dollars! Ha! You almost forgot, did you!" Regina threw up her hand and gave Nicole a high five. "You're the woman, Nicole. You are the woman." Then Regina picked up her spoon and spoke into it. "The officers of Fresh, Inc. will arrive in the Motherland with both barrels loaded."

While they were eating and rejoicing over their good fortune, the evening news caught their attention.

"Tonight at the top of the local news," the anchor reported, "a house fire in Maywood leads to a horrific gas explosion that could be witnessed for miles. Let's go to Randy Winters, who is at the scene of the explosion."

As the reporter spoke, the camera panned the area. "I am standing in front of what remains of the home of Alice Plunkett. It has been ascertained that Miss Plunkett was in her home at the time of the fire and perished in the explosion." The reporter went on, reporting Alice's recent retirement and her lifelong employment at the bank.

Nicole and Regina were horrified. The blood rushed to Nicole's head, causing a loud pounding in her ears. Tears streamed from her eyes.

"Alice, Alice," she cried. "Oh, God, no. This can't be true—I just talked to her tonight!"

Regina grabbed her friend to comfort her.

Nicole's eyes focused on the Horus Crystal Ball. In amazement, she watched beads of water run down its sides as if it were crying. She moved to the staircase. Regina followed and watched Nicole wipe Horus dry.

"Oh, Gina, why do I feel that Horus is grieving for Alice? And why do I feel like I'm responsible?"

***

Friday, Nicole and Regina stood with the small congregation at Alice's funeral. When the former bank president completed the eulogy, Regina and Nicole each placed a rose next to Alice's urn. After the service, Alice's ashes were sealed in a catacomb under the mausoleum.

It rained most of that morning, and a cloudy gray overcast still remained as Nicole and Regina started to leave the grounds.

"Regina, would you mind if we visited my parents' graves?"

"If I had known they were here, I would have suggested it myself," Regina said, holding her near. "Show me the way."

Nicole guided her down a path and up a hill. There, the two stood looking at Marion and Joseph Johnson's headstones.

"Daddy, Momma, since my thirtieth birthday, my life and Regina's life have been filled with a series of extraordinary and unexplainable events. What is our fate? We need your guidance. Please give us a sign?"

They heard distant thunder as the sky began to darken. Regina took her friend by the arm. "Nicole, we'd better get going before we're caught in the storm."

"Gina, don't you see?" Nicole said in desperation. "We are already caught in a storm." The thunder grew louder. Blue's face flashed before Nicole's eyes. Then a harsh rain began to pour. Nicole did not move. "Gina, say it with me! Give us a sign. Please, Gina. *Please!* Trust me. Just hold my hand and say it with me!"

Regina wondered about Nicole, but she acquiesced. "Give us a sign!" Regina said with Nicole in unison.

Suddenly the rain ceased and the clouds broke. The sun shone brightly and the air warmed.

Nicole looked to the heavens and smiled. "This must be our sign." Nicole sighed in relief and started to leave.

Regina stopped her.

"Come on, Gina, we can go now."

With an unyielding tug, Regina pulled Nicole back and pointed at Joseph's headstone. "Look, Nicole!"

At first, there was a slight bubbling gurgle releasing a thick red substance from the peak of Joseph's headstone. The flow rapidly increased, revealing the substance to be blood. It soon drenched the entire stone and saturated the ground. Finally it was absorbed into the earth. Only then did they see that Joseph Johnson's epitaph had been expunged from his tombstone. In its stead, an inscription materialized in Joseph Johnson's own handwriting.

My
Children
Beware
Of
BLUE

At that same moment, words formed in the Horus Crystal in Nicole's foyer.

Regina and Nicole, take hands
Before your births, your destinies were delivered
From the Motherland.

Regina saw the words in her mind's eye. She reached out for Nicole's hand.

"What is it, Regina?"

Regina was staring at Nicole's palm as she told Nicole what Horus had said. "Look, Nicole! Your hand. The impression is gone!"

Nicole rubbed her palms and looked carefully at her hands. The impression had definitely disappeared. "What does it all mean, Regina?

First my father sends us a sign, and now this. It must be a communication from my momma. My parents must be looking out for us from wherever they are for some reason. We just have to figure out why."

Part II

From the Motherland

Bertrand Lwanga and Eleni

Hatshepsut and Kabaka

1936, Botswana, Nigeria, Sudan

Chapter 9

1936

Bertrand Lwanga sat impatiently in his automobile, waiting in the long line of vehicles that stretched for miles to Ethiopia's capital of Addis Ababa, where he and his wife, Eleni, lived. The Second Italo-Ethiopian War had begun. For the first time in its history, the Italian Army occupied Ethiopia. The Italian soldiers guarded the city's border thoroughly and searched every vehicle that entered.

Bertrand was agitated by this delay. His wife was due to deliver their first child any day and she had come to him in a dream, terrified and calling for his help. Bertrand was overwhelmed. His wife was the most courageous person he had ever known. So he had departed immediately and had been traveling for three days nonstop.

***

Eleni Dessalgn Lwanga, a scientist and inventor and the daughter of a government official, had been born in Awasa, the Great Rift Valley, and raised in Addis Ababa, Ethiopia. Educated in Europe, Eleni held doctorates in both engineering and physics. Even in her male-dominated culture and country, her genius was too vital and vast to ignore. Many African and European governments were watching and waiting for this flower to completely bloom. Eleni had recently designed and built a vehicle that was fueled by an alternate energy force and could traverse land, mountains, water, and desert. Bertrand had funded her secret project and was searching for a location to build their manufacturing plant.

Bertrand Lwanga had been born in the highland of Mount Kenya north of Nairobi, Kenya. As a child, his intelligence and physical prowess far surpassed those of other children his age. When Bertrand was ten years old, his uncle, a master diamond cutter, recognized his nephew's potential and wanted to take him from the village. Bertrand's father trusted his brother to raise and educate his son.

By age fifteen, Bertrand was a master diamond-cutter prodigy. Jewelers all over the Motherland and Europe sought out his services. Along with his unbelievable dexterity, Bertrand was gifted with a business acumen that far exceeded his years and education. His business flourished. At twenty, he purchased a small diamond mine of his own. Ultimately, Bertrand presented his uncle with a cache of diamonds as a gift of thanks, which his uncle accepted with great pride and joy.

At twenty-one, Bertrand traveled north to Ethiopia in search of new opportunities. They were scarce, but he found something much more valuable. It was early evening on May 3, 1931, when Bertrand was admiring St. George's Cathedral in Addis Ababa and Eleni Dessalgn walked out of the cathedral door. Their eyes locked.

Bertrand joined her. "I am Bertrand."

"I am Eleni," she replied.

"Eleni, would you like to walk with me?"

"Yes, Bertrand, I would."

One month later, Eleni and Bertrand were married where they had met, at St. George's Cathedral. It was said that they were the most exquisite couple ever to walk down St. George's aisle.

***

After five years, the Son of the Mountains and the Daughter of the Valley awaited the birth of their child. Since her husband's departure, Eleni had slept restlessly and was exhausted. She ascended the staircase of their palatial mansion to the master suite. Feeling a slight contraction, she had decided to rest, when a presence in the room startled her. At first, she thought it was her younger brother Akim checking on her, but the ominous figure at the foot of her bed was dressed in a long white tunic with a turban wrapped around his head. One would only have known the intruder was Blue disguised as the Stranger from his deadly cold menacing blue eyes.

"Who are you?" Eleni asked as she reached over and grabbed a brown pouch from the night table. "What are you doing in my home?"

"Silence, vassal. You should have remained asleep."

"Do you think I fear you?"

Even this close to childbirth, Eleni was remarkably spry. She secured the pouch by putting the loops around her wrist. Then she sprang from the bed and positioned herself in a combative stance.

The Stranger roared with laughter. "I will make a believer of you, infidel."

With that statement, he viciously snatched the pouch from her wrist, throwing her off-balance. With his right hand, he dropped the pouch into his robe and tried to send a rapid back-left-hand slap across Eleni's face, but Eleni dodged the blow and stuck two fingers in the Stranger's eyes. Furious, The Stranger stepped back, trying to refocus. Eleni rushed down the stairs.

Suddenly, Eleni felt her head jerk back as this perverse fiend dragged her up the stairs, slamming her back against the edge of the steps, causing her water to break and strong contractions to begin. The pain was excruciating. She screamed out for Bertrand while the Stranger dropped her onto the bed, placed his hands on her stomach, and began to incant:

"Of sky and water, of water and sky
Mother of the mother of my son
Slave beasts chained as one.
The world order will be governed by Blue
Reign on, future son of Blue."
***

Without warning, a blinding light flashed before Bertrand's eyes, and he heard a whining siren reach a deafening crescendo. He grabbed both sides of his head. Then the vision of Eleni screaming for help overcame him.

The line of traffic remained at a standstill, but Bertrand could wait no longer. He flung open the auto door, removed his shoes, and ran with the speed of a leopard to his house fifteen miles away.
***

Eleni never lost consciousness. She heard all of the Stranger's chants and the information he was trying to transfer into the subconscious of her unborn child.

Eleni's spine had been damaged and her birth canal altered. During her last contraction, the infant struggled to enter the world. The hellish intruder reached inside her womb and snatched out the infant. Eleni screamed in agony.

***

Akim Dessalgn, Eleni's sixteen-year-old brother, had lived with Eleni and Bertrand since the death of their parents in the early stages of the Italo-Ethiopian War.

Akim was walking home from school when he noticed an unusual darkness in the sky over the Lwanga mansion. The murkiness gave him an uneasy feeling, and he ran to reach his sister. Inside, the sound of indistinct murmuring was coming from Bertrand and Eleni's bedroom. Akim found his sister lying in a pool of blood.

"My baby!" she cried. "He has taken my baby!"

Akim rushed to her. "Eleni, who did this?"

Eleni withered in pain. "Do exactly what I tell you, Akim. I have little time. Bertrand must save our baby."

"Eleni, I don't understand."

"Little brother, you must be brave. Hurry, go to my desk and bring my journal and pen! Write down everything I am about to tell you."

***

Bertrand burst through the front door and charged up the stairs to the bedroom. Akim sat sobbing next to Eleni's bed, where her blood-soaked and lifeless body lay.

"Eleni, Eleni!" Bertrand cried out, lifting his beloved wife into his arms. He stared at her, uncomprehending, touched her face, kissing her, holding her. "Eleni, I am here, awaken."

Akim screamed out, "She's dead, Bertrand! He murdered my sister and has stolen your baby."

"Dead! She's not dead! She's sleeping!" Bertrand said, trying to grasp reality.

"No, Bertrand, she's dead! Don't believe me. Look at her instead. She's with child no more. The savage Stranger took the baby from her womb and killed Eleni!" Trembling, Akim opened Eleni's journal. "It's all in here. Eleni would not allow me to seek help." Akim explained about Eleni's dying wishes. "It was horrible, Bertrand. You must kill the demon that has done this!"

Bertrand dropped into a chair, cradling Eleni in his arms. "Tell me everything! Everything!" he said, not taking his eyes off her face.

Akim read Eleni's account of their infant's abduction while, for hours, Bertrand held Eleni in his arms. Somewhere in Bertrand's mind, he knew he would have to overrule his emotions and zero in on his enemy. But not now. He could not give her up. Not yet. He held her so close, he didn't even notice that she was cold and stiff. She was his Eleni, and if he held her close enough to him, he knew she would feel his warmth and come back to him.

Watching Bertrand finally broke Akim. He sobbed hysterically. "Bertrand, you have to find your child! Please. I promised Eleni. You must let her go. She's dead!"

Bertrand looked from Eleni to Akim. Reality hit him, taking his breath away. For a moment, it seemed like he might let go of Eleni, then he pressed her to his chest and his eyes turned black with rage. "I will avenge Eleni's death!" he told his brother-in-law. "I will save my child. This I promise!" Bertrand gently placed Eleni on the bed and spoke to her. "I promise you, my love, we will have our baby once again."

Bertrand knew he wasn't in his right mind, but he went through the motions. As he covered Eleni in their bedding, he asked Akim to get ready to travel.

"You will transport Eleni to the Lwanga family plot in Kenya." He drew Akim a map with instructions and gave him diamonds and a large sum of money. "Now you must prepare. Go pack and leave me alone with my wife."

Bertrand spent the rest of the night studying Eleni's journal and planning his mission. Before the sun rose, he loaded up the multi-terrain vehicle Eleni had invented.

When Akim returned with servants and a coffin transport, Bertrand faced his young brother-in-law. "You take Eleni's journal. I have memorized it. I know all about the Demon Blue. He changes from the Azuroid to the Stranger. I know the journey. I know I must use an incantation to summon a fortress to materialize. This demon has no idea what a brilliant mind Eleni had. She has taken in his whole history. Now she has shared it with me. I will find our child." He handed Akim the journal. "I need a few more minutes." Without waiting for an answer, Bertrand walked back up the stairs and closed the bedroom door behind him.

Eleni, Eleni, he thought as he held her hand. *Never fear, my brave love. I will find our baby and we will return to you, and we will be a family again.*

When he kissed her, he felt the cold. For the first time, he realized his thoughts were untrue. Eleni was gone. How could he think of life without her? It was all too much for him. He stood and turned from her with tears streaming down his face.

He opened the bedroom door, then paused. Akim was right outside. He embraced the younger man.

"Take care of her, Akim," he said, his voice quivering with tears.

Without another word, Bertrand Lwanga departed on his journey to find their child.

Chapter 10

Bertrand Lwanga followed his wife's directions. For days, he traveled through the mountains, the rivers, and the jungle and down into the valleys until he stood in the center of a great desert. There he found an oasis his beloved Eleni had described.

I am here, Eleni, to rescue our daughter. Never fear. I will find her.

With an incantation from Akim's journal, he summoned the fortress.

> *"Of sky and water, of water and sky*
> *Mother of the mother of the ancient daughter*
> *The new world order shall bring them to slaughter*
> *Reign once more, will you*
> *Reign once more, Blue*
> *Come forth, house of the last*
> *Open the door to the child of the past."*

A pyramid materialized. Finding extraordinary strength, Bertrand forced open the colossal stone entrance. Behind this door, the murderer of his wife stood, still shrouded in his white tunic. His azure eyes were piercing.

"I have been waiting for you, sub-creature. I need someone to clean and feed your larva."

"I do not know what kind of creature you are. Someone as evil as you cannot be human." Bertrand removed the machete strapped to his back. "I did not come here to talk to you, Blue. I came for my child and to end your life." Bertrand charged his enemy.

Blue raised a shield, and the blade of the machete shattered on impact. Bertrand stumbled backwards.

Blue laughed. "You are not my equal. Bow to your master."

Bertrand was upon him, literally running up Blue's torso, pummeling Blue with a flurry of kicks and blows. Bertrand could see that Blue was stunned. It drove him on to inflict more pain on the evil one. Blue crashed into the walls of the pyramid, collapsing to the floor.

"What manner of human are you?" Blue asked.

Bertrand escaped through a passageway into a dim cavern where there were no other openings or doorways. Against one wall he spotted a stone table where a bowl of meal, a jug of water, a jug of mammal's milk, and pieces of cloth were set. On the opposite wall, he viewed several chains with shackles. His enemy was nowhere to be seen, but Bertrand heard his voice.

"Son of the Mountains, what is it they call you?"

"I am Bertrand Lwanga."

"Bertrand Lwanga, you are above your kind. But you are far beneath me. You shall serve me as I order you."

"You are evil and insane. I will never serve you."

All at once, a bright orange light shone from above. Bertrand raised his eyes to behold the most macabre, bizarre spectacle he had ever seen. Hanging several feet above him in midair was a large muscular man with sky-blue flesh, massive white wings, and the facial features of a child of the Motherland. His azure eyes were menacing. At shoulder height, his arms were stretched out to each side. In one hand he held a flaming ball of fire, in the other an infant.

"Behold your daughter, Bertrand Lwanga," Blue said, bring his hands closer together. "Tell me, Bertrand Lwanga, will you serve me as your master, or will I set your child aflame and let you watch her burn to death? The choice is yours."

Bertrand had to control every fiber of his being. "Do not harm my child. I will serve you."

The evil one brought the infant closer to the flame. "I did not hear my title."

The infant began to cry.

Bertrand bowed his head. "I will serve you, Master."

"Very well," Blue replied. He spread his arms apart and continued to speak. "Remove your shirt and your shoes. Step back to the wall at your rear. Attach the shackles to your ankles, wrist, and neck."

76

Bertrand did as ordered.

The evil one extinguished the ball of fire and descended. "Here," he said, laying the infant on the stone table. "It must be cleaned and fed." Then he departed.

Bertrand hurried towards the table, but the weight of the heavy chains nearly pulled him down. Their length only allowed him to travel to the edge of the table. He had to strain to pull his daughter into his embrace. Once she was in his arms, he felt a love and strength that he had never known.

"Hello, my precious one. I am your father, Bertrand Lwanga. You are my daughter and you will have my mother's name, Zinzi Lwanga. I will never be a slave and neither will you," he said, knowing from that moment forward, he had to plan their escape. "Your mother is…" He choked on his words and held his baby to his bosom. "Your mother was a magnificent woman. I will tell you all about her as we make our plans."

The water, milk, and meal were affixed to the table. Bertrand was undaunted. He reached over to the water and cloth and cleaned and wrapped his child. He then tore a small piece of cloth, twisted a tiny end, and dipped it into the milk for his daughter to suckle. With each movement, the shackles cut deeper into his flesh. But he continued to dip until he was sure his child was nourished.

Blue watched with concern from the darkened doorway. There was danger in Bertrand Lwanga's influence on his daughter, Zinzi, but someone had to raise the baby until she was old enough to fulfill her role in the destruction of The Freedom Code.

Blue looked ahead. Next he would capture the child of the Daughter of the Desert and the Son of the River. Surely, within their tribe, he would find a suitable slave to act as nursemaid for the two girls. Then he would take Bertrand Lwanga's life.

Chapter 11

The wings of the enormous bird glided over the Kalahari Desert, casting an ominous shadow. The creature decided to rest where the red sands met the grassland. As it descended, the mighty downdraft of its feathered limbs pushed huge clouds of sand up from docile sleep.

Blue, now disguised as the Traveler, emerged from those clouds to stand on the desert floor. No beast of burden or sustenance protected him, yet he traveled the desert unscathed. He came in search of a second child born with traits found only in the purest human pedigree. Walking the grasslands, he reached a village of African purity. The people of this village were unaffected by the outside world. The gods of Africa prevailed and all living creatures possessed souls.

The council of Elders sat in a circle in the center of the village. The Traveler walked to the circle and sat as if he were a delegate. All eyes turned to him. The most venerable Elder was the first to speak.

"You come to us as if you know us. I have seen the desert rains a hundred times. Not once have I seen you amongst us. Your face has child's texture, untouched by the wind or sand, yet your eyes have seen more than forty rains. You may be of our tribe, but I am not certain. May I ask your calling?"

"I am born of this land, as are you," the Traveler replied. "I have come here as an envoy of the gods. For the first time in two thousand rains, a son of the Okavango River has fertilized a Daughter of the Desert. From this union, a child has been conceived. Through me, this child must be channeled." The Traveler smiled inside, for he had also channeled the child that was conceived when the Son of the Mountains fertilized the Daughter of the Valleys. Soon he would have two heirs.

"Around you sit Elders of many villages. We all are descendants of the Okavango River or the Kalahari Desert. All of us are children of the ancients. Who amongst us are the children you seek?" the Elder asked.

"The true son of the river is called Kabaka, and the desert's daughter is called Hatshepsut," the Traveler replied.

The council fell silent as the Traveler recounted the history of Kabaka and Hatshepsut. "Young Kabaka is the bravest of hunters and wise beyond his years. His family once migrated from Uganda to the grassland forest at the curve of the Okavango River. He is a direct descendant of the western Bantu dynasties. Hatshepsut, his beautiful wife, is a direct descendant of the true Egyptian pharaoh and named after the woman pharaoh of the dynasty of 1500 BC. "Then, of course, there are the secrets," the Traveler said smoothly.

With each word the Traveler spoke, the council members grew more anxious, glancing at each other for support. His knowledge of the couples' preordained destiny to protect The Freedom Code unnerved every one of them. How did the Traveler know about Kabaka and Hatshepsut's importance to The Freedom Code when it was a secret that only they had known?

Amin, a nephew of the senior Elder and the most worldly member of their council, spoke at last. "Unlike others here," he said, "I have crossed the desert to the corners of our land. Yet I have not heard of this channeling of which you speak. I call the gods for healing. They send the power, not the person. I have the medicine and the rituals."

"I am also a doctor," the Traveler replied. "The gods have given me the power of healing hands, and I am bound to fulfill this mission. I must give warning. If this child is not channeled through me, it will signal the beginning of drought, famine, disease, and the onslaught of our enemies until we are no longer. I am simply the courier."

"What proof do you give us of your power?" Amin demanded.

"You have a boy here in the village," he said. "He is not yet seven rains. Since his birth six rains ago, his legs have been twisted. He cannot walk. Bring him to me."

Shortly, the child's father carried him to the circle of Elders. The Traveler instructed the father and son to lie beside each other on the ground. The Traveler knelt at their feet. From his knees to his ankles, the boy's legs were like twisting vines. His left foot pointed to the right; his right foot was completely backwards. The Traveler placed his right hand on the boy's left knee and his left hand on the father's left knee. Simultaneously, he ran his hands from the knee to the ankle of both father and son. When he reached the ankles, the boy's left leg was as straight as the father's. He repeated the same ceremony on the right leg. The entire village gathered and watched in astonishment as the boy's right foot rotated forward. The Traveler commanded the father and son to stand. They did with joy. Overwhelmed with gratitude, the father fell to his knees.

"Thank you, thank you, healer from the gods."

"It was not by me. It was the gods through me. Now take your son's hand and walk with him."

As the father and son paraded around the village, the Elders and the villagers cheered. Although Amin was seething, he joined in. The villagers were all impressed with the Traveler's humility. His benevolence quickly endeared him to the entire village. Word of the Traveler's deed was already en route to neighboring villages.

***

The sage Elder studied the Traveler interacting with his newfound admirers. Although the Traveler projected the humility of a servant of the gods, his eyes were that of a cunning, victorious conqueror.

As if feeling the Elder's stare, the Traveler joined him. "One of wisdom and time," the Traveler said with respect. "I know that the others will follow what you decree. I have only three days to perform my task. Will you help me?" The Traveler knelt on one knee before the Elder.

The Elder gazed deeply into his eyes and placed his hand on top of the Traveler's head. His powers collided with the Traveler's. The Traveler blinked first and recoiled, exposing two medallions hanging around his neck in the opening of his robe. Immediately, the Elder stood and addressed the assembly.

"Let us all welcome our guest. Do everything to make him comfortable after his long journey. He will stay in my hut. My daughter Ade has room for me," he said, turning back to the Traveler.

"That isn't necessary, wise one," the Traveler said, trying to get away, just as the Elder had anticipated.

"I insist. Amin show him to his quarters. I must pray to the gods and ask them for guidance to help him with his mission. When the sun rises, I will return to the circle with the answer."

The Traveler reluctantly entered the Elder's grand hut. At least for a few hours, the Elder knew the evil one would be forced to sleep, entrapped in the goodness of the Elder's ancient ancestors.

The Elder entered Ade's hut and covered the door. His daughter was sitting on the floor, legs and arms folded. Ade was her father's closest friend, advisor, and confidant. She had never married and had no children, but she was the official aunt to everyone in the village and had raised many children.

In perfect health, Ade stood five-foot-four-inches and was unusually strong for her size and age. She had the mystic powers of sight. Because she had witnessed so many tragedies in her life, her age was beginning to show. The lines under her eyes, on her forehead, and next to her nose had deepened into her round face. Her short, tight curls were now sprinkled with gray. Curiously, the "eyes that saw all" remained crystalline, and her spirit stayed pure.

She was counseling Mpho, her young pregnant cousin, a direct descendant of the Twin Oracles. Recently, Mpho had lost her husband, Aliko, to the killer crocodile. The Elder noticed her travel satchel packed beside her.

"You are leaving us, Mpho?"

"Only until my child is born. Remember, Hatshepsut and I are having our babies a few weeks apart. We vowed to be together. Ade will help us."

"I remember," the Elder said gently. "Ade, I do not want to interrupt a private moment you are having with Mpho."

"We were talking about her loss. I was reminding Mpho that the killer crocodile has taken the lives of many great warriors, including Kabaka's father," Ade said. "Now she must think of her dear Aliko as transitioning to a better life as only a warrior of his stature would be granted by the gods.

"I have encouraged Mpho to join Hatshepsut. New surroundings will be good for her. Don't you agree, Father?"

Usually Ade was joyful. Now the Elder saw a coolness in her eyes, a warning. As a descendant of the Oracles, Mpho should not be seen by Blue. The Elder took his niece's hand and helped her to stand. Although the Elder tried to hide his sense of urgency, he knew Mpho, with her keen intuition, had picked up on it immediately.

"I can't wait to see Hatshepsut. I must go," Mpho responded, trying to speed things along. "You think it's a wise idea too, don't you, Uncle?"

"How is it that you and Ade know my thoughts before I say them?" he asked, holding her hand. "I want Amin to accompany you to Hatshepsut's. It is a long journey."

"Do not worry, Uncle. Women from the village next to Hatshepsut's are walking with me. If I need help, they will provide it."

The elder looked outside. A group of villagers was waiting for Mpho. He glanced at his grand hut. His ancestors were doing his bidding. Blue was still under their spell and nowhere in sight. The Elder ushered Mpho outside as Ade called out.

"I will not be far behind, Mpho."

From the doorway, the Elder watched Mpho and the women until they disappeared into the forest. Only after he glanced one last time at his grand hut did the Elder return to his daughter.

Ade whispered to him, "That was wise of you, my father. Your powers keep Blue from Mpho and me while he's in your hut, but he must never see my face or hers. Father, place the hand that touched him over my eyes."

The Elder did as his daughter requested, holding his palm in place. Ade began to moan and tremble.

"I hear the screams of a baby writhing in pain. What manner of sadist is this I see? He has taken the baby's skin and made it his own. He has sheathed himself to disguise his origin. He is a danger to all humankind."

The Elder removed his hand. "When I was but a child, my father warned me of this day. The prophecies of the female our ancestors have come to pass."

"He is Blue?"

"Yes, and he has returned as the Traveler with the face of a child of Africa. At first I could not see his blue skin and wings, but his evil touch removed his disguise in my mind's eye, and only then did I see him for what he was."

"I need to know everything about him now, Father. You never did tell me how he stole The Freedom Code from our twin aunts, the Ancient Oracles."

BLUE

"Blue had been the leader and sole survivor of his small race of fallen angels known on earth as the Azuroids," the Elder said, "a race so gifted with powers that they could have ruled and enhanced the earth with beauty and peace, freeing all of humankind. Instead, the fallen Blue used his powers for evil, enslaving his people and usurping the power of freedom.

"All of Africa, every nation, every tribe, every person rose up and waged war against Blue. Blue's army and the rebels' armies fought in Freedom's War and perished.

"The all-powerful Blue was the only Azuroid to survive. Flesh torn from his body, bones broken, limbs rendered useless, wings severed, he was left blinded as an evil, brooding, soulless spirit. His fate? Over the generations, he was given a second chance to reflect on the evil he had inflicted on our world.

"The twins prophesied that he would never consider redeeming himself. His incarceration only bred more hate in his heart. Entombed in the far-off Sudan, he furiously waited for his body to regenerate. Then he discovered he had an untapped power. He relished in using it against all descents of Africa as revenge against our ancestors for having destroyed his civilization.

"Infiltrating the minds of our people with destructive thoughts, he caused our people to feel inferior and pitted our ancestors against one another. Many families were stolen and enslaved and taken to a land far away. With every freedom lost, the self-love of Africa's descendants diminished, and Blue's power grew out of our mayhem.

"Now some of us have again seen the light, but if Blue has his way, he will destroy our flame before we can light up the world for our people to see.

"It is written that when Blue's body is once again whole, he must produce children to recreate his kind in order to prevent his extinction. Our ancestors prepared for this.

"First they created The Freedom Code to save us from a final enslavement by Blue, but Blue stole the Code from them and now wears its spirit in the sword and shield medallions hanging around his neck.

"Our ancestors countered by preordaining that Blessed Children, descendants of the Ancient Oracles, would be born at the same time as Blue's heirs. Those Blessed Children would face the children of Blue to determine the fate of all of African descent in this world. This now is your task, my daughter, to make sure these Blessed Children are aware of Blue and his powers.

"Hear my words and do as I say. You have a powerful gift. I believe the reason for your gift has come to fruition. Blue must only procreate with the most perfect of our race and those free from enslavement to once again enslave the free. Such a child of perfection is soon to be born. The gods have shielded Hatshepsut and Kabaka from Blue's sight, but he will find them. You must go and warn them and save their child. You will ultimately travel to a distant land and you will meet more of our family there, descendants of your great-great-great twin aunts, the Ancient Oracles. There are three sisters. Two will help you."

"And Mpho? She is a descendant of the Oracles, and we have sent her to Hatshepsut!" Ade shivered and looked around as if trying to hear if anyone were nearby. Suddenly she leaned in to her father and spoke softly. "I feel his presence outside your hut. He can gaze into your mind. My father, I cannot leave you alone. Let me stay with you tonight. I will go to Hatshepsut and Mpho as the sun rises."

The Elder held Ade's hand. "My daughter, he awaits my answer at sunrise. I must stay here, and you must go now. You cannot deny your destiny. You have to save Hatshepsut, Mpho, and their children. Our people's future depends on it. Don't worry about me. I was alone when I first saw the light of life. It is fitting for me to be alone this night. Always remember, my daughter, I am part of you."

***

Everyone in the village slept, except for Amin. Filled with deferred ambitions and lost dreams, he was haunted by his own restless spirit. He walked late into the night to tire his body. For seven years, Amin had worked the worst of minimal wage jobs to remain in the city as he tried to educate himself. The city had laughed in his face. He returned to the bush, the only place he would be given authority and respect. For Amin, it was too little by too few. He knew better than anyone in the villages that the outside world was at their door. For years, he had been trying to prepare the people of the villages, especially his young cousin, Kabaka.

Amin had thought that after the Elder's passing, he would lead their people, but, over the years, the people's allegiance had turned from him to Kabaka. Somehow, the fact that Kabaka was of Amin's own family made the loss of power more poignant.

"I see that I am not the only one the night will not allow to sleep."

The Traveler was sitting outside of the hut the villagers had prepared for him. Amin joined him.

"Might I walk with you, Doctor? I need to speak with a man of the world. I wish your counsel."

"Healer, you are welcome to walk. I know not what I can share with a man who is worldlier than I."

"Amin, your return from the outer world back to the village was the will of the gods. But the gods must be certain you have remained a man of vision. Are you willing to satisfy the gods? They ask of you no blood or suffering."

"I will always do as the gods decree."

"Very well. It shall be. Close your eyes. When I order you to open them, you must gaze out upon the desert, study the scene, and tell me all you see. Open your eyes."

Although Amin couldn't believe what he saw, he told the Stranger of all that lay before him.

"My beautiful village is gone. It now sits on lumps of clay. The trees are few and decaying. The huts lie shattered. I recognize no one. The adults are in rags without shelter. They look like skeletons. The children, oh my, it's difficult to look at their bellies, they are swollen. The children are emaciated and starving. It's terrible!"

Amin could no longer talk. He could barely catch his breath. Human feces, crawling worms, and swarming flies covered the ground. Desperate moans of pain and anguish echoed in the air. The smell was putrid and made Amin gag. He fell to his knees and began to regurgitate.

Once again, the Traveler asked Amin to close his eyes. When Amin reopened them, all was back to normal, but he was not. His heart was heavy as he tried to readjust to what he now saw from what he had seen.

The Traveler had abilities beyond Amin's understanding, hypnotic and telepathic powers which created illusions that were tactile and three-dimensional. Amin marveled at how the Traveler had drawn him in to such an extent that he experienced the vision with all his senses. His smell, taste, touch, even his sense of feeling had been awakened. It was horrible.

"What was that all about?" Amin asked the Traveler. "It was so real."

"It is real," the Traveler assured him. "And you must now choose what the future brings. The vision you saw begins at the moment the Elder dies. When attacked by outsiders, Kabaka defends the villages with ancient weapons. Your villages are destroyed and your people perish from this earth. The invaders murder you and Kabaka's child."

"How do I prevent this from happening?"

"You must seize power to stop the catastrophe."

Amin faced the Traveler. "I cannot allow the vision to come to pass."

"The time grows near. Before the sun rises, the gods will take the Elder. Kneel before me."

Amin knelt.

"Amin, the gods demand the channeling of the child. Bequeath to me the route to her."

"In the fourth village to the west, you will find the hut of Hatshepsut and Kabaka. It is the largest hut and lies away from the village. The lions often walk in guard when Kabaka is on the hunt. The distance can be traveled from the time the sun goes down to when it rises again."

"You have served your master well. You shall be rewarded." The Traveler removed two of his necklaces and placed them over Amin's head.

Amin was a member of the council and was one of the guardians of The Freedom Code and its secrets. These medallions displayed a sword and shield, like the medallions Blue had stolen from his ancestors. The thought was fleeting. The Traveler distracted him with his words.

"Behold Amin the Protector. With these medallions, you are empowered. With these symbols, you will vow to protect the child, the mother, and the future of humanity. You have but to call upon the shield and the sword around your neck. As long as these symbols are worn, no harm can penetrate you. Rise, Amin the Protector."

Amin returned to his feet. Strength emanated from his body, more strength than he had ever before known. Amin was heady with the new power and forgot about The Freedom Code.

The Traveler reached inside his garment and placed a pouch in Amin's hands. "You will use these gems to build your kingdom. In two moonrises the baby will come. You will rest, and then you must go and watch over the mother. I will return for the child's birth. Thereafter, you will teach and guard the child, and you will rule this land. I must go now and fulfill the gods' orders."

***

As the sun rose, the Elder opened his eyes. Hovering over him were the plumes of huge wings. The Elder smiled a radiant smile. The wings began to lower and wrap themselves around him. The wings' grip tightened more and more. They engulfed the Elder's entire body. Shortly, the Elder drew his last breath.

***

Ade traveled through the forest with miles yet to go to Kabaka's and Hatshepsut's hut. Suddenly, she was struck with a mournful pain in her heart. Tears began to roll from her eyes. She fell to her knees and then her father's voice came to her.

"Ade, Ade, get up, my daughter. He draws nearer with every moment. Call upon a kindred soul to help you."

Ade rose to her feet and cried out, "Oh, my father, I never should have left you. He has taken you from me."

Ade pulled together all of the strength she could muster and released the calling roar of a lioness. In seconds, she heard the sound of breaking branches. Leaping through the thicket, a colossal lioness landed a few feet in front of Ade.

"Sister of the forest, I beg you for your help. Blue has returned. He is after the child of your mistress, Hatshepsut."

The lioness lay on the ground. Ade mounted the lioness's back and wrapped her arms around the animal's massive neck. The lioness raced with her rider through the forest.

"Thank you, my sister, thank you," Ade told the lioness as the bush whipped past.

***

87

The moon was edging down to the horizon as Hatshepsut lay asleep in her hut. Her baby, so near birth, rested evenly between the hips of her slender five-foot-seven-inch frame. Pregnancy had only enhanced Hatshepsut's beauty. Her flawless, satin ebony complexion was more radiant than ever. Her full lips framed her heartwarming smile, only eclipsed by her onyx eyes that shone like gems set in alabaster globes. Her regal posture and delicate gaze gave the appearance that she was floating as she walked. She was an African angel. Many villagers believed she and her husband, Kabaka, were children of the gods.

Before the sun rose, the lioness delivered Ade to the door of Hatshepsut's hut. Ade quickly rushed in. Mpho was sleeping beside Hatshepsut. They awakened, startled then happy to see Ade.

"Ade!" Mpho exclaimed. "I just arrived a few hours ago. You made it with the gods' speed."

"You are here for my baby's birth as promised," Hatshepsut said, smiling.

"No, I am not," Ade said firmly.

"What is wrong, Ade?" Mpho asked at once.

"A powerful and evil being is on his way here. We cannot stop him. He is after Hatshepsut's baby. He wants to lay his hands on your belly to send a message to your unborn. If he finds you here, Mpho, he will find great satisfaction in taking the life of a descendent of the Oracles with child. You must leave at once. Take your things. I don't want him to know you were here. Hide in the forest as far from here as possible. I will come for you after he leaves."

"But how will you protect Hatshepsut and yourself?"

"It's your child the evil one will wish to kill, because of the Ancient Oracles' prophesies and your child's part in The Freedom Code. He does not know of you now. We must protect you. I will tell you everything later. You must go. We will be safe."

Mpho hurried to pick up her satchel with water, food, and a knife and clothing. She kissed her best friend and her Aunt Ade. "I will go to the forest." Then she was gone.

Hatshepsut stood up and tried to force Ade out of the hut. "You must run away too, Ade."

"There is no time. He approaches your home as we speak."

"How will we fight him? Kabaka is away hunting. He won't return until the moon sets."

"With the gods' help, we will fight. Kabaka has a cloak from his ancestors. I saw him wearing it here. It has been passed down from father to son since ancient times to protect his family from danger and evil. Quickly, get it for me."

Hatshepsut hurriedly retrieved the quilt from under a zebra hide. Ade instructed her to get on the floor. Ade first tucked the quilt snuggly under Hatshepsut's left side and then her right. The weight of the pregnancy held the quilt tightly beneath Hatshepsut as she lay on her back.

Ade prayed as she rubbed her hands in a circular motion over the quilt.

"Ancestors of this child not born, protect your child from the evil power that comes. Oh, cloak of the Ancient Oracles, take the spell within your fibers. Save your family. Save us all." Then Ade placed her hands over Hatshepsut's eyes and prayed. "Gods, bring sleep to her. The evil Traveler Blue will know if she pretends." Hatshepsut fell into a deep sleep.

Ade fled the hut to hide. Baba, a boy child carrying a drum Kabaka had made for him, was just entering the clearing. She scooped him up and found a place to conceal them in the bush as the Traveler appeared. Approaching the entrance of the hut, the Traveler moved his head from side to side, scanning all around him. His eyes lingered where Ade and Baba were hidden. The Traveler paused. With a scowl on his face, he turned and walked in their direction. A thunderous, deafening roar filled the air.

In the next instant, Ade and Baba felt a violent wind pass over their heads. The lioness hurdled the bushes twenty feet in the air and fiercely descended upon the Traveler. The Traveler extended his arms and clamped the attacking lioness's head between his hands. With one ferocious turn, the lioness fell to the ground, headless. Holding the decapitated head, the Traveler looked into the lioness's eyes, released a mighty roar, and laughed. Dropping the head, he turned and walked triumphantly into the hut. Ade's heart raced so fast she almost fainted, but Baba was shaking with such fear she was jarred back to reality. She cupped her hand over Baba's mouth to keep him from crying out in terror.

***

Inside the hut, the Traveler saw Hatshepsut sleeping alone and was pleased. *I will do this deed and none will know.*

He knelt beside Hatshepsut and tried to loosen the cover. It would not move. He knew if he pulled with more force, it might awaken her. So he left the quilt in place. He placed his hands on Hatshepsut's belly and began to speak the words of enchantment.

"Mother of the mother of my daughter
Slave beasts chained for the slaughter.
The world order will be governed by Blue
Reign on, future daughter of Blue."

The Traveler closed his eyes and raised his head upward. A glow of blue light appeared where his hands lay. When the light paled, he removed them.

"It is done. It has begun."

As the morning broke, he quickly departed the hut and disappeared into the forest. Ade waited several minutes before leading Baba out of their hiding place.

"Hatshepsut!" the boy cried, looking at her hut.

Ade held the boy close and looked into his eyes. "Our beloved Hatshepsut is fine. Go to your parents, Baba." Ade placed him on his feet. "Warn them about the Traveler!"

"Yes, Ade!" The boy ran in the opposite direction from the Traveler, into the forest.

Inside the hut, Hatshepsut was still asleep. Ade reached under her shoulders, lifted her forward, and tugged the quilt until it loosened.

"Awaken, Hatshepsut. Awaken. We have much to do."

A sudden darkness startled Ade, causing her to release the quilt. An awesome figure had appeared at the entrance of the hut, casting a huge shadow where she knelt. As Ade turned to look, the man rapidly approached.

"Ade, why are you here? Has the time come? Hatshepsut, what is the matter? Who brought the lioness to such an end?"

The voice behind these questions brought Ade a sigh of relief. It was Kabaka, returned early from the hunt. Thoughts of his wife and child had hastened him to them. Tall and strong like the trees, with stalwart limbs and unyielding roots, Kabaka had been born with the innate presence of a great chieftain. His broad 6'5" frame cast an enormous shadow. Wisdom, courage, and kindness projected from his eyes. His square jaw, broad nose, and ample lips were impeccably sculpted. All admired Kabaka, but he only required the love of Hatshepsut.

"She is sleeping. I have much to tell you. But first, you must help me remove this quilt from around her."

Ade warned Kabaka not to touch the face of the quilt. It was full of evil spirits. Carefully, Ade folded the quilt inward. Only then did she hand it to Kabaka with instructions to take it from the hut.

"Later, we will burn it. And Kabaka, Mpho is hiding in the forest. Please look out for her. If she isn't nearby, we'll find her later."

Although Kabaka did not understand, he trusted Ade. He traveled more than a mile looking for Mpho. He left the quilt in the high grass of the forest and regretfully returned without Mpho.

"Hatshepsut, are you all right?" he asked, entering the hut.

"I am now that I see my husband's face." She took his hand as he knelt beside her. "You did not find Mpho?"

Ade interceded. "We will find her as soon as your child is born and you are safe. I know Mpho. She is protecting us all and her child, making sure Blue does not find her."

Hatshepsut placed her husband's hand on her stomach. "Your child is anxious."

"Like I have been, but last night the voice of my mother came to me. She said not to worry—my father was guarding you and our child until I returned home," Kabaka said.

"I just had a dream about your father!" Hatshepsut exclaimed. "With the heart of a hundred lions, he was fighting a great battle with a demon Traveler. Then he came to me, holding a baby in his arms. He told me to have no fear. He had stopped the demon and his grandchild was unharmed. He said my adopted aunt would be of help us."

Ade lifted her arms to the sky and cried out, "Thanks to the gods."

Ade's outburst surprised Hatshepsut. "Ade, in my dream you were protecting my child. I didn't understand its meaning. Are you afraid of a demon Traveler?"

"Tell me now," Kabaka demanded. "What has happened? Who or what dares to threaten my family and home? They will perish!"

Ade took one of their hands in each of hers. Then she described the chain of events that had occurred from the moment the Traveler had arrived in their land.

***

Mpho was suddenly disoriented. Having walked over twelve hours yesterday, she was weary, and the more so because her labor pains had begun and were coming closer and closer together. *My child! Why do you come so early? I will love you just the same, but what complications!*

She struggled through the dense bush of the forest, wishing she were back in the safety of the Elder's hut. All of her life he and Ade had taken care of her. As she forged forward, she felt a sudden softness underfoot.

It was a quilt. *What good fortune. If my baby comes before I reach the Elder's, he or she will have a comfortable place to rest.*

She took the folded quilt and felt it familiar. She held it from her and smiled. *It's Kabaka's quilt!* The gods were smiling down on her. She was not far from Hatshepsut! She wondered if it were safe to rejoin her best friend. Smiling, she knew it was. The gods would never have sent her this sign if it weren't.

She rolled up the quilt, placed it under her arm, and continued down the path. In her weakened state, she had become disoriented, and unbeknownst to her she headed in the wrong direction for several minutes.

Suddenly pains ripped through her body, and she crumbled to the ground. Nothing had prepared her for this. Trying to catch her breath, she attempted to gain some control of her body, but it was useless. Nature had its way with her. In her mind she told herself over and over, *You must not scream! What if he's nearby? You must not scream!*

It seemed like hours before she pushed her baby through the canal. Head first, then the tiny body. When she heard her little girl's first cry of life, she wept with joy, but she was also fearful of any noise that would alert Blue to their whereabouts. Hurriedly, she took water from her satchel, washed the child, cut the cord, and wrapped the baby in Kabaka's quilt. The quilt quieted her newborn.

At last, Mpho held her baby to her breast and nestled down in the grass with her gift from the gods. Nature took its course and her baby fed from her breasts. Her body grew wearier by the hour as her child grew stronger from her nourishment.

I wish you could see her, Aliko! She is so beautiful!

Mpho had no idea she was bleeding. She only thought of her baby and the wonder of it all as she lost consciousness.

Chapter 12

Amin awoke with the sun. He was having second thoughts about his imminent reign of power. His heart was heavy as he began his journey to the home of his young cousin, Kabaka. If he served his new master, he would betray his family, even if it were by decree of the gods. Amin felt the wealth of diamonds tied within his robe that he would use to build his empire. Was he being honest with himself, or was he tricking himself into thinking he was pursuing his destiny when in actuality he was betraying everyone he loved?

Along his way, Amin came to the Elder's hut and looked inside. The Elder was sleeping. Amin noticed his peaceful smile. He did not detect that the Elder had passed away.

Amin continued on his sojourn, remembering the day the Elder had saved his life. The Elder had found him just as a snake was about to attack. Amin had no idea how, but he was suddenly airborne and landed safely in the high grass. The Elder held the snake, hanging lifeless in his hand. Though the Elder had slain the serpent, it had closed its fangs on the Elder's forearm and released its venom. The Elder instructed Amin to take his knife and cut where the snake had bitten. Amin was afraid, but he did as the Elder ordered. The Elder sucked the poison from his arm and tore his robe to make a bandage with magical herbs. Together they walked back to the village.

Along the way, the Elder said, "Someday, my young Amin, you will be a doctor and save many lives."

Amin stopped for a moment to rest. He looked around the forest and realized that he was standing in the very spot in which the Elder had saved his life from the serpent.

He heard the Elder's voice in his mind and shivered. "I could not stop the serpent. This time he has bitten you."

***

In the hut, Ade, Hatshepsut, and Kabaka planned their strategy for the Traveler's return. They didn't know when or how he would come. But they knew he could be fooled. He had underestimated their intelligence once. They knew his weakness was his prejudice. Kabaka devised an escape vehicle. In order to create it, he had to go to the river.

Hatshepsut could sense her husband's disquiet. "I know you fear for our safety, but the gods will protect us until your return."

"Hatshepsut is right. You know all I know now," Ade confirmed. "You must prepare passage and destroy the quilt. Another day has passed. You must find Mpho and bring her to safety before her child is born."

Kabaka conceded. He strapped his hunting knife around his waist and took his spear in hand. He raised his arm to the sky and prayed. "Gods of all, send protection to my family."

When he walked out of the hut, he noticed movement in the bush. He held his spear tightly and drew his knife, ready to attack. Then, out of the forest, Amin appeared. Kabaka dropped his weapons, ran to his cousin, and wrapped his arms around him.

"The gods have answered my prayers," he shouted. "All will be safe. My Elder cousin has come. No harm can come to our family now."

As Kabaka held onto his cousin, Ade and Hatshepsut appeared at the entrance of the hut. Ade's eyes met Amin's. Ade bowed her head. Amin's face was stone.

"The wise Elder of my family is present. Now I go without fear," Kabaka bellowed. "Ade will tell you all that has happened."

Amin did not reply.

"I, too, must leave to prepare the place of my father's rest," Ade said to Amin.

"What do you mean, Ade? I saw your father sleeping this morning."

"It is a sleep from which he shall not awaken," Ade said. "I saw it. The Traveler beast took his life. My father laughed in his face."

Amin and Hatshepsut were stunned by Ade's announcement. Ade put her arm around the weeping Hatshepsut.

"It was his last duty on this earth that your baby be kept out of harm's way. Now we must all do as the gods will. I must go. I will return before the end of the coming moonrise. Amin, will you walk with me to the forest's door?"

Ade and Hatshepsut embraced. Amin then escorted Ade to the forest's edge.

"There are no gods who order betrayal of the family," Ade said. "The snake has bitten you. But its poison has not completely entered you. It cannot flow, because you are not evil. Its venom requires an evil host."

"I do not know what you speak of, Ade."

Ade placed her hand on Amin's face. He quickly moved his head from her touch. With that, Ade walked into the forest. As she disappeared within the greenery, Ade shouted, "Amin, look at your forearm."

Amin looked and saw the wounds of a serpent's bite.

***

Along the route to recover his father's quilt, Kabaka searched everywhere for Mpho. He wanted to call out to her, but Ade had warned him to keep quiet. Blue would be listening. When he reached the high grass, the quilt was gone and Mpho was nowhere to be found. Kabaka looked to the heavens for guidance. Maybe his father's spirit had claimed the quilt. It was too ancient to be destroyed. But what of Mpho? Returning without her weighed heavy on his mind. Hatshepsut would never get over it, but he had no choice.

Only after Hatshepsut and their baby were safe would Kabaka resume his hunt for Mpho.

Chapter 13

In the darkest depths of the river's swamps, there lived the father of all crocodiles, who had devoured hundreds of the bravest hunters, including Kabaka's father and Mpho's husband. From the tip of its monstrous jaw to its tail, it measured nearly twenty feet and was as broad as the deck of a three-man raft. Its layered teeth were ten inches in length. This crocodile was feared more than any lion. It was as if it were created to destroy man. It would attack, even when its belly was full.

Kabaka was going to meet this executioner and challenge his right to live. He could not tell Hatshepsut and Ade his plan. They would have been terrified. This was a day of reckoning and reciprocity. This amphibious beast had murdered the bravest hunters Kabaka had ever known. Now Kabaka would face their killer in order to save his wife and child and The Freedom Code.

My true courage will be born with your birth, my child, he thought proudly of his unborn infant. *May the gods be with me.*

When Kabaka reached the marshy swamps, the sun was at its highest point.

He stepped into the murky water. "Ancient demon of the sea, it is I, Kabaka, son of Tau, who summons you here."

A pair of enormous, liquid, evil eyes broke the surface of the muddy water and glared at Kabaka. The creature had the senses of a seasoned hunter. Its perverse nature found satisfaction in the death of the weak and terrified. It waited for Kabaka to cower.

Unafraid, Kabaka slowly submerged into the water. Soon, only his eyes and the tribal bandana wrapped around his head were visible. He dared to opposite direction and hastily swam away, then disappeared from sight.

The crocodile's retreat was a cunning ploy. Moments after its departure Kabaka stepped out of the water. He took mud and wet leaves and molded them into a ball. Mounting the ball on a branch, he tied his bandanna around it, and then firmly planted the decoy in the swamp. He perched in a tree to watch for the crocodile's attack. His father had taught him to think as his enemy.

Many minutes passed, and the demon crocodile still did not break the water's surface. Then, without warning, the crocodile appeared on the shore. It spotted Kabaka's bandana and slithered silently and methodically into the water. Once within striking distance, it charged into the water, jaws fully extended, exposing its spiked teeth, which closed on Kabaka's bandana.

With the force of a lightning bolt, Kabaka's spear entered the top of the crocodile's snout. The thrust was so powerful the blade passed through to the crocodile's underside, locking the creature's jaws together. Struggling frantically, the writhing crocodile tried to free its mouth. Kabaka held fast to the spear, jumped on the crocodile's back, reached to its underside, and repeatedly plunged his knife into the reptile's heart. When the crocodile had breathed its last breath, Kabaka dragged the creature to shore.

Kabaka's time grew short. He took his knife, slit the crocodile's underside, and gutted the creature. Then he gathered wood, twine, and sap from a rubber tree to prepare the crocodile for its mission of salvation.

***

Amin stood guard in the doorway of the hut. He offered no conversation to Hatshepsut. She sensed his anxiety.

"My heart aches too," she said, breaking the silence. "We all loved the Elder, but we must accept the gods' decisions. We have you here to lead us now."

"What are you talking about, Hatshepsut? The villages have chosen Kabaka as their leader. He will rule."

"That is not what Kabaka has said to me, cousin Amin. He says you were the future leader of our people, and he is still learning from you. I agree with my husband. You have seen the outside world and are the only one truly prepared. Ade told me, when you returned, you even taught her to speak English so that she would be prepared to live in their world. You taught us all. You have opened our minds and healed our bodies. You are our leader.

"And Kabaka loves you so much. When his father was killed, you embraced him as your own son. He has never forgotten. He told me he would exchange his youth and courage for a small portion of your knowledge."

"My young cousin is naïve," Amin said. "He sees me with a child's vision. His love is nothing more than a remembrance of isolated kindness shown. Love is an illusion."

"Amin, you are an Elder. You are wiser than I am. But to me, a child's vision is the clearest. Love is something simple and natural."

"Hatshepsut," Amin interrupted, "you think love is simple, harmless, and free. Perhaps you should rest. I can make no sense of what you are saying. "

"That saddens me, because you are loved by so many."

Amin gave no reply. She had stripped him of his self-pretenses. With her words, Hatshepsut had brought him to the crossroads. He had to decide which path to take.

***

It was late in the afternoon when Ade returned to her village. No one had seen the Elder or the Traveler. Most assumed the two were together, deliberating in the Elder's hut. Even though Ade knew what she would find, her heart and mind were not prepared for the sight of her father lying lifeless inside his hut. Holding her hands to her heart, she slowly walked to him and dropped to her knees. His smile brought tears to her eyes. She placed her hands on the sides of his face.

"Oh, my father, beautiful in life, beautiful in death, I will prepare you for your new life."

Ade cleaned her father and wrapped him in his favorite robe. Her time was short, but she sat with her father. It was only a moment. She took his hand and brought it to her check. Her visions told her his spirit was safe. Then she set his hand down at his side gently, and went to the huts of the Elders, and told them of her father's passing.

She was at peace as she watched them view her father. Men she had known her whole life. They nodded to her. She left the hut to gather the village people to announce the Elder's death.

The villagers crowded around their beloved Ade to give their condolences. She heard some of the villagers ask where Mpho was, but they politely left her only with their well-wishes, not their questions. She could not speak Mpho's name for fear Blue might hear her. Finally the boy, Baba, said he had seen Mpho at Hatshepsut's, and the questions stopped. Everyone knew they were best friends.

Keeping with tradition, the women finally returned to their huts while the men of the village performed the ceremonies of death. The villagers didn't notice that Ade had slipped away with her few articles of clothing and her most prized possession—an English-language book Amin had given her years ago.

As she approached the edge of the forest, she turned to stare at the village where she had lived her entire life. Her people would miss her, and she was sad she was unable to say farewell, but she had no choice. Blue was nearby.

Ade's mind spun into thoughts of love, her father's love, Hatshepsut and Kabaka's love, and the one love in her life that was never requited. Ade had loved a man since she was a very young woman. She knew no one else could fill her heart. Now she doubted the words confirming that love would ever come from his mouth to her ears.

As her father had told her, she had another journey, and she hastened now to undertake it.

***

The moon was high above when Ade reached the hut. Amin still stood guard at the door. Sullen and silent, his brow was deeply wrinkled by troubling thoughts. He did not speak to Ade as he stepped aside for her to enter then followed after her.

"All is prepared," Kabaka said. "We will travel tonight to the den of the lions to hide. When the baby is born, we will let Hatshepsut rest, and then we will travel the river. We should leave very soon. Is all ready, Hatshepsut?"

Hatshepsut tried to answer; instead she balled over, holding her stomach. Amin watched Ade and Kabaka run to her side. Hatshepsut's water had broken.

"Hatshepsut!" Kabaka said.

"Your baby will not wait. It is coming into this world. Get her to the ground, Kabaka," Ade ordered.

Kabaka guided his wife to the floor as her contractions rapidly intensified. She told the men to leave. Amin did as he was told, but Kabaka remained.

"I will watch my child arrive."

Ade prepared Hatshepsut for her birth.

While Hatshepsut breathed and pushed, Amin ran through the forest, trying to rid himself of the demon. At the moment of Hatshepsut's last contraction, she screamed from the hut's floor while Amin raised his arms to the sky and released a deafening bellow of penitence. When all at last was quiet, a beautiful baby girl had entered the world and the demon had departed from Amin's soul.

Amin rushed through the forest back to the hut. Kabaka was sitting on the floor next to his wife, with the new baby in his arms.

"You must all leave at once!" Amin blurted out. "The Traveler will soon come. I have betrayed you and I am sorry."

Kabaka was shocked.

"I will stay here and stop him," Amin continued, "but you must flee now. I beg you, go!"

"I love you, Amin," Kabaka said. "I don't know what demon possessed your mind, but had you been another man, my knife would be buried deep in your chest. Now you are willing to sacrifice your life for ours. You are forgiven."

Hatshepsut took the baby from Kabaka and called Ade to her. She handed the baby to Ade.

"I cannot travel. I give you charge of my baby's life. You must protect her. You must make sure she is loved. Save our baby's life."

"Hatshepsut will rest a short time," Kabaka said. "Then I will carry her. Ade, take our baby to the river. If we have not arrived by the time the moon sits on the water's edge, you must leave without us."

Kabaka further described where to find the unique vessel for her escape and instructed her how she should use it. Ade took the infant and exited the hut.

"Ade, please wait," Amin called out, following her.

"You have come back to me," Ade said, her heart filled with pride.

He removed the two medallions and placed them around Ade's neck. "The Traveler gave these to me. As long as you wear them, you and the baby will be protected."

Could this really be? Ade thought in astonishment. *Do I possess The Freedom Code?*

Amin had been watching her. Quickly, he said, "They are what you would think. Protect them and the baby with your life. They must be preserved until the Blessed Children face the children of Blue."

Ade watched Amin reach into his garment and pull out a pouch of diamonds.

"Exchange these for money in the outside world. Do not be fooled. Each one of these diamonds is worth a fortune. Use one at a time. And let no one know you have more."

"Amin, I know nothing of the outside world. You have taught me the language, but I don't know where to go or what to do."

"Hold the baby with one hand and place the other across my eyes. You will see all I have seen. Just call upon my memories and you will know where to go." Ade did as Amin instructed. A surge of energy warmed her head as thousands of images, thoughts, and writings streamed behind her eyes at lightning speed. Amin's memories were now hers.

"I must go now, Amin."

"Before you leave my sight for the last time, I must tell you I have loved you for nearly all of my life. Only the gods know why I have waited until now to say these words."

"And I have always loved you."

"Goodbye, Ade."

"Goodbye, Amin."

Ade secured the diamond pouch in her clothing and hastened into the forest.

In the early morning, Amin looked out of the hut. In the distance, over the tops of the trees, he saw the glow of high flames. Amin called out to Kabaka.

"The Traveler comes closer, Kabaka. This fire is a warning from the gods. Hatshepsut can rest no longer. You must go now."

Kabaka picked up his wife. Although her pain was excruciating, Hatshepsut remained silent. "Amin, come with us," Kabaka said as he exited. "There is nothing here you must do."

Amin looked deep into his cousin's eyes and smiled. "You know what I must do." Amin placed his hand on the back of Kabaka's neck and pulled his head to him until their faces touched. "I love you, my son."

"I love you," Kabaka said.

"Goodbye, Kabaka."

"Goodbye, Hatshepsut."

"Goodbye, Amin."

With his wife in his arms, Kabaka hurried into the bush.

After traveling no more than twenty minutes, they heard a baby crying. Hatshepsut told Kabaka to stop. Kabaka placed his wife gently on the ground. A few feet away, he discovered the baby alongside the mother, who was lying face down on the ground.

"It's Mpho! Why didn't I see her here?"

He gently rolled her to her side with the baby still in her arms and put his ear to Mpho's heart. She was dead. Kabaka didn't know what to say to his beloved Hatshepsut.

"Mpho! Come to me. Bring your child!" Hatshepsut called out weakly.

Kabaka rushed back to his wife and held her. "The gods have taken her."

"How can that be, Kabaka? I don't understand!" Hatshepsut cried uncontrollably. "I love you, Mpho." Hatshepsut held onto Kabaka. "Blue killed her and her baby just like Ade said he would!"

"Her baby is here, Hatshepsut! The baby lives!"

Hatshepsut gulped back her tears. "Bring the baby to me."

Kabaka disengaged the baby from Mpho. Then stopped.

"It's wrapped in my quilt. Didn't Ade say it had evil spirits?"

"The quilt is your family's, and Mpho's child is blessed. I do not fear the quilt."

The child did not cry, appearing content when in Kabaka's arms and at last in Hatshepsut's.

Kabaka was once again in the moment and saw the fire in the distance. "We must go. Mpho would understand. Do not look back," he said as he lifted his love and Mpho's baby.

They continued their journey. Hatshepsut fed Mpho's baby from her breast, just as she had her own infant. *I have your child, Mpho. I will protect her with my life.*

***

The crackling fire, the snapping and popping sounds, and the smell of burning embers all were precursors of Blue's arrival. From earth to sky, Blue had set the world ablaze in a wall of gold and orange flames.

103

Blue appeared, wrapped in white from head to foot. His robes were without char or soot. Only his cruel eyes were visible. Strapped to his side was a mighty sword. Its handle was laden with jewels.

Amin stood outside of Kabaka's hut, blocking its entry.

"I've come for the child," the Traveler called out from the end of the path. "Step to the side."

Amin did as ordered. Blue charged past him into the hut and as suddenly was confronting Amin.

Blue had thought it ironic that Amin would do his bidding. While betraying his own people, he would be wearing the spirit of his people's freedom in the medallions. Blue had gloated. Now he was enraged that his plan had been uncovered before he had control of the baby.

"You insolent fool, where is the child? Answer me, vermin!" With a powerful backhand blow, Blue knocked Amin to the ground.

Blood poured from the gaping tear in Amin's lip.

"You should have been protected by the medallions. What have you done with them?" Blue demanded, his anger intensifying.

Amin only smiled. "The child will never be yours, nor will the medallions of The Freedom Code. Do what you must, vile serpent Blue. Yes, I know who you are, and I do not fear you, or death!"

Blue drew back his sword.

The snakebite had disappeared from Amin's forearm. "My Ade!" he called out, seconds before his head was severed from his body.

***

Blue's rage governed his thoughts. He had wanted Dr. Amin to be the infant's teacher and caregiver. He searched Amin's body and found that Eleni Lwanga's diamonds were also gone. In a fit of rage, he torpedoed the hut and forest with flaming balls of fire.

Blue surveyed all around him with his cold, steel-blue eyes. Suddenly, hawk-like, his eyes fixed on a faint azure glow in the distant woodland.

Chapter 14

Even in the arms of her husband, this journey was devastatingly painful for Hatshepsut. Kabaka moved at such a feverish pace, he had not noticed the blood on her garments.

"Kabaka," Hatshepsut mumbled, barely conscience. "We must stop, I cannot go on."

"Hatshepsut," Kabaka said, still running, "the moon will soon touch the river. If I move faster, we will make it. I cannot stop."

"You could make it without me."

"What are you saying?"

"I do not believe it is in the gods' plan for me to make it to the river."

"Do not speak that way. I will not stumble or fall. You will rest on the river. We will not be much longer."

"My husband, look at me."

For the first time, Kabaka looked down at Hatshepsut drenched in blood and felt it dripping from his hands. Tears ran down his cheeks. In his heart, he refused to believe his beloved would die. He increased his pace.

"Kabaka, stop!" Hatshepsut raised her hand to wipe the tears from his face. Kabaka came to a halt. He carefully sank to the ground and cradled Hatshepsut and the infant in his lap.

"I can go no further. You must take this infant with you. Raise this baby with ours. Tell my daughter I will always watch over her and I will always love her."

"Hatshepsut, I could never leave you. We are one. I cannot live half dead."

"You must protect our child and teach her. You are a father now, Kabaka, and I live through her. Now, would you lay me on the ground? I want to feel Mother Earth." Kabaka did as his wife wished. He remained next to her, on his knees.

"Today, we have been given two daughters," Hatshepsut said, handing Kabaka Mpho's infant. "The gods had a reason for this child to be wrapped in the cloak of your ancestors. You must respect their wishes and mine. Now, my bravest of hunters, and the man I will love through all my lives, rise to your feet."

With every fiber of strength in his body, Kabaka rose.

"Take my love and your new daughter," Hatshepsut ordered, with the loudest voice she could muster, "and be gone."

"The child belongs to me," a sinister voice boomed behind Kabaka before he could move.

Blue had arrived, following the emissions of the ancient cloak. Kabaka returned the infant to Hatshepsut.

"No one here belongs to you," Kabaka declared. "Leave these grounds. You have no role here."

Blue moved closer to Kabaka. "You give no orders to me. You may be the best of your breed, but you are far beneath me. Now, step aside so I may pass."

Kabaka stood fast. When the Traveler Blue reached Kabaka's spot, he flailed his backhand to Kabaka as he had to Amin. But Kabaka avoided the hit and sent a powerful blow to Blue's stomach, followed by a kick to his chest that sent him stumbling backwards. Infuriated, Blue hurled a ball of fire directly at Kabaka. Once again Kabaka dodged his wrath, then grabbed a heavy stone from the ground and threw it at Blue, hitting him in the head with a resounding wallop. Blue was stunned momentarily, then he drew his sword.

"A man cannot hurt a messenger from the gods," Kabaka declared. "You may not be a man, as I am a man, but the gods do not favor you. I do not fear you, evil one!"

His sword extended, Blue charged Kabaka. Kabaka sidestepped him, caught Blue's wrist and delivered another powerful kick to his midsection. Again Blue stumbled backwards, steadied himself, and stood back. Slowly, he began to circle Kabaka, poking his sword at him.

"I have chosen well. You are a worthy opponent, but now you shall die."

Blue stepped back. His shoulder hunched forward. Suddenly there was a ruffling sound. From his back sprang enormous white wings.

Kabaka and Hatshepsut watched in amazement as Blue ascended straight up and then circled the sky over them.

Kabaka turned and turned, trying not to lose his enemy's position. Hatshepsut slowly dragged herself to her husband to aid him. Dizzy and disoriented, Kabaka stood still to find his equilibrium. At that moment, Blue hovered in front of Kabaka, and with an accelerated dive thrust his sword into Kabaka's chest, splitting his heart in half.

Hatshepsut cried out, "No, no Kabaka, Kabaka, Kabaka!"

Hatshepsut was midway between her husband's body and Mpho's baby. She had promised Mpho she would protect the child with her life. When Blue approached the infant, Hatshepsut dug her fingers deep into the earth and pulled herself towards the child.

"You will not take my baby!"

"I have selected well. You too remain fearless to your death. I have no patience for battle with you. Be with your husband."

Blue lifted Hatshepsut's enervated body over his head and hurled her to where Kabaka lay. She collided with the ground with such force that her bones cracked. Using her last ounce of strength, Hatshepsut placed her trembling hand on Kabaka's arm before she perished.

Blue swept the bundled infant into his arms. The fire had reached this parcel of forest. Drumbeats filled the air. Animals scattered. Towering clouds of thick smoke followed after Blue and the infant as they escaped into the sky.

The Mother of the Father and the Mother of the Mother, I own you both now. Blue will continue to reign! I am triumphant.

Chapter 15

Ade sat with the infant at the river's edge, waiting for Kabaka and Hatshepsut. Several lionesses stood guard. The moon fell closer and closer to the water's surface. The tiny newborn was hungry and began to cry. One of the lionesses had given birth to a litter a few days earlier. She lay on the ground and turned on her side. Ade got down on her knees, uncovered the infant's head, and held the baby to the lioness's underside to be nursed. When the baby was full, the lioness allowed Ade to fill her canteen with milk.

When the moon met the Okavango River, Ade knew only she and the child remained. Her heart ached. She and the lionesses viewed the not-so-distant fire and knew the world of the forest was coming to an end. The lionesses bid her farewell and began their exodus down the river with the lions and their cubs. Ade walked to the Okavango's bank, placed the sleeping infant on the ground, and removed the thicket that hid the vessel for their escape, the carcass of the floating crocodile.

Even though Kabaka had assured her the creature was dead, the crocodile still appeared to be alive. Its body bore no wounds and its eyes were open with that cunning look reptiles show before attacking.

Ade's heart pounded against her chest as she stared at the creature. Maybe this was Kabaka's intent. Blue would not seek out this creature, and others would fear the crocodile and would stay clear of it and therefore of her and the child. She reached out with a trembling hand and touched the ancient beast to assure herself it was dead. Finally her heart steadied. It was a perfect lifeline for their escape.

She checked to make sure the two medallions were around her neck and the pouch was secure in her garment. Following Kabaka's instructions, she broke a short, sturdy branch from a tree, using it to prop open the crocodile's mouth for air and to view their voyage. Then she saw the fatal wound on its side. Kabaka was a craftsman.

Holding the infant close to her breast, Ade carefully crawled into the crocodile's mouth, trying not to scrape herself on its teeth. In a kneeling position, she untied the twine Kabaka had secured to a tree and tied to the deck of the raft. As soon as the twine was released, the Okavango's current took hold of the raft. Ade eased back into the creature's hull and watched through its open mouth as they were swept down the river.

"Sweet infant," Ade told the baby, "I know not the destiny planned for you, but I will find ways to protect you. I will be your guardian and your decoy. But you cannot know of your beginnings. This knowledge could bring the demon to you. He must never look into your eyes or hear your voice."

Several moonrises passed before the crocodile raft floated to the Okavango's end. Seconds after they disembarked, the raft loosened itself from the shore and returned to the water. Ade did not know why, but she sensed this was her destination. She gave the infant the few remaining drops of lion's milk. The child fell asleep. Ade laid her on the ground and began to meditate.

Amin, husband of my heart, come to me now. I need your guidance through this land of mystery.

Soon Amin's voice sounded in her mind. *Fill your canteen with water. You will travel the desert for many moonrises. Then, you will come to a place called Orapa. There they speak both Bantu and English. In Orapa, you will go to the marketplace and seek a man named Baruti. His eyes see no light. He will help you. He is a thief with honor. I saved his life from robbers. Tell him you are my wife. He will sell one of the diamonds for you. He may still cheat you. It is his nature, but he will secure you with enough money for your travels.*

Ade, I am traveling to the next life. You will not be able to call upon me again. Listen carefully to what I tell you about your travel with the infant. You must cross the vast sea. You will go to the country that took our people away in chains. There you can hide from Blue and find safe haven for the girl child. Ultimately, it will be too dangerous for you to stay with her. She must never know who she really is. Most importantly, you must understand the power of the shield and the sword. To call upon them, you must…

Ade could no longer hear Amin's voice. *Amin, how do I call upon their powers? Amin, come back to me!* Did he know of The Freedom Code? *Amin!*

Amin had traveled too far into the beyond. Ade was now left to her own devices. After she prayed, she stored water and began the journey to Orapa.

***

Far north, on the sacred Ethiopian plateau, the Traveler Blue stood in the waters of the Al-Bahr Alazraq. As he began to remove the quilt from the infant, he realized something was amiss. The child was gaunt and sickly. By some miracle, the powers within the quilt had kept her alive. Her imperfect form showed no signs of the superior lineage of Hatshepsut or Kabaka. Blue realized the azure glow emanated from the cloth, not the child. His fury built into an insane rage. With all of his strength, he flung the infant, still wrapped in the quilt, into the Blue Nile and watched the river wash the infant downstream.

"Let the waters swallow your useless life!" he yelled. "Curse you and your gods, Kabaka. Your trickery will not stop me. I will find the girl child. I will find my riches and my medallions! I swear The Freedom Code will not prevail. None have powers greater than mine!"

Chapter 16

The halo of the sun was just emerging from the east when Ade and the baby reached Orapa. *This truly is an extraordinary child,* Ade thought. Through desert heat, raging rivers, and little nourishment, Kabaka and Hatshepsut's child had survived. *Father, you said she would be perfection, and she is. She is our hope. I only wish I knew what happened to Kabaka and Hatshepsut.*

Ade held the baby close, feeling an overwhelming sadness which only an indomitable spirit such as hers could overcome. Although heavy hearted, she forged ahead with determination.

By noon, she and the child had found their way to the marketplace, where she marveled at the buildings and bustle of the city. She had never seen so many people clustered together. They reminded her of herds of charging antelope.

Amin had told her of the different races and hues, but his explanation had not prepared her for such a visual challenge. Everyone was talking, but it did not appear anyone was listening. People in booths lined the streets, selling everything imaginable from pots, clothes, and jewelry to rugs and tapestries.

It was fortunate that she and the infant appeared to be paupers from the bush land in the eyes of all that viewed them. Their modest clothing was tattered from the trip, and they reeked of the crocodile's scent. Their lives would have been in grave danger if any of the local miscreants had had the vaguest notion that Ade carried a wealth of diamonds.

Ade walked over to one of the booths and asked a woman vendor if she knew the blind man named Baruti.

The woman covered her mouth and nose. "Go, your odor sickens me."

Ade was unaware of their pungent smell and was surprised by the woman's rudeness. She wondered if everyone in the outside world acted in this manner. Ade heard deep, hearty laughter behind her. She turned around and found it was coming from an older man in the next booth. He had the face of a person from her village. He noticed Ade's dismay and stopped chortling.

He gave a broad smile. "You must ignore her. Many of us have forgotten from where our parents came. Sister of the forest, what or whom do you seek?"

"I am looking for a man without sight. His name is Baruti. My husband said I should meet with him."

"Did your husband tell you that this blind man has the honor of a serpent?"

"My husband told me many things. From your description, this is the man I seek. Can you tell me where I can find him?"

"Everyone knows Baruti. You will travel a short distance until you reach the end of this road. There, you will find Baruti's mansion guarded by an assassin. I do not speak harshly when I say to you I am sure you do not have the money that Baruti would require for his audience. May the gods help you."

Ade remembered Amin's warning not to let anyone know of the wealth she carried. She thanked the merchant and headed down the road.

Minutes later, Ade and the infant stood before the guard in front of Baruti's home. The guard was massive, with deep scars carved into his face. He had a rifle strapped over one shoulder and a sword at his side.

"I have a message from my husband for Baruti," Ade told the guard. "If he hears my words, Baruti will meet with me."

The guard looked at Ade as if she were a complete fool. "Baruti is not interested in you, peasant woman, or your message. Leave at once, or I will slice off your ear!"

Ade positioned herself in the middle of the road, directly in front of the entrance to the house. In her loudest voice, she called out, "Baruti! I am the wife of Amin, the man who saved your life. I demand an audience with you at once."

The guard drew his sword and charged in her direction. "Peasant woman," he screamed, "I will teach you with this blade."

Ade placed the infant on the ground behind her. As she turned back, the guard's sword was falling upon her. She instinctively raised her hands over her head to block the weapon's fury. To her amazement, a golden shield suddenly appeared in her left hand and a colossal sword in her right. The guard's sword came crashing down on the golden shield. Upon impact, the blade shattered like glass.

The guard was shocked. He immediately pulled the rifle from his shoulder. With one slash of the sword, Ade split the rifle in two before he could aim. The impact sent the guard to the ground. He looked up only to find the tip of Ade's mighty sword pressed tightly against his throat.

"You will take me to Baruti or I will remove your head from your body. I swear this before the gods."

A voice came from a frail silhouette shadowing a second-floor window of the house. "Escort her to my quarters. Do not try to harm her when she releases you. You would not want me to also humiliate you."

Ade removed the sword. The guard stumbled to his feet and walked to the entrance of the house. Just as they had appeared, the sword and shield mysteriously vanished. Ade picked up the infant and followed the guard into the house.

The house was decorated with beautiful pictures, tapestries, vases, and rugs. Fragrant incense burned in every corridor. Ade was unaccustomed to such opulence. She had never even walked up a flight of stairs. When they reached the second floor, another guard was posted in front of regally carved ebony doors. He opened them. The guard from the street stood with Ade and the infant in the doorway. The slender figure stood in the shadows.

"Have a bath prepared for the wife of Amin and his child. Then find nourishment and clothing for them. From this odor, I can tell they have traveled the sea. I will meet with the wife of Amin when this is done. Be gone now and do as I have instructed."

Ade and the baby were taken to a room filled with women lounging on tasseled pillows and feather mattresses. The women were dressed in fine silks. Golden bracelets and rings adorned their arms and hands. The guard gave them instructions to prepare Ade food and ready her bath.

Ade did not understand when they tried to bathe her. She had never smelled such wonderful aromas as from the soaps they used to bath her body to the shampoos used to lather her hair. She was washed, rinsed, washed again, and lathered in lotions and ointments. When the women had completed their task, not only did Ade not recognize her own scent, her soft, smooth body felt foreign to her touch.

When she and the baby were taken to the dressing room, Ade had no idea how to put on the clothing she was given. She thanked the gods that the women helped her. She had so much to learn. She prayed that she would learn quickly.

The women prepared a feast for her and had somehow procured mother's milk for the baby. It was obvious that Baruti had become a very wealthy and powerful man.

Several hours passed before Ade and the infant were led back to Baruti's private quarters. This time, when Ade entered the room, the scene was quite different. Surrounded by fragrant candles was a minute, elderly man, perched on several overstuffed pillows. His neck, arms, and hands were frail. His fingers were twig-like. His eyelids were wide open. But his eyes were haunting white globes.

Baruti ordered the escort to leave the room and close the door. Then he gestured to Ade to come forward and be seated. Ade sat on a pillow a few feet in front of him and cradled the sleeping infant on another pillow next to her.

"Did my servants provide you with good nourishment and clothing?" Baruti asked.

"Yes, they did. I would like to thank you for your generosity. I am not accustomed to this kind of life. I wonder if I am prepared for the journey I must take."

"You are not. That is why Amin sent you to me. He looks after you even in death."

"How did you know Amin had passed from this life?"

"His voice came to me in my sleep. It had been so long since I heard his voice that I did not recognize it at first. He told me to take care of his wife and the child of his blood. Until I heard you call from the street, I ignored the dream. As a man ages, his mind travels to all the stations of his life. I thought Amin's voice was just a reminder of the only

114

true friend I have had in this life." Baruti smiled. "So, Amin told you that he saved my life."

"Yes, he did."

"I am sure he was thinking of the night he rescued me from the young boys who were beating me with clubs behind the marketplace. Amin just happened to be on his way home from work, heard me calling for help, and rushed to my aid. He did not know me, nor did he know anything about me. If he had known what a scoundrel I was, he probably would have let them beat me to death. You see, I had cheated those boys out of their rightful share of a burglary. The boys of the city were no match for the powerful young man from the grassland. They took a greater beating than I did that night.

"Amin picked me up and carried me to my home. There he cleaned my wounds and brought me food every day of the following week. I told him I would pay him for his help. He laughed. Later, he came by one night and asked me if the stories he had heard about me being a thief were true. I was angry, and for the first time in my life, embarrassed.

"'Yes, I am a thief,' I told him. 'I am a great thief. I can steal better than most with sight. You think you are better than I am. I could buy your entire village, jungle man. I told you, I would pay you for your help.'

"'I asked you for the truth, not payment,' he said. 'You told me the truth. Now, as a friend, I can always trust you.'

"Amin came around very often after that day. He would read to me. He opened my mind to a world of knowledge I never would have known otherwise. When this world became unbearably ugly, it forced him back to the forest. He still would not take my money. He wanted to build and lead with honor.

"I am sure he taught you English. He was generous to many. I am positive that Amin never realized he was my hero and a hero to many others. No one paid tribute or returned his generosity."

Ade's eyes swelled with tears. "Baruti, I have loved Amin for as long as I can remember. I did not show him by my words or actions." Ade held the pouch in her hands. "He even provided the child and me with protection and the means of safe passage. He gave me these diamonds and instructed me to give one of them to you. He said that you would be able to get money for the gem and I must travel across the great sea. Then—"

Baruti interrupted. "You need not tell me any more. This child's life must have a significance that exceeds the importance of my life, yours, and Amin's." Baruti placed his hands across his chest. "Now, I shall repay you, Amin. Put away what you are about to give me. Baruti will pay for all. You must leave this land soon, and I will teach you what to do. You will travel to a country known as the United States of America. When you arrive, all will think you are an African queen."

For years, Baruti had paid scholars from every corner of the world to teach him. Now he imparted some of that knowledge to Ade to help her on her sojourn. From the brutal years of the English colonies to the slavery in Louisiana, Ade learned part of the history of the United States.

"Ultimately, the French settled in Louisiana," Baruti told her. "They were slave owners, but viewed slavery differently than the English. If children were born of Africans and Europeans, the children were the responsibility of the fathers. Slaves could even be freed.

"When the French or Spanish had children with American Indians, they were called Creoles. When Creoles had children with the Africans, these children became second-class Creoles. Over the years, these different classes of Creoles became one. Yet Creoles with African blood held closely the secrets of African spirits. Although Creoles look very different from the Africans you have seen," Baruti told her, "they may have the power to help you the most. What do you think of the United States of America, Ade?"

"The people frighten me. How can I take this child to a place that enslaved our people?"

"There are many reasons you must go to this land. The Europeans are on the edge of war. Our motherland won't even be safe. Countries will fight over our riches. The United States is the only place for you and the baby."

Baruti continued Ade's lessons, improving her English and teaching her to manage United States currency. Baruti filled expensive luggage with a wardrobe fit for royalty. He taught her how to dress and how to walk in shoes. Her stance, her posture, and her expressions were all important. Her regal demeanor would keep people from approaching her unless she was interested in talking to them.

Finally, he gave Ade thirty thousand dollars. It was more money than most Negroes in the United States earned in their lifetimes. Just like with the warning about the diamonds, Baruti cautioned Ade not to let anyone see her money.

The night before their departure, the child, Ade, and Baruti dined together for the last time. They had grown close. "There is so much more I want to tell you, but there is no more time. As the sun rises, the child and you will begin your journey. I have much to do in the next hours. You are an excellent student, Ade."

"No, Baruti, you are an excellent teacher. In my life, I've had three teachers—first my father, then Amin, and now you." Ade walked over to Baruti and knelt in front of him. "My teacher, I have a gift for you." She took both of his hands and placed them over her eyes. Then she placed her hands on his eyes. "Baruti, recall when you and Amin were together. Think of nothing else."

Baruti did as Ade instructed. In moments, his mouth gaped open and he began to laugh with joy. "Ade, Ade, I can see! I can see myself! I can see Amin. We are beautiful! We are magnificent! I cannot believe this!"

In seconds, the images faded. Ade removed her hands and took Baruti's hands in hers. Tears rolled from Baruti's eyes.

"Ade, you have given me what I have yearned for all my life. The picture still remains in my mind. I will leave this earth seeing it. I did not know you had this gift. With your gift and what you have learned, you will conquer any dangers you will face. I thank you. And I thank Amin for sending you to me."

Part III

The Protectors

Ade, Melinda, Lula, Bernice, and Jesse

1936, New Orleans, Alabama

Chapter 17

Melinda sat at the kitchen table sipping her morning coffee. The sunlight beaming through the window cast an almost angelic light on her. Unlike her elder sister, Cora, Melinda was the true heart and head of her family. Cora was much too vain and self- serving. Melinda also stood taller and was more buxom than her petite sisters, Cora and Lula. Lula was very fair, with raven eyes and hair. Cora shared Melinda's light caramel complexion and hazel eyes. Melinda and Lula loved one another and shared a mutual respect. It was different with Cora, but she was their sister.

Melinda greeted her younger sister with a warm smile. "Lula, I could have sworn I woke up this morning hearing the distant sound of drums. I even got out of bed and went outside. I wish I knew where they were coming from."

"Maybe you should ask the Horus Crystal Ball that Big Momma left you when she died," Lula said as she poured a cup of coffee. "She always said you had the power, and I have always believed it." Lula joined her at the table.

"Maybe it wasn't drums. Maybe some of those old sugarcane stalks were rubbing together in the wind." She was suddenly on her feet. "I'll tell you what. Let's go to the French Quarter and take another look at my fantasy store. I've almost saved enough rent money for the first few months."

"Big sister, your store is no fantasy. You're going to be a huge success."

"*We* are going to be a huge success," Melinda said, winking at her favorite sister.

It was Christmas Eve, 1936. The two sisters drove their faithful old pickup truck into downtown New Orleans.

***

Ade was an hour away from New Orleans. Over the last two months, she and the beautiful, healthy, alert child had shared a lifetime of experiences. Ade deeply loved the baby she held in her arms. Baruti had been right. They were treated like royalty. Some whites still did not want to serve her, but they were forced to because they were not sure if she were an emissary of an African government. To avoid questions, she often pretended not to speak English. Transferring from an ocean liner to a smaller ship to a steamboat, she and the baby now traveled up the Mississippi River. They had not stepped on United States soil yet, but within the hour, their new lives would begin.

***

Lula and Melinda parked the truck and walked down Bourbon Street. Even this famous avenue was suffering the effects of the Depression. Buildings had gone without paint or repair. More people stood in soup lines than worked in the sugar factories. But Bourbon Street still had a spark. With President Roosevelt's New Deal, Melinda sensed the fire would return. Since it had taken her five years to save two hundred dollars, she hoped it would be soon.

Lula walked with Melinda toward the shop she wanted to rent. The owner, Roth, was sweeping it out.

Melinda whispered to Lula, "You know he knows that I'm interested in his building. We've been playing cat and mouse for nearly a year. Watch his reaction." She smiled and called out as they approached, "I see you still don't have a tenant, Mr. Roth."

"Well, hello, Miss Melinda and Miss Lula," Roth said. "Yes, my property is still vacant, but not for long! I'm cleaning it now because a nice white gentleman from Baton Rouge is coming down to take a look at it the day after tomorrow. He is willing to pay fifty dollars a month, plus two months in advance."

Melinda smiled. "Well, best of luck, Mr. Roth, but you never know, someone local may make you a better offer."

"Well, most of the white folks around here are barely holding on. The only colored people I know with any kind of money run the Creole Cathouse. I'm not going to rent to them. Do you know somebody else, Miss Melinda?"

Melinda took her sister's hand. "You never know who's capable, Mr. Roth. You never know. You have a good day now."

"You two do the same."

Melinda felt Roth's eyes on them as they walked away. She whispered to Lula, "I can just hear him now. 'That little colored girl has a plan and I'm going to make her pay double if she wants my shop.'"

"Do you think so? He said he had himself a tenant," Lula said.

"He doesn't have anyone coming to see that shop. He knows I want it. I know that he charged his last tenant thirty dollars a month and they left because the rent was too high, but I am just an ignorant little colored girl to him. He wants to take my money with one hand while he sticks his other under my dress. But he'll learn. Now, let's go find ourselves a Christmas tree."

"You're a smart woman, Melinda, except when it comes to picking out trees. Last year that doggone tree was as dry as your sister Cora."

Melinda laughed. "The Lord does not like ugly talk. I'm going to tell on you. Besides, Cora is your sister, not mine."

"If she had it her way, she would have been an only child."

"Cora is too mean to ever have been a child."

"Now that's the truth," Lula agreed, 'but I'm picking out the tree!"

They continued to laugh as they walked toward Bourbon Street. Suddenly, Melinda stopped dead in her tracks.

"Do hear them?"

"Hear what?"

"The drums, Lula! The drums! They are louder than this morning. Don't you hear them?"

"I swear, I don't hear anything, but don't panic. Remember when Big Momma would hear sounds and voices. You have the power. I knew it."

Lula took her sister by the arm and guided her several feet to the north.

"Are the drums getting louder?"

"No."

She guided her southwest towards the docks.

"It's getting louder!"

"We've got to follow the sound of the drums, Melinda!" Lula urged.

Melinda did not move at first. "Maybe the sound will go away."

"I know this must be frightening for you," Lula said. "I know it would scare the hell out of me. But we are here together. If the drums stop, that's fine. But if they don't stop, we have to find out where they're coming from, okay?"

"All right, Lula. I don't think they're going to stop by themselves. The beat is too strong. Just keep holding my arm."

"You know I will."

The beat of the drums grew louder as the sisters drew closer to the bank of the Mississippi River. Suddenly, the steamboat whistle filled the air with a deafening blast.

"Lula, the drums stopped after the whistle blew." Melinda sighed in relief.

"There is someone on that steamboat you must meet."

The steamboat pulled into the dock.

"I think you're right, Lula. I wonder who it could be."

A lively crowd began to gather at the dock, looking for their holiday visitors. Melinda and Lula watched and waited as the passengers disembarked.

"Do you hear anything?" Lula asked.

"Nothing. No, wait. I hear a single drumbeat!" Melinda exclaimed, watching a stunning woman carrying herself like an African queen carefully walk down the gangplank with a child in her arms.

"Is she the one?" Lula asked.

"We'll have to wait and see," Melinda said, never taking her eyes from the woman.

Chapter 18

Ade's eyes scanned the crowd and stopped immediately on Melinda. *Can I trust my instincts? There's only one way to find out.* Holding the baby close, Ade maneuvered her way through the throng of people.

Ade reached the sisters and stood directly in front of Melinda. "When the sun awoke this morning, my heart began to race. As the boat came closer to the shore, it raced again. The pounding in my chest has now stopped as I stand in front of you. Last night I dreamed of two young women. They were dressed as I am dressed. One had skin the color of sand such as yours," Ade said to Lula, "and the other had skin the color of honey such as yours"—referring to Melinda. "The woman with honey-colored skin carried a ball made of crystal. When we both touched this ball, light came from it."

Melinda and Lula were momentarily speechless.

Then Melinda spoke. "I don't know you. But I feel connected to you. I heard your heartbeat. I thought it was a drum. My sister told me the beats were a sign. I didn't want to believe her. I was frightened. And truthfully, I still am."

"Please do not fear me. I wish no harm to anyone. I am also frightened. I am a stranger in a strange land where I do not know anyone. I have come to ensure the safety of this child. You must have the same gift as I. There is no other way you could have heard the beating of my heart."

"My grandmother told me," Lula said, "that Melinda would inherit my grandmother's ability to see the future and I would save a baby, and afterwards have a baby of my own."

The baby began to cry. Without thinking, Lula reached for the child. Unconsciously, Ade released the child to her. Once in Lula's arms, the baby relaxed and cooed joyously. Melinda studied this scene. "My name is Melinda Bovine, and this is my sister, Lula."

Ade introduced herself.

"Ade," Melinda asked, "have you made reservations at a hotel?"

"I do not understand."

"My sister is asking if you have made arrangements to stay in the city. It is a holiday here. If you don't have reservations, it will be very difficult to find a room to sleep."

"I did not know this. If we must, the baby and I will rest on the earth."

"Believe me, that is not a good idea," Melinda said. The two sisters looked at each other. "Ade," Melinda continued, "it is Christmas Eve. You and the baby are welcome to stay at our house. It probably is not the kind of place you are used to staying. It is very humble. We aren't royalty."

"I'm not royalty," Ade said, smiling. "My teacher taught me to act as a queen. He told me if I did not, I would be treated as a nigger. I was not sure of the meaning of this word, but I understood being treated like a nigger was not a good thing."

Melinda and Lula looked at each other and laughed.

"Your teacher definitely told you the truth," Melinda said.

Lula held the baby while Melinda and Ade went to claim Ade's bags. They loaded the luggage into the pickup truck. When Ade tried to climb into the back of the truck, Melinda stopped her.

"No, you and the baby will ride inside with us."

Ade looked puzzled. "I was wondering how big the horses were in America. It must be very hard to pull a cart this heavy. Do you need help bringing them out?"

Melinda chuckled slightly. "This is called a pickup truck. It has a motor. It does not need horses to pull it."

"Are you telling me this cart can move on land as the ship moves on water?"

"That's right," Lula answered.

"I have so much to learn about this world. This baby knows as much as I," Ade said, shaking her head.

When Melinda pulled off, Ade grabbed the dashboard and didn't let go until Melinda parked the truck and turned off the motor. Ade's legs were wobbling slightly after the ride.

"Not everyone drives an automobile like my sister," Lula whispered in Ade's ear. "I've just started to open my eyes when I ride with her. Don't worry. Next time, I'll drive."

Lula burst into laughter. Ade tried to cover her smile.

***

Lula and Melinda lived in a small but comfortable two-bedroom log house. It had been a mere shack behind the sugarcane fields when they were children, but their parents were skillful and hard working. Their father saved for years to purchase this small strip of land. He completed the work on the cabin just a year before he died. Their mother was a talented seamstress. She made all of their clothing, the curtains, quilts, tablecloths, and rugs. It was quaint and picturesque. When they were children, the entire Bovine family had lived here.

"Your home is beautiful," Ade said.

"Thank you," Melinda said, rather surprised. "Our parents built it for the family."

"You can feel that this house was built with love," Ade added.

"Ade, you and the baby can sleep in my room," Lula said.

"I cannot take you from your sleeping quarters. The baby and I have slept many nights on the ground."

"Well, you aren't going to tonight. I'll just sleep in my old bed," Lula said, pointing to the open loft above. "You take my parents' old room."

"This is quite a privilege, to sleep in the room of your parents. I am honored." Ade said. "I must pay you for your kindness."

"Our momma taught us that you can't pay for kindness. So I guess this is just your Christmas gift from the Bovine sisters," Melinda said.

"We can't take your money, Ade," Lula added. "You need every penny you have to support yourself and the baby." Lula carried Ade's luggage into her bedroom. "But if you have a couple of thousand dollars to spare in your pocket," Lula said, jokingly, "Melinda would be more than happy to make you her business partner."

Melinda walked into the room with the baby and laid her on the bed. Ade had her back to them for a moment. When she turned around, she had at least three thousand dollars in her hand.

"Would this be enough to make Melinda's business happy?"

"Lord have mercy," Lula exclaimed, as she ran over to the window and pulled the curtains shut. "Ade, where did you get all of that money?"

"Baruti gave it to me for my traveling. He told me not to show it to anyone. But you two have treated me as family. This is not all of the money. Lula said a couple of thousand dollars would make your business more than happy. I would like to see you more than happy."

"Ade, there are people who would take your life for this kind of money."

"You are warning me, as did Baruti and the husband of my heart, Amin. I believe you, Melinda, as I believed them."

"Ade, you've only known us for about three hours," Lula said.

Ade sat down on the bed next to the baby. "Kill me here and now on your parents' bed, Melinda and Lula Bovine. Take this money, lay this baby in the grass for someone to find. No one knows the child or me. No one will look for us."

The sisters stood dumbfounded. "What are you talking about, Ade? Melinda and I aren't talking about us. We just want you to be careful who you trust until you get to know them better."

Ade just smiled.

"That's the point, Lula. Ade is telling us she is no fool. Am I correct, Ade?"

"Perhaps. I have seen more moons than both of you. There are good and evil people all over the world. Others have held this baby in my travels. The only times she did not cry were when her mother, her father, Ade, and Lula and Melinda Bovine held her. I trust her judgment. Do you trust your own? You have only known Ade for three hours," Ade replied.

The sisters were quiet for a few seconds, and then Lula tucked her chin. "If Melinda's driving didn't kill you, I'm surely not going to try." Ade covered her mouth, trying to conceal her laughter from Melinda.

"Well, if you think my driving is frightening," Melinda said with her hands on her hips, "wait until you taste my cooking."

Lula hurried to the bedroom door as soon as Melinda walked out. "She wasn't joking. She cooks worse than she drives. I may not be able to save us. But at least I can prepare some pabulum for the baby."

Ade walked over to her bag and removed clean clothes for the baby. She poured water from the pitcher into the basin to bathe the infant. After her bath, Ade laid the child on the bed and talked to her.

"The Gods are with us, my beautiful little one. Ade will miss you so much when I find a new mother and father for you. I love you as if you came from my body. I must be sure the Traveler Blue never finds you. I hope the great water we have traveled is too far for his eyes to see you and its roar too loud for your voice to be heard.

"Lula and Melinda will help us. Lula has a heart and mind that shine like the diamonds we carry. Melinda has the vision and wisdom. I will teach her to use them. Just as you will learn to walk and talk, she will learn to walk and talk in the world of spirits." The baby's eyes began to close. Ade's voice always soothed her into a peaceful sleep. "So it shall be."

***

Lula and Melinda had prepared chicken, biscuits, and red beans with rice. Before they ate, Melinda said the blessing.

At the end, Ade raised her hands. "I thank the gods for Melinda and Lula Bovine."

Then she started to eat and noticed they were watching her. "I learned to eat with a knife and fork on board the ship. The first time I ate with my hands, I heard the laughter around me. Then I watched to see what I was doing wrong. I took a knife, fork, and spoon to my cabin and practiced."

"You know, I never thought about that, Ade. We were waiting to see how you liked the food," Lula said.

"It is very good. You use the spices the way women in Baruti's house used them. Many things on the ship had an odd taste to me."

"Well, wait until you taste a real New Orleans feast. The food here is enough to make you stay forever," Melinda bragged.

"I believe you," Ade replied.

"Please get some sleep, Ade. Melinda and I want you to go to midnight Mass with us. It is a Christmas tradition in our family," Lula said.

"I do not know what midnight Mass is, but I am sure I will enjoy it," Ade said.

"Melinda will explain it to you while I'm gone." Lula got up from the table and walked to the front door. "Ade, before we met you today, we were on our way to get a Christmas tree. So I am going back to town to pick one out."

When Lula departed, Ade helped Melinda clear the dishes.

"You and Lula share many good times together."

"Lula is only twenty-one, but she is my best friend in the whole world."

Ade smiled. "That is clear. Melinda, what about your special gift?"

"I've never told anyone this, Ade. I'm afraid of it. I have known I was different since I was a child, when my grandmother tested all of her grandchildren to see which of us would inherit her power to lift the veil of sight. I was able to light up the globe with the touch of my hand, but I refused to develop my powers, even though Big Momma told everyone in the family I was blessed.

"Years later, when I finally mustered up enough courage to touch the Horus Crystal Ball, nothing happened. I use it now around Mardi Gras and pretend to tell fortunes. What I really do is give advice. My grandmother was quite a legend, so I used her name, Madam Bovine, to make extra money. Truthfully, today when I heard the drums, I was more willing to believe I was going crazy than to believe I had the power. I still don't really believe it's true."

Ade smiled. "I understand. I inherited the power from my mother, who died when I was very young. I always could see things before they happened. After many years of hiding this gift, I told my father the gods were unhappy with me. Sometimes they made me have frightening dreams.

"My father was also a gentle man. He told me the gods had given me a gift. He helped me overcome my fear, and now I will help you. Your vision will never go away. If you do not know how to use and control it, it will frighten you for the rest of your life. You want to believe it isn't true. I can prove to you it is."

"How can you prove I have the power, Ade?"

"The same way your grandmother did. Will you show the Horus Crystal Ball to me?"

"It's in my bedroom. Follow me."

Ade did as Melinda directed. As soon as they entered the room, Ade saw it sitting on its wooden tripod throne. Big Momma's chair was still stationed behind the globe.

"Bring that other chair here. We must sit across from each other." The women sat down. "Melinda, you have reached the rite of passage. You must sit in your grandmother's chair." The women changed chairs. "I am here to open the eyes of the crystal light. Follow my words and do as I say. There is no fear or pain where there is knowledge. Do you trust me, Melinda?"

"I don't know why. But yes, I do."

"Then we are free to begin. Place your hands over my eyes, Melinda, and I will place mine over yours." Once Melinda had complied, Ade began. "Today, we call upon the elders of our families to bring back the light of life to the Horus Crystal Ball and to instruct us. Relieve Melinda of her fears. Help us, we beg of you. Melinda, place your hands on the Horus Crystal. I will place my hands on top of yours." Melinda followed her instruction. "Come to us, twins of light and knowledge, and show us our destiny," Ade said.

At first, there was just a flicker of light from the Horus Crystal Ball. Then, it completely awoke with radiant beams of golden light. Ade pressed Melinda's hands to the globe, making it impossible for Melinda to snatch them away.

"Thank you for the return of the light," Ade continued. "Show us your will, and we shall follow."

Letters began to float inside the Horus Crystal. Melinda watched in amazement as one word at a time flowed to the top. *Melinda, the vision of light is yours.* The message disappeared. The letters floated again to form a second message. *Ade, entrust the baby to my descendants, Melinda and Lula. They will protect her.*

The light of Horus faded. Ade released Melinda's hands. "How do you feel now, Melinda?"

"Ade, I no longer fear my gift. It is a privilege. I understand it now. I also understand my message. But I do not understand yours. What did it mean?"

"I will explain it to you when Lula returns. She plays the most important role, although I know not what it is yet. Melinda, you must understand, you are now the light of the Horus Crystal. Your touch will bring it to life, and it will tell you what the other side wants you to know. It will not always tell you what you want to know."

Ade decided to wait to tell Melinda about the twin oracle sisters of her tribe, who were separated as teenagers in the seventeenth century when they traveled from the village to the western coast. Slavers on the coast captured one sister. The other sister escaped. With the help of the other captives, the captured twin smuggled her Horus Crystal onto the slave ship and hid it well. The captured oracle was the first matriarch of the Bovine family, Melinda's great-great-great-grandmother. The twin that remained in the Motherland was Ade's great-great-great-grandmother. She was married to the Elder who had passed down The Freedom Code. *Free Restraints Eliminate, End Domination of (the) Master!* Ade's ancestors had known that they were blessed with the true meaning of what it was to be free—the freedom Blue wanted to destroy to remain master over the descendants of the African race, no matter where they were, and to seek vengeance against them for rising up against him and destroying his world.

She had to pass on her knowledge carefully. Otherwise Blue would discover her and the baby girl who would become the mother of one of the Blessed Children. Ade and the Bovines were linked in spirit and in blood.

One thing at a time, Ade cautioned herself. *Melinda has enough to think about right now.*

Chapter 19

Melinda and Ade helped Lula bring in the enormous tree. They set it up next to the stone fireplace Russell Bovine had built in the living room. Melinda convinced Lula to wait until the baby was awake to dress the tree. Melinda warmed some hot chocolate and started a fire in the fireplace. They sat on the old sofa and told Lula about the re-lighting of the ball and the messages it had sent. When they came to the part about Ade's message, Ade partially explained why she had to wait for Lula.

"The message the crystal sent to me was from the Elders. They said they would guard the child. I'll tell you more later, but for now, Melinda is the Messenger and somehow, Lula, you are the Protector. I just have not been told how."

"I know how," Lula said. "I'll show you after midnight Mass tonight. But, Ade, you have not told us everything. You brought the child here to save her life. What danger is she in? What danger do you bring? You must tell us the whole true story. Only the complete truth will allow us to make the decision of whether we should get involved."

Ade told them the story of the Traveler Blue, from the moment he came into her village to the moment she stepped off the steamboat. She made it clear that The Freedom Code had secrets which would never be revealed until the Blessed Children were safe. Then she waited for their reactions.

"You said the child is not to know where she came from or the history of her family?" Lula asked.

"She must think she was born right here," Ade said.

"Then it would be best if she believed her parents were her real blood parents. She must look like them. And they must be of the highest character."

"That's right, and only one of us will be able to watch this child from afar," Lula said. "Ade, you are connected to her spirit and Melinda is connected to yours. The Traveler Blue could trace either of your thoughts to her. That leaves me. I know what to do and where this innocent baby will be safe." Lula laughed at the expression on Ade's face. "I'm more than a pretty face. Everyone says I'm the problem solver of the family."

Ade nodded seriously. "I am lucky you are." Lula and Ade smiled at each other with respect.

"Melinda," Lula continued finally, "do you remember my friend, Bernice, and her husband, Jesse?"

"I sure do," Melinda answered.

"Who are these people you speak of?" Ade asked.

"Bernice and I grew up together. Her family used to cut sugarcane. Jesse's a mechanical genius, and people with money bring him cars to repair from other states. Bernice met Jesse three years ago when he drove a car he repaired from Alabama to New Orleans.

"Lightning struck that day. Bernice and Jesse are inseparable. Their only sadness is that they have no children. Bernice has had three miscarriages. Jesse is kind and talented like my father. Bernice is bright and good of heart. Both would make perfect parents for this child. The baby looks like she could be their natural child. She would never think otherwise."

"Let's ask the Horus Crystal," Ade suggested.

The three women went into the room. Ade and Melinda laid hands on Horus. They asked the question and the orb replied. "Lula has spoken what is written. Bernice wanted a baby girl and she was going to call her Marion. So be it."

"That's right!" Lula exclaimed. She was going to name her little girl Marion!"

"We must contact Bernice and Jesse immediately," Melinda said. "Should we send a telegram?"

"We can't do that. Ade was sent here so that she would be beyond the eyes and ears of Blue," Lula said. "If we send a message about this child, Blue might pick up the signal. Ade, I'm a little confused about Blue. Is he Caucasoid, Negroid, or Mongoloid?"

"He's a demon in blue skin with super human powers. He comes from the hearts of men. He might even be the Devil himself. Melinda, he

BLUE

must never find this child," Ade said. "We must watch out. We must beware of the demon Blue."

***

When the infant awoke, they decorated the Christmas tree. Melinda explained the holiday to Ade. But Ade was so enthralled by the decorations, she only half heard.

"We better start getting dressed for Mass," Melinda said at 10:30. "I didn't get anything ready. Do you know what you are going to wear, Lula?"

Lula thought for a second. "I've got an idea. Ade, do you have any more dresses?"

"Baruti purchased more than I will ever need."

"Can Melinda and I wear two of them tonight?"

"That would be wonderful! Come, let us select your garments."

The three women went into the bedroom and selected their ensembles for church. Once dressed, they all stood in front of the mirror together.

"This is how you looked in my vision," Ade said.

"I think I'll dress like this more often," Melinda said.

"This is perfect. We are the three wise women," Lula said as she picked up the baby and brought her to the mirror. "I present Marion, our mother, child, and spirit."

They made it to the church about three minutes before the service began. All eyes turned to them as they walked in the doors. Coming down the aisle, they could have heard a pin drop. They sat in one of the front pews where their sister, Cora, and her daughters were perched. Cora gave them a stare of disdain.

"Ade," Melinda said, "I'd like you to meet my sister, Cora, and her children."

"Lula, this is your doing. Are you just trying to embarrass me?" Cora stood up, turning her back on her sisters. "Lorraine, take Lucinda's hand," she told her daughters. "We're going to find somewhere else to sit." Cora hurried them to another section of the church.

Melinda looked at Ade. "I'm so sorry."

"There is no need for you to say this. We all are who we are. She does not know or understand who or what I am. There is no reason she should."

135

"Our sister doesn't know who or what she is. That's the problem," Lula added.

When the priest and altar boys entered from the sanctuary, Ade smiled. "I feel better now. At least that man and those boys are dressed as we are."

Melinda and Lula held back their laughter.

After Mass, many of the parishioners introduced themselves to Ade. Even the priest welcomed her to the country. Cora stood in the vestibule with her daughters and signaled Melinda to come over to her.

"Melinda, what is the meaning of this? How could you bring that jungle person and her child to our church? Look at how she dresses. I would expect this kind of foolishness from Lula, but you know better. What is that jigaboo's name? Ade?" Cora paused for a second. "The name certainly fits! And her color! She looks like a slave pickaninny."

Melinda held her temper. "Cora, who do you think you are?"

"I am Russell Bovine's daughter."

Melinda felt the blood rushing to her head. "You're wrong to talk and act this way in front of these children. Ade is a sweet and kind woman, and that child is an innocent. No one pleases you, Cora. Russell Bovine was Creole. He loved all of us, and he was always respectful of our mother. Although you find it an embarrassment, our father could have cared less that Momma had been a slave. And you never talk about Momma because she was too dark, like Ade, where Lula was too white. If you couldn't look white, you hated anyone who did. Lula never did anything to you except to treat you with the same kindness Momma did, but you always belittled them both. I am sick to death of it. If you insult my little sister one more time, or say anything else disrespectful about our momma, I'm gonna slap you down on Christmas Day and disown you as my sister!"

Melinda watched Cora throw her nose up in the air. "Humph." Then she took her children and stormed out of the church.

***

When Melinda returned to Ade, Lula and baby Marion, the church was empty.

"Have I caused a problem in your family?"

"No, Ade. My sister, Cora, has problems she doesn't even understand. Although I wish she would, I don't believe she'll ever change."

"Cora is Cora," Lula said, taking the baby from Ade, "and right now she's irrelevant. We have a very important ceremony to perform."

Lula told Ade and Melinda to come with her to the holy water fountain. She instructed Melinda and Ade to stand on one side. She and the baby were stationed across from them. Lula uncovered the baby's head and prayed.

"Lord, I stand before you in your house. I hold, in my arms, Marion. I pledge to you now that I will accept the responsibility you give to me. I will protect this child to the best of my ability. I wish to be her godmother. This Christmas Day, Melinda and Ade act as witnesses to this baptism. Melinda, please say the words and anoint this child."

"Marion," Melinda said, "Lula has asked the Lord to be your godmother. Please accept her into your soul." Melinda scooped the holy water into her hand. She let the droplets fall on the baby's forehead. "Marion, I baptize thee, in the name of the Father, the Son, and the Holy Ghost. Amen." Melinda stepped back.

"Ade, please say your words," Lula said.

Ade raised her arms with her palms to the sky and prayed. "Woman is water. Water is life. It is fitting. The gods look upon us. Lula has pledged to be the Protector of this child now called Marion. Stay with them. Stay with their children and their children's children. Give them the courage to fight the final battle." With those words, Ade dipped all of her fingers into the water and ran them across the baby's face. Then she looked at Lula. "The gods of my world are with you now, and so are our ancestors."

Then Ade told Melinda and Lula what her father had told her, that they were descendants of the Elder through the twin great-great-great-aunts and thus were the guardians of The Freedom Code. Lula and Melinda looked at one another in utter wonder. The three women were suddenly one as they accepted their destiny to protect the future through the baby called Marion.

Chapter 20

Very little was said during the ride home. They went to sleep soon after their arrival at the house, each contemplating what would transpire in the next few days. Around 6:30 a.m., Ade climbed the ladder to the loft where Lula slept.

"Lula, Lula, please wake up."

Lula rubbed her eyes. "Is something wrong?"

"Would you take me into town before Melinda and Marion awaken?"

"It's Christmas, Ade, nothing is open."

"There is something I wish to look at closely. I saw it when we were driving to church last night. Take me."

Lula got dressed and drove Ade to town. When they reached Bourbon Street, Ade asked Lula if she would park the truck. She wanted to walk.

"There are many buildings with wood across the doors. Does this mean that no one is inside?"

"Yes, it does. It's been very hard times for the last five or six years. Many people have gone out of business. Melinda says all of this is going to change in the next couple of years. She is very bright when it comes to business. She wants to lease Mr. Roth's building. I'll show it to you."

"What do you mean when you say Melinda wants to lease the building?"

Lula explained leases and rent to Ade.

"I saw three buildings that said 'For Sale,'" Ade said. "In time, would you not pay as much or more in rent than the cost of the building?"

"That could happen, Ade. But if you do not have enough money to buy, you must rent."

"It would be better to own than rent, would it not?"

"Yes, it would."

As the two women approached Roth's building, Ade asked why Melinda wanted this particular location. Lula explained that it was at the end of Bourbon Street and at the beginning of the French Quarter. The second floor could be converted to apartments for tourists, especially during Mardi Gras. The first floor had enough room for a store, a room for fortune telling, and a private office.

"Melinda has put a lot of thought into this business."

"Oh, yes she has, Ade."

The two stood in front of the building and continued to talk. A few minutes later, the front door opened and Mr. Roth appeared.

"Good morning, Miss Lula," Mr. Roth said.

"Good morning, Mr. Roth. What are you doing in the building on Christmas Day?"

"I don't celebrate Christmas, Miss Lula."

"Oh."

"Are you going to introduce me to your friend?" Roth asked.

"I am Ade," Ade said, "Melinda's business partner. Lula was kind enough to show me this building that we might use for our business."

"Really. Well, I am sure Melinda has told you this building is for rent."

"Melinda said to look at your building. It is much smaller than others I have seen. I have not entered, but much of the outside is not pleasing to the eye."

Lula hid a smile. Roth seemed rather taken aback by Ade's candor—Lula guessed he wanted to defend his property, but also to force Ade to humble herself. Lula applauded Ade for refusing to let him do either.

"Well, you'd better consider yourself lucky that I'd even consider renting my building to colored," Roth said at last. "I'd be doing you a favor. I would only consider it because I knew these Bovine girls' father. Some of the people in town never realized Russell Bovine was a Black man. You're not from this country. But I think you'd better learn your place."

Ade looked into Roth's eyes. "Thank you for that information. I am learning many things about your country. I also regret that I led you to believe that Melinda and I wished to rent your building. I have only been looking at buildings that are for sale."

Roth laughed aloud. "I don't know any Negroes around here or anywhere else that could buy one of these buildings."

Ade smiled. "As you yourself said, I am not from here. I did not even know I was a Negro until just this moment. Thank you for this knowledge. I will tell Melinda Bovine what you have taught me. Goodbye."

Ade took Lula's arm and began to walk away. Roth followed behind them. "Hold on there. Lula, is this woman staying at your house?"

"Why do you ask, Mr. Roth?"

"Well, if she's got enough money to buy a building, it sure isn't safe sitting in your house."

"I was taught never to keep money in a house. Some people will try to hurt or kill you for your money in this country. Is that not true, Mr. Roth?" Ade answered.

"Ah, ah, well, that's true."

"Thank you once more for trying to teach me how to act in this country. Goodbye."

"I'll be here until three o'clock," Roth called out. "If you want to talk some about the building, you can see the inside. But if you're not here by three, you can forget it."

"I will talk with Melinda. It is Christmas. She may not be interested today. We must go now."

Ade took Lula's arm again. This time she walked at even a faster pace. Roth stood in the middle of the street, shaking his head and tapping his fingers on the sides of his legs.

When the two women got back in the truck, Lula laughed. "You're something else!"

Ade just smiled.

Melinda and the baby were already awake by the time Ade and Lula returned. Lula told Melinda about the conversation with Roth. Melinda was amused by the way Ade had outwitted him. Still, she would not accept Ade's money.

"Melinda," Ade finally said. "I have no home to go back to. Where I came from, I did not need money. In this world, I must have it to live. I don't know what you know. I will give the money to you, thereby taking care of you once, and you in turn will have to take care of me forever. I think that sounds like I am getting more from it than you."

Melinda sat thoughtfully. "OK, Ade, I accept the terms of our partnership. We will go to Roth today. I promise you this business will succeed."

Lula and Ade were so excited by Melinda's decision that they jumped up and down.

Melinda was holding baby Marion. "Of course they're happy," she told baby Marion. "I'm the one that's going to do all the work."

The baby smiled, and Melinda kissed her forehead.

***

Just to keep him anxious, Lula drove Melinda and Ade into town to meet Roth after 3:00 p.m. Melinda pulled out a stack of Bank of Lafayette envelopes. She told Ade to put twelve hundred dollars in one envelope and five hundred in the other. She explained to Ade how her father, who had never had a bank account, took stacks of these envelopes. Whenever he made payments or purchased anything, he would retrieve his money from hiding places in the house and put the cash in these envelopes. He said it made people think he had more money than he really did. Everyone thought his bank was far away in Lafayette. Most folks figured he had another business there.

Melinda didn't want Roth to see them coming. Lula parked the car on the next block. She and Ade carefully peered around the corner of the building before showing themselves. They saw Roth's head bobbing back and forth, staring out of the window.

"It's time to cut the cane," Melinda said.

Melinda took the bank envelopes from Ade. She put them in her purse and fixed the flap just enough to expose part of one of the envelopes. Roth spotted the two turning the corner. He grabbed his hat and hurried outside. As soon as they were near, Roth started to lock the front door.

"Mr. Roth, I told my partner we were too late. I'm sorry. Well, at least we won't be late for our next appointment. Have a good day, Mr. Roth."

Roth turned around so quickly the keys flew out of his hands. Ade caught them, smiled, and handed them back to him. Roth took a moment to regroup.

"Well, I had some paperwork to do," he said. "You're lucky you even caught me. I guess I can still let you in, since you're here."

As they passed through the open door, Melinda immediately noticed that Mr. Roth had been cleaning. Huge circles of perspiration drenched his shirt under his arms.

"As you can see," Roth said, "the inside is in a lot better condition than the outside. Truth is, all the outside needs is a good coat of paint."

After touring the building, they sat in the back office. None of the women said a word during the entire tour.

Roth spotted the bank envelope in Melinda's purse and tried to initiate a conversation. "I see you're still using your father's bank."

Melinda acted surprised and quickly fastened the flap over the envelopes.

Roth smiled. "Don't you worry any, Miss Melinda. You're safe here with your old friend Mr. Roth. And I do believe you and your partner lady here are serious. That's why I have decided to help you ladies out. I know there are some unscrupulous people who would take advantage of your limitations. I, personally, have never believed in that kind of thing. Therefore, I'll sacrifice this prime location for a mere two thousand dollars."

Melinda knew that Roth's price was at least five hundred dollars over the market value. She took out the first envelope, exposing the second to Roth.

"Mr. Roth, all we have is twelve hundred dollars."

"Miss Melinda, no property is that cheap on Bourbon. What's in the other envelope?"

"It's the money I saved to stock the store."

"How much is it?"

"It's five hundred dollars. It's all I have to start the business."

Roth put his hand on his head as if he had a headache. After a minute, he looked up. "Melinda, I was in business before you were born. You don't need that much money for startup. I want you to have this building. Add three hundred to the twelve and the building's yours."

"Mr. Roth, that is so generous of you. Thank you so much." Melinda smiled. *I thought you wouldn't agree to anything less than seventeen hundred.*

Roth had the deed to the property waiting in the top drawer of his desk. Within the next five minutes, the building was Melinda's and Ade's. Madam Bovine's House of Mystery was born on Christmas Day, 1936.

This was a momentous Christmas for all who dwelled in that house. After this day, none of their lives would ever be the same. Before they turned in that night, they prepared for the morning's sojourn. They would leave before dawn to deliver baby Marion to her new life and parents.

Chapter 21

A t four the next morning, they were on the road. The drive to Huntsville, Alabama, would take over sixteen hours. Most of the roads were not paved. They knew traveling in the South late at night wasn't safe for Negroes, especially the women.

Once they were in Alabama, Lula did most of the driving. She had visited Jesse and Bernice two years earlier and knew the quickest roads to their farm. It was close to 10 p.m. when they reached the road in Huntsville that led to Bernice and Jesse's house.

***

A tall man with a broad chest stood on the front porch lighting his pipe. He yelled into the house as they approached. "Bernice, there's somebody coming down the road. Take a look, darlin'. See if this truck looks familiar to you. I can't place it."

Bernice came out on the porch and stood next to her husband. "It sure does look familiar, Jesse. You know what, honey, I believe that's Lula's truck."

"Did she write you and say she was coming?" Jesse asked.

"No, she didn't."

The truck drew closer and Jesse could see the frames of the people inside.

"Something has happened. Otherwise she would have let us know she was coming. She's not alone. She's got some other people with her," Jesse said.

Jesse knocked the ashes out of his pipe, put it in his pocket, and followed his wife. Bernice ran up to Lula and gave her a big hug. Then she hugged Melinda. Jesse lumbered over wearing a big grin.

"What in tar-nation brings my favorite little bitsy person all the way to Alabama?"

Lula ran over to Jesse and gave him a hug. "You and Bernice brought us here, my favorite giant person." Lula took his hand and

Bernice's. She walked them over to where Ade stood, silently holding the baby. "Bernice and Jesse Wilson, I'd like you to meet Ade and baby Marion. Ade, these two are my best friends in the whole wide world."

"Baby Marion?" Bernice exclaimed.

Lula smiled. "Yes, Baby Marion."

"It is very nice to meet you, Miss Ade," Bernice said.

"It's a pleasure, Miss Ade. But don't believe Lula. Bernice is little bit's best friend. She only likes me because she can stand behind me on a sunny day to block the sun off her. She thinks I'm some big old shade tree," Jesse said with a laugh.

"Jesse, Miss Ade might take you seriously. She doesn't know how you joke around," Bernice gently scolded.

"I understand," Ade said. "Humor is a good thing in a man. A man who wants to make you happy is a man who tries to keep you from pain."

"You see, Bernice. Miss Ade knows what she's talking about." He looked over at the truck and saw Melinda struggling with the luggage. "What are you doing, Melinda? I'll get those bags."

"Thank you, Jesse. You get used to doing everything yourself when there isn't a man around."

Bernice walked over to Ade. "Miss Ade, may I hold the baby?"

"You may. Please call me Ade."

Bernice carried the baby into the house.

Jesse followed Lula and Melinda in with the bags. "Why don't you all sit at the table? Bernice was brewing up some hot chocolate right before you came. I'll get it. I know my wife won't be letting go of little Marion anytime soon."

Jesse had the fireplace blazing, and it was rather warm in the house. Bernice removed Marion's blanket.

Lula walked over to the fireplace. "This wasn't here the last time I visited."

"Ever since Jesse saw the fireplace your daddy built, he's wanted one. He worked all summer on this one. Child, it's been lit every night since he finished it," Bernice said.

A work of art, the fireplace was formed in an eight-foot arch of stone, enhanced by a beveled five-foot mahogany mantle that extended to its base.

"I won't say it too loudly, but I believe Jesse Wilson's fireplace outshines Russell Bovine's," Melinda said.

"You know how men are always trying to outdo one another," Bernice said.

Jesse brought the hot chocolate to the table and served a mug to everyone.

Bernice could not take her eyes off of the baby. "Honey, come and look at this baby. She is the most perfect child I've ever seen."

Jesse bent over to take a closer look. "You know all babies are beautiful to me. But I've got to agree, little Marion here is the prettiest one I've ever seen. Don't take this wrong, darlin', I swear she favors you!"

"That's strange, Jesse. I was thinking she looked a lot like you."

Lula had chosen well. Bernice was only 5'3" with a medium build, but she was well proportioned, with smooth, deep reddish-brown coloration and rather sharp features. Combine her traits with Jesse's, and no one would ever question whether Marion was their child.

Jesse straightened up and looked at his guests seated around the table. "It's always a pleasure to see Little Bit and you, Melinda. I am very happy to meet you, Miss Ade. And this beautiful baby could bring a smile to a hound dog's face. But it is the day after Christmas, nearly midnight, and without warning you appear at our gate. Ladies, would one of you be kind enough to tell Bernice and me why you are here?"

"Bernice," Lula said, "we've been friends most of our lives, and I love you and Jesse. I wouldn't even consider toying with your emotions. I—"

"We understand, Lula," Bernice interrupted. "Just say it."

"All right, I will. That wonderful little baby you're holding came here from Africa with Ade. The man who killed her parents and Ade's husband was trying to kidnap this baby. He is a powerful and dangerous person." Lula went on to tell them about Ade's adventure in coming to America and why she could not keep the baby. Then she described the Traveler Blue in detail and why they had not called. "Baby Marion must think that she was born right here. Bernice and Jesse, behold your daughter, Marion Wilson."

Bernice gasped. Jesse leaned forward. "What did you just say, Lula?' he asked.

146

Bernice answered for her friend. "You heard her, Jesse. She brought little Marion to us. She wants us to be the parents of this precious baby."

"What Lula has told you is true, but there is more to this story. I don't want you to think it is that simple. We must tell you everything," Melinda said.

As she talked, Jesse opened the window, sat on the windowsill, and lit his pipe. When she had finished, Jesse put out his pipe and knelt on one knee before Bernice and Marion. His eyes fixed on Bernice. Silently, she nodded her head.

Jesse stood up. "I have listened to everything that has been said. I don't let my head rule my heart or my heart rule my head. So I want you all to listen to what I am about to say. Ade, you left your country to escape a demon. People like us were raised on demon lies.

"When I was a boy, I woke up one night under a pile of sticks and twigs. My ankles were tied together. My hands were tied behind my back. My mouth was gagged. From between the branches, I could see torches. There was a lot of yelling and cursing. I heard one man holler, 'Get that nigger on his knees.'

"Then, I saw my daddy. The men were trying to wrestle him to the ground and tie his hands. There were at least ten of them. But they couldn't hold him down. One of the men pulled a shotgun from his saddle and shot my daddy in his knees. He fell to the ground. They tied his hands behind his back and put a noose around his neck. A short time later he was danglin' in the air.

"My momma ran from the house, screaming with a club in her hand. The man with the shotgun reloaded and took aim. When they were sure my father was dead, one of the men pulled out a hunting knife and cut off his manhood."

Jesse paused. The women were stunned silent.

"My momma and daddy were murdered because my daddy made my momma a rocking chair and the white lady of the Big House wanted it. My daddy told her it was for my mother and the new baby. Mrs. Green took it anyway. My daddy was powerful mad. He walked up to the Big House and took it right off the front porch and returned it to my momma. She asked him why he had gotten the chair.

"He answered, 'I'm tired of the demon lies. No more lies. What comes will come.' And that night, he paid for the truth with both of their lives, not to mention the baby that wasn't born. My daddy was the one who tied me up in my sleep and hid me under those sticks.

"Tonight you speak of one demon man. Well, you can all believe this. It would take more than ten of these demons to stop me from protecting my daughter, Marion Wilson."

Jesse sat next to Bernice and took Marion in his massive arms. Bernice laid her head on his chest.

Ade watched Jesse, Bernice, and Marion with great joy. Then she saw a golden aura of light surround them. Ade took Melinda's hand and shared the vision. In the golden light above their heads, the images of Hatshepsut and Kabaka appeared. The apparitions slowly descended, superimposing themselves over Jesse and Bernice. Soon the images of Hatshepsut and Kabaka began to ascend. Melinda and Ade watched as the two spirits rose to the ceiling. Before their departure, they looked down at Ade, nodded their heads, and vanished. She bowed her head and covered her eyes for several minutes. For the first time, she felt the exhaustion of her long journey.

"Ade, are you feeling ill?" Bernice asked.

Ade raised her head. "No, Bernice. I will rest for the first time in many moons."

"I think you all should get some sleep. We can talk tomorrow," Jesse said.

"Jesse, we are leaving at sunrise," Lula said.

"You can't be serious. It's almost one a.m. now," Bernice said.

"Lula is correct, Bernice. When Marion awakens, she shall see us no more. She is your daughter. There is no woman from Africa. There was no village, no world but this world," Ade said as she lifted the sword medallion over her head. "There are two more things you must know. This medallion will assure Marion's safety. If she must use it someday, she will be given a sign. You must promise me now she will always have it on or near to her. I wear the shield medallion. I will pass it to Lula. She will become the Protector."

"We promise," swore Bernice and Jesse.

Ade reached into her garment and removed the pouch and opened it. Slowly, she poured the diamonds onto the table. "These stones may be used to provide for Marion. I have been told that one jewel alone will provide great wealth."

Everyone at the table was speechless.

"Ade, Jesse and I will provide for Marion. We can't accept these diamonds," Bernice said at last.

"They belong to Marion. I can never see her again. Melinda can never see her again. Lula will visit very little. They must be wherever she is."

Jesse walked over to the fireplace and turned the cornerstone in the rear of its base. He walked to the other side of the fireplace, slid out a hollowed section of stone.

"One side unlocks the other. It is a secret safe. I built it into the fireplace. I still don't trust the banks. Now, we will use it for the diamonds only. Once I put the diamonds in here, it won't be opened again until Marion is a grown woman. She won't have to ever worry about money. I wanted all of you to see how to open it. In case something happens to both of us, any of you can get Marion her diamonds."

Ade returned the stones to their pouch. Jesse placed the pouch in the hollowed stone and reinserted it. Then he walked to the other side and locked the compartment, turning the cornerstone counter-clockwise.

***

It wasn't long before sleep overcame Lula, Melinda, and Jesse. Lula rested at one end of the sofa, Melinda at the other. Jesse was sleeping so soundly that it would have taken a crane to remove him from his easy chair. Baby Marion had been sleeping for hours in Bernice's arms. Only Ade and Bernice remained awake.

"Aren't you sleepy, Ade?"

"I will rest when we drive."

"You will never know how great a gift you have brought to this house."

"Bernice, you are a gift to me for loving this baby as your own. All is well. Sleep."

Bernice lay next to Marion and fell fast asleep. Ade stared at her momentarily, and then with tears in her eyes, she walked to the door. *All is well,* she thought, smiling through her tears.

***

149

Ade quietly took their luggage to the truck, removed one of the bank envelopes from the stack, took twenty thousand dollars from the remaining twenty-eight thousand, three hundred, and placed it in the envelope. Thereafter, she packed the truck.

She felt her medallion and took it out to look at. She wanted to explain everything to Melinda, but she was so tired, she knew she would forget if she didn't remind herself. She took her medallion off and placed it on the dashboard as that reminder. Back inside, she awakened Melinda and Lula. Quietly, they dressed while Ade placed the envelope near the sleeping Jesse. Outside, Ade walked between Lula and Melinda and took their hands and raised them to the rising sun. Their mission was done.

Chapter 22

Melinda was the first to drive. Ade sat beside her waiting for Lula to fall asleep. She had wanted to tell Melinda how they gained their powers in the spiritual world and how it was linked to the real world. By the time Lula went to sleep, Ade was already out. Having not slept for three days, she was almost comatose.

Melinda drove the entire state of Alabama before she awoke Lula. She had overextended herself by driving nine hours nonstop. Melinda passed out before Lula took over the wheel. Ade never budged a muscle. It was dusk when Lula reached the outskirts of Biloxi, Mississippi. Darkness set in as she reached a quarter tank of gas.

It was close to 8:30 when she spotted a gas station. As Lula stopped at the gas pump, she got an eerie feeling. At first she tried to awaken Melinda and Ade. When neither responded, Lula decided to ignore her uneasiness.

The filling station attendant walked out, wearing overalls covered with oil. He looked as if he had been drinking. His face was beet red.

"Hell, I thought you were a white gal 'til I seen them two," he said, peeking into the car. "You're a pretty little octoroon, ain'cha."

"Thank you, sir. Could you fill me up?" Lula only rolled the window down just enough for him to hear her.

"I sure could fill you up. And the gas might even be free."

Lula didn't reply. He walked back to the pump and started to fill up the tank. There were two other men sitting in front of the station.

"Harvey, Jack, come over here. There's something I want y'all to see."

"What is it, Charlie, my feet hurt," one of the men said.

The attendant pulled the nozzle from the tank. "Just get over here."

The two men walked over to the pickup truck. Lula watched them out of the side-view mirror. She couldn't hear what they were saying. But she wasn't going to roll the window down any farther. Charlie returned the nozzle to the pump and started walking back to her window. She didn't notice the other two men walking around to the other side of the truck. Lula quickly dug down into her purse to get the money to pay for the gas. *I'm pulling out of here the second I hand him the money.*

Charlie tapped on the window. "That'll be a dollar ten." Lula was startled by another voice from the passenger side.

"Well, lookee here. Chocolate, caramel and vanilla. Which one do you want, Charlie?" Harvey asked.

"I like the little yella one."

"Well, I never had no jungle woman before. I wonder if she can hang by her tail," Harvey said.

"The one in the middle is appealin' too. You get her, Jack," Charlie said. Jack did not speak.

Lula tried to hand the money out of the window, but Charlie wouldn't reach out and take it. Lula eased her one foot onto the clutch and covered the accelerator with the other. She dropped the money out of the window, quickly shifted the gears and took off.

***

"Did you see that? That nigger bitch tried to run us over," Harvey bellowed, pointing to the truck tracks in the dirt.

"We was just havin' some fun with her," Charlie said.

Jack spoke with hesitance. "I think we was scarin' her."

"We didn't say nothing to her she ain't heard before, Jack. Them colored gals like it, 'specially from a white man," Charlie replied.

"Well, somebody needs to teach that uppity coon her place," Harvey said.

"You know, Harvey, you're right. She ain't from around here. We need to teach her how niggers act in Mississippi."

"Whatcha say, Jack?" Harvey asked.

"Well, well, I don't rightly know. I…"

"What are you, Jack, some kind of nigger lover?"

"No. Hell no."

***

Lula drove down the main road as fast as the old pick-up would go. This time she shook Melinda. "Wake up! Wake up! Come on now! We're in trouble!"

The sky was black. Gusts of winds from the delta seemed to blow in from nowhere. There was a rumbling in the sky. Suddenly a tremendous bolt of lightning tore across the sky. As it ripped the heavens, the sound reverberated like a thousand cracking whips. It took nature's awesome energy to finally awaken Melinda.

"What's going on?" Melinda said, still half-dazed. "Where are we?"

"I'm trying to get the hell out of Mississippi. Some rednecks gave me a hard time back at the filling station. They were really getting ugly. I think they may follow us."

"Damn it, I knew we should have packed Daddy's shotgun. Lula, be calm, but drive as fast as you can! The last thing we want is for us to get caught on this deserted road."

Melinda yelled in Ade's ear. Nothing. She shook her. Nothing. Melinda thought for a moment, then she took both of Ade's hands in hers and concentrated. Ade felt Melinda's message like an electric shock. There was a frightened look in her widened eyes.

"No! No!" Ade yelled, as the truck darted out into the middle of the road ahead of them.

Lula turned the steering wheel sharply to avoid crashing into the vehicle. Their pickup went out of control, veering off into the forest. Lula was able to maneuver the truck out of the path of several trees and stop on the edge of a shallow ditch. Several flashes of lightning blinded the women from seeing their enemy approach.

Without warning, the driver's door flew open. "Did you think we was gonna let you get away with disrespecting us?" Charlie ranted as he pulled at Lula's arm.

During the brief moments Ade had held Melinda hands, she had seen all that was to happen. When Harvey snatched open her door, she leaped on him like a lioness defending her cubs. Harvey stumbled backwards and fell to the ground. Ade turned to help Lula and Melinda. Harvey jumped up and slammed his lantern across the back of Ade's head. She turned around completely dazed, blood gushing from her scalp. Harvey hit her hard with his fist. The blow sent her plummeting to the ground.

Jack had come around to the passenger door to pull Melinda away from helping Lula. As Melinda and Jack wrestled, Charlie was able to lock Lula's arms together and drag her from the truck. Lula and Charlie tugged back and forth. Lula bit deeply into his hand and rammed her knee into his groin. In a furious rage, Charlie lifted Lula and hurled her to the earth. She landed on a jagged rock that protruded from the ground. She felt excruciating pain as it pressed against the nerves in her spine. Charlie unzipped his pants and got down on his knees where Lula lay. He lifted her skirt and tore off her undergarments.

Melinda still struggled with Jack. He kept trying to force her back onto the seat. Finally he whispered, "I ain't gonna hurt you. Just lay back and be quiet."

Melinda looked at him with disdain. "If you know this is wrong, why did you let it happen? I've got to help my sister and my friend." Melinda conjured up the strength to push Jack away.

But he grabbed her again and pushed her back to the car door. "What's the matter with you, stupid bitch? I'm trying to help you."

Melinda was able to push Jack enough for her to look over his shoulder and witness Lula being raped. The red heat of rage soared through her body. She freed her right hand from Jack's grip and punched him in the face.

"You stupid Black bitch." Jack drew back and punched Melinda in her stomach. She fell to her knees. He came across with another blow to the side of her head that knocked her unconscious. Realizing what he had done, he lifted her up and laid her on the car seat.

Harvey was on his knees zipping up his pants as Ade drifted back to consciousness. When he saw her eyes opening, he leaned forward. "Did you like that, jungle nigger?"

Ade formed her hand in the mold of a lion's claw. She reached up, jamming her fingernail into the flesh of Harvey's forehead. She raked her hand down his face, splitting his skin into paper-like sheets. His blood began to pour like water from a spigot. He stood up screaming as the pain hit him all at once. He ran over to Charlie, who was smiling down over the unconscious Lula.

One look at Harvey's face and Charlie rushed over to the bag he had laid next to his lantern. He pulled out a Colt .45 and handed it to Harvey. The two walked back over to Ade. She had reached the truck and was scrabbling inside for the medallion. She finally grabbed it, but crashed to the ground.

154

"Come here, Jack," Charlie called out. "Charlie's gonna kill this bitch."

Melinda's eyes opened, but she could not focus.

Jack looked at Melinda. "I'm sorry, lady."

Charlie yelled out again. "Come on, Jack. What's keepin' ya?"

"You're as guilty as they are, Jack," Melinda yelled out. "Run away, you coward. Run away." Melinda tried to lift her head, but she passed out again.

Jack hurried over to Harvey and Charlie. Ade looked up and saw the gun pointed at her. Jack stood speechless. Ade held the medallion in her left hand. As Harvey squeezed the trigger, Ade raised her right hand in a motion to block the weapon, and the golden shield appeared. The bullet hit the shield and ricocheted.

Charlie cried out in agony. "My eye! She shot me in the eye. Somebody get me to the damn hospital."

"What the hell," Jack yelled in disbelief at what he had just seen. He grabbed Harvey and Charlie. "Let's go!"

Ade could hear the wheels of their truck screeching as they pulled away. The shield disappeared and Ade fainted once more.

The rain poured in through the open truck window, the harsh shower of water splashing against Melinda and waking her up. Getting up slowly, she felt the swelling in her face and the bruises on her body and moaned. When she tried to get out of the truck, pain shot from her stomach to her internal organs.

Still, she persevered. The torrential rain and the pitch-black night made it nearly impossible to see.

She stumbled into Ade.

Half-conscience, Ade had somehow propped herself against a tree. She was fumbling to put on the medallion while talking to herself in a foreign tongue. Melinda did not understand what she was saying, but she helped Ade put on the medallion. Then Melinda lifted her up and helped her to the truck.

"Amin—is here," Ade mumbled, now talking in English. "I did not wish to leave my father that night. Oh Amin! Where is Hatshepsut? We must hurry. Melinda tell Amin to hurry! The Traveler Blue comes!"

Melinda held Ade, soothing her fears, while noting that the blood had clotted in an enormous gash on the back of Ade's head. Finally

Melinda laid Ade on the seat. Then, with dread, she went to search for her sister.

Several yards from the truck, Melinda found Lula floating in a puddle of muddy water. She lifted her tiny unconscious sister in her arms. As Melinda carried her back to the truck, Lula screamed out in agonizing pain. Tears rushed from Melinda's eyes. She laid Lula next to Ade and closed the passenger door. Before she opened the driver's door, she looked up at the sky.

"We did as you asked and look how you treat us! Why, why?" Melinda grabbed the steering wheel and tried to climb into the cab. She had exerted all her energy helping Ade and Lula and she had none left for herself. She fell to the ground, beginning to cry, but stopped abruptly. She had to get them to safety. She clawed her way to her feet and held onto the steering wheel for dear life. Then she was in and somehow she was driving them all away.

They all were to learn that they had permanent damage. Melinda was informed she would never bear children. From the blows to her head, Ade suffered from disorientation. From time to time she lapsed into her past, believing that she was still in her village. She would hold conversations with her family and friends. When she made trips to the shop, children would make fun of her dress and wild-eyed expressions. Her only constant was her time with Melinda. She did not remember the baby Marion or how she had come to the United States.

Lula's spinal cord was severely damaged, and she walked with a limp. One month after the attack, she discovered she was pregnant. The weight of the child during pregnancy caused her harrowing pain. During the last three months, she was completely bedridden. The trauma associated with childbirth further exacerbated her condition.

On September 1, 1937, Emma Bovine was born. Lula suffered a stroke causing partial paralysis to her left side. She lost all feeling in her left leg and walked from then on with a cane. Her left arm was limp. Often her speech was slurred. She was twenty-two years old. Lula never went to visit baby Marion. She could no longer drive.

With Melinda's gifts, she could not risk seeing baby Marion either for fear her mind would be read and the baby would be put in jeopardy. Her business was very successful. By World War II, it was a major tourist attraction. In time, her gift of vision became as powerful as Ade's. She purchased a house on Basin Street.

Ade returned to the family's old cabin. With the expansion of the levy, the river reclaimed the land surrounding Ade's home. Now located on a tiny island and isolated from everything, she lived as a recluse in harmony with the alligators that migrated to the swamps around her cabin. Melinda took care of all of Ade's needs until the day she died.

Chapter 23

Blue was a cruel master. Early in Zinzi and Bertrand's captivity, Blue realized that any bond between Bertrand and Zinzi had to be severed. Envy, hatred, and fear were the only emotions that he would allow slaves to develop—especially fear.

Whenever Bertrand made any attempts to nurture or show love to Zinzi, Blue beat him. Zinzi witnessed this brutality, but Bertrand would never cry out. This infuriated Blue. As time passed, Blue shortened Bertrand's chains in tiny increments to increase Bertrand's pain and minimize his physical contact with his daughter.

On an autumn morning in 1936, Bertrand Lwanga learned how brilliant his child was when he awoke to find his six-month-old lying on his chest. She had taught herself to walk. He had to act quickly. He knew that Zinzi would also be in chains if Blue knew she could walk. Bertrand decided to teach Zinzi to protect herself by concealing her potential.

Bertrand held Zinzi close. "My daughter, I love you more than life itself, but I must teach you how to survive this bondage."

He carried her across the room, sat her on the table slab, placed his opened hand in front of her face and ordered her to stay. Every time Bertrand walked away from the table, Zinzi climbed down and followed. Finally, he placed her on the table, and when Zinzi started to get off, he yelled "No, Zinzi!" and flashed a horrid scowl at her.

Zinzi, hurt and frightened, reached out her arms to her father. When he did not respond, she released loud, pain-filled tears, but she did not move. Bertrand witnessed his daughter suffering without changing his expression. In the corner of his eye, he felt a single tear. He turned his head from his daughter the second before it fell.

Next, he taught Zinzi to walk only when he gave special eye and hand signals. From that day forth, they developed their own special nonverbal language.

Despite Bertrand being careful, Blue saw the relationship between him and Zinzi growing with a special love reserved only for the two of them. Being outmaneuvered by a human was inconceivable. Soon Bertrand would outlive his usefulness, and Blue would make him pay.

During their first year, Blue brought clothes, food, and water, but he hardly spent a moment in their presence. Bertrand knew he had to make the most of his time with Zinzi while Blue was otherwise preoccupied. When Zinzi could take care of herself, he would be executed. Bertrand did not fear for his life. He feared for Zinzi's life without him. Zinzi's only weapon against Blue would be the knowledge that Bertrand left behind for her. Whenever Blue was absent, Bertrand held his daughter close and quietly taught her about her survival.

***

Zinzi's development was unprecedented. At one year, she had physical coordination, mental capacity, and speaking ability surpassing a three-year-old's. Bertrand worked hard with Zinzi and was crushed when his training came to an abrupt halt a month after Zinzi's first birthday.

"What is wrong with your larva, Bertrand Lwanga? Have I wasted my time on an unworthy specimen?"

Blue reached for Zinzi. The sight of his massive blue hands moving toward her sent Zinzi instinctively leaping from the table and running to her father.

Rage swept across the blue demon's face. He charged the chained Bertrand and grabbed him by the shackle around his neck and squeezed until Bertrand could no longer speak. Thereafter, his vocal cords were permanently damaged.

The next day, one-year-old Zinzi was chained to her table.

***

Never getting over that a sub-creature had duped him, Blue verbally and physically abused Bertrand. Despite his discomfort, Bertrand continued to educate his daughter through their sign language. At two years old, she had all the attributes of a highly intelligent six-year-old. Zinzi knew how to prepare her own food, clean and dress herself, and bury her waste. Bertrand traced images in the air and on the

159

floor, teaching his daughter to draw and write. Bertrand was not preparing Zinzi for a life of servitude. He was preparing her for how she would live in the world after they escaped.

It was 1938. Zinzi's second birthday was approaching. For two years, Bertrand had been wearing down the hinges of his shackles by rubbing them against his chains. The day had finally come when Bertrand could break through all his shackles with minimum effort.

"I've tired of you, Bertrand Lwanga," Blue said one day. "Soon, your little maggot will not need you, and neither will I. I will take great pleasure in killing you."

When Blue turned to leave, Bertrand freed himself from his shackles and leaped upon Blue's back. For a second, Blue was disoriented. Then he spread his wings and propelled himself upward to the pinnacle of the pyramid. Before Blue could crush Bertrand against the pyramid's apex, Bertrand locked the wings in his powerful arms. This sent Blue spiraling downward onto the pyramid's floor. Bertrand held fast to the wings and rode the creature's back. Upon impact, he heard the cracking and crushing of Blue's innards. Kneeling on Blue's back, Bertrand clamped one hand under Blue's chin and the other on the back of his head. In a wrenching twist, Bertrand wrung Blue's neck. Blue lay lifeless. Bertrand sprang to his feet and rushed to his daughter.

Held by her chains, Zinzi stood with arms widespread. "Father, I love you."

Bertrand leaned over and kissed his daughter on her head. Then he pointed to himself, clutched his heart with both hands, and pointed to her and smiled. But the instant he leaned back, the blade of Blue's sword plunged through his back, piercing his heart and splitting open the cavity of his chest.

Blue's body had regenerated and attacked before Bertrand could harm him further. He lifted Bertrand's slain body over his head with the sword. Then he dropped the body to the ground. He knelt down on one knee next to the body.

"I must have a trophy."

Zinzi watched as Blue skinned her father. Blue took the skinless body and propelled it out of the pyramid entrance to rot in the desert sun. Then he put on Bertrand's skin and paraded around Zinzi, taunting her.

"Do you still love me?" he asked.

The toddler crouched in the corner of the pyramid walls. Though she trembled from the inhuman barbarity that had transpired, she kept her sanity by recollecting the love of her father, Bertrand. But the Blue vermin never heard her voice again.

***

In the recess of Blue's twisted mind, Bertrand Lwanga remained a fascination, although Blue would never accept that a mere human had brought him to his knees. Even Bertrand Lwanga's flesh did not deteriorate like other humans'.

No longer would Blue be the Traveler or Stranger. To the world, Blue disguised himself as Bertrand Lwanga, the champion of human freedom, when in reality he was the antithesis of Bertrand.

Chapter 24

During the years that followed, the Wilson family was blessed with prosperity. Jesse saved the money Ade had left until a real opportunity arose. At the beginning of World War II, a bright young mechanic named Bill Beddington brought his wife and baby boy to Huntsville. Bill was from the Appalachian Mountains of West Virginia. He came to Huntsville with his life savings—one thousand dollars—to seek a career in the auto repair business. Considered poor white trash, he was treated just slightly better than a Negro. He wanted to better the lives of his family.

It wasn't long before he heard about the colored mechanic who could fix anything. Bill's curiosity soon led him to Jesse's front door. Both men shared the same passion for machinery. Soon they shared their professional secrets. In time they became close and trusting friends.

The two were a highly unlikely pair, given where and how they were raised, but in less than a year they had decided to become partners. Each man invested a thousand dollars. Of course, the people of Huntsville, Alabama, weren't ready for a Negro entrepreneur. Everyone thought Bill Beddington owned the business. Jesse was a silent partner. Jesse was the true talent, and Bernice kept the books. Bill was the front man for the white clientele and business deals. They planned everything together and the profits were split evenly. With their hard work, dedication, and skills, Mechanical Enterprises became a real success.

Marion grew to be both a lovely and intelligent child. In school, she exceeded all of her peers in skills and intelligence. Bernice had been a sincerely loving mother. She was Marion's idol and best friend. Jesse was an excellent father. He brought a feeling of warmth and security to their home. Marion respected him for his wisdom and loved him for his kind and giving nature. She was blessed.

By 1952, Mechanical Enterprises had expanded and diversified. Jesse and Bill had two buildings in Huntsville. One building housed their auto repair and body shop while the other was the headquarters for their construction business. As the years passed, Jesse bought more land around his home. Ultimately, his construction skills surpassed even his auto-mechanical skills. Bill also fronted for this business, but Jesse ran the operation almost exclusively.

It was June of 1952 when a nineteen-year-old Negro boy from Chicago walked through the doors of Wilson's Mechanical Enterprises Construction seeking a summer job. Before the young man was shipped off to basic training September 1, he had to work for the Negro, Jesse Wilson, whom he had heard so much about.

Jesse was away at a construction site. When he returned, a foreman told him that Joseph Johnson had slept behind the building for two nights just waiting to see him. Jesse offered the young man an apprentice job and the storage room to sleep in. Three weeks later, Jesse was sitting at the dinner table talking to Bernice and Marion.

"I've got this Northern boy from Chicago working for me. He's not that much older than you, Marion. I tell you, the boy is smart as a whip and works like a Mississippi mule."

"I never heard you go on about any of the other boys this way," Bernice said, smiling. "This boy must be something else. You should invite him to Sunday dinner."

"I might just do that, darlin'. I'm sure you both would like him."

"Looks like Daddy's found the son he's always wanted. What do you think, Momma?"

"You might be right about that, Marion. I guess he's just tired of the female company in this house. Is that true, honey?" Bernice teased.

"No, no. It's nothing like that. I just think the boy is special." Jesse realized he couldn't win. He shook his head and took out his pipe and laughed.

The following Sunday, young Joseph stood at the Wilson's front door. He had grown to idolize Jesse. Yet he was nervous about having dinner with the Wilson family. The handsome, copper-toned, sinewy six-footer was usually pretty confident. His great aptitude was only surpassed by his wonderful attitude. He had strength, yet a kindness of character. He finally mustered enough courage to knock on the door.

"Come on in, Joseph. Make yourself at home," Jesse said with a broad smile.

"Thank you, Mr. Wilson."

The room had been expanded over the years, but the fireplace remained the central piece of interest. Joseph was very impressed. Jesse had gone into the kitchen to get Bernice.

The moment Bernice looked into Joseph's smoky gray eyes, she had a good feeling about him. "I'm Bernice, Jesse's wife. I've heard a lot about you, Joseph."

Joseph shook Bernice's hand. "It's a pleasure to meet you, Mrs. Wilson. You really have a beautiful house here."

"The house should be nice. My wife has had me working on it for eighteen years."

"I really like your fireplace," Joseph said.

Jesse looked at Bernice and laughed. "See, darlin', I told you I should have stopped with the fireplace. It's the first thing I built and the only thing anybody notices."

"I noticed more than the fireplace, Mr. Wilson—"

"Joseph, relax, I'm just funnin' you."

"Whew, I thought I had messed up already."

Jesse and Joseph laughed

Joseph's back was to the door when Marion stepped into the room.

"Here's my baby girl," Jesse said.

Joseph turned around, and once Marion's and his eyes had met, their lives were never the same again. That moment in time was the epilogue of the Elder's journey and the destiny of the cherished Freedom Code.

Chapter 25

On January 17, 1945, Lula Bovine died from complications of poliomyelitis and pneumonia. Melinda painfully mourned her sister's death for the next decade. Melinda's only consolation was Lula's daughter, Emma. Every ounce of love Melinda held for Lula was transferred to Emma. She raised Emma as her own.

On August 15, 1959, the Traveler Blue found Ade. She told him nothing. She had no memory of him. She had no idea why he had come or why he wished to harm her. The Traveler killed her.

On March 4, 1960, a boy was born in the Motherland.
On April 7, 1960, a girl child was born in the United States.
On July 15, 1960, a girl child was born in the United States.
On June 6, 1961, a boy was born in the Motherland.

The births of these four children sealed the cherished Freedom Code, and their inevitable unions were to determine the fate of Africans and American Blacks, which would also influence the fate of humankind.

The true story now begins.

Part IV

The Children

Nicole, Regina, Segun, and Sotonye

1990, Botswana

Chapter 26

August 3, 1990, arrived before Nicole and Regina knew it. They had spent the last two weeks preparing for their trip to Botswana. First, they upgraded their laptop computers, purchasing the necessary software and equipment to create state-of-the-art presentations. Hours were spent researching every aspect of African tradition, geography, art, history, and economic development. Since Q.P.S.'s product was a deeply held secret, they created a myriad of possible test products and developed prospective marketing and advertising plans as an exercise.

The night before their departure, Regina sat on the edge of Nicole's bed while Nicole finished some last-minute packing.

"I was thinking about my mother," Nicole said. "There's so much about her life that I don't know. My grandmother used to tell me this tall tale about three wise women who came with gifts to give her the first Christmas after my mother was born. My mother's godmother, Lula, was one of the women. Listen to me rambling. It's a long story. Never mind."

Regina scooted back on the bed, kicked off her shoes, and propped a pillow between her back and the headboard. "Unlike another person in this room who shall remain nameless, I have completed all of my packing. Now tell me the story. It will keep your mind occupied as you labor."

"You know, I cannot stand you."

"I can live with that."

"If you insist," Nicole continued while she packed. "My grandfather Jesse was a very talented artisan and businessman. He owned a construction business. Around 1957, my Grandpa Jesse's partner, a man named Beddington, came to the house and told my grandfather there was a problem at one of their construction sites.

"For some reason, Grandpa Jesse and Beddington decided to climb up and check the beams on the roof. Both men had to be in their fifties. A beam broke under their weight. Mr. Beddington was killed. My grandfather was paralyzed and a head injury caused him lapses of memory. The Beddington family took over the business and left Jesse and my Grandma Bernice penniless. Mr. Beddington's wife was ignored when she told the relatives that Mr. Beddington and Jesse had a verbal agreement. Eventually, the family even cheated Beddington's wife out of her share of M.E.I."

Regina interrupted Nicole. "Hold on a second. Did you say M.E.I.? You're telling me Grandpa Jesse was one of the founders of Mechanical Enterprise Incorporated, one of the largest mechanical engineering companies in the world? The company that builds aerospace centers, rocket components, and launching pads?"

"One and the same," Nicole said. "Grandpa Jesse had one of life's pleasures and vices. That was his pipe. One day, while my grandmother was at work, Grandpa Jesse was lying in bed smoking. By the time the fire department arrived, the house was almost destroyed. My grandmother discovered my grandfather had returned inside to get his tobacco pouch… but it wasn't a tobacco pouch Grandma took from his hand…" Nicole looked up, startled and wide-eyed. "Gina!"

Nicole glanced over to the bed. Regina had fallen asleep. "I guess I'll tell you tomorrow. Goodnight."

***

"I can't believe that I'm up and ready before you, Gina," Nicole called through the bedroom door.

Twenty minutes later, Regina entered the kitchen to a breakfast of hash browns, eggs, sausages, orange juice, and coffee. After breakfast and cleaning up, they finished the last of their packing before calling a cab.

"Well," Nicole said as the two sat on the floating staircase steps, "usually it's you that makes sure we stay on schedule. The first time I make a real effort, we sit here with nothing to do."

"I'm happy we have a few minutes," Gina said. "I didn't tell you everything about my conversation with my Aunt Melinda." She glanced at the Horus Crystal Ball in the foyer. "Horus is not an ornament or a simple prop for a carnival act. It has mystical powers. If I tell you my secret, it will make you a part of its destiny…"

"Tell me! This is the way it should be," Nicole said.

Regina reached into her blouse and pulled out the medallion. "This medallion is in the shape of a shield. It's a part of my legacy." She glanced at Nicole. "Now it will be a part of yours."

Nicole was afraid to touch the medallion, but she examined it as Regina continued.

"When Melinda placed it around my neck, she declared that I was the Protector. I had to swear I would wear it always."

"Gina, this shield matches the designs on the handle of the sword I saw in my dream! It's unbelievable." They sat in silent for a moment trying to sort it all out. "I need to show you something, too." Nicole reached into the pocket of her apron and handed the pouch to Regina. "My mother left me more than the diamond I sold. Open it."

Regina loosened the drawstring and parted the fabric. Diamonds cascaded into the morning light.

"Nicole! These are priceless!"

"I know! I can't believe it, Gina. I have so many questions. If each of my family's generations had access to these diamonds, why did my grandparents struggle? Why did my parents have to scrimp and save all of those years until their construction business became a huge success? If my mother sold one of those diamonds for fifty thousand dollars, that money was more than they needed to live on. Alice said my mother was in a panic when she came for the box. Why? Last night I realized my Grandpa Jesse didn't die for a pouch of tobacco. Did you hear that part, or were you already asleep?"

"I remember."

"You're holding the pouch Grandma Bernice took out of Grandpa Jesse's hand. Gina, he went back inside to get the diamonds for my mother!" Nicole was still trying to understand it all. "It's frustrating how slowly our ancestors' secrets come to us. Hopefully, before it's over, the truth will be ours. We witnessed the blood message my father sent on his tombstone. Do you remember what was inscribed?"

"Of course I do, Nicole. 'Daughter of my body and daughter of my choice. Children beware of Blue.'"

"That's right. It didn't say, 'Nicole beware of Blue.' The message was for both of us. Gina, our meeting, our friendship, our partnership and connection were not accidental. I am beginning to think there is a connection amongst our ancestors."

"I'm not even afraid of Horus any longer. I believe it will help and guide us!"

"You know, Gina, I've got something to confess to you."

"What is it?"

"It's puzzled me since the day we met. I've never been able to figure out why you were so familiar—I trusted you right away. Of course, it might have been that you quoted my father, but I don't think so. It's more the way you said things. It's like I'd watched you my entire life. Now, we've put together a business and a partnership in a remarkably short time. It's as if we're acting out a play that was written just for us."

Nicole followed Regina's eyes to the Crystal Ball at the bottom of the stairs. "Let's do it."

They walked down the stairs and faced each other with the ball between them.

"I'll place my hands on the Crystal Ball. Then you place your hands on top of mine. You ask the question. Only one of us can speak and only one question can be asked. If the ball doesn't answer right away, do not take your hands away. I remember it answers in its own time."

Regina placed her hands on the surface of the globe, closed her eyes, and bowed her head. She meditated for a few minutes, then raised her head, opened her eyes, and nodded to Nicole to ask the question.

Nicole placed her hands firmly on top of Regina's. "Horus, Regina and I are about to travel to a place we've never been. Who will watch over us?"

The Horus Crystal Ball remained transparent. Regina could feel Nicole begin to lose her grip. Regina raised her fingers without removing her palms from the crystal and interlocked Nicole's fingers with hers. In the next moment, a faint golden light began to glow in the crystal. As the light grew stronger, black letters began to appear. Soon words began to form against the golden background. Nicole and Regina watched in amazement as a golden scroll appeared in the orb.

Daughter of my body, daughter of my choice,
Both of you are now in my heart.
Your father watches over you.

Nicole smiled. "My father is now your father. He has given me the perfect sister. He's the best father. My mother said he was a guardian angel."

"That is so beautiful, Nicole!" She suddenly stopped. "My mother! We haven't called her!"

They hurried to the telephone. "Hi, Momma Emma," Nicole said. "We're leaving for the airport in a minute, but we wanted to say goodbye!" The cab horn blew outside.

"Have a safe trip," Emma said. "I know you two will dazzle them in Africa!"

Regina took the receiver. "We've got to go, Momma!"

"I love you both," Emma said.

Regina heard the pride in her momma's voice. "The Horus Crystal Ball is working again," she blurted out. "Nicole and I received a message from her father. He's adopted me. Isn't that something? Did you hear me, Momma?" The cab driver blew the horn again. "I love you, Momma. Don't worry about us! We'll call!"

Regina hung up the phone and hugged Nicole. "Wherever all this is leading, I'm so happy I'm going down the path with you!"

They walked arm in arm to the cab. "To our journey, Gina. Our first step is to go back to the home where we've never been."

Chapter 27

I t was evening by the time their jet landed in New York to refuel. In a short time, they were staring down at what seemed to be an endless ocean.

"It's hard to imagine how people have traveled by ship across the Atlantic. I suppose we all must cross uncharted seas in quest of our dreams," Regina said.

"It's funny," Nicole said. "When I was a child, my parents and I traveled all over the United States. We even went to Mexico and Canada. But they refused to cross the Atlantic. After all of these years, I still wonder why."

"You never know why parents feel so strongly about things."

***

Nicole and Regina arrived at London's Heathrow Airport on schedule. Their flight to Botswana was delayed for six hours, so they spent most of their time in the airport reviewing strategies. After a five-and-half-hour layover, the boards finally showed their flight's scheduled time of departure.

"I want to make sure our luggage was transferred," Nicole said. "I'll also make sure our equipment is there when we are!"

"I'll pick up some postcards for Momma and Melinda."

Regina was thumbing through the postcards when she heard a familiar name. Outside the store, cameras began to flash and anxious fans were calling out "Big El, Big El," shaking their pens and papers in the air.

"Uncle Elbert!"

"Sugarplum!" He addressed the crowd the same way he had on Bourbon Street. Once again, the sea of people parted. El lifted Regina off the ground with a hug. "I'm back to the States for a few days to see your Momma."

Regina laughed happily, wishing Big El were her father instead of a faceless one-night-stand soldier on furlough.

"How did you get to London so quickly, Uncle Elbert?"

"Sugarplum, I have my own jet." El pointed out of the window to the Lear with a "Big El" insignia on the tail.

"When I grow up, I want to be just like you."

"I know you're funnin' me, Sugarplum, but that still means a lot to me."

"I wouldn't kid my Uncle Elbert. I spoke to Momma from New York, but tell her I'm fine! You know how she worries! Don't forget. Tell her I love her! I've got to go. I don't want to miss my flight!"

"Miss Melinda told me about your business in Africa. Good luck, Sugarplum. Next week, I'm starting my world tour. Your Momma has my number. Call me if you need me. I mean that."

"I will, Uncle Elbert." They hugged, and Regina kissed El's cheek then hurried to the plane.

***

Several passengers were checking to make sure their luggage was loaded on the flight. Nicole was one customer away from the front of the line.

"It is very wise indeed to secure your luggage on these international flights."

Nicole had learned not to encourage male strangers with conversation. But this voice, except for the accent, seemed very familiar to her. When Nicole turned her head and met the eyes of the man, she momentarily fell speechless.

Although dressed modestly in a loose-fitting white shirt and slacks, he was striking. Standing about six feet two inches, with a solid frame, he had a medium mocha complexion, smooth and unblemished. His facial structure was strong, yet free from harshness. His kind, deep-set eyes were the hue of a black pearl. It could have been an awkward moment for Nicole, but he, too, gazed upon her admiringly.

"I hope you don't think I was forward," he said. "Sometimes, one looks and speaks before thinking."

"Don't worry, I didn't take it that way at all. You were only saying what we both were thinking."

The next moment, the attendant called Nicole to the desk. She was assured their luggage and equipment were loaded on the connecting flight.

As Nicole walked away, she felt the eyes of the man on her.

"I am glad all is in order. Have a safe trip," he said.

"Thank you. You have a safe trip too," Nicole said, walking away, smiling.

The man watched after Nicole so intently that the attendant had to call out to him twice before he responded.

***

"Did you get lost?" Regina asked.

Nicole did not answer. She was in a world of her own as she sat down.

"Earth to Nicole. Come in, Nicole."

Nicole shook her head slightly. "I'm sorry, Gina. I was thinking about a conversation I just had with a man I met in the baggage loading area."

"What did this guy say that was so earth-shattering?"

"Nothing. He just seemed to be a very interesting, well-mannered man. It was refreshing."

Regina raised a brow. "You look extremely refreshed."

There was a sudden flurry of activity as a late passenger boarded.

"Please, find your seat, sir. We'll be taking off momentarily."

"Look at this late freight. Why can't people be on time?" Regina complained.

Nicole looked up at the straggler. He was the man from the baggage area. As he removed his backpack, he happened to glance across the aisle at Nicole and Regina.

"We meet again. How very fortunate."

Nicole responded with a partial smile and a brief upturned palm. The young man responded to her cool response with a slight bow of the head. He was saved from further embarrassment by the voice on the public address system instructing all passengers to fasten their seat belts.

"Mr. Refreshing, I presume."

"Shh, Gina. You don't need to broadcast to everyone on the plane."

"He's definitely not painful to the eyes, but he doesn't quite appear to be an African prince or even an oil magnet. Is this some type of *opposites attract* thing?"

"That's pretty superficial of you, Gina. When did you start judging people by their bank accounts? Besides, I don't even know the man."

"That wasn't me talking," Gina teased. "It was the ghost of my Great-Aunt Cora. You have to admit, I've never seen you react to any man this way."

Nicole decided not to defend this stranger any more. It would give Regina too much ammunition.

It wasn't long before Regina was asleep. Nicole decided to review her notes one more time. No one was sitting next to the young man, so he took the liberty of sitting sideways across the entire seat. He appeared to be writing vigorously and peeked at her over the back of his seat. Nicole didn't understanding her feelings. Normally, intrusions on her privacy would anger her, but she found this man's attention endearing. She closed her notebook and her eyes to rest. The words *Beware of Blue* crossed her mind as she fell asleep.

***

"You know, Gina, our timing is so perfect, sometimes I can't believe it myself."

They had beat the crowd to the restrooms, freshened up, and now sat back to relax as they were asked to buckle up for landing.

"When you're good, you're good."

The young stranger was one of the last to awaken and was slightly disoriented. Whatever was in his lap started to fall. He fumbled to catch it before it hit the floor.

"Graceful, isn't he," Regina said.

"Are we starting where we left off last night?"

Regina just laughed.

As soon as the plane landed at the Sir Seretse Khama International Airport in Gaborone, Botswana, the young man unbuckled his seat belt, removed an 11" x 15" sheet from a pad, and carried it over to Nicole's seat. He handed the sheet to her.

"I'd like you to have this."

It was a drawing in charcoal and pastels of Nicole in the traditional ceremonial garb of an African princess. He had even drawn a diamond crown on her head that appeared to sparkle. Nicole's likeness was uncanny.

Regina was the first to speak. "This is magnificent. Sir, you have a rare gift. It's just breathtaking." No one had ever given her such an unexpected, beautiful gift.

"I know artists seldom receive the compensation they deserve. Your talent is exceptional. I couldn't accept your lovely work without paying you." Nicole picked up her purse and started to unsnap it.

"Please," the young man said, "I could not accept remuneration. I am not an artist by profession. It is merely something I do for relaxation. Please accept it in the spirit it is being given. I apologize if I made you uncomfortable"

"Well, I certainly would love to have this drawing. Therefore, I suppose I accept your apology, even though it wasn't necessary. You were just being friendly. Thank you so much. I really appreciate it," Nicole said.

The young man flashed a broad smile. "You are more than welcome. I hope you both enjoy your stay in my country. I'd better collect my belongings before the stampede begins down this aisle. Goodbye." The young man maneuvered back to his seat through the crowd forming in the aisle.

"Goodbye," returned Nicole with a smile.

"Nicole, I take back everything I said about him. He is refreshingly sincere. Not to mention good looking and talented. There is something about him that is so familiar."

***

At Sir Seretse Khama International Airport, a blue Mercedes limousine left a restricted area and approached the terminal on the dusty public service road. It stopped just inside the gates of the guard tower. The driver got out of the car, walked around to the rear passenger door, and opened it.

"Welcome home, Doctor. It is so good to see you again."

"It is good to see you, Raheem."

"How was your flight?"

"It was quite exhilarating. I'm rather surprised you asked. I'm in the air so often."

"You know me too well, Doctor." The driver confessed, "I noticed the smudges on your shirt and pants. I thought something might have fallen on you."

The doctor looked down at his clothing and laughed. "I had not noticed. I must have dropped the charcoal. No wonder she tried to pay me."

"Pardon me?"

"It is of no importance, Raheem," the doctor said, getting into the limo.

"As you say, sir." Raheem closed the door, put the bags in the trunk, got behind the wheel, and drove the limousine out of the airport.

***

On the far side of the airport's main lobby, an African man wearing a chauffeur's hat, short pants, and a short-sleeve shirt with a crest on his chest pocket was holding a sign that said "Fresh, Inc." The other man was white and dressed in a summer suit and straw hat. He caught sight of Nicole and Regina and waved.

"Hello, Miss Johnson," the man in the suit said, greeting Regina. "It is a pleasure to finally meet you. I am Raymond Oliver. We spoke on the telephone."

Nicole and Regina returned his greeting. Then, graciously, they let him know that Nicole was Miss Johnson.

The girls noticed that Oliver was embarrassed that the lighter-skinned Regina was not Nicole Johnson. They could see he had an instant liking for them because of the tactful way they let him off the hook.

***

Oliver's main function at Futrob was to act as a liaison between Futrob and international interests, which included Q.P.S., potentially one of Futrob's most valuable international investments. The business community considered Q.P.S. to be the future technological leader on the African continent. Futrob wanted to be the first to secure an investor's shares in Q.P.S., which was still a private company. Oliver had been instructed to tell Fresh, Inc. that Q.P.S. was a subsidiary of Futrob's and to seek favor with Fresh, Inc.'s owners, for Fresh, Inc. was

179

one of the few agencies the President of Q.P.S. had requested to interview. These young women might be of tremendous benefit to Futrob if Fresh, Inc. landed the Q.P.S. account.

Once the three were settled in the company Rolls Royce limo, Oliver began to brief Regina and Nicole. "I hope you both are well rested. You are about to enter a fast-paced, no-holds-barred foot race. You will meet the President of Quantum Protection Systems, Segun Bada, at three o'clock. That gives you less than three hours to get settled and prepare.

"Futrob has reserved two connecting suites at Gaborone Sun Hotel. Simply sign for anything you need—equipment, meals, clothing, personal items, long-distance phone calls, and transportation. I know you thought you'd be responsible for the bill, but Futrob wanted to weed out the faint of heart. Your confidence and willingness to take the financial risk impressed us.

"A word to the wise. Do not underestimate Segun Bada. He was educated in Africa and England and received his PhD in engineering at MIT at twenty-three. Although he held the highest academic standing in every university he attended, he refused any recognition and ignored his graduation ceremonies. He's very private and secretive.

"At twenty-five, he created Quantum Protection Systems. His mother and brother are his silent partners. They are a very close-knit family.

"Segun is the elder son and extremely protective of his mother and brother. He possesses the keen and cunning business sense that is normally found in a man decades his senior. At thirty years of age, he's a gifted engineer. Many consider him a genius. Isaac Embel is his right-hand man and Vice President of Operations. Isaac balances Dr. Bada's executive and research development responsibilities. Q.P.S. is Dr. Segun Bada's sole creation."

"Well, I'm impressed. What about you, Gina?"

"Impressed is the word."

"A note to the wise. Dr. Bada takes great pride in staying two steps ahead of any Futrob strategy or research. He is a master of logistics and anticipates our every move. Bidding agencies have been given varied assignments. Sometimes, he creates an imaginary product and gives half a day to produce a campaign. At times, he requires detailed analysis of certain African traditions and customs. He even asked one company to design a state-of-the-art security system for the Bureau of African Affairs in Washington, DC."

"Well, his pattern is obvious."

"What do you mean, Miss Johnson?" Oliver asked.

"During the interview process, Mr. Bada looks for points of weakness. His questions are designed to uncover the interviewees' Achilles' heels or their greatest fears. Giving a limited period of time, he forces the interviewees to overcome their own obstacles. If they fail, they lose. Since he holds all of the cards, it's his game. During our interview, we won't try to win. We just want to force him to show his hand. Mr. Oliver, where are the interviews conducted and how are the parties seated?"

"I don't understand the relevance of your questions, but I have to admit, no one else has asked them. The interview will be held in Bada's office."

"Can you walk us through the interview?"

"Mr. Bada will walk in, open the blinds, and allow the bright sunlight into the office. He may or may not acknowledge your presence. He never shakes your hand. He's always the first to speak. His voice is strong and intimidating. He sits behind his desk. I'm usually seated to the side. You will be seated closely together, directly in front of Bada."

"Have any of our competitors taken notes during the interview process?" Regina asked.

"I've never seen anyone take notes." Mr. Oliver smiled. "I have a feeling the meeting this afternoon will be unique."

"You can be assured of that, Mr. Oliver. We didn't come here to fail," Nicole said.

***

Both of their lavishly decorated suites had private sleeping quarters, dining space, and living room space with a desk and a small conference table. The east walls were floor-to-ceiling windows that boasted a breathtaking panoramic view of the city.

Regina parted the adjoining doors of their suites. "I hope you are as overwhelmed as I am."

181

"Not to worry. I haven't closed my mouth since I walked through the door."

At 2:00 p.m., Regina and Nicole walked across the lobby, carrying matching brief cases with the Fresh, Inc. insignia embossed on each side. The Rolls Royce limo pulled up and the driver opened the door. Regina and Nicole thankfully slipped into the air-conditioned backseat. Oliver was on the telephone to Q.P.S. reporting the afternoon itinerary to the corporate office.

At 2:10 p.m., they saw the exterior complex of Q.P.S.'s ultramodern headquarters through the front windshield. Inside, the main lobby was in stark contrast to the building's exterior. The floors were mosaic tiles set in designs depicting centuries of African countries' battles for independence. An abundance of plants representing rare and colorful African flora were set around a magnificent fountain. Birds of every African species flew freely, from terns and lilac-breasted rollers to crested barbets.

"I have never figured out how this lobby stays immaculate with all these birds. They never disturb anyone or soil the premises," Oliver said.

Nicole and Regina were inspired. That feeling was only surpassed by the pride they felt that all of this had been the creation of a Black man.

"Mr. Oliver, is it possible for you to take us to the office where the meeting will be held?" Regina asked.

"It's rather early, but I'm sure that wouldn't be a problem."

Oliver escorted Nicole and Regina to the elevator. The entire top floor was designated for Segun Bada's exclusive use, from his offices, private research lab, and library and conference room to a workout room and private suite for the times he stayed overnight. Oliver was allowed entry into Segun Bada's office. His secretary informed Oliver that Mr. Bada was in the factory. He was expected at exactly 3:00 p.m.

Segun's office reflected the building's interior and exterior motifs. The furnishings and computers were ultramodern. The walls were adorned with African paintings and tapestries. Every table showcased an African sculpture, vase, or item of colorful pottery.

"This office is lovely," Nicole said. "Yet I feel it could use a woman's touch."

"I couldn't agree more, Nicole."

"What exactly do you mean?" Olivier asked, slightly nervous.

Nicole walked over to the windows and opened the blinds. "I would hate to begin our meeting with a sudden burst of sunlight. It would be very distracting to have the momentary impairment to our vision. It might impede our concentration. Do you share my feelings, Gina?"

"We are in total agreement. Now, tell me if you share mine on the seating arrangements, Nicole. These chairs are pushed too close together. It's like being in the disciplinarian's office. We're trapped together, while he maintains a combative authoritative position, placing us directly in his line of fire. If I separate these chairs and place them slightly at an angle, we create a triangular balance and a peaceful equality amongst all parties. Not to mention that it looks so much nicer."

They noticed Oliver was smiling, showing his appreciation for their teamwork. A look of acknowledgement passed between them that they were on the right track. Then they continued with their preparations in high spirits.

***

At one minute to 3:00 p.m., Segun Bada arrived. He walked with perfect posture, and his entrance and overall presence created an automatic kinetic reaction. He was 6'4", with broad and powerful shoulders that tapered into a slender waist. His arms were a continuous network of tightly knit muscles ending with massive palms and long, thick fingers. His face was strong, his jaw perfectly square. His deep coffee complexion was smooth and flawless. When Segun Bada spoke, his baritone voice vibrated over glistening white teeth.

As he passed the window, he glanced at the blinds. Once in his chair, he noticed the seating arrangement, but his expression remained inscrutable.

"Good afternoon," Nicole said.

Bada looked up from the paper he was examining on his desk. "Good afternoon, Miss Johnson, Miss Bovine, and Mr. Oliver. Since our session has now begun, I want to clarify the reason for our meeting." His eyes lingered on Ray Oliver.

The snake has revealed itself, Segun thought. *I'll live with my mistake. I was too anxious, too impatient. I wanted Q.P.S. launched securely into the international market place. I was caught off guard, but I'm going to make Futrob pay for underestimating me.*

"My first order of business is to disavow any erroneous information imparted to you by Futrob Corporation. Foremost and contrary to what you've been told, Quantum Protection Systems is *not* a subsidiary of Futrob. Q.P.S. is the Bada family's privately owned company. Along with most European and American conglomerates, Futrob wants to take over my company."

Segun looked directly at Ray Oliver. "I can guarantee you that this will never happen. I own all patents. None of the Q.P.S. stock is for sale. I have not received foreign or domestic government aid of any kind. In the final analysis, I would burn down this building and everything in it before I would allow a foreign invader to steal another African creation. This is nationalism, not racism. I recognize that Africans around the world have historically created product without receiving any profit or market share.

"Q.P.S. has hired Futrob Corporation to market and advertise one product for Q.P.S. Security Systems. That product will be built and exported from this factory under the direct auspices of Q.P.S."

Segun stared directly at Nicole. "I want you to understand where your allegiance should lie. Futrob will try to entice you with unlimited funding, perks, and bonuses. It stands to make one hundred times its investment in less than three years. Its ultimate goal is to use Q.P.S. to reestablish its presence on the African continent. If you are chosen as our advertising agency, you will wield a lot of power. Futrob wants eyes and ears on the inside; they want the agency that wins to be beholden to them. I don't intend for that to happen, and I alone will select the advertising agency. If Futrob continues to misinform the groups I contract for service, our deal will be terminated."

Segun paused to glare at Oliver. Even though Oliver was aware of Segun's psychological game, Segun watched him involuntarily nod his head. Segun took note of this as he proceeded with the interview.

He could tell that Nicole's adrenaline was pumping. She had a counterpunch for every combination he threw at her. When he questioned the newness of their agency and limited experience, Nicole cited a list of successful campaigns she and Regina had masterminded. Each of the clients had more than tripled their profits as a result of those advertising blitzes. She also mentioned the twenty-two million dollars of new business that she and Regina had brought in to the Brummel Agency. Segun asked what actual experience she had in the industry.

"As you have developed your own business, Regina and I have developed ours," Nicole said. "I learned from the best. My grandfather was one of the founders of M.E.I., and my father owned Johnston Constructions."

Bada raised an eyebrow. Every hole he poked, Nicole filled. He couldn't rattle her or find a defect in her logic. Finally, Segun sat back in his chair. "I have one last question for your partner, since she has remained silent through the entire interview. I am wondering if Miss Bovine is the silent partner, or is she the secretary?"

Regina had been taking notes in shorthand. She had not raised her head from the pad since the meeting began. After Bada's comment, Regina folded back her notes and placed her pen on the pad in her lap. Sitting erect, she looked Bada directly in the eye. "Do you really want me to answer that question, Dr. Bada?"

"No. I'd rather you answer this. I have asked many professional business people the question I will ask you. So far, no one has given me a satisfactory, let alone correct, answer. What is the only reason to go into business?"

Regina never blinked or lost direct eye contact with Bada. "The answer is both obvious and simple. The only reason to go into business is the continuance of business. If a business continues, all personal and financial goals will be met. None of this will occur if the business is not self-perpetuating."

Bada was intrigued. "What if market conditions change?"

"If owners of a business have not planned for future change, then they have not planned for their business to continue."

"Then what does it mean if I sell the business or diversify?"

"It means that you wish the old business to end and a new business to continue. No matter how the business is altered, it must continue."

Bada sat back and rubbed his chin. Nicole and Oliver were trying their best not to smile. Bada stood up.

"It is clear that the partners of the Fresh, Inc. Agency are astute businesswomen. It still is not clear to me why you would take the risk of coming to this country. How does this venture ensure the continuance of your business? More importantly, I do not have adequate time today to assess your creativity. By tomorrow at noon, I want you to compose a song that will explain to me why you are here. Your completion of this task will show me if your creativity extends beyond redecorating other's offices." Bada walked toward the side exit. He paused at the window, closed the blinds, and then exited.

***

The instant the door closed behind Bada, both Nicole and Oliver sprang to their feet. Nicole gave Regina a hug. "Girl, you were phenomenal."

"Nicole, you had him on the ropes through the whole interview."

"Maybe so. But you delivered the knockout punch!"

"I would like to commend both of you," Raymond Oliver said. "Miss Bovine, I haven't witnessed many summations as excellent as yours. Please understand, this is Raymond Oliver speaking, not Futrob."

"Thank you, Mr. Oliver," they both replied.

"I am going to make arrangements for your transportation. The car will be in front of the building whenever you are ready. You two have a busy night ahead. Good luck. By the way, please call me Ray." Oliver left the office.

Regina put her pad and pen back into her briefcase.

"What do you think of Segun Bada, Gina?"

"At first he scared me, but the more I listened to him, the more my respect grew. I was impressed that he would rather burn down his life's work than have it compromised or stolen. That means he won't compromise values, his friends, or his loved ones. He's like you,

186

Nicole. You can feel confidence in his word and his loyalty. I like his style."

"I think you're right, Gina."

They put their cases under their arms and marched out after their first victory.

***

In the small room adjoining Segun's office, he sat viewing the post-interview activities on a closed-circuit television. After listening to Nicole and Regina's conversation, Segun turned off the television, put his hands behind his head, and smiled.

"I'm rather partial to your style too, Miss Regina Bovine. You were the first ever to give me the correct answer."

***

As Regina and Nicole's limo pulled up in front of the hotel, a nurse pushing a fragile old disfigured man in an umbrella-covered wheelchair stopped to check her patient. Apparently, he had been badly burned in a fire. Both of his legs had been amputated. Regina was the first to get out of the car.

When Nicole came into view, the man in the wheelchair cried out. "Ah, ah, aaaaaaaaaah!" He pointed to her and pounded on a small drum he carried on his lap. Then he tried to push the wheel of his chair with his free hand.

The nurse had never seen him act in this manner. "What is wrong, Baba?"

"Hatshepsut! Hatshepsut! Hatshepsut!" the old man yelled weakly.

The man was calling out to Nicole, and she was drawn to him. Regina followed.

"What's wrong?" Nicole asked.

"I believe Baba has mistaken you for someone in his past," the nurse said.

"You say his name is Baba?" Nicole asked.

The nurse nodded. Nicole stooped down in front of the wheelchair. Baba grabbed Nicole's hand and pressed it against his face. Tears began rolling from his eyes.

"No, Baba," the nurse said.

"It's all right," Nicole assured her.

187

Once more Baba repeated the name Hatshepsut and began to speak rapidly.

"What is he trying to say? Would you please translate?"

"He's thanking the gods that you were spared from the Traveler Blue. Years ago, his village was burned to the ground. All of his people perished. He has mistaken you for his friend, who was probably your age the last time he saw her."

The man released Nicole's hand and tried to hand her his drum.

"I don't believe what I am seeing. I was told that Baba carried that drum out of the fire. He has kept it all of his life. Now he wants you to have it."

"I cannot take your drum, Baba."

Baba placed one hand on his heart and the drum on the ground.

"He will not take it back," the nurse explained. "You will shame him if you do not accept it. Please take it."

Finally, Nicole picked up the drum. The old man raised both of his arms to the sky.

"Why don't I visit Baba tomorrow. I'll bring the drum too, just in case he changes his mind. Where is he staying?" Nicole asked the nurse.

"The Princess Marina Hospital, only a few blocks from here. Here's his room number."

After the nurse handed Nicole the slip of paper, Nicole leaned over and kissed Baba on his scarred forehead. A smile of unadulterated joy graced his lips.

***

As the nurse rolled Baba away, he closed his eyes and remembered his boyhood. Kabaka had made the drum for him. Finally, after all these years, one of his own came to him, Hatshepsut and Kabaka's baby girl.

***

Back in their suites, Regina unpacked her briefcase while Nicole looked out the window.

"Gina, I wonder who Baba thought I was?"

"Even when you were right in front of him, he never stopped believing you were Hatsep...say the name again, Nicole."

188

"Hatshepsut. I read about her in a history class. She dressed like a man in order to become the ruler of Egypt. You know what's strange, Gina? I felt it was my duty to talk to him. It was like a voice inside me said, 'Relieve his burden.'"

"As I keep saying, after the things we've witnessed, I don't second guess any compelling feelings. Not to change the subject, I think we've got a song to write."

Nicole called room service. They showered and put on their creative uniforms—jeans and tee shirts. After eating, they sat at the conference table in Nicole's suite.

***

For hours they worked on the lyrics. None were inspirational. Nicole got up to stretch her legs and picked up the drum. Regina was jotting down ideas on her pad. Deep in thought, Nicole started to softly beat on the drum, playing a very moving series of drumbeats. Regina stopped writing. Suddenly on her feet, she started to dance.

"Play, Nicole! Play!"

"It's just a beat I've always heard in my head."

"What do you mean?" Regina asked as she swayed her hips from side to side.

"Sometimes, I hear the sounds of drummers in the distance. I heard them the moment I agreed we would come to Africa. The drumming seemed to call me to action."

"That's it," Regina shouted. "Don't stop, Nicole! Don't stop!

"What is it?"

"But first we need to squander some of Futrob's money!"

Regina shared her plan with Nicole and they jump into action. Regina telephoned Futrob and asked for a car and driver while Nicole called a contact at the American Embassy to ask a favor.

They started their journey by going twelve miles northwest of Gaborone to the Oodi Village to purchase two of the company's fan palm *mokolane* baskets created by the Lentswe-la-Oodi weavers.

Quickly, they drove on to the Maitisong Cultural Center and Fair Grounds, where an international trade fair was being held. They were thrilled by the performance of a young student dance group dressed in traditional tanned leather skirts and tops, performing the *Borankana*, a popular dance celebrating the rain and harvest. The accompanying musicians played the drums and the *mbira*, a thumb piano. They were amazing.

After talking to the group's leader, Nicole and Regina left for a meeting scheduled at Botswana's second legislative body, the House of Chiefs, set up by Nicole's contact at the embassy. The leaders were very receptive to their plans. Nicole and Regina were all smiles when they left and hurried to their last stop.

The Main Mall was just east of the government buildings and was the true center of Gaborone. There they purchased a carpet, silk fabric, pottery, garments, and delicacies like wild plums, *tsama* melons, *marula* fruit, honey, and wild cucumbers. They returned to the hotel and continued to plan and prepare for their presentation. They had a long night ahead of them.

Chapter 28

The next day, a nervous Ray Oliver sat alone in Segun Bada's office. His palms were perspiring and his head pounding. It was 11:45 a.m. and Nicole and Regina were nowhere to be found. When the driver arrived, no one was waiting in the lobby and their suites were empty. Oliver had his assistant ringing their rooms every five minutes.

At 11:57 p.m., Segun Bada arrived at his office through his side entrance. Isaac Embel and Mr. Rolls accompanied him. Without speaking, Segun stared directly at Oliver.

As Oliver was about to render an apology, an echoing gong suddenly resounded loudly, vibrating the front doors of the office. It was exactly 12:00 p.m. when the doors swung open.

A carpet was released from a low angle stand, racing through the office until it unrolled and rested directly in front of Segun's desk. It created a perfectly aligned aisle from the doorway to where Segun's chair was positioned. Attached to the top of the carpet was a flowing blue silk veil that shimmered and billowed like the rolling ocean. Suddenly, a musician began playing the *mbira*. A beautiful melody was accentuated by the pulsating beat of drums. Musicians lined up playing on either side of the flowing runway and opened the stage to a group of beautiful children. The young dancers performed the *Borankana* and ended the dance by sitting in front of the executive desk. There was a moment of silence.

A lone soprano voice sang "Sometimes…" in a sweet melodic tone. An alto voice picked up the cue and sang "I hear…" Then, in cherubic tones, the two voices blended in harmony, singing the lyric line, "Sometimes, I hear the sound."

From the Maitisong Cultural Center and Fair Grounds, two elderly vendor women dressed in traditional brown and blue *leteisi* garments led the parade. They carried Oodi baskets abundant with fruit and flowers. Their aromas filled the room.

Regina and Nicole appeared from opposite sides of the doorway and moved to the middle of the blue runner. Clad in stunning traditional African dress with heads wrapped in matching silk turbans, they were breathtaking. A conga drum was strapped over Nicole's shoulder and an acoustic guitar was hanging from Regina's. Nicole began to pound the pulsating drumbeat and Regina strummed a haunting rhythm on the guitar.

To the beat of the music, they began their journey down the flowing blue runner. They were followed by a group yet unseen. Their syncopated movements billowed the chiffon, created the illusion that they were dancing atop the tide of an ocean's current. Accenting their forward motion, they swayed like the leaves of the willow in a whistling breeze. Midway through their procession, Regina began to sing the song they had composed. Nicole sang harmony. Their audience was already marveling at their beauty and their presentation, but the lyric line and musical ability of the two women blew them away. Segun Bada paid particular attention to the lyrics Regina sang:

Often I hear the sound of distant drums
calling from long ago and far away
This is what I hear them say
Come back home, come back home,
where your people understand you.
Come back home, come back home,
your Motherland commands you.
Come home, Come home.
Come home, to the Motherland, come home.
Like the seeds from a windblown tree,
We were carried across the sea.
In the new land we grew,
Despite being planted in bitter soil feeling Blue
We always knew to truly grow,
To our Motherland's garden we must go.
Come back home, come back home,
Your Motherland's arms will surround you.

Come back home, come back home,
Lost, now your Motherland has found you.
Come home, come home,
Your Motherland commands you to come home.

On that ending note, Nicole and Regina each gracefully went down on one knee, revealing the rest of their procession, the eight members of the House of Chiefs.

Segun could not believe his eyes as the Heredity chiefs of the principal tribes of Botswana spread across his office and raised their hands to the sky, reciting in one voice, "Come back home!"

In respect, Segun immediately sprang to his feet to greet these advisors to Parliament. Everyone applauded and cheered.

The chief of baTwana spoke to Segun. "*Dumela rra*, young Mr. Bada. You have done well to bring these brilliant African American women back home. We are positive that your combined efforts will show the world that our beloved Botswana encourages ingenious inventions and innovations such as yours."

"Thank you, sir," Segun said, bursting with pride. Then the chiefs of the baKgatia, baKwena, baMalete, BamaNgwato, baNgwaketse, baRolong, and baTiokwa gave their congratulations to Segun with further endorsements of Nicole and Regina. Thereafter, the House of Chiefs departed the office to another burst of applause.

"I have come to my decision," Segun said. "Fresh, Inc. will represent Q.P.S. in this venture to promote our product in an international advertising and marketing campaign. Excuse me. I will return shortly."

He and Isaac quickly exited through the side door. Segun locked it behind them. Then he unlocked the hood of the roll-top desk to reveal his closed-circuit television.

"Isaac, watch how they work."

Nicole and Regina were bursting with excitement. Ray shook Nicole's hand and congratulated her. The Senior Vice President took Regina's hand. "Welcome to the Futrob team. That was an outstanding presentation!"

Regina's smile ceased. She seemed to realize this was her cue to inject a reality check.

"I am sure you and Mr. Oliver discussed the details of our meeting yesterday with Dr. Bada. He made it clear to all of us, and we all were in agreement, in the event Fresh, Inc. was selected, we would become contractual employees of Q.P.S., and Q.P.S. will hold exclusive rights to any and all of our creations. We are to report to Q.P.S. only. Please, correct me if this has been changed. Has Dr. Bada changed his position?"

The Senior Vice President from Futrob was a veteran business negotiator. He was not about to get caught in his own web.

"Doggone it," he replied with a toothy grin. "You are absolutely right. I am so used to Futrob acting alone in business that it slipped my mind that this is Q.P.S.'s ballgame. Saying 'welcome aboard' has just become a habit of mine."

"I am certain your association with Segun Bada will cause you to rethink many old habits," Nicole said.

After Nicole's comment, Ray Oliver turned away before he smiled.

In the next room, Segun Bada sat back and placed his hands behind his head. "They stood up to the giant. I am proud of them. Isaac, I want you to make sure these two women get any and everything they request. Do not second-guess them. The creative mind needs space and a rather large margin to make errors. We must ensure their success. Our loyalty to them must be equal to, or greater than, theirs to us. My mother always told me, 'We are all a part of a greater family. When the mother calls the daughters home to help her put the house in order, it is the inherent responsibility of the sons to protect the daughters.' I have always answered my mother's call. Therefore, I shall not deny my Motherland's call. That was truly a magnificent presentation."

Isaac was twenty-five years Segun's senior. He had watched Segun, this creative genius, this man with the technical acumen, build Q.P.S. singled handed. Not once had Isaac heard Segun speak in such emotional, philosophical terms. For the first time in their relationship, Isaac placed his hand on Segun's shoulder. The contact startled Segun, but he did not protest.

"Segun Bada, you never cease to amaze me. With each day I grow prouder of your accomplishments. Today, I am just proud of you. I pledge to you these daughters will never fail under my watch."

There was a swell in Segun's chest. "Isaac, for some unfathomable reason, I have an overpowering feeling that my life is on the threshold of a dramatic change. And, as I say that, I realize I have never said thank you—thank you, Isaac, for all you've done."

"You are welcome. This has been a conversation I will cherish." He placed his hands at his side. "You have many battles yet to fight. I will go now and prepare everything you'll need. I know you will want to meet with Nicole and Regina this evening."

***

Segun stood behind his desk. He spoke directly to Nicole and Regina.

"The contract is being prepared as we speak and will be ready this evening. I require at least one family member to sign a contract with me. The other member of my family is only available in the evening hours, and I want him to meet you. I recognize the inconvenience. Therefore, we will combine business with dinner.

"This evening at seven o'clock, I will send a car for you two at your hotel. You may need a day or so to evaluate the terms of the contract. I will expect an acceptance or addenda within a forty-eight-hour period. This meeting will also allow me to demonstrate the product you will promote to the world. Are there any extenuating circumstances or pre-engagements that would prevent our meeting this evening?"

"None whatsoever, Dr. Bada," said Regina.

Then Segun made a gesture that shocked everyone in the room. He extended his hand first to Nicole. "Welcome to the Q.P.S. team." And then he repeated the welcome to Regina. He held onto Regina's hand slightly longer. "Try to rest before our meeting. The production of today's spectacular presentation must have required a sleepless night."

Segun was right. For their presentation, Regina had searched the stores for similar attire to the beautiful design the artist had created for Nicole to wear in the pastel portrait. Afterwards, Regina had insisted they find a fabric and carpet store. Back in Nicole's Gaborone Sun suite, Regina had hand-sewn blue silk chiffon to the new runner. Once all their props and costumes were ready, she had begun working on the lyrics and composing the music inspired by Nicole's words and drumbeat. Afterwards, she had choreographed their routine. By 7:30 a.m., she had woke Nicole to practice.

Now, Regina smiled at Segun. "You are right. I am exhausted."

Segun released her hand. "Until tonight," he said, and he took his leave.

The Executive Vice President of Futrob excused himself to report the day's activities to the corporate office.

Regina, Nicole, and Ray were left standing in the office.

Ray spoke first. "Over the last twenty-five years, I have rarely witnessed true creativity. I'm so sick of copycats, cornballs, ass kissers, and self-proclaimed business wizards that at times it takes every ounce of strength I have not to get up and walk out. You two have restored some of the faith in this cynical old company man. Now get some rest. The car is waiting."

***

When Regina and Nicole returned to the hotel, Regina went upstairs to rest and Nicole entered the hotel gift shop.

A half hour later, Nicole unlocked her suite, her arms full of flowers and packages. She set the flowers down and walked over to the end table where the drawing lay. She fastened the picture into a new wooden frame. The beauty of the picture and subtle elegance of the frame were in perfect harmony. She took a card from the bag and wrote on the inner flap:

Dear Gina,

I may have gotten us here, but you are the one who has ensured our stay. You captured this account. You'll never know how much I respect you. I am truly blessed that you are my partner. We are an unbeatable team. I'm not twice blessed. I am thrice blessed. You are the best friend I have ever had. I thank my father for making you my sister. God could not have created a more perfect sister for me than you.

Love always, Your Sister Nicole

Nicole attached the card to the flowers and took them into Regina's suite, taking one more admiring glance at the drawing on her way out the door. Her best friend was sound asleep, so Nicole placed the flowers and card on the nightstand.

At 3:00 p.m., Nicole stood before the Princess Marina Hospital information desk getting directions to Baba's room. She was upset she had forgotten his drum on the end table but vowed to herself that she would bring it on the next visit.

As Nicole approached the fourth-floor ward, Baba's nurse was coming out. Her expression was somber and her eyes were very sad.

"I am very sorry to tell you," the nurse said, taking Nicole's hand, "Baba died a few minutes ago."

Even though Nicole hadn't known the man, she felt a deep sense of grief. She asked the nurse if she could see him. The nurse was rather surprised by Nicole's request, but she escorted Nicole into his room. Lying motionless in his bed, Baba looked serene and at peace.

"Baba, I will take care of your drum," she told him softly. "Perhaps you were the distant drummer who called us here. I am honored you delivered the drum to me."

Back in Nicole's hotel suite, the drum began to rock back and forth on the end table until it toppled to the carpet. It rolled across the floor and came to a stop directly under the table where Nicole's portrait was stationed. The drum stood itself on its end as if it were standing guard over its grandchild.

***

It was nearly 5:30 p.m. when she returned to the hotel. Regina met her with a hug.

"The flowers are beautiful and the card—it made me cry. Thank you so much, Nicole. I am on a natural high. Never did I think things would go our way so quickly."

"You know, you couldn't be more right, Gina. This has been like a fantasy come true. Somehow, I think the best is yet to come. It must be our time."

Regina started for her suite. "It was getting kind of late, so I went ahead and picked out our outfits for the dinner meeting. Yours is on your bed. I'm going to shower."

"That's great. One less thing to think about."

"Don't get too relaxed. You've got a contract to dissect tonight."

"Not to worry. While I was out, I had my contract scalpel sharpened."

Regina laughed. "By the way, I love that frame on your portrait. And putting the drum under it was a nice touch."

Nicole looked over at the picture. She didn't remember putting the drum there.

***

The Q.P.S. limo arrived at 7:00 p.m. The driver helped the ladies into the car.

"Do you know where we will be dining this evening?" Nicole asked the driver.

"Yes, madam. All has been prepared at the Bada estate."

Nicole and Regina spoke in low tones. "Gina, I meant to ask you this earlier. Correct me if I'm wrong. I do believe I detected a flow of electricity between you and one Segun Bada."

"You are letting your imagination run wild, Nicole."

"Then explain to me why my hair stood on end when I walked between you two. I was wondering if he was ever going to let go of your hand. Was he checking to see if you washed, or what?"

"I respect the way the man does business. I believe he was impressed with our presentation. That's it."

"I see. I am way off the mark. Good of you to clear it up for me. Whew! I feel better."

Nicole's sarcasm was interrupted when the driver announced, "Ladies, we have arrived."

A twenty-foot-high stone wall that extended a half-mile in each direction surrounded the Bada estate. Huge iron gates automatically opened to palatial grounds. As the limousine drove towards the mansion, Nicole and Regina looked at the cobblestone paths leading to magnificent gardens and fountains. Animals and birds of the wild roamed freely. Lions, zebra, giraffes, monkeys, and elk peacefully cohabited.

"Do not worry about the animals, ladies. They are tame and docile. As you can see, predator and prey live in harmony. This is the only life they have ever known. Do not be alarmed if any of them approach you."

"Thanks for telling us. I was a little afraid of getting out of the car," Regina confessed.

198

"You are most certainly welcome, madam. I haven't had the opportunity to speak of the animals for some time. We have not had guests at the house since Mrs. Bada's illness. I am sorry, I am speaking too much."

"Not at all. We will not mention it to anyone," Nicole said.

"Thank you, madam," the driver replied as he entered the circular drive leading to the front door.

The Bada mansion was as opulent as the lavish grounds. The driver parked and opened the limousine door for the ladies.

"Look around, Nicole. A man as young as Segun Bada, who has accomplished so much, has no time or inclination for anything other than his work."

"I didn't say anything else about the man. You seem to be pretty defensive as far as Segun Bada's concerned."

They walked to the stairs.

"Segun Bada is not the kind of man you have to defend or take care of, Nicole. He doesn't get crayon smeared all over his little white shirt and pants after naptime." Regina placed a victorious grin on her face and confidently ascended the stairs.

Nicole laughed. "That was low, but a good one. You're the woman, Gina. You're the woman."

The two reached the top of the stairs. The double doors parted, and they were greeted by Segun's voice over the PA system.

"I will be with you momentarily. The sitting room is to your left. Please make yourselves comfortable."

The interior decor was more understated than Segun's personal quarters at the Q.P.S. building. In all of its grandeur, the house was homey, with a woman's warm, personal touch.

Within a few minutes, Segun came down the winding staircase and entered the sitting room. He was wearing a black tuxedo. It fit him to perfection.

"I must apologize for not meeting you at the door. I was trying to contact my brother. He is in transit. I have your copies of the contract in the next room. If you'll pardon me, I'll get them."

"Certainly," Regina said.

"I love the way he says 'Hello, how are you ladies this evening?'" Nicole said.

"Well, he's not as gracious as crayon man. But his tuxedo alone more than makes up for it."

Nicole composed herself before Segun reentered the room.

"I was not sure of your procedure for contract evaluation," Segun said, handing Regina and Nicole individual copies of the contract. "I made a copy for each of you." Segun paused, looking at Regina. "I did not wish to make the same error as at our first meeting."

Regina smiled slightly to acknowledge Segun's attempt at an apology.

"To be perfectly honest, Dr. Bada, Nicole is in charge of contracts. She can reduce the best to putty."

"I hope I do not have reason for concern. I dictated the terms of our contract to my lawyers. I'm confident they put together a fair and equitable agreement. Personally, I consider haggling over a contract that is designed to cheat one of the parties a waste of time and energy. I may be tenacious in business; sometimes, I'm even ferocious. But, you both can be assured, I am always honest."

"I'm anxious to read it," Nicole said.

"Why don't we adjourn to the dining room first?"

The elegant table was set for four. A beautiful floral centerpiece graced the table, complemented by crystal wine and water goblets and sterling silver place settings. Lighted candles flickered beneath a dimly lit chandelier. Segun sat at the head of the table with Regina to his right and Nicole to his left. The chair opposite Segun was reserved for his brother. The servants were bringing out serving dishes when Segun heard the front door open.

"That must be my brother now."

"I'll be with you in a moment, Segun," a voice from the entrance called out loudly. "Let me wash up. I was told you are wearing the tuxedo that cost more than our first house. Is that true?"

"Yes, I am, Sotonye. You do realize our guests are here."

"Of course I do. Why else would I be making such an effort to embarrass you?"

Nicole and Regina looked at each other and tried their best not to smile.

Segun was fighting back a smile himself. "What my brother lacks in social grace, he more than makes up for in humor. He's actually one of the few people who can make me laugh."

Regina and Nicole both noticed the change in Segun's demeanor. The love he felt for his brother was obvious. Segun heard his brother's approaching footsteps. He stood up.

"Ladies, I would like you to meet the real Dr. Bada. He is the MD, not the PhD."

Dr. Sotonye Bada entered the room and a feather falling would have sounded like thunder. Segun quickly noted the shocked expressions of all.

"It's crayon man," Regina blurted out.

"Pardon me?" Segun asked.

Regina waved her hand. "Pay no attention to me. That was a slip of the tongue."

"Well, Segun, in an effort to embarrass you, I have made a complete fool out of myself for the third time in front of these two women."

"Do you all know one another, Sotonye?"

"Remember, the drawing on the plane…"

"You mean to tell me…" Segun paused.

Nicole and Regina watched Segun move his hands from side to side, as if to ask Sotonye whom he had drawn.

"Your brother created an absolutely gorgeous picture of Nicole while we were on the plane," Regina said, noting Segun smiled despite himself at the news.

"Really," Segun said. "Sotonye, you forgot to introduce yourself on the plane, so let me do the honors. I would like you to meet the partners of Fresh, Inc., Nicole Johnson and Regina Bovine. Fresh, Inc. is in charge of our company's international advertising and marketing campaign. Once again, ladies, it is my pleasure to introduce my thoroughly humiliated brother, Sotonye Bada."

Sotonye walked over to Regina and shook her hand. "Hello again. My brother tells me you are quite creative."

"It's nice to see you again. And thank you."

Sotonye joined Nicole at the other side of the table and took her hand.

201

Nicole spoke first. "I bought a frame for your drawing today. I am so happy to have the opportunity to thank you again. "

"You are an inspiration. It was my pleasure." He smiled, lost in her eyes. "I'm very happy your agency won the bid. I know my brother is in good hands."

Segun looked from Regina to Sotonye and Nicole. "Sotonye, you may release Miss Johnson's hand. She might possibly need it to eat."

Everyone was seated. The servants placed the remaining serving dishes on the table and left quietly. Segun stood up and grandly uncovered the platter.

"Fried chicken, sweet potatoes, collard greens, cornbread, and red beans and rice." The girls applauded and he laughed. "I told myself that you might not be ready for our traditional African cuisine, which gave me the perfect excuse to ask the chef to prepare the meal I most enjoyed when I studied in the United States."

"It is really considerate of you to go to all of this trouble for us. I feel right at home. I must tell you, red beans and rice are my favorite," Regina said.

Segun smiled. "That is amazing. They are also mine."

"I see Miss Bovine shares my brother's health fetishes."

Segun looked at Nicole and Regina. "This is the type of dinner conversation one must endure when there is a doctor in the family."

"Do you eat dinner together often?" Nicole asked.

"Whenever we are not traveling, we always eat together," Sotonye said. "It is our mother's rule. 'Families that do not break bread together become strangers living in the same house.'"

"Your mother is very wise," Nicole said.

"We think so," Segun replied,

"I think you girls are being very considerate, but I know both of you have the same question, so I'll answer it for you.

"Earlier this year, just before Segun's birthday, our mother had a severe fall and lapsed into a coma. She is at the Mayo Clinic. I was returning from Minnesota when I first met you in London. We have the finest researchers and diagnosticians trying to find a way to bring her out of the coma. So far, we have been unsuccessful."

"Your mother's illness must be extremely difficult for you both," Regina said.

"Our mother spent her entire life working to ensure that Sotonye and I would be successful. Our father was an officer in the Nigerian Army. Assassins killed him before the war in Biafra began to escalate. Mother was still carrying Sotonye when our father died. With the money father left her, Mother built an import/export business. She's an artist of many talents. You'll see many of her paintings and sculptures on display here in our home. She also designs and weaves tapestries and traditional African garments and quilts. Her creations are all one of a kind. Even her jewelry designs. If I am not mistaken, Miss Bovine, this afternoon you were wearing one of her necklaces. I noticed it when you were singing. Usually I can spot my mother's work. Do you remember the name on the tag?"

"Actually, I do. It said *An original design by Nafisa*."

"That's our mother, Nafisa Bada," Sotonye said.

"You won't believe this! I have a statue of a servant girl at home. The carving is so realistic I can actually feel the hardship and pain the servant girl has suffered. The name Nafisa is carved in the base. It originally belonged to my parents," Nicole said.

"I don't doubt that at all. It sounds like one of her earlier works," Segun said. "My mother was a servant before she met our father, who she said was sent to her from the gods. If it weren't for our father, her art would never have been known. I'm sure he would be very proud that all of her work has been in demand for nearly thirty years."

"What an amazing woman," Regina said.

The brothers nodded in agreement.

Their conversation never lulled. It was as if they had all known one another for years. When they had finished their meal, Segun asked Nicole if she still wanted to look over the contract.

"Of course."

"I would like to take a look at the contract myself," Sotonye said.

"You have never been interested in our business. What has changed?" Segun teased.

Sotonye laughed. "I want to know exactly what we are paying Fresh, Inc. I am reconsidering a payment offered to me for a picture I drew."

Segun noticed a hint of embarrassment on Nicole's face and decided to play along with his brother. "That is an excellent idea, Sotonye. Everyone knows how a young, struggling artist, such as you, is in need of money. Take payment in gold. The dollar has devalued."

"Very funny," Nicole said.

The brothers laughed.

"If they are going to read the contract," Regina told Segun, "I would really like to take a look at the product Fresh, Inc. is going to make world renowned."

"An excellent idea! Before we separate, it has occurred to me that at least three of us in this room will be working together for quite some time. I would feel more comfortable if you called me Segun."

While Nicole and Sotonye reviewed the contract in the sitting room, Regina and Segun remained in the dining room.

"Do you store your inventions in a special room?" Regina asked.

"Actually, I could show you my invention without leaving this room, but I would rather take you outside. You may have noticed I am making every effort to impress you. It is my nature to quantify everything I do. So, Regina, on the 'impressive' barometer, with atmospheric pressures from one percent to ten percent, where have I gauged?"

"I'd say around eight percent."

"Sotonye reduced me from nine percent, didn't he?"

"You did that all by yourself."

Segun hid a smile. He walked over to the china cabinet and removed a miniature remote control. "Come with me. I will redeem myself."

Regina walked with Segun. He pushed one of the buttons on the remote and the front doors swung open. As they were stepping outside, Segun called into the sitting room.

"Nicole, in a few seconds, the house will be completely black. If you hear whimpering, do not be disconcerted. Sotonye is afraid of the dark."

Walking down the stairs, Regina said to Segun, "Nine percent."

"Thank you. Now I will strive for a perfect score."

Segun escorted Regina to the outer perimeter of the driveway, where they could view the entire mansion. He pressed a button on his remote and the house turned pitch black. He pressed another button and illuminated every window in the house. Bars of golden light appeared from the tops of the windows down to the sills.

"The light is brilliant. I don't understand how you've made it form such perfect columns. They actually look like the security bars you would find on windows of a store or house. Is the light encased in some sort of tube?" Regina asked.

"No, it is not."

"Are they some type of laser beam that would burn an intruder?"

"That would be very dangerous. Could you imagine a small child sticking his hand into such a powerful beam?"

"Okay, Segun Bada, I'll give you your ten percent if you tell me what I am looking at."

"I do not want points by default." He took Regina by the hand and led her to one of the ground-floor front windows. "Touch one of the bars."

"It's solid and hard as a steel bar. How can this be? It's just a beam of light."

Segun smiled at her. "Let's go inside. I'll explain."

He turned on the lights and left the bars of light operational. They reentered the mansion, and Regina went directly to the windows.

"Nicole," she called out, "come in here and touch a light beam! You won't believe this. They are solid. Don't worry, there is no heat or shock."

Nicole was bolder than Regina. She raised her palm with the intention of pushing her hand through one of the bars. Nicole's hand was stopped cold. She touched the other bars, yielding the same result. She extended her arm through the space between the bars of light. The bars stopped her at the shoulder. When Nicole stood up straight, Segun pressed a button on the remote and the bars disappeared. Nicole and Regina simultaneously waved their hands and arms in the open window space. How had a solid mass suddenly disappeared? Regina was regrouping, but Nicole was still sticking her head out of the window.

"Give it up, Nicole. This is payback for a surprise Segun Bada experienced around noon today. Am I correct?"

"You are correct."

"I can safely assume this is the product that we'll market and advertise to the world."

"You are also correct, Nicole."

"Segun, explain," Sotonye said.

"When I was in the United States working on my doctorate, I slipped away from Cambridge every once in a while and walked the streets of Boston. I couldn't believe there were bars on the windows of homes and apartment buildings. They posed a greater danger to people on the inside than intruders on the outside. In a fire or an emergency, locked gates create death traps. The inhabitants were prisoners. On the other hand, a thief in the night could easily force the locks. There had to be a better answer.

"Although I am an engineer, I am also a student of physics and chemistry. As a child, water and light fascinated me. Water exists in all three physical states—as a solid piece of ice, a liquid like the rivers, or steam, a gas. I wondered if light was transformable. Light did not exist in any of these physical states, but what physical properties did it exhibit?

"Well, we know that light can bend, refract, and reflect, just as solids can. Through molecular reconfiguration, with the absence of heat, water becomes ice. I thought to myself, what would be the conditions required to transform light into a solid mass? I am sure you remember as children watching the sun's rays through your window or through the trees in the forest. You also may recall watching the dust particles flow through light rays. They looked like light poles shooting at an angle from the sun.

"I was fascinated with all of this light. As I grew older and learned about ionization and fission, the concept finally crystallized. It would take weeks for me to explain the quantum engineering involved. Just pretend I've replaced the dust particles that are flowing through a sunray with microscopic iron particles. These particles are ionized, yet they do not require an alternating current. There's no electric shock. I force these microscopic particles through a beam of light at quantum speed. At the same time, the light beam is accelerated to a rate faster than quantum speed. The light is moving too quickly for the infinite number of ionized iron particles to pass outside of the tubular walls of the light beam, creating iron-like bars of light. When the system is turned on, the light beam is followed by the iron particles. When I turn it off, the process is reversed."

"No wonder Futrob is so excited. These light bars will revolutionize the entire security industry," Regina said.

"Yes, but they're more than enthusiastic," Segun said.

Nicole noticed he was about to tell her something but was hesitating. "Is there more about Futrob you'd like to tell me?"

"I didn't know that reading minds was one of your talents," Segun said, amused.

"I know you won't appreciate hearing this, but for a moment you were transparent. You looked like someone had tried to cross you." Seeing Segun was surprised and uncomfortable, Nicole smiled. "I'm sure they didn't succeed, however."

"I will have to be careful around you," Segun said, laughing. "My mother and brother are usually the only ones who see so much."

Nicole turned serious. "For some unexplainable reason, I think you know me, too. I don't like it when people try to take advantage. I have been known to get highly offended. Maybe you'll tell me what you're really thinking one day and we'll compare notes," Nicole said, smiling. "For now, just know that Regina and I will be proud to work on this project, Segun. It's brilliant! I don't know why you hired Futrob when all you needed was us!"

"I have you."

"Yes, but you still have to pay Futrob," Nicole said.

"Not for long." He turned to Sotonye. "I'll tell you about it later, brother. Better yet, you might want to talk to Nicole. She knows more about me than I'd care to admit."

"I hate to interrupt," Sotonye said, "but we're short staffed at the hospital. I have to get back."

Regina looked at her watch. "I didn't realize how late it was. We'd better be on our way too."

Before Regina got into the car, she turned to Segun. "Oh, by the way, eleven percent."

On the way to the hotel, Sotonye told them his practice was affiliated with the Princess Marina Hospital.

"I was there this afternoon, visiting Baba," Nicole said.

"I knew Baba well."

"What do you mean, you *knew* him?" Regina asked.

"Gina, I can't believe I didn't tell you. Baba died a few minutes before I got to his ward. It was so strange. I don't know why I didn't feel sad. I was suddenly tranquil."

"In traditional African religion, when a person has suffered most of his or her life, he or she is rewarded with a new, happier life. Maybe there was a kinship between you and Baba, and instinctively you knew Baba was going on to a better life."

The limo pulled up to the Princess Marina Hospital entrance. Sotonye got out of the car.

"This has been a most enjoyable evening. I can't remember the last time I saw my brother so relaxed. Hopefully the contract meets with your approval. I know you can help capture Segun's dream to make Africa a major player in the global economy."

"I promise we will do our best," Nicole said.

"Then I am sure success is inevitable." Sotonye bid the two ladies farewell.

***

Nicole and Regina retired to their separate suites lost in their own thoughts.

In the chair next to her bed, Nicole sat down to read the contract and went through page after page without lifting a pen. The terms of the agreement were more than fair. Fresh, Inc. had a free hand and an enormous budget. There was even a consent allowing both parties to dissolve the contract. If Q.P.S. terminated the contract, Fresh, Inc. would receive full payment.

Once she told Gina about Segun's generosity and honesty, the two of them wouldn't sleep again until Q.P.S. products were in demand worldwide.

Her thoughts drifted to Sotonye. There was no doubt she was attracted to him. *Pull yourself together, Nicole. You didn't even act like this in high school. You've always been level headed and in control. This time, I don't know if I should control myself.* She laughed and went to bed.

***

Segun Bada never slept more than five hours a night. If involved in a project, he wouldn't sleep at all. This night, he sat at his worktable in the research lab down in the sublevel honoring his mother's wish that their home be a home and not an industrial complex.

He recalled when he had first told his mother he wanted to build the company in Botswana, the country with the greatest growth potential. She had asked what he expected of his family.

"I want you and Sotonye to move with me, of course," he said without thinking there was any other option.

Although Sotonye had been in his last year of medical school and his mother had a lovely home and a booming business in Nigeria, he remembered his mother placing her hand on his.

"If this is the road you must travel, you will not travel alone. We will come when you call."

Q.P.S. had shown a seven million dollar profit its first fiscal year. By the fifth year, most governments and businesses on the continent sought Q.P.S.'s services or bought its products. Segun built the Bada estate after the first year. His mother had left her native Nigeria, and when Sotonye had finished his residency at Luth Lago University Teaching Hospital in Lagos, Nigeria, he had followed.

Segun suddenly thought of Regina and heard a drum beating in his head. She was walking towards him across the waters of the ocean, her arms outstretched. She was singing, "Come back home." He sat back in his chair and closed his eyes.

***

The expansive window in her Gaborone Sun Hotel suite was several stories lower than the apartment window in the housing projects where she had watched the world go by as she grew up. What a different perspective she had now!

The odds had been stacked against her standing here, but even as a child, Regina had known she had a right to dream and believed her dreams would come true. Emma had instilled this faith in her.

As she grew up, Regina had begun to identity the common thread amongst the successful people she knew. Despite the degradation in which they lived, the darkened stairwells filled with trash, the hallways of broken glass, the stench of pungent urine, the addicts, the gangs, the violence, these people looked ahead, willing to work, refusing to be hindered by self-doubt and self-hatred. They were free and proud and strong.

In the past, she may have made some bad decisions, but she had accepted her mistakes and learned from them. Now she looked to the future, like those she had admired in the projects.

Gone were the hopeless stares of the projects. Gone were the dingy barred windows. Gone were the bitter-cold Chicago glass panes frozen opaque, distorting all outside images of the world. Now, in clear view of the star-filled ebony sky of Africa, she saw the bright light that shone on the future.

Part V

Joseph, Blue, and the Mothers

Zinzi, Emma, Marion, and Nafisa

1959–1961, New Orleans, Ethiopia, Sudan,

Washington

Chapter 29

It was around 11:00 p.m. when Emma finally decided to call it a night. The Madame Bovine staff had developed a great respect for Emma and her business savvy. In less than three weeks, profits had risen thirty-seven percent.

Emma walked down Bourbon Street toward Big El's Club. A group of tourists crowded around Big El's limousine. How far Big El had come from the days when he ran errands for Aunt Melinda. Big for his age, white but with a ruddy complexion, he had a lock of hair in the back of his head that never lay down. Elbert was the only child of an abusive alcoholic father and a much abused young mother. Melinda had taken him in. His allegiance to her was undeniable.

El had been five years old when he first heard Satchmo play the horn on Bourbon Street and knew he had found his calling. For El's thirteenth birthday, Melinda bought him the trumpet in the pawnshop. From that day forward, Elbert was never without his horn. By the time he was twenty-one, El was called Big El, for no one could blow a horn like him. His career skyrocketed.

El never forgot where he came from. When he heard about Melinda's family reunion, he canceled a European tour. He loved Melinda as a son loved his mother.

Big El signed autographs, towering over most of the people standing around him.

"Where are you headed, Emma?" he called out.

"You're back already! I'm just on my way home," Emma shouted back.

"Come on. I'll drive you!"

"I'll be fine, El. It's not that far."

El spoke loudly over the crowd. "You know Miss Melinda would tan my hide if I let you go home unescorted. Come on, Emma, please don't get me in trouble."

Emma had to laugh. This silver-haired man of nearly sixty, dressed in a thousand-dollar suit, was begging like a mischievous child.

"Folks, please step aside and let Miss Emma through," El said to his admirers.

The crowd parted like the Red Sea. Big El opened the limo door, took Emma's hand, and helped her into the car.

"It's hard to believe," El said as the limo pulled away. "Here we are, thirty years later, both back in New Orleans. You're running Miss Melinda's shop and I own a club. Who would have thought? I bet you never knew that a week after you left for Chicago, I got on a bus and headed out to Los Angeles. You were my inspiration. I said to myself, if Emma's got enough nerve to get out in this world, then so do I."

"And look at you. You're rich and famous and you've never let your head swell. You've dedicated your entire life to sharing your music and your good fortune with the world. I'm so proud of you."

"I must confess something to you, Emma."

"What is it, Elbert?"

"Emma, I've spent my entire life alone. I've never been married, nor have I had any children. If I'd had the courage to tell you how I really felt about you thirty years ago, I might have been able to share my life with you and that beautiful baby girl of yours. I could always use the excuse that it was the times we lived in or that I was young and foolish. But if I had told you the way I truly felt, maybe I would have had a chance for my own personal happiness."

El handed Emma a card. "I've already given you my private number. If you need me for anything at all, even if you just want to chew the fat, just punch in the numbers. You'll reach me no matter where I am in the world."

The limo pulled up in front of Melinda's Basin Street house. El started to open the door to let Emma out.

"Wait a minute, Elbert." El released the door handle. "I always knew how you felt about me, but I knew that life had a plan for you. If you had stayed here, the world would never have had the benefit of sharing the gift you were given. I wasn't destined to travel that road with you, even though I wanted to."

El opened the door, took Emma's hand, and walked her to the front door. "I'll never forget that night you came to the club, and

214

afterwards, I walked you to this very same door. You told me you were pregnant. I thought about it all night. That next day, I put on my old suit, bought a bunch of fifty-cent flowers, and headed over here to ask you to marry me. But you were gone."

"Oh, Elbert, you were going to make an honest woman of me!"

"Emma, I wasn't going to ask you to marry me because you were pregnant. I was going to ask you to marry me because I've always loved you. And I've never stopped. When I get back from Europe, we're going to finish this conversation, and I mean it. We won't have to leave New Orleans to get married either, like we would have back in '60. We'll have the finest wedding New Orleans has ever seen!" El bent over to kiss her hand.

"I love you too, El," Emma said joyfully. Then she rubbed her fingers across his unruly locks, smoothing them down. The hairs stayed in place. "I'll be waiting."

El straightened and put his hand on the tamed patch. "I'll be damned. I've been trying to do that all my life." He walked back to the limo. "I'll call you before I'm due back in the country in case you have a hankering to cook up—"

"A batch of red beans and rice..." Emma smiled and waved goodbye.

Lucinda brushed by her and out the front as Emma entered the home.

"Was that the wicked stepsister I heard leaving?" Melinda called out from her bedroom.

Emma laughed, kissed Melinda on the forehead, and sat down beside the bed. "Lucinda looked like she was running from a perpetrator."

Melinda's eyes twinkled. "When the carpenters came today, I told the foreman that Lucinda was almost deaf. The crew shouted at her the entire day."

"You are really bad, Auntie."

"I know. How was your day?"

"Elbert drove me home."

"I thought I heard his voice."

"After talking to Elbert and Gina, I'm forced to do some serious soul searching."

Emma's mind wandered off. Melinda asked her twice if she had heard any more from Gina in Africa. The third time, Melinda raised her voice. "Emma, I'm talking to you. Have you heard from Gina?"

Emma snapped out of her reverie. "Gina told me she and Nicole received a message from Nicole's father through the Horus Crystal Ball. Why didn't you tell me my baby inherited the power?"

"I told Gina the vision was hers before she left. I didn't think it would manifest itself before I left this earth. It's never happened that way in the history of our family. I had a mentor. There must be a new configuration forming to destroy The Freedom Code. Maybe there's a child of whom we are unaware. If so, it will be the task of the children."

"Auntie, what in the world are you talking about?"

"Do you remember the message in the Crystal Ball?"

Emma told her what she remembered.

"The children have a mission," Melinda said thoughtfully. "The Freedom Code. *Free Restraints Eliminate, End Domination of (the) Master*. The Elders wrote this code."

Melinda explained why. Emma was stunned.

"I have seen that Regina and Nicole will return at New Year's," Melinda said. "It is then that Regina must be told the truth about her father. She must begin to prepare her path to fulfill her destiny.

"Every generation has played a role in our quest to achieve The Freedom Code, including your mother, Lula, my beloved sister. Now, my sweet Emma, you must finally learn the truth about your beginnings. Otherwise I won't be able to share the vision of your future. You must be free."

With tears in her eyes, Melinda released the painful secrets of the three wise women and that fateful night in Mississippi over fifty years ago when Lula was raped and Emma was conceived. Then Melinda told Emma of her vision on Emma's future.

Afterwards, Melinda was exhausted. As Emma cradled her auntie in her arms, she tried to think about how she felt being the product of a violent act, but the violation of her mother, aunt, and Ade was much more important to her. They had suffered that night. They had suffered for years! A sudden rage burned deep in Emma's heart.

Suddenly she felt the memory of her aunt's embrace. It calmed her down and cleared her mind. Her mother and aunt had transformed evil into good and hate into love. In turn, they had passed on their love to her. Now, after all these years, she was taking the first steps to love herself, which was the truest form of freedom.

There was time to think of her history later. For now she realized with crystal clarity her true life's purpose and the future role she would play as the mother of one of the Blessed Children.

***

Although Melinda's spirits were high, her physical condition was slowly deteriorating. She greeted each day with a smile and thanked God for each sunrise.

Emma helped Melinda sit up in bed. "How are you feeling this morning, Auntie?" Emma asked.

"Light as a bird and fit as a fiddle."

"That sounds good to me. I've got our breakfast ready. I'm going to bring it in here so we can eat together."

Emma placed Melinda's tray across her lap and sat down next to the bed with news of Regina and Nicole and their new contract. Melinda had already seen this in a vision. Her exquisite niece was delighted for the girls, yet melancholy.

Finally! Melinda thought to herself. *Now I can help Emma.*

"It's shameful my daughter is out in the world achieving her dreams and I am caught in my own self-indulgence," Emma continued. "I can't seem to let go of the past. What's wrong with me?"

"Emma, I remember when Gina would come to visit as a little girl. We would sit and talk about her ambitions. I'd ask how she planned to achieve her dreams, and she would say, 'My Momma always tells me, as hopeless as life sometimes seems, always believe in and save your dreams.' "Gina believed in and lived by your words and still does. You did a great job raising her. Remember, your children may have come from you, but they are not yours. There are plenty of mountains left for you to climb. Sometimes you get stuck on plateaus; other times a loose rock can fall on your head; other times you hold on for dear life. Believe me, Emma, your climb isn't over until you reach the mountaintop. That's when you see the light. Sooner or later our eyes adjust… Emma, I don't believe that your life haunts you as much as your secrets."

"What secrets, Auntie?"

"I know the real reason you left. You felt I'd betrayed you by taking the one thing you wanted most in life. It's taken you thirty years to forgive me. That's why you never came to visit." Melinda paused, and then tears began rolling down her cheeks. "I had to tell him, Emma, but I would have given anything not to hurt you."

Emma tried to console the weeping Melinda. She wrapped her arms around her. "It's true. Everything you've said is true, except that I forgave you long ago. And you've explained everything to me now. The mystery of The Freedom Code. Regina's role to protect it. I just have to have the courage to talk to Regina about her father. Now that I'm back home living with you, the mother I love, I think I will find the courage to tell her."

Melinda rested her head on Emma's chest. Life had reversed their roles.

When Melinda fell asleep, Emma carefully removed Melinda's tray to the kitchen. Out on the porch, she sat down to think, looking over the garden. Memories spiraled back in time to the night of the Fourth of July, 1959.

***

Finding a special celebration on Bourbon Street is the easiest thing in the world. In 1959, there was an "End of the Decade Fourth of July Celebration" planned. The decade's last Independence Day had to go out with a bang. The street was packed with tourists and locals. Dixieland music filled the air. By 10:00 p.m., it seemed like every kid in New Orleans had found a closet full of firecrackers. Firecrackers thundered and sparklers lighted the sky. The Mississippi River hadn't seen this many projectiles since the Civil War. It looked like Mardi Gras had been moved to the summer. The crowds were so busy watching the lighting display that the local shops were virtually empty.

Twenty-two-year-old Emma stood behind the counter of Madame Bovine's House of Mystery. Only one customer was in the shop. A sergeant in the United States Army browsed through the bookshelves. Around 11:00 p.m., a pair of good ol' boys came stumbling in, smelling of whiskey.

218

"Lookee here. It's one of them Creole gals I've heard these New Orleans folks talkin' about. Ain't she pretty, Lester?" one of them said loudly.

"She sure in the hell is, George. Let's go talk to her."

George leaned on the counter and started to speak directly into Emma's face. The foulness of his breath made Emma step back.

"What's the matter, little Creole gal? You ain't gonna serve your customers?"

"What can I do for you?" Emma asked.

"You can do a lot for me back up in my room," answered George.

The two men laughed.

"I think you gentlemen have had a little too much to drink. Why don't you just leave," Emma said.

The soldier put the book he was looking through back on the shelf and walked closer to the counter. George was angry and reached over the counter, trying to grab at Emma. She stepped further back.

"Come here, you little nigger whore. You don't tell me what to do."

The soldier walked up next to him. "The lady asked you to leave."

George turned to the soldier. "Lookee here, Lester. The colored toy soldier done come to the little whore's rescue." George looked to the side and grabbed a statue off the counter. He swung it full force at the soldier's head. "You Black son of a bitch."

With his left hand, the soldier blocked the blow and sent a powerful right cross to George's jaw, sending him spinning to the ground. Lester lunged at the soldier. Before his feet left the ground, a huge fist crashed down on top of his head like a fifty-pound sledgehammer. The blow knocked him out cold.

It was Big El. He had been in the back room talking to Melinda when he heard the commotion. El's face was fire red. He picked up both George and Lester, slammed their bodies into each other, and then dragged them by their collars to the door. He threw them into the street one at a time. He was on his way out to finish them when Melinda called out to him to stop. The two drunks were now lying in the street stone-cold sober and shaking in their boots. Elbert stared down at them. Rage was in his eyes.

"If it wasn't for that woman standing in that doorway, I would have stomped you two pieces of poor white trash shit to death. I don't know where you're from, but if I ever see you in New Orleans again, I'll kill you both with my bare hands." Elbert turned his back. He could hear George struggling to get up on his knees. El raised his knee and kicked back. The bottom of his boot met squarely into George's face, sending him crashing to the ground once more.

"Elbert, I told you, that was enough," Melinda said.

Big El walked back toward Melinda with his head down. "I'm sorry, Miss Melinda."

Just then, the police arrived on the scene. They took one look at the two men lying in the street and another at Big El and shook their heads.

"I guess you two boys are stupider than you look. Big El must be feeling generous tonight," one officer said, cuffing George.

The other trooper cuffed Lester. "Yeah, you boys are still breathing."

When Elbert reached Melinda in the doorway, she brushed the dirt off of his shoulder. "Are you all right, Elbert?"

"I'm fine, Miss Melinda." El spotted the soldier's cap on the floor. He picked it up, dusted it off, and handed it to the soldier. "I want to thank you, Sergeant, for looking out for Miss Emma. She and Miss Melinda are my family. What I did was natural. You, sir, are a man with honor. I respect that."

"I should be thanking you. I forgot about the second guy. He had the drop on me."

El shook the soldier's hand. "You could have handled that sorry son of a gun, too. I'm Big El, and you are?"

"Joseph Johnson. Nice to meet you."

El looked at Emma. "Are you okay, Emma? They didn't put their hands on you, did they?"

"They tried, but Sergeant Johnson stopped them. Did you hurt your hand? Are you going to be able to play tonight, Elbert?"

"My hands don't have a scratch on them. We are going to rock the riverboat tonight. Miss Melinda, are you coming?"

"I've had enough excitement for one night. Next year, when I'm sixty, I'll watch the fireworks."

"I understand, Miss Melinda. I have enough time to see you home before the show. I'll come back for you, Emma," El said.

The soldier saw they were having a private conversation and headed for the door.

"Elbert, you won't have enough time. It's after eleven now. I'll make it to the riverboat," Emma said.

El called out to the soldier. "Sergeant Joseph Johnson, do you like jazz and Dixieland music?"

The soldier turned around. "Yes, I do."

"Are you busy tonight?"

"Not really. I'm just a tourist here. I have no set plans," the soldier answered.

"Well then, I'd like you to be my special guest tonight. My band is playing on the riverboat during the big fireworks display. There will be plenty of good food, drink, and music. It's all on me. When you come, please escort Miss Emma. I don't want her to walk alone."

Emma interrupted. "Elbert, Sergeant Johnson is going to think the only reason you invited him is to babysit me. We have imposed on him enough tonight."

"I don't take it that way at all, ma'am. I'd be more than happy to see you safely to the riverboat," the sergeant said.

"I told you this man had character. Thanks, Sergeant," El said, shaking his hand again.

Melinda walked over to the soldier. "In all of the excitement, I forgot to thank you." She extended her hand.

When Melinda felt the soldier's grip, she felt a sense of urgency. She couldn't quite figure it out. However, she did have the overwhelming feeling that Emma couldn't be in safer hands.

***

"Well, knight in shining armor," Emma said, coming from around the counter, "everyone has thanked you except the person you really saved. I can't tell you how much I appreciate you coming to my aid."

"I could never stomach a bully. I hate it when a man thinks he can take something that hasn't been offered. No offense intended, ma'am."

"None taken, Joseph. If you would excuse me for a few minutes, I'm going to start closing the shop for the night."

"Do you need any help?"

"No, thank you. Here, have a seat," she said, gesturing to a chair, "and finish looking at that book you had before the chaos." Emma found the book and handed it to him. He accepted it in surprise. "When you've been working in a store all of your life, you don't miss anything any customer holds that belongs to you. I could have picked out this book if there had been twenty people in the store. It's second nature to me."

"Amazing. I wish I had your instincts. Maybe I wouldn't have spent three years of my life in Death Valley, a Korean POW camp."

Emma collected her receipts. "Three years?"

"Three years, and when I was released, I found out the war had been over for two of those three."

"Are you kidding me? How in the world did that happen?"

"The camp was isolated, thirty miles southeast of Pukchin, North Korea. The Koreans were never notified, and our captors were almost in as bad shape as we prisoners were. I was sent to the colored ward at the Eleventh Evacuation Hospital in Korea, where most of my former Korean prison guards were my roommates."

Emma turned off the lights in the back and the sign out front. She pulled down the shades and put the "Closed" sign in the window. "How long were you in the hospital?"

"Nearly six months."

"I don't know how you endured all of that."

He stood. "I wanted to live."

"That sounds like a good reason, but it is still a terrible ordeal." She could see he didn't want to discuss it now. "Well, I'm ready to go."

The soldier handed the book to Emma. "All right. But you'll have to put this back. I've forgotten which shelf it goes on."

"Were you enjoying the book?"

"It's my favorite work, by Khalil Gibran. I lost my copy when I was overseas."

"Then I want you to have this copy. *The Prophet* is one of my favorite books, too."

The soldier pulled out his wallet. "How much is it?"

"You must have been in Korea too long. Don't you understand English? This—is—a—gift. I—am—giving—it—to—you."

"Thank—you."

The two burst into laughter.

***

On Bourbon Street, the crowd walked shoulder to shoulder.

"Tonight is a pickpocket's heaven. You'd better put your wallet in your side pocket and then twist the pocket lining."

The sergeant did as instructed.

Emma put her arm through his arm. "Follow me. I know all the shortcuts."

Emma led the sergeant through a couple of side streets and an alley. Before he knew it, he was standing on the bank of the Mississippi River. Emma pointed to the riverboat. It was lit up like a Christmas tree. The pipe organist on the upper deck was entertaining the long line of passengers waiting to board.

Emma led him to the front, where the crew boarded. She unfastened the guard rope and stepped onto the ramp. As they passed through the galley, all of the cooks and waiters greeted Emma. Big El was on stage at the other end of the ballroom and didn't see Emma and the sergeant. A new first mate stood at the ballroom door entrance.

The first mate stopped Emma and the sergeant. "The colored section is being used tonight. Step back and let the white folks through."

The captain's voice came from behind them. "Mr. Henderson, I need to speak to you."

The first mate joined the captain.

"I know it's your first night on the ship, but you see that colored girl? She is a very close friend of Big El Hunt. She and that colored soldier are his guests. I want you to seat them at his guest table."

"You want me to sit them up front with white folks, Captain?"

"The high-spending crowd Big El Hunt attracts in one night is enough money to pay this crew's salaries for a year. If you want to keep your job, I advise you not to cross him. Have I made myself clear?"

The first mate grudgingly nodded his head. "Niggers being treated like white folks. What is the world coming to? I'm going back to Georgia."

He escorted Emma and the sergeant through the crowd. At Big El's Table, he stood apart from Emma, refusing to look at her or to pull out her chair. The sergeant helped Emma instead and unobtrusively sat down opposite her, looking quite uncomfortable.

"What's wrong?" Emma asked.

"You may be used to this, but I'm not."

"Don't you think we have the right to sit up here?"

"We've got the God-given right to sit and go wherever our freedom takes us. Unfortunately, America's laws haven't caught up with God's laws. I don't scare easily. But I don't like to feel I've got to watch my back every minute, especially when I'm supposed to be out having a good time."

"You don't need to concern yourself about that, Sergeant. Big El will stop anything before it starts."

"Emma, I like you. You are bright, friendly, and generous. It's probably none of my business. So stop me if you think I'm out of line."

Emma was puzzled. "Have I said something to offend you, Joseph?"

"No, not at all. What I am trying to say is this. There aren't many Negroes with a powerful white man as a friend who comes to their defense whenever racism rears its ugly head. If El hadn't finished that fight tonight, I could have been hanging from a tall tree. You aren't always going to have a Big El Hunt around. Don't think for a second that you'll be treated differently than any other Negro in America just because you have light skin, keen features, and Caucasian hair."

Emma was about to respond when a drumroll began, followed by Big El's voice.

"No one's going home disappointed from this Fourth of July celebration! By popular demand, there will be a second show. For now, though, let's enjoy this one!"

El blew a high note and a set of rockets lit up the sky in red, white, and blue. All the doors opened. The whistle blew. The paddle started turning and the gala began. People stood on deck watching the fire display as the boat paddled down the Mississippi. The band had them tapping their feet, clapping their hands, and dancing in the aisles. The food was plentiful and the alcohol flowed like a mountain spring.

The sergeant finally loosened up. To Emma's surprise, he was really smooth on the dance floor. Before they knew it, the riverboat was pulling back to the dock. After Big El's last song, he received a standing ovation. El took his bows and headed over to Emma and the sergeant.

"Man, you sure can blow a mean horn," Joseph said, shaking El's hand. "I can't remember the last time I had this much fun."

"Well, I sure am glad you enjoyed yourself, Joseph, 'cause Big El has another favor to ask of you. I promised these good folks a second show. Can you walk Miss Emma home for me?"

"It would be my pleasure. Thanks again."

Emma hugged Big El. "Show these folks a good time."

Emma and the sergeant exited. The streets had quieted down. Most of the remaining tourists were on the riverboat with Big El and his band.

"He is one fine musician, and a real nice guy too," Joseph said as they strolled down the River Walk.

Emma faked a startled expression. "Do you mean to tell me that my powerful, big, white body guard might be more than a crusading abolitionist? He might be a decent man, just like you. He might be a man that can't stomach ugly-acting, evil people."

"I apologize if I offended you, Emma. The first mate reminded me why I wasn't in a hurry to come back to the United States. When we sat down, I could feel the eyes on us. I guess I took it out on you."

"You don't need to apologize. I decided to show off instead of acting embarrassed. And I'm really sensitive when it comes to Elbert. He's my Aunt Melinda's godson. Did you notice that old trumpet he plays? It was his first trumpet. Aunt Melinda bought that for him when he was a boy."

"So your Aunt Melinda is responsible for that great performance I heard tonight. That's remarkable."

"The three of us have always been close." She paused and looked at him. "You have a heavy heart, Joseph. I can see it in your eyes. I feel like you're looking for something and I'm supposed to help you."

Joseph was surprised. "I'm looking for a piece of property south of town. I've never seen it. I only have a description of what it used to look like." He described it to Emma.

"I know the area. It's not far from my grandparents' old house."

"This is great! Can you tell me how to get there?"

"You'd never find it on your own. I'll show you. I have to ask you one question."

"What is it?"

"We can only get there by boat. Are your rowing arms in shape?"

The sergeant laughed and flexed his muscle. "Feel this."

Emma reached around the sergeant's arm and placed her hand on his bicep. "This will do just fine. Why is this land so important to you?"

"I'll tell you when I see it."

"We'll go tomorrow. Nine a.m.?"

"That sounds perfect. Where should I meet you?"

"Right here. This is where I live." Emma pointed to the house. "See here on the mailbox, it says Bovine, just like the store."

Joseph walked Emma to the door. "I guess you saw in my eyes that I've had some pretty rough times the last five years and a lot of disappointments, but I want you to know that tonight was the most enjoyable time I've had in years. I'll see you at nine a.m."

"I'll tell you what. Come by at eight. I'll fix you some breakfast."

Chapter 30

A t 7:00 the next morning, Emma was in the kitchen. Fresh-cut flowers were displayed on the table. Coffee was brewing. Bacon and sausage were frying. Grits were boiled and homemade biscuits were in the oven. Freshly squeezed juice was in the cooler.

Around 7:47, Melinda walked into the kitchen, rubbing her eyes. "Why do I get the feeling we're having a guest?"

"Joseph is coming over for breakfast, and then I'm going to show him the area around your old house."

"Okay. Let's start with Joseph. Who is Joseph?"

"The soldier at the shop last night. Before you ask any more questions, I'll answer all of them. I told Joseph I'd cook him breakfast. It's the least I can do after he came to my rescue. I don't know why he wants to see this land. But it is very important to him. Auntie, he is one of the nicest men I've ever met."

"Is he bringing his whole troop with him? There's enough food here to feed an army."

The doorbell rang.

"Oh Lord, he's early. Auntie, would you get the door? I'm a mess. I've got to fix myself up."

Melinda shook her head and went to the door as Emma rushed up the stairs.

"Good morning, Miss Bovine," Joseph said. "I believe Emma is expecting me."

"Oh Lord, did she invite you to breakfast? She always does that. The fella shows up the next morning, and she's gone. What makes it worse is she can't even cook."

"Pardon me. Ah, I, I don't know what to say."

"Don't say anything. I'm just teasing you. Come on in. Emma will be down in a second."

"I believe the Bovine women are a little too clever for me," Joseph chuckled.

"As an overly protective parent, I've always tested anyone Emma or Elbert invited to the house. You've got a sense of humor. I like that. "

"Well, the way they both treated me, and the way they talked about you, shows me Emma and El couldn't have been raised by a better parent."

Melinda smiled her special smile. "Joseph, if you're trying to make me like you, I want you to know you're doing just fine. Come on and have a seat in the kitchen."

As Melinda poured Joseph's coffee, Emma walked into the room, looking radiant. The apron tied around her waist was the only clue she had been in the kitchen that morning.

"Good morning, Joseph."

Joseph stood up. "Good morning, Emma. It sure smells good. You must have been cooking all morning."

"It was no trouble at all. Just sit down and drink your coffee. I was just waiting to see how you liked your eggs."

"Sunny-side up. This is really great!"

"Okay, Auntie, would you help me serve?"

"Sure, Sugar. Let me go get my galoshes. What you're shoveling is getting kind of deep."

Emma laughed. She looked over at Joseph, who was amused.

"Auntie, I knew you were going to wisecrack sooner or later. Joseph, the truth is, I've been cooking all morning. So if you don't like something, pretend you do."

Emma's humor was the final icebreaker. They all sat down and enjoyed each other and the delicious meal.

"I haven't eaten this good in seven years. Not since I left Huntsville," Joseph said, pushing back from the table.

Melinda put down her coffee. "Are you from Huntsville, Alabama, Joseph?"

"No ma'am, I'm from Chicago originally. I spent a summer in Huntsville before I went into the army. I worked for a man named Jesse Wilson. He was the closest person I ever had to a father. He kind of adopted me. He was the greatest man I ever knew." Joseph's expression reflected the sincerity in his words.

Just as on the night before, Melinda's senses were heightened. This time the message was clear.

"Bernice and Jesse Wilson were close friends of my sister, Lula, Emma's mother. Didn't they have a daughter? I believe her name was Marion," Melinda said, knowing very well who Marion was.

When Marion's name was mentioned, Joseph looked pained.

"Are you all right, darlin'? It looks like your mind has taken you somewhere else. Or are you just bloated from Emma's cooking?"

Joseph stared at Emma and Melinda.

"Marion Wilson is the main reason I came back to the United States. We were engaged to be married. I was going to start my construction business when I returned from the war and after she graduated from college. Our love was magical. She used to say it was our destiny to be together."

Joseph paused. "When I got out of Death Valley POW Camp and was hospitalized in the Eleventh Evacuation Hospital, I wrote Marion every day. I even tried to telephone her long distance, but the line was disconnected. Soon my letters came back marked 'Return to Sender.' I was devastated. You see, I sat in that dark little prison shack thinking of Marion. I finally realized she might have gotten married and started a family."

He went on to tell them about his release from the hospital and decision to reenlist. He was stationed in Europe. The army pinned a few medals on him and added some stripes. Ultimately he ended up back in Korea. A private from the PX gave him an old sack of mail filled with letters from Marion. Then he knew he had unfinished business.

He returned to Chicago for some documents and headed to the Wilson's home in Huntsville, never suspecting it had been burned to the ground. Only the grand fireplace Jesse Wilson had built remained, and it had become his headstone.

"I felt like my father had died, and I cried like a baby. In town, the folks acted like the Wilson family never existed. After a week and a half, I left Huntsville without any answers. I arrived here in New Orleans the day before yesterday to see the property described in those documents I read about in Chicago. Then I met you all last night. Emma said she would help me. So here I am."

"Joseph, for a young man, you've traveled a mighty long road. I sincerely hope you find what you're looking for. I believe you will."

Emma had been very quiet. "Auntie, I don't remember you ever mentioning Bernice and Jesse Wilson. If they were close friends of my mama, why didn't I ever meet them or their daughter, Marion?"

Melinda looked at the wall clock. "It's almost nine thirty. Help me with the dishes, Emma. I don't want you two in the row boat when the sun gets high." Melinda smiled at Joseph. "You relax and store up that energy for rowing. This won't take long." Melinda ushered Emma into the kitchen and closed the door. "I need to tell you something, Emma."

"Why didn't you answer my questions, Auntie?"

"Joseph Johnson is a fine young man."

"Believe me, Auntie, I already know that."

"I can tell by the way you look at him you've already got feelings for Joseph, but you heard him just like I did. He isn't trying to hide his feelings. His heart belongs to another. She also still loves him, even though she thinks he's dead. He's very lonely and very vulnerable right now. Please don't pursue this. Save your love for someone who can return the same love to you."

"He was talking about a puppy love, Auntie! I've finally found the kind of man I've always dreamed of, and you want me to back away."

"Emma, I love you. I would never intentionally hurt you. I'm just telling you that this man is not yours to have. Please believe me. It's best you don't get involved in any of this."

"Auntie, there's a lot you're not telling me and I don't appreciate it. Bernie and Jesse—Marion. We'll talk later," Emma said, taking off her apron. "I don't know what you've seen. All I know is that Joseph was sent here for a reason. Don't mess up this chance for my happiness."

***

"You've been quiet ever since we left," Joseph said, smiling at Emma. "Did I say something to cause such deep thought?" Joseph was rowing down the Mississippi to where it narrowed at its mouth.

"Several things, but right now I'm thinking about what you said about Big El protecting me. I get the feeling if I ever left here, I might find out how most Negroes in this country really live. I'm afraid that the real world might make mincemeat out of me."

"Negroes in this country are divided in so many ways," Joseph said. "I think it's part of the divide-and-conquer plan that we are so many different shades of color and our hair and features are physically diverse. Although we're descendants of Africans, we are taught to see Africans as savages and ape-like creatures. So the part of us that looks like Africa is something we hate in ourselves."

"My Aunt Cora is living proof. She tries to look white. She's invited to every social gathering and thinks she's better than other Negroes. She turns her back on Negroes and people talk about her behind her back."

Joseph nodded in agreement. "Lighter-skinned Negroes versus darker-skinned Negroes. No one stops to think what this self-prejudice does to us as a race. We begin to act like the characters created for us, like we are different instead of understanding that we are the same."

"White folks, like the men yesterday, might have called me Nigger many times, but you should hear the names my own people have called me! My auntie has an African friend," Emma said, tossing her head in frustration. "She's very dark skinned and a little off. When she comes to town, the little Negro children laugh at her, throw rocks and spit at her and mock her. They even make grunting sounds and insinuate she acts like a monkey. Rumor is that she was African royalty. I hate the way people treat her!"

"We've taught our children to hate who we are and where we're from," Joseph said. "We have a war raging inside us, too. We don't trust each other. We are cruel to each other. We don't believe in each other. Certainly, we have been taught not to believe in ourselves."

Joseph looked at Emma thoughtfully. "It's 1959, just short of one hundred years since the Civil War ended. Although the chains came off our bodies back then, they are still attached to our minds. I can't really tell you what's worse, being a slave fighting to be free or being set free, still thinking you're a slave."

Joseph continued to row the boat to a bend in the Mississippi. Another rowboat was a coming in their direction. Emma recognized the passenger.

"It's Aunt Melinda's friend, the woman from Africa I was telling you about."

Ade's rowboat was about fifty feet away when the two boats passed. When she caught sight of Joseph, she stood straight up in the boat, pointing. "The baby, the baby, the baby!"

"What is she doing? She's going to turn the boat over!" Joseph said.

"Ade! Sit down!" Emma hollered.

Ade responded, but continued to stare back at Joseph until she had disappeared around the bend.

"I could swear she was saying, 'the baby' and pointing at you. Do you know what it means?"

"I have no idea."

They continued down the river in silence until Emma saw the sugarcane fields off of River Road. She instructed Joseph to follow her directions very carefully.

"There are gators all through here. I don't want us to get stuck in the mud. Ade gets along real well with the gators. I don't."

Emma pointed to a narrow stream of water, where Joseph turned. Up a few hundred yards, Emma pointed out her grandparents' cabin. Five hundred yards past the cabin, Emma was about to tell Joseph to stop, but he had already put the oars in the boat.

"This is it. This is where it happened."

Joseph explained that he had picked up his original file at the orphanage in Chicago where he was raised. A migrant family of farmers had found him in one of these Mississippi sugarcane fields wrapped in a blanket with fifty dollars tucked inside. The family had ended up in Chicago and left him at an orphanage.

Emma had never seen such pain on a man's face. "I want you to row backwards about three feet." Joseph did as Emma asked. "Now, look to your left and then your right. You will see how the land slopes in a straight line almost a mile in each direction. Do you know what that means?"

"No."

"I've been around sugarcane all my life. That straight line tells you where the crop line ends. Your mother placed you where she knew you would be found. Those fifty dollars were probably her life savings. I do not know what was going on in your mother's life, but I know she loved you."

Joseph rowed the boat with incredible celerity out of the waterway. Deep in thought, all his power suddenly turned to his rowing. It was nearly noon and the sun beat down mercilessly. Joseph was drenched in his own perspiration. Emma knew he was going to dehydrate or pass out from sunstroke.

"Enough, Joseph," she said, putting her hands on top of his. "There's a shady patch just around the next bend. You're going to get out of the sun and rest awhile."

On shore, Emma picked up a tarpaulin and carried it over to a patch of wild grass. They sat down. Joseph took off his shirt. Emma wrung it out while Joseph lay back with his hands under his head.

"I spent my whole life trying to prove I was just as good as everyone else, Emma. I needed to hear people say, 'Joseph really learns fast. He works harder than two people. He's going to be somebody one day.' I drew my confidence from others' opinions of me."

"We aren't so different," Emma said, sitting beside him. "I'm an orphan too. Although I was blessed to know my mother before her death, and Auntie became like my second mother, I still had my questions. No one would tell me how my beautiful mother ended up crippled. No one would talk about my father either, and I was always curious why I don't have my father's name."

Joseph pulled her close. Without thought, Emma gave Joseph a passionate kiss. He returned it.

"Emma, you're very special, and I don't want to hurt or mislead you."

"I'm not asking for a commitment. You still think that Marion is out there waiting for you. You haven't lied or tried to fool me. I am twenty-two years old. I want to share this special part of me with you. You aren't taking anything. It's being offered to you. If you think I'm so special, then make it special for me. At least then I'll always know how it should be."

Joseph took Emma in his arms. In the rapture of the moment, their bodies soon intertwined as one. Joseph fulfilled Emma's desires and she his. Enthralled in the rhythm of their love making, their bodies glistened from the heat of the sun's rays peeking through the trees of the bayou.

Chapter 31

I n the back room of Madame Bovine's House of Mystery, Melinda and Ade sat with the Horus Crystal Ball between them. Ade had a different aura this day. She placed her hands on Melinda's and spoke. "I saw the daughter of Lula and the orphan boy today. It is one of the signs of the beginning. The crystal will lead us now."

Melinda knew a cataclysmic wind was about to blow and change the course of their lives. Ade was again the Messenger. The two placed their hands on the Crystal Ball. Its message began with their touch.

He heard her voice in the wind and followed it. Blue has come. Today, the mother of the world order will be conceived. Twelve months shall pass before her birth. On her thirty-first birthday, she will be born anew, reborn Blue. Then, the children's love will transform into hate. Mortal enemies may be their fate. The child's Protector is also conceived on this day. The father must now go. He is the only one who might save the child. The baby Marion will face the demon alone. Joseph will carry her safely home.

"When Joseph comes to you, you must tell him where Marion has gone. She dwells with her mother, Bernice, in Washington, DC. He must leave tonight to save her."

Horus grew dim. The two women recited the incantation:

"Not Negroid, not Mongoloid, not Caucasoid.
It is Blue that must be destroyed.
From father to daughter and son
Each must protect the mother one."

The apparitions of the golden shield and sword appeared over the Horus Crystal Ball. When the image dissipated, Ade stood up and removed the golden shield medallion from around her neck. She reached over the crystal and placed it around Melinda's.

"Soon, he will come for me to seek his revenge. This shield will protect you. I do not have the strength to continue, Melinda. I'm so sorry. You will have to become the Protector and the Messenger. There is no other way. The shield will protect you from harm, but it will not keep Blue from hearing your conversations as a Messenger and a medium. Pass along information you learn as you always have, but please be careful not engage in conversation unless you are protecting The Freedom Code or one of the Blessed Children. You will know when the time has come to pass it on to the new Protector." Ade took her hand. "Before I leave this earth, Melinda Bovine, I want you to know Ade loves you and thanks you. *You will Free Restraints, Eliminate, End Domination of (the) Master;* and Ade will always smile down on you with gratitude until we meet again."

Melinda could not believe this transformation. All these years, Ade had lived in a state of mental confusion. The only words she had uttered were during their incantation. Ade opened her arms and smiled. The women held each other tightly. Suddenly, Ade's embrace grew limp. Melinda leaned back and gazed into Ade's face. She had left once more. Her expression was blank. Her eyes wandered and twitched spastically. Ade stepped back from Melinda and rushed out of the back door. Tears rolled down Melinda's cheeks.

"Goodbye, Ade. I'll never see you again, my dear friend."

***

In her office, Melinda racked her brain, trying to figure out how she was going to explain to Emma about Joseph. Why did she have to break Emma's heart! She remembered how Lula had looked at her when Ade told them they were all linked in blood and spirit to each other through their twin great-great-great-grandmothers. The three women were suddenly one as they held each other and protected the child and accepted their destiny to protect the future through the baby called Marion. She was still protecting Marion, now at the emotional expense of her own daughter. Would this never end?

***

Emma and Joseph parted in the middle of Basin Street. He was going back to his room to clean up. Emma kept clothing at the shop.

Melinda had stepped out of the back door when Emma came sauntering into the shop with a song.

"You're looking mighty happy there, Miss Emma," the clerk said.

"I've had a lovely day. But I was in an old rowboat. I get the feeling I might smell like the bottom of the river. Would you hang around a little while I freshen up and change?"

"No problem, Miss Emma. Take your time."

"Where's Auntie?"

"I think she went out the back door a few minutes ago."

Twenty minutes later, Emma came out of the washroom as Melinda walked through the front door. "Hello, Auntie! I have so much to tell you!" She smiled at the clerk. "If you want to go…"

Melinda nodded that the clerk could leave, then shut the front door behind her and put the "Closed" sign in the window.

"Emma, we've got to talk. It's serious."

The cloud Emma was floating on suddenly burst.

"I know what you're feeling for Joseph."

"I knew it. I knew this was about Joseph. Auntie, I'm not pushing anything. He's a wonderful, kind, gentle man. I want to let him come to his own decision about us."

"Baby, I'm proud of you. That's what a real woman does. But that's not the issue. Ade visited today. She actually focused. She said she had seen you and Joseph. When we went to the Horus Crystal Ball, it told us where Marion Wilson was. She's in Washington, DC. The ball also told us that she is in grave danger. Only Joseph can save her." Melinda paused and rubbed her face. "I was instructed to tell Joseph he must leave tonight. Tomorrow, Marion will face some horrible vision. Joseph must be there to help her."

Emma shook her head. "Auntie, you haven't raised a fool. A man like Joseph will protect a stranger. Have you forgotten last night? You and I both know what he will do when he finds out the woman he has loved is in danger." Emma's emotions seethed at the thought of losing him before they began. She stood up and raised her voice to Melinda for the first time in her life. "Your Horus Crystal Ball and your mumbo jumbo talk to the spiritual world are a bunch of crap. You do what you have to, Auntie. Your magic is more important than your family. Joseph will be here in a few minutes. He was going to keep me company tonight. Tell him to go save the damsel, Marion. I'm going home." Emma stormed out of the shop.

Melinda tried to catch her, but Emma was too fast.

Halfway down Bourbon Street, Emma ran into Joseph. He could see she was troubled. "Emma, what's wrong?"

She turned her head. "Auntie has something urgent to tell you."

"What is it?"

"It's not for me to tell you. Go to the shop. Go right now. It can't wait. You don't have time to talk to me." Emma placed her hand on Joseph's chest and pushed away.

"I'll go. Then I'm coming to talk to you. Where are you going?"

"I'm going home, Joseph." Emma hurried away.

***

An hour later, Joseph ran down Basin Street toward the Bovine house. Emma was standing in the doorway with her arms crossed. When Joseph raced up the walkway, she stepped out onto the porch. Joseph placed one foot on the porch and one on the top stair as he caught his breath. Emma lifted his chin and stared at him.

"Joseph, you may have traveled the world, but I'm sure not like you have today."

"That's the truth without a doubt. Emma, I have to—"

She put her finger over his mouth. "I know what you're doing. You asked me how I would feel if you left tomorrow. I'll never know, because you're leaving today. I just want to look into your wonderful eyes and lock them in my memory. What I had today is more than some women feel their entire lives."

Joseph gazed at Emma's face. "Oh, Emma Bovine."

"I like the way you say my name. But, Joseph Johnson, it's time for you to go." Emma kissed Joseph's cheek and returned inside the house, closing the door.

***

Nine months later, on April 7, 1960, Emma Bovine lay in the maternity ward of Cook County Hospital on Chicago's Westside. She gave birth to a baby girl and named her Regina Melinda Bovine.

***

Twenty-one years later, on April 7, 1981, Emma finished cleaning rooms at Palmer House on Michigan Avenue, where she was employed.

238

She and Regina were going out to celebrate Regina's twenty-first birthday. She rushed for the elevator.

A huge crowd was gathered in the foyer. Regina walked through the revolving doors. She heard a man's resonant voice, which she listened to very carefully over the crowd as she hastened to meet Emma.

"The only reason to go into business is the continuance of business. If a business continues, all personal and financial goals will be met. None of this will occur if the business is not self-perpetuating."

I'll have to remember that, Regina thought. *Very smart answer.*

The elevator doors opened and Regina waved. She and Emma hugged and exited the door on Michigan Avenue as Marion and Nicole cut through the crowd to proudly watch Joseph Johnson alongside the mayor.

A reporter called out, "Mr. Johnson, step in closer to the mayor. I need you in this shot."

Joseph, looking very distinguished in an expensive suit, stepped forward. His construction company had won a major bid to renovate the hotel and was the first Black-owned company ever granted a government subsidy of this magnitude.

The following morning, Emma was surprised as she looked at the handsome photo of Joseph in the morning *Chicago Times*.

We must have just missed him, Emma thought. *I didn't know he lived in Chicago! Gina looks just like him!* Her heart sank.

***

Now she was in New Orleans and Regina was thirty and she considered Nicole to be like her second daughter. In essence, Nicole was. Joseph had two beautiful daughters. She asked herself for the hundredth time—when was she going to tell them they had the same father?

Life's coincidences were all on her doorstep in a surreal reality. Emma reached into the pocket of her apron and pulled out the newspaper photo of Joseph.

"You would be proud of your daughters, Joseph. They are beautiful girls, and Regina looks just like you!"

Chapter 32

On March 1, 1959, from Blue's pyramid in the Sudan, beautiful, young Zinzi, the infant ripped from Eleni Lwanga's womb, cowered in the corner against the pyramid wall, trembling uncontrollably. With one hand, she covered her mouth. With the other hand, she held her throat.

Blue laughed at her pain as he leaned over her, wiping drool from his lips. "I have made you immortal. I will not destroy the mother of my children. You will bear my first son."

Blue was interrupted by a disturbing sound. He demanded silence from the whimpering young woman and followed the sound to the great stone block that barred the pyramid's entrance. With both hands, he pushed and moved the stone that had taken hundreds of Egyptians to set into place. With one motion of his wings, he ascended to the apex of the pyramid. In seconds, his face formed into a grotesque expression of elation. He raised his arms to the sky.

"I hear your voice, Daughter of the Desert. I hear it from across the great sea. Soon, I will come to you. We will consummate the destruction of The Freedom Code."

***

Hours later, in Washington, DC, on March 1, 1959, Marion Wilson, then an assistant professor at Howard University, took a group of her freshman students on a field trip to the White House. Local reporters from the *Washington Post,* television networks, and news commentators from local stations WMAQ, WBBM, and WFLD TV and the national news NBC, ABC, and CBS covered the educational conference spurred by Admiral Rickover's articles and the controversy over what he called "the failing educational system in America." Network reporters questioned Howard University students leaving the White House, asking who was in charge in order to get an interview on the Negro perspective on the conference.

"Is there a leader in this group?"

A couple of students pointed to Marion and said, "Miss Wilson is our instructor."

"This is perfect." He signaled to his cameraman. Other reporters became curious. In a few seconds, several microphones were shoved in Marion's face.

"Are you an educator?"

"I am assistant professor of economics at Howard University," Marion answered.

"Are you aware of Admiral Rickover's position on Negroes?"

"As always, the education and contributions of the Negro in America are treated as separate issues. From the Admiral's article, one would assume Negro achievement would peak at a lower level than its white counterpart. This misconception is spun into the fabric of the American culture. Until the American public is reeducated, they will never truly understand how the American Negro has been the greatest unsung hero of this nation."

There was rumbling amongst the reporters. Most were reporting live. None had expected Marion's response. When the cameras left, Marion's students applauded her.

Far across the ocean, atop an ancient pyramid, Blue roared proudly. Ade's forewarning had come to pass. Marion had worn the medallion through childhood and had grown tired of its weight. Often she would leave it at home in her jewelry box, unaware of its power. The demon now heard the voice of the child of Hatshepsut and Kabaka, unprotected by the medallion. The ocean barrier had been broken.

***

"Miss Wilson, Miss Wilson!"

It was July 3, 1959. Marion was leaving her classroom when she heard her name called out. It was the chancellor of Howard University. He was walking toward her accompanied by an elegant gentleman.

"How are you, Chancellor? I thought you were on hiatus for the summer session."

"Well, Miss Wilson, as they say, the best-laid plans of mice and men…"

"I understand, Chancellor," Marion replied.

"Miss Wilson, I would like you to meet Bertrand Lwanga, philanthropist and entrepreneur from the Ivory Coast. Mr. Lwanga, may I introduce Marion Wilson, one of our professors of economics."

Lwanga extended his hand. "It is a pleasure to meet you, Miss Wilson. I admire your oratory prowess."

The chancellor interceded. "Mr. Lwanga saw the television interview you gave a few months ago. He was very impressed."

"Thank you, Mr. Lwanga."

"You are most welcome. The chancellor has taken time from his busy schedule to give me a tour of the university. I am very interested in sending students from my country to the United States to be educated. I honestly had not considered the Negro institutions before I heard you speak. I am now convinced they will prove beneficial in developing an understanding between our peoples of our historical bond and our future international business endeavors. Your university sits in your nation's capital. I cannot think of a more appropriate setting for my students."

Mr. Lwanga's visionary plan had long been one of her own dreams. "I couldn't be more excited, Mr. Lwanga."

"You are very generous, Miss Wilson. I thank you. If you are not otherwise engaged, I would appreciate your company on the remainder of my tour."

"I have no plans for the next few hours."

Marion assumed the role of guide. The chancellor was impressed by Marion's knowledge of the university and her powers of persuasion.

Mr. Lwanga ended his visit on the front steps of the library. "There is a saying in my country. 'A foolish man searches for what he already has found.' My search is over. This university will be offered a proposal to implement my plan. If accepted, endowment funds will be transferred to the university. Miss Wilson is an asset to your institution, Chancellor. I hope tenure is in her near future."

"There's no doubt, Mr. Lwanga." The chancellor smiled.

"This is an historical moment," Marion said.

"More than you realize," Bertrand Lwanga added.

"Are you leaving tomorrow?" the chancellor asked.

"I have heard so much about the fireworks display celebration on your Independence Day that I am compelled to partake. I've postponed my departure another day."

"Do you have friends here?" Marion asked.

"I am afraid not. I will view the Potomac River display alone."

"Well, we can't have that. How would you like an escort?" Marion said.

"That would be marvelous, Miss Wilson."

Marion opened her note pad, wrote down her address in Logan Circle, and handed it to Bertrand.

"Do you have transportation? If not, I can meet you in the lobby of your hotel."

Bertrand pointed to his Thunderbird convertible parked in the Howard University Library parking lot. "I've purchased an automobile. I will come for you at eight p.m., if that is acceptable?"

"That will be just fine, Mr. Lwanga."

Bertrand started down the steps. "As of this moment, I am officially on a one-day vacation. Therefore, I would appreciate it if you would call me Bertrand."

"Very well, Bertrand. Then you must call me Marion."

Lwanga bowed. "Excellent, Marion. I will see you tomorrow."

The chancellor and Marion watched Lwanga drive away.

"Miss Wilson," the chancellor said, "you are an asset to this university. Believe me when I tell you, the board will be apprised of the crucial role you played in this negotiation. "

"Thank you, Chancellor."

"I'm hoping you plan on making your career here at the university. Don't run away with some rich African chief."

"Why, Chancellor!"

"I'm old, but not blind, Miss Wilson," the chancellor said. He shook Marion's hand. They walked down the stairs and parted.

***

Twenty minutes later, Marion walked up R Street NW to her building. She climbed the stairs and unlocked the door to the small two-bedroom apartment she shared with Bernice Johnson.

"Momma, I'm home."

Bernice called from the kitchen. "How was your day, baby girl?"

"It started out to be ordinary, but it ended with an exciting bang."

Marion told her mother about the African, Mr. Lwanga, the endowment promised to Howard University, and the accolades she had received from the chancellor.

"You'll meet Bertrand tomorrow night. He is interesting."

"Marion, you just met this man," Bernice said, proud of her daughter but cautious of strangers. "What do you know about him?"

"Just what I told you. Besides, the chancellor introduced us. This is not a date. I am just being hospitable to someone from another country who wants to help our university."

"All that's fine and good, baby girl, but he still has to pass my inspection."

"I know, and that's why I'm not worrying, Momma," Marion said as she gave her mother a kiss on the forehead.

"Go wash up. Dinner will be on the table in a minute."

On the roof of Marion's apartment building, Bertrand Lwanga loomed in the shadows. *You will never have the opportunity to inspect Bertrand Lwanga, Bernice Johnson,* he thought with satisfaction.

***

That night, before Marion went to bed, she walked over to her dresser and picked up her most treasured possession, a picture framed in brass of a fuzzy black-and-white snapshot of Joseph in his army uniform. He had sent it to her a few days before he was shipped overseas. Marion lay back on the bed. She placed the picture on her chest and closed her eyes. It was the only photograph she had of Joseph. *I know I am crazy. I still love a man who died years ago. You only get one of those. Just like you only get one heart. Joseph Johnson and I were soul mates.*

Marion placed the photo on the nightstand. Before she reached over to turn off the light, she traced Joseph's face in the air and kissed it goodnight.

***

Bernice had seen her daughter struggle with her unresolved pain. How could she not? For the loss of Bernice's beloved Jesse had left a hole in her heart, too.

Bernice sat up most of that night. When day broke, she decided to brew herself a pot of coffee, but she was out. Years earlier, Lula had introduced Bernice to New Orleans-style coffee with chicory. Bernice

244

wrote a note to Marion and walked down R Street to Logan Circle's neighborhood grocery store, the only place where they stocked chicory.

Bernice walked down the coffee aisle, but found no chicory. At the counter, a Black man stood behind the cash register.

"You're new here, aren't you?"

"Yes, I am," the cashier said.

"I'm looking for an herb called chicory. I didn't see any on the shelf."

"Let me go and check." He tightened his apron strings and went to the stock room. "You're in luck," he said, returning with the herb. "This is the last bag we have."

After Bernice had paid the clerk, he came around the counter and opened the door for her. She thanked him and bid him a good day. Once the door was closed, the clerk removed his apron and placed the "Closed" sign back on the door.

"Sleep long and well, Bernice Wilson," he said.

When Bernice returned, Marion was up preparing breakfast.

"I got your note, Momma. You sure made good time."

"I'm just one of those folks who'll be spry until the day they die."

"Preach, Momma, preach."

"Marion, you'll never believe this. Terguson has hired a Negro clerk, and he had opened the store early!"

"Times are changing, Momma." Marion watched her mother make the coffee. "Come shopping with me today. I need a nice summer dress for tonight."

"Seems like a lot of bother for one night," Bernice said as she sipped her coffee.

"This endowment will be a major coup for the university. I don't want Mr. Lwanga to change his mind because I'm dressed like a country schoolmarm. Please come with me."

About 10:00 a.m., they finished their cleaning and got dressed. Marion drove to Virginia to shop. It was nearly 3:30 by the time Marion decided on a dress. Bernice looked tired. By the time they returned to the apartment, Bernice was ready for bed.

"Momma, I'm so sorry for dragging you out."

"Baby, it's not your fault. I must not be as spry as I thought."

Bernice went into her bedroom, got undressed, and instantly fell into a deep sleep.

Chapter 33

At precisely 8:00, Marion's doorbell rang. She buzzed Bertrand in. He presented her with a bouquet of two dozen pink and yellow long-stemmed roses.

"Thank you, Mr. Lwanga! Please come in."

"Are you ready, Marion?" he asked, closing the door.

"Just about. My mother wanted to meet you, but I'm afraid she isn't feeling well. I just want to check on her before we go."

"Of course," Lwanga replied.

Bernice was still sleeping. Marion wrote her a note.

***

The convertible top was down. The warm air was soothing as it rushed across their faces. Marion initiated conversation.

"I really think your plan is exciting. I can't wait until all the agreements are signed and the first African students arrive on campus."

"Your contribution was the deciding factor for me. You are above your breed."

Marion decided not to overreact. "I am not sure I understand your meaning."

Bertrand, realizing the time was not right, retraced his steps. "I consider myself a fair linguist. At times my phraseology does not match the thought I wish to convey. I believe I should have said your breeding impressed me. Education is enhanced by the qualities one receives from his or her parents. I regret not meeting your mother. I wanted to compliment her. I hope my meaning is now clear."

Marion felt better, but she was unable to understand the uneasy feeling forming in the pit of her stomach.

They reached the Potomac River as the fireworks began. Behind them was the Lincoln Memorial. While they walked through the crowd, Marion closely observed Bertrand Lwanga. His movements were guarded, almost as if he were repulsed by being in such close proximity to the other Negroes who stood behind the section roped off for the colored. Why would he postpone his departure for the Fourth of July celebration when he obviously had no interest in it?

Before the finale, Lwanga turned to Marion. "I am ready to leave."

Marion couldn't have been happier. They were about to get into the car when a drunken vagrant staggered up to Bertrand.

Before the man could speak, Bertrand yelled, "Do not dare to approach me, you vile SOS!" With a slight thrust of his hand, Bertrand sent the man tumbling to the ground.

Marion rushed to the man's aid and helped him to his feet.

"That son of a bitch is crazy!" the drunk said to Marion and ran away.

Marion was fuming when she got in the car. Bertrand backed up the Thunderbird and took off, peeling the tires. Marion realized Bertrand was headed in the opposite direction from her home, to Virginia.

"You're going the wrong way. Turn this car around at once."

"How dare you give me orders? You will go where I want you to go and you will do as I tell you."

"You are crazy!"

Marion grabbed for the door handle. Bertrand took a viselike grip around her wrist and pulled her back toward him. Marion struggled to free her arm. In seconds, the car was exceeding 100 miles per hour. They reached an expanse of tall grass on the side of a deserted road. Bertrand cut the steering wheel sharply, sending the car plowing deep into the field. The car came to a jerking halt. The instant Bertrand released Marion's wrist, she sprang out of the car and took off through the willowy grass. Bertrand pursued her, taunting her with laughter. Soon, he tired of the game. Marion suddenly found herself locked within his grasp.

Without forethought, Marion formed her hands into the shape of a lioness's claws. Prepared for attack, she plunged her fingernails into his forehead and face with all her might. To her surprise and horror, the skin loosened and slid down, revealing a face the color of the blue cloudless sky. Bertrand—or this creature—had African features with Asian eyes of Anglo steel and hair of silver.

Suddenly, his shirt began to draw tightly against his chest. The sound of the ripping cloth echoed in Marion's ears. His monstrous white wings emerged over his shoulders. With one awesome flap, he thrust the two of them straight up into the star-filled sky. Against the night, he held Marion prisoner. His arms welded around her waist. Marion's arms fell back, dangling limp and useless.

He raised his head and proclaimed, "I now consummate my dominion."

He stretched his mouth. His blood-red tubular tongue flitted toward Marion's mouth and split and separated into two rod-like tentacles with suction tips. Marion tossed her head from side to side, straining to keep her mouth clamped shut. The tentacles attached to her lips, and she was unable to combat the incredible sucking vacuum. The tentacles tunneled down her throat into her body. Her threshold of pain was far exceeded. She grew dizzy, then nauseous. Red flashed before her eyes, white followed, and she blacked out.

***

An eerie silence hovered over Marion as she lay motionless, sprawled across her bed. Lurking in midair outside of her window, Blue watched her, chanting:

> *"Of sky and water, of water and sky*
> *Mother of the mother of the ancient's daughter,*
> *Now hear, these beasts of the earth shall die.*
> *The new world order will bring them to slaughter.*
> *Reign will you, my daughter DOM*
> *Reign will you, Mother of World Order*
> *Reign once more, Blue.*

"After four hundred suns and moons, I will return for both of you." Then Blue was gone.

***

With every degree of upward motion, Marion felt a hammering, pounding, relentless pain in her head. When she had pulled together enough courage to open her eyes, she was relieved to find herself in her bedroom. An unusually cool breeze came through her open window. Marion felt a slight chill. Her arms were weak, but she pushed herself to her feet and walked over to the window. Her legs were wobbling, her head throbbed, and when she tried to swallow a cutting pain shot from her

249

throat to her eyes. She closed the window, saw her reflection, and realized she was still dressed. She inspected the apartment. Nothing was out of place. Her mother appeared to be sleeping peacefully.

Could she have been as exhausted as her momma? She remembered getting dressed. She sat on the bed. Maybe she fell asleep with the window open and got sick. If Bertrand had come, he would have left when no one answered the door. It was all a feverish nightmare!

Marion had perspired heavily and decided to take a bath. In the bathroom, she turned on the light and looked into the mirror.

God, I look awful. Her eyes were puffy and her complexion was chalky. There were odd bruises on her upper and lower lips. Her mind flashed back to the horrifying tentacles. She regrouped. *They're fever blisters.*

Marion walked over to the tub and turned on the water. She unbuttoned her dress and let it fall to the floor. After she removed her bra, she turned back to the mirror. Her reflection left her staring in total disbelief. Her nipples were completely blue. Her mind could not handle it. Marion snatched up her slip and ran to her mother's bedroom.

"Momma, wake up! I'm going crazy!" When her mother did not respond, Marion shook her. "Momma, what's wrong with you?" Marion put her ear to her mother's chest and heard only a faint heartbeat. "Oh my God, she must have had a stroke!"

Marion reached for the phone. In her haste, she frantically yanked the cord from the wall.

"I've got to go find help!" She struggled back into her dress and raced into the deserted street. In the distance, she saw a lone figure. She ran toward the silhouette. When saw his face, she stopped dead in her tracks.

"No! It can't be! Lord, why are you doing this to me!"

"Marion! Marion, is that you?"

The sound of Joseph's voice terrified her. She definitely had lost her mind.

Joseph dropped his duffel bags and chased her. "It's Joseph! Marion! I am alive!"

He caught her half a block away. "Marion, I've been searching for you. You're not crazy. It's me, Joseph." He loosened his grasp and lifted her head. "Marion, I don't know what's going on, but I'm here now. I'll take care of it."

Marion pounded his chest with her fist. "Where have you been? Oh God, where have you been!" At the end of her tirade, she wrapped her arms around Joseph's neck, buried her head in his chest, and released a flood of tears. "Momma's in some type of coma. I can't wake her up."

***

"I saw this kind of reaction when I was in the Orient," Joseph told Marion. "It's like she had too much opium. Run the cold water and soak some towels. If you have any ice, get it. I am going to sit her up to change her breathing."

After several cold compresses, Bernice began to respond. The vision of Joseph holding her in his arms graced her eyes.

"Are we in heaven, Joseph? Where is my Jesse?"

"You aren't dead and neither am I," Joseph said as Marion came through the door.

"Oh, God, thank you!" Marion cried. "Thank you!"

***

Joseph told them of his imprisonment and his search for them.

Marion told Joseph and Bernice about her night of terror with Bertrand Lwanga. In private, she showed her breasts to Bernice.

Bernice told Marion and Joseph about Marion's parents, Hatshepsut and Kabaka, and their trust in Ade to cross the Atlantic to find a new life for Marion away from Blue. Lastly, she spoke of the three wise women, Melinda, Lula, and Ade, who had brought Marion to her and Jesse in Alabama.

"I saw the woman Ade. She isn't in her right mind anymore. Is that a result of this *Blue*?" Joseph asked.

"I don't know. How strange you ended up meeting Melinda and Ade. Was my dear friend Lula there?" Bernice asked. "She's Melinda's sister."

"I am sorry, Bernice. Lula died many years ago, but I met her daughter, Emma."

Bernice was saddened to hear of her best friend's death and mystified that Lula had a daughter. She wondered what had happened to Ade. She looked at Marion and Joseph.

"I know this vile Blue is disguised as Bertrand Lwanga. Were you wearing your medallion, Marion?"

"No, Momma."

"I never stressed the importance that you wear it," Bernice said sadly. "Ade asked your father and me to follow the Elder's instructions and not to tell you about your heritage, but she made us promise we would see to it you wore the medallion or had it nearby. I should have..."

"I did have it nearby, Momma," Nicole said, trying to comfort Bernice.

"But not near enough," Bernice said, wiping her tears. "Blue has found you, and now we must leave Washington."

Before the end of that week, Joseph had moved them to Chicago. The following week, Marion and Joseph were married. The first night of their honeymoon, Marion's nipples returned to their natural color. Three months later, Marion began to have morning sickness. She was pregnant. Marion's nipples again turned blue.

The birth of her child would take twelve months.

Chapter 34

March 4, 1960

A petrified Zinzi lay on a stone slab, writhing in pain. She had no idea she was about to give birth. With the final surge of pain, the baby's head popped out and a pair of blue hands reached in and guided the newborn infant into the world.

Blue held the baby. "Welcome to the world, SOM. In time, you will shed the skin of the sub-creatures." He walked away with the child, leaving the mother to her own devices.

***

It was July 15, 1960.Unsure of what to expect, Marion lay in her hospital bed at Grant Hospital on Chicago's North Side, preparing to give birth. Joseph and Bernice were with her. Her contractions came rapidly, as did the birth of her infant.

The infant cried, and Marion closed her eyes. The doctor allowed Bernice to clean the baby daughter and wrap her in blankets.

"She is unbelievable!" Bernice exclaimed, handing the baby to Joseph.

He looked at the infant and smiled broadly. "Marion, I've never seen a more beautiful newborn baby girl in my entire life."

When Marion's eyes fell upon her stunning infant, she was filled with love and joy. Nicole was named after the mother of Jesse Wilson.

***

It had been over twenty-three years since Melinda had traveled from New Orleans to Huntsville. Once again, she had to travel the roads of her discontent. Ade had come to her in a dream and given Melinda a message to deliver to Bernice at Jesse's grave. They were taking a huge risk having this meeting, but Bernice had to be warned.

Melinda spoke to Joseph, knowing he would ensure that Bernice wore the sword medallion to their meeting for her own protection.

Melinda stopped Joseph from telling her anything about Marion or their lives. Melinda could only deliver Ade's message to Bernice.

***

It was August 19th. Infant Nicole was slightly over a month old. At 8:30 p.m., Joseph was putting Bernice's suitcase in the car. Bernice was taking a train to Huntsville. Every year on August 20th, the day Jesse Wilson had died, she returned to visit his grave. This year, Melinda was joining her for a secret meeting.

Before her departure, Marion and Bernice stood over the crib, watching Nicole sleep.

"She really is beautiful, isn't she, Momma," Marion said.

"She surely is, baby girl," Bernice replied.

"Joseph calls Nicole 'baby girl' now, Momma. I guess I'll have to give the name up."

"I know. She wears it well." Bernice kissed Nicole's forehead.

Joseph came into the room. "We'd better get going, Momma."

"Have a safe trip," Marion told her mother. Before Bernice could protest, Marion took off her medallion and placed it around her mother's neck and tucked it into her blouse. "For your safety, Momma. He must not find you or know you've met Melinda."

Reluctantly, Bernice accepted the medallion and kissed her granddaughter, Nicole, goodbye.

Out at the car, she blew Marion a kiss and got inside with Joseph, and off they drove to the train station.

***

Marion checked on the sleeping Nicole and decided to take a nap. The crib was at the foot of her bed. Whenever the baby awakened, so would Marion. An eerie sensation overtook Marion in her sleep. The moment she opened her eyes, all she could see was the plumage of enormous white wings. She sprang from the bed as Blue lifted Nicole from her crib.

"You won't take my child!" Marion charged him, screaming. "I'll kill you first!"

Blue held the infant in one hand and pushed the attacking Marion with the other. "She will not be alone. You are coming too."

Blue reached down to grab Marion. She pulled at his wings in a rage, and he almost dropped Nicole. Thinking better of being too close to Marion, he backed away until he was pressed to the window.

"I've warned you. You will die!" Marion screamed, clawing him to release her baby.

In that split second, Blue shoved the baby out of the window, suspending her in midair. Marion watched in horror as her crying infant dangled four stories above the ground.

"Back away, or this child will meet her doom."

Marion knew this creature was without conscience. She stepped back, and in the blink of an eye, Blue was out of the window with baby Nicole. He moved his wings just enough to hover out of reach. She ran to the window.

"Don't hurt my baby. Please bring her back. I'm begging you! Please! Please!"

Blue caressed the infant, cradling her in both arms. "You stupid inferior sub-being! Did you think I would harm my own child?" He looked down at Nicole. "It is time for us to leave, DOM." With those words, Blue flew with the child into the darkened sky.

When Joseph returned from the train station, Marion was on the verge of a nervous breakdown. When he finally calmed her down and heard what happened, he was beyond rage. He stood erect with clenched fists.

"I will find them. Then I will destroy him, and I will bring home our child to safety. There is nothing in heaven or on earth that can stop me. This I swear to you, Marion. This I swear!"

Chapter 35

*B*rrring, brrring!

"Hello, hello," Marion answered.

"Marion, it's Momma."

"Oh, Momma, he came, he came and got my baby! She's gone! She's gone!"

"I know, Marion," Bernice said, filled with remorse. "That's why Melinda wanted to talk to me—Ade foretold that Blue would take your baby. I am so sorry, Nicole, I was too late! I would do anything to spare you this pain! Where is Joseph? I must speak to him."

Marion handed the telephone to Joseph.

"I'm here, Momma."

"Joseph, get a piece of paper and write down what I am about to tell you."

He did as he was told and learned about the land of Africa where the Blue Nile met the White. He was to travel there, and a messenger would give him further direction.

"You must first free the one enslaved," Bernice continued, "before the infant can be saved. In the Motherland, you will travel sixteen degrees north of the equator and thirty-three degrees east of the meridian. Once there, you cannot turn back."

With that, Bernice asked to speak to Marion again.

"Everything is going to work out, Marion. I'm catching the next train back. You must be strong for Joseph and Nicole. It is time to use the diamonds. He must be on a plane before the next sunrise."

"I'll take care of everything, Momma," Marion said, rallying her strength.

Joseph prepared for his trip while Marion found a buyer for one of the diamonds.

Around 8:00 p.m., Marion returned home. Bernice was waiting and spoke to her and Joseph.

"I have a message from the Elders. The enslaved you free will clarify the importance of your journey. You must protect The Freedom Code. *Free Restraints, Eliminate, End Domination of (the) Master.* Then rescue Nicole and come back to Marion."

"I promise you, I will find our daughter."

Bernice left the medallion with Marion, allowing the young couple privacy.

Marion handed Joseph fifty thousand dollars, a thousand of which he carried in his wallet and the remainder of which he placed securely in money belts taped to his thighs. His destination was near the capital of Sudan. That night, there was one flight to Europe with a connecting flight to Lagos, Nigeria.

At 9:00 p.m., Joseph and Marion were ready to leave for the airport. Marion placed the medallion around Joseph's neck.

"I pray it will protect you and Nicole." She stared at the medallion, lost in guilt. She should have kept it to protect Nicole! But then what would have become of her mother?

"You could not protect Nicole," he told her, reading her mind. "Don't torture yourself. Melinda as much as said it was preordained. Whether the medallion's magic works for me or not, I will defeat this demon. I'm supposed to do this for some reason, Marion. I will return to you with Nicole."

"You are willing to risk your life, and you know of Nicole's true father."

"Nicole is my child, not his," Joseph said. "I am so thankful for her. We need never speak of that again."

"I love you so," Marion said, coming into his arms. "Bring our daughter home, my guardian angel. Come back to me."

***

Twenty-four hours later, Joseph was catching a train in Lagos, Nigeria. For the next five days, he traveled by rail, air, and beast of burden. As morning broke on the sixth day, he stood on the outskirts of Khartoum, Sudan, to begin his journey to the Nile.

Joseph walked down a dusty dirt road. The sun was rapidly heating the earth. In the distance, he saw a woman at a well filling a large clay pot with water. His throat was parched.

Joseph picked up his pace. He was still over two hundred yards away when the woman looked up and noticed him approaching. She quickly collected her sack of goods, placed them over her shoulder, and hurried down the road. Joseph wondered why she was frightened. At the well, he dipped his hands, drank a few swallows, soaked his handkerchief, wiped his face, and then tied the handkerchief around his neck. All of a sudden, he heard a woman cry out.

Joseph snatched his duffel bag and ran toward the shrieks. Three thugs surrounded the woman from the well. They hit her with sticks while trying to pry her sack away, but she bravely held onto it. Joseph yanked a stick from the leader, placed him in a chokehold, and lifted him off the ground. The other attackers watched their leader dangle and struggle to breathe. Afraid they might meet the same fate, they ran away.

Joseph felt the leader falling limp. When he released him, the leader dropped to his knees, gasping for air. Before Joseph could raise his stick, the man scrambled to his feet and took flight. Joseph turned to the woman, who was checking the contents of her sack. She was frail, probably in her early twenties.

"Are you hurt?" Joseph asked.

"No, I am not."

"You speak English."

"I have been the servant of an English family all of my life."

"I hope whatever is in that sack is worth risking your life."

The woman held her possessions tightly.

"I'm the one who just helped you, remember?"

The woman bowed her head. "I have treated you with disrespect. Forgive me."

"Don't give it another thought, but you need to be more careful."

"I know this road is dangerous, but it's the fastest way to the market where I sell my art."

They were heading in the same direction. Joseph could accompany her to the market and continue on his journey.

"Do you come to the marketplace often to sell your work?" Joseph asked as they began their journey.

"I am allowed one free day each month. I work every day from five in the morning until nine at night. Often, I work through the night on my art. I have at least ten pieces to sell each month. I am saving to purchase my freedom."

Joseph stopped in his tracks. "Did you just say 'to purchase your freedom'?"

"Yes. Years ago, the Carlyle family purchased my contract. In order for me to leave their services, I must pay the value of that contract. I've saved for ten years. I have one fourth of the cost saved. In twenty more years, I will have enough to pay them."

Joseph was totally incensed. He asked how much she had to pay. She told him the cost in pounds.

"That's five thousand dollars. It took you ten years to save a thousand dollars?"

"I receive no salary, just food and supplies."

It was afternoon when the two reached the marketplace. She picked out a space on the ground and displayed her art. Joseph was amazed at the detail of her wooden sculptures and her jewelry. He picked up one of her carvings. "This word inscribed on the bottom, N-a-r-a?"

"Nafisa is my name."

The sun was now scorching the earth. Joseph was perspiring heavily. He unbuttoned his shirt, exposing the golden medallion.

Nafisa caught sight of it. "You have come to save the child. The DOM!"

Joseph grabbed her shoulders. "Where is my daughter? What do you know?"

"Joseph, I am not your enemy. I will help you. I know of the demon you face."

Joseph removed his hands. "I am sorry. I did not mean to hurt you. You must be the Messenger I was told I would find."

"I believe I am. The enemy you will face is ancient, powerful, and mystical. Tonight at midnight, he will bring the infant girl to the sacred river for her first anointing. The moon will station itself where the White Nile meets the Blue Nile. This is the baby's first cleansing, and it must be completed in one hour, for the child must be returned to her tabernacle before one a.m. The second anointing will come in ten days."

"Thank you, Nafisa. Tonight, Blue will meet his doom."

"You are not ready to meet Blue on this night. There is much you must learn. I will teach you. Then I will go with you in ten days when he returns with the child."

Joseph stared into Nafisa's eyes. "I will go tonight. I will go alone. This is my child, my battle. I will not wait so that he might harm her more."

"I beg you, listen to what I am saying, Joseph. You must think like a soldier."

"I am a soldier." He lifted his bag and swiftly departed. His only vision was infant Nicole crying for him.

He checked maps, recalled Bernice's directions and Nafisa's description. At 11:00 p.m., Joseph reached the connecting rivers. He had his revolver in its holster and a machete strapped to his leg. He took off the medallion, placed it in the bag, and covered it in the bushes near him. Scooping up a handful of dirt, he camouflaged his clothing with mud. Afterwards, he hid in the thicket awaiting Blue's arrival.

At exactly midnight, the gargantuan white wings eclipsed the moon. In moments, Blue glided to the riverbank. In a cloth of blue silk, Blue carried baby Nicole. He turned to the river and removed the cloak from the infant. He held Nicole in his hands, outstretched over the water. Joseph rose from the ground. From about twenty feet away, he took his revolver from its holster and aimed it directly at Blue's back.

"Give me my child or die where you stand."

Blue slowly rotated in Joseph's direction. He placed Nicole in one arm, cradling her next to his chest. "You mutant, vile sub-creature. Do you think I did not see you slithering in the grass? Do you think I cannot smell your foul, putrid odor? Do you think you're capable of my level of cognition? You are the least of your species, Son of Slaves. You are the mongrel of the earth. You are excrement. This is my child. You could not create a child such as this. Now, I will teach my child how she must treat an SOS mutation." Blue looked down at Nicole. "Watch carefully, DOM."

Joseph paused, knowing he and Nicole were in jeopardy and every second counted, but he couldn't fire. He did not have a clear shot.

Without one, he might wound his daughter. He could not take the chance.

Blue flung a ball of fire directly at Joseph's revolver. The sphere jolted the gun from his burning hand. Joseph went to the ground to smother the flame. When he looked up, Blue stood over him. Ignoring the pain in his hand, Joseph ripped the knife from his leg. Blue caught Joseph's wrist and lifted him by his arm to his feet. Joseph swung at Blue with his other fist. Blue caught Joseph's other wrist. Holding Joseph above the ground, Blue spit putrid bile in his face. With one powerful yank, Blue flipped Joseph over his head and catapulted him through the air, smashing Joseph's head into a tree. Every time Joseph tried to stand, his body was met with kicks and punches. Every blow was accented with insults. Finally, Joseph lay face down on the ground, nearly unconscious.

Blue twisted vines and willowy branches into a whip-like bundle and immersed them in the river. Once they were soaked, he ripped the shirt off the battered Joseph. Blue beat Joseph until the skin on his back was in bloody strips. Joseph was motionless. Blue walked back over to baby Nicole. He picked her up, stepped into the river, and completed the ceremony of water.

"Now, my daughter, I will show you how the sub-creatures are to be treated." He released a ball of flame, setting the whipping vines on fire. He picked up Joseph's machete and held the blade in the flames until it was white hot. Blue walked over to the motionless Joseph and positioned Nicole so she could see him take the burning blade and brand him, carving "SOS" into his back. The burning incision jarred Joseph awake. He screamed out in agony.

"Now you see how weak these sub-creatures are, my daughter," Blue said. "Others of his kind will find his body. It will be a sign for them to prepare for their destinies. This mutant has taken our time. We must return to our temple at once." Blue dropped the blade and bolted into the sky with Nicole in his arms.

Joseph lay waiting to die. The odor of his smoldering flesh filled the air. Suddenly, there was a rustling in the bush. A horse whinnied. Nafisa emerged from the woods with the Carlyle's bridled horse and cart.

Nafisa hurried to Joseph. The sight of his seared flesh made her grimace, but she found the strength to maneuver him onto a blanket and drag his nearly lifeless body to the cart. Collecting herself, she hoisted Joseph up and into the cart.

Why didn't the medallion protect him? Nafisa thought, knowing all about Blue and the medallions from Kabaka's quilt. Joseph wasn't wearing it. Had the medallion dropped, or had Blue taken it? She hurried back to where she had found Joseph. Moving around the area covered with bushes, she noticed broken branches. Perhaps Joseph had waited there for Blue. She looked around and was suddenly drawn to an area fifty feet away. She reached into a bush and out came Joseph's satchel. She found the medallion inside. She rushed back to the cart and placed the medallion around Joseph's neck for his protection.

Before the break of dawn, Nafisa reached her hut on the Carlyle estate. She laid Joseph on the floor on his stomach and covered his legs. With less than an hour before she began her daily duties, Nafisa created a poultice from herbs and plant leaves and applied them to Joseph's wounds. Joseph remained unconscious, with a soaring fever. Nafisa would sneak away to check on him.

Three days passed and Joseph's fever continued. Delusional, he would call out to Marion, Bernice, Nicole, and Jesse, or rant about his days in the prison camp. On the fourth day, his cold sweats began. By the fifth day, chills set in with constant shaking. Nafisa kept feeding him warm broth and natural medicines. She covered him, but nothing seemed to stop the chill.

When Joseph's shaking became more spastic and uncontrolled, Nafisa searched her mind for the answer. Rolled against the wall of the hut was her solution. Her quilt. Nafisa removed her frock, lifted the quilt from the floor of the hut, and placed it around her shoulders. She removed the blanket from Joseph and lay on top of him, wrapping the quilt around them both for heat. It was not long before Joseph's chills subsided.

On the sixth day, Joseph's eyes partially opened. He caught a blurred glimpse of Nafisa's face. "Marion, Marion," he called out. He clung to Nafisa in a tight embrace, and his body began to gyrate. At first, Nafisa tried to free herself, but her body began to respond. Joseph called out Marion's name again and again. Nafisa relaxed her legs and allowed them to open. She was caught in the rapture until Joseph fell still. Minutes later, Nafisa also succumbed to a heavy sleep, lying on Joseph through the night. Before dawn, she slowly eased herself from his body. He was still unconscious, but his fever had broken.

All of Nafisa's life, the quilt had protected her. It was the vessel that had navigated her safely to the shore of the omnipotent Nile after Blue had thrown her as an infant into the river to drown. Nomads had found her and sold her to the slave traders. The quilt had stayed with her and given her strength. It had been her mother, her father, and her family, and now it had saved Joseph.

***

On the seventh day, Joseph awoke from his long slumber. The medicines and care he had received from Nafisa had saved his life. He opened his eyes.

"The gods have brought you back, Joseph," Nafisa said.

Joseph took both of Nafisa's hands and kissed them. "Thank you, Nafisa, thank you."

"You need not thank me. If you had not survived, I shudder to think of how it would change our destiny. You must continue to rest. Tonight you must begin your lessons. I will teach you all you need to know."

By evening, he was able to stand and walk. His duffel bag sat at the end of the cot. Nafisa must have found it in the bush. He took out his clothes. Slowly, he pulled on his pants. The cloth of his shirt met the blistering wounds on his back. The discomfort was too much to bear. He removed the shirt. He suddenly noticed he was wearing the medallion. Had Nafisa put it on him? He knew now he should never have taken it off.

He reached behind himself and traced the scars. The night of his torture flashed before his eyes. Euphoric, Blue had gloated over Joseph's suffering.

When Nafisa returned to the hut at nightfall, Joseph was waiting for her. "I realize the mistake I made," he told her. "I let my emotions take over. I paid for my ignorance. Now, I'm filled with fears and doubt. I am not sure if I can defeat such an enemy."

Nafisa sat on the floor in front of Joseph. "If you study and understand your enemy, you will be victorious in battle. Fear will teach

263

you never to underestimate anyone or anything. Your physical strength does not compare to his. With the medallion, you would have had a chance. But you weren't wearing it. You must call on its powers."

"Its powers?"

Nafisa stood up. "Since you didn't know how to use it, maybe it is fortunate Blue did not see it. He would have taken it from you.

"Pay close attention, Joseph. Blue is the last of his kind. He wants to crush The Freedom Code, which is about to transform our people all over the world with the true knowledge of what it is to be free. Blue mated with the best of us, the women who have already broken from his mental and physical chains and tasted that sweet freedom. By controlling these women and their children, he will enslave the best and purest of us. Then the spirit of real freedom will be suppressed. All who have never felt true freedom of spirit will be enslaved forever. Those who knew of the freedom spirit will only have a lingering memory of its sweet taste. Blue has thirty-one years left to prevail. When we face him, we can only temporarily destroy his body. The labyrinth of his mind will live for thirty-one more years. The Freedom Code predicts:

In the final engagement, Blue will try to enslave those who are free and keep bound those who never knew freedom. Africans and all their descendants in America must break the shackles which they are unaware still bind them. The journey to freedom starts in the Motherland and ends in the Motherland.

"Joseph, all is not in Blue's favor. He has selected who he believes are the only humans perfect enough to bear his children. The children he has sired will remain of our humankind until they reach thirty-one years of age. We must influence those children with humanity.

"In three days, Blue will return to the anointing waters. You and I will face him together and free the progeny. We must prevail. Ask your questions, Joseph," she finally urged. "We can have no secrets."

"Nafisa, you are a puzzle whose pieces don't fit. I was an orphan raised in an orphanage where I was cared for and educated. You've been enslaved all of your life, yet the way you speak, your artistic skills, your knowledge of the world, require education. Where did you learn about Blue? Who taught you these secrets?"

Nafisa handed the quilt to Joseph. "This quilt holds the secrets of Blue and of Kabaka's family. The knowledge of Blue's history channeled to the Blessed Child was instead transferred to me. At five months old, I walked. I can remember that step. At the age of one, I could talk and read. I carved my first wooden statue at five. The quilt taught me all of these things. I know Blue's whole history.

"Channeling also awoke the other spirits of Kabaka's family, the blood father of Marion. After all, this was his quilt. Although touched by Blue, Kabaka's ancestors made this quilt. Therefore, I learned of goodness, virtue, and humanity from those noble spirits. I knew someday you would come. I knew it would be my duty to teach and help you. Joseph, I have told you my secrets, now let us plan. The quilt makes me the only person on earth who truly knows how to destroy Blue. We must begin!"

Chapter 36

On the morning of the tenth day, Nafisa left for work, and Joseph went into town to purchase African robes, the type worn by chieftains to declare wealth and prestige. Then he bought one of the few available finer automobiles for sale. Before noon, Joseph was parking in front of the Carlyle estate. He walked up the stairs and knocked. Nafisa opened the door. She was shocked. Joseph acted as if he had never seen her.

"I have come to see one Mr. Carlyle. I have business of importance."

Carlyle happened to be passing the door. He dismissed Nafisa.

"I am John Carlyle. What business do you have with me?"

"I have been commissioned by the US government to assist the Bada family in their search for their missing niece. It seems she was abducted and illegally sold into servitude as a very small child. Her family has been searching for her for over twenty years. Their investigators have concluded she is in your employ. According to our information, her name is Nafisa. The Bada family presently resides in the United States. The safe return of their niece has become of interest to the Central Intelligence Agency. Our government is interested in procuring Nigerian properties now owned by the Bada family, of which Nafisa is an intricate part. No, please no questions. I can't tell you any more, except, in order to keep this matter out of the press and expedite her safe return, I have been sent."

Joseph opened his wallet and displayed his identification photo in his army uniform as a member of the US Army Division of International Affairs. Joseph asked if he could come in. Carlyle allowed him entry and escorted Joseph into his den, unsure how to handle this situation.

"I have no idea why you have been sent to my home. I am a citizen of the United Kingdom, not the United States. I have a legal and binding agreement for Nafisa's services."

"Please do not misunderstand, Mr. Carlyle. The reason I have dressed in this manor is to perform my duty without drawing suspicion. Neither my government nor the Bada family wish to implicate you in any wrongdoings. On the contrary, everyone feels they owe you a debt of gratitude. I am here simply to offer a fair and equitable payment. Our research indicates the current value of Nafisa's contract is five thousand American dollars. I am prepared to pay this fee immediately."

Carlyle felt he had the upper hand. "At five thousand dollars, I don't sense gratitude."

"I have been authorized to pay twice the value of the contract. If that amount is unsatisfactory, I am instructed to retract all offers. My retraction will be followed tomorrow by visits from officials representing both of our governments. An investigation will be opened. I am sure such measures are unnecessary. You are a reasonable man."

Carlyle knew he had overplayed his hand. "Ten thousand dollars is fair. Nafisa deserves to be with her family. If you will excuse me, I will bring her contract to you."

Carlyle returned with Nafisa and her contract. Nafisa looked totally mystified by Carlyle's friendliness. Until now, he had only spoken to her to give orders. He was not cruel, just oblivious of her or any aspect of her life. She was a servant, nothing more.

"Nafisa, this is Mr. Johnson. Your real family has sent him. It seems they have been searching for you. Once Mr. Johnson and I finish our business, you will be leaving with him. He will take you to your family. Now, go and gather your belongings."

Nafisa was speechless. Joseph extended his hand to her. "Nafisa. I will find your quarters. We must leave immediately."

Nafisa held her hand to her mouth. Tears of joy ran down her cheeks. She scurried from the den and ran to her hut.

***

When Joseph entered the hut, Nafisa hugged and thanked him. "Why and how did you do this?"

"Bernice told me I was to 'free the one enslaved.' My wife escaped from Africa as an infant. I believe that somehow, when you were taken, Marion escaped. Now justice has been served, Nafisa. Marion just paid for the freedom you allowed her."

Joseph removed the contract from his sleeve. He signed it over to Nafisa Bada. Nafisa read the document and held it close to her heart.

"Who are the Badas?"

"I had to come up with a name. The man who sold me these robes was a traveling merchant. He was very nice. I believe he said he was from Nigeria and his last name was Bada. It was the name that came to mind when Carlyle opened the door."

"I am fond of the name. From this day forward, I am Nafisa Bada."

On their journey to the river, they stopped at the marketplace for supplies. Night had fallen when they parked the car miles away from their destination. They walked along the riverbed where Joseph had been left to die. They marked the exact position where he had lain and began preparations. Nafisa removed all of her clothing. With camelhair brushes, they painted her entire body sky blue. When her paint dried, they rubbed the riverbank moss all over her. Its odor disguised her human scent. She placed a wig woven from horsetail on her head. Finally, they attached the wings she had created onto her back. Joseph removed his shirt and rubbed manure and fish oil on his skin. Then he put on the clothes he wore the night of the first battle. All was ready for the midnight hour.

"Joseph, the time grows near. Remember, when I speak, you will not understand. But at the exact instant I stop speaking—do it. We have one chance. We cannot fail."

"We will not fail."

At midnight, Blue's wings cast a shadow over the sky. Blue landed at the river's edge, holding Nicole, the child of Marion, and Segun, the child of Zinzi. Blue glanced at Joseph's body.

"Children, smell the decaying subgenera."

Suddenly, a blue glow of light emanated from the thicket. A voice was heard. It spoke the ancient language of Blue. The words continued as Nafisa walked from the bush. She looked to be of his kind. Blue smelled the air and listened to her speaking in his tongue.

"You are not alone," she said. "I have been searching for you, my brother. Come to me. Come to me."

She watched Blue lay the babies near the riverbank and curiously walk toward her. Standing at Joseph's feet, Nafisa saw Blue scowl. He knew she was a fraud. In that instant, Nafisa spoke no more.

With lightning speed, Joseph sprang to his feet. As he raised his arms above his head, the sword appeared in his hands. With one swipe, Joseph sliced through Blue's neck, and he kicked Blue's body from under him. Blue's head fell, plummeting to the ground.

"He is still watching, Joseph!"

Joseph gouged out Blue's eyes. The eyeballs rolled to the ground. Using the mammoth blue diamond on the sword hilt, Joseph pounded the orbs in. He exerted so much force the blue diamond broke from its setting and fell to the ground. Joseph put the stone in his pocket while Nafisa retrieved the metal box they had hidden in the bush. Joseph lifted Blue's head by the hair and placed it into the box. He closed the lid, all the while feeling Blue's temples pulsating.

"Remember, Joseph, he is not dead."

Joseph placed the metal box on the ground. Nafisa was now holding both of the children. Joseph took Nafisa's costume wings and laid them in a small clearing. He grabbed Blue's feet, dragged the decapitated carcass over, and laid it on the wings. He gathered dry twigs and wood, built a pyre around the body, and set the pyre alight. When the last flame flickered out, Blue's remains were a pile of volcanic ash and rock.

The plan had worked. From the quilt, Nafisa had learned Blue's language and knew he held his sister sacred. His own light, the quilt, had fooled him.

Joseph took baby Nicole in his arms. "My daughter, no harm shall come to you as long as I am alive." Joseph looked at the other baby. "Whose child is this?"

"I fear we will never know his mother. We must care for him."

Joseph took the baby in his other arm. "I will ensure your future also."

They collected their gear and traveled back to the car. Driving nearly a thousand miles, they only stopped for fuel. Along the way, Nafisa told Joseph about the true burial ground for Blue at the Kibo Volcano, the highest point in all of Africa. Finally they crossed the border into Kenya. Joseph found accommodations for them at an inn.

The next morning, he woke Nafisa and gave her money to pay for an extended stay.

"I must go now to finish this. I don't know how long it will take, but I will return."

Joseph purchased climbing equipment and traveled without rest. In three days, he found himself at the base of Kilimanjaro. He had scaled mountains in the army, but none as formidable as this. He fell to his knees and asked God and all of the ancestors to watch over him.

Each time he drove the pick into the stone or a rock broke away after his step, Joseph looked to the sky and gave thanks. As he gained altitude, the weight of the metal box seemed to grow. He may have severed Blue's vocal cords and blinded him, but Joseph knew Blue was still alive, aware and waiting. Joseph reached the snowy plateau, Mawensi, fifteen thousand feet up. He still had more than four thousand feet to climb.

Day became night and night became day. The bitter cold and wind, the jagged edges and the erosion made his climb even more harrowing. At over nineteen thousand feet above the Motherland, he reached the apex of Kibo.

He dropped the metal box into the eye of the volcano and watched it sink into molten lava.

"The final battle is yet to be fought. I know your powers will regenerate in thirty years. We will meet again. I will be prepared next time. No one is meant to be a slave."

***

Joseph returned to Kenya. He had no concept of the time that had passed, only that both children looked older. Nafisa had lovingly nurtured and cared for them.

After resting a few days, Joseph drove them to Lagos, where he purchased airline tickets. Fifteen minutes before it was time for takeoff, he and Nafisa said their goodbyes.

With sadness in her eyes, Nafisa stared at Joseph. "These children cannot be raised together. It is far too dangerous. Take your daughter back across the ocean. The boy will remain here. I will be his mother." She lifted the baby to her face. "We are both children of Africa. His face is not different from mine. He will never know I am not his natural mother. My love will keep him from doubt."

Joseph understood. "Nafisa, you have a gift. Your art brings beauty to this world. You must continue." Joseph had thirty-two thousand dollars left. He gave thirty thousand to Nafisa. "You will be able to build a business and a future for your child. If you are to stay here, you will need protection." He took the medallion from his neck and placed it around Nafisa's. He reached into his bag and took out the mammoth blue diamond.

"No, Joseph, you must keep the diamond. Keep it for the final day."

Nafisa reached into her bag and removed a wooden statue. "I remember how you admired this. I want you to have it. It was my first carving of myself. I am the servant girl."

Joseph searched his own bag to give something personal of himself to Nafisa. *I forgot I had brought this!* He handed her a manuscript.

"This is a Christmas story that Marion and I wrote and illustrated. You can read it to your son at bedtime."

"Thank you, Joseph," Nafisa said, taking the book. She looked at Nicole in Joseph's arms and then to the baby boy in her own. "We must raise our children with a sense of humanity and love, and they will overcome their heritage. This we must promise one another."

"You have my word," Joseph said.

The engines of the jet began to fire. Joseph and Nafisa embraced.

"Thank you, Nafisa. I will never forget you."

"Nor I you, Joseph Johnson. Until we meet again."

Chapter 37

Three-fourths of a year had passed since Joseph, Marion, and Nicole were happily reunited. Marion and Joseph had opened a small construction business.

At the beginning of the New Year, Bernice had a massive heart attack. It was only a few days before she joined her beloved Jesse. She left this earth a joyful woman.

***

Trapped in a pyramid, Zinzi mourned the loss of her son. He was taken away and never returned. She didn't know where he was, if he was safe or even alive.

***

Nafisa cared for Zinzi's son, Segun, and they prospered. Within a year, she had opened her own shop in Lagos, and Nafisa was thrilled that her art was received with such enthusiasm. She became an extraordinary success.

Often she thought of the man who had given her the freedom to change her life. Today was the greatest reminder. Nafisa Bada lay in her bed with her son, Segun, beside her. In her arms she held her newborn, the son of Joseph, Sotonye Bada.

**The Children of the Master and
The Children of Freedom
will become one. These
children will unbind the
shackles of slavery from our people who are unaware the
chains bind them.**

Part VI

Segun and Sotonye

1991, Botswana, New Orleans, Rochester, Chicago

Chapter 38

"You Know You're Safe on the Other Side of the Golden Guard" became the marketing slogan that brought notoriety to Segun Bada's light bar security system. Nicole and Regina decided initially to target the African market. They had Segun replace every fence, gate, security entrance, and barred window at the Q.P.S. compound with the Golden Guard Security System. The system not only proved to offer maximum security, it also aesthetically enhanced the architecture. The impenetrable light amazed sightseers who dared to touch the bars. At first, the articles about the Golden Guard appeared only in local newspapers. In a month's time, it was featured on BBC television all over the African continent.

Regina and Nicole hosted presentations for financial institutions, government leaders, military officers, and corporate executives from every nation on the continent. Sales skyrocketed. It seemed that the Golden Guard Security System was being featured on every new blueprint submitted by architects designing office buildings or apartment complexes.

When United Press International caught wind of the burgeoning security innovation, Q.P.S. and Golden Guard received exposure before any funds were spent on the international campaign. From October 15 to November 30, Nicole and Regina traveled to England, France, Italy, Greece, Japan, and Russia. In each country, they helped to secure millions of dollars in contracts.

International joint ventures were also offered, along with incentives to build factories in countries on every continent, but Segun insisted that the African nations in the greatest need of economic and industrial development would become the home for Q.P.S. factories. If such development required transportation systems, he would build new roads and landing strips and purchase fleets of trucks and cargo jets.

In December, a snide reporter tried to corner Segun. "Why invest so much of your capital into developing business in Africa? Won't your profit share be less? Is that really the most intelligent business strategy?"

Segun smiled. "It is in my interest and in the interest of everyone of African descent to invest in and ensure the economic furtherance of our people and continent. Historically we have done most of the work and received the least profit. Contrary to popular belief, profit is not the reason one goes into business." Segun winked at Regina. "Rather, it is the continuance of business."

Fellow journalists ribbed the thwarted reporter. Segun left the stage thinking how extraordinary it was that he had met Nicole's father all those years ago. Joseph Johnson had influenced Regina, too—with just those words. Regina hadn't known at the time, nor had he, that they would meet the man's daughter, Nicole, who would become their sister. Life amazed him.

Nicole took the podium to make a comment and field any additional questions.

"Q.P.S. has a presence in Africa, Europe, and Asia. Does the company plan to expand their markets to the Americas, specifically the United States?" a reporter asked.

"Q.P.S. is planning a major promotional exhibition in the US shortly after the New Year," Nicole answered, creating quite a stir.

The reporters asked for details.

"A news release will be forthcoming. This concludes our session."

The next day, the headline read, "Q.P.S. Will Open the Golden Guard in US." By the second week in December, the details for the exhibition were finalized. On January 10, 1991, Segun Bada would demonstrate the wonders of Q.P.S.'s Golden Guard Security System in downtown Chicago, Illinois.

***

Segun was behind his desk in his office picking up his telephone to call his brother at the Princess Marina Hospital. Sotonye had just completed his rounds.

"Segun, there must be something brewing for you to call me here."

"Actually, I was hoping you could get away this evening. I want to take Regina and Nicole out to dinner. You realize they are making us very rich."

Sotonye laughed. "I thought you had already made us rich."

"So did I, before these two came along. I haven't asked them if they're available tonight. I thought I'd call you first."

"If they want to go, call me back. If the answer is yes, get your tux ready and leave the arrangements to me."

"Shall I tell them to dress formally?"

Sotonye laughed again. "I would not advise you to make any suggestions to Nicole Johnson or Regina Bovine. Your feelings might get hurt."

"Excellent point, my younger brother. I'll go to their office now and call you back in about fifteen minutes."

***

Nicole and Regina were in their office discussing the campaign. Somehow they had become sidetracked and started talking about the holidays.

"This will be the first Christmas I've ever celebrated without Momma."

"I've spent many a Christmas alone, Gina."

"I'm sorry, Nicole, I hadn't thought about that."

"No, it's me. I didn't think about you. I guess I was so excited about spending Christmas with you and possibly Sotonye and Segun, I forgot about Momma Emma."

"I know she's thrilled to be with Aunt Melinda, and I am so happy about spending Christmas with you all. "

"Gina, what is the custom here? Do Sotonye and Segun celebrate the holidays? "

"I don't know. But we want to celebrate. Therefore…"

"We'll talk them into it," they both said and slapped each other's hands.

There was a knock at their office door and Segun walked in. "I'm relieved to find you in high spirits. I have a request."

"I am sorry, Segun, we are all out of miracles this week," Nicole said.

277

"You've surpassed the miracle quota for this year, which brings me to my request. Sotonye and Segun Bada would like to take you out this evening to a fine restaurant to show our gratitude for your extraordinary work."

"Where are we going and what time?" Regina asked.

"We will pick you up at seven. I have no idea where we are going. Sotonye told me that he would make all of the arrangements. Surprising as it might be, there is a possibility that my brother may wear a suit and tie."

"Your brother is going to wear a suit. This is a major celebration!" Nicole said.

"Sotonye wore his hospital whites to the opening celebration of Q.P.S. It was black tie or traditional African only. When I asked if I should mention attire to you two, he suggested I would most likely have my feelings shredded and handed to me."

"You're allowed this time," Regina said.

"Thank you, Regina," Segun said. "You always—"

Nicole interrupted. "Segun Bada, we have some negotiating to do."

Segun looked at Regina for help. "She never stops."

Regina raised her hands, shrugged her shoulders, and said, "I'm sorry, dear, you are on your own."

Segun released a sigh. "What are your conditions?"

"Regina and I have on blue jeans and tee shirts. It's one thirty p.m. For the first time in your brother's life, he is going to wear a suit."

"Actually, he told me to have my tuxedo ready."

"Oh, this is far more serious than I thought. You shouldn't have held back such a vital piece of information. This is an entirely new scenario. Do you know how much preparation a woman goes through for this type of evening? Since the Bada brothers have given us this last-minute invitation and because they are feeling so generous, here are the conditions of our acceptance. One. Gina and I will leave immediately after these negotiations. Two. Everything we need for tonight will be charged to Q.P.S."

Regina broke in. "Oh, Nicole!"

Nicole waved off Regina's protest. "They can afford it. Where was I?"

"You had just completed condition number two," Segun chuckled.

"That's right. Three: we don't want to be chauffeured. I am sure you both know how to drive. Four: seven is too early. Make it seven forty-five. Five: please pay close attention. This is the most important condition. Neither Gina nor I went to our high school proms. Therefore, you two must find the most gorgeous corsages on this entire continent to pin on us tonight. Based on these conditions, we accept your invitation."

As Segun nodded his head in agreement, Nicole grabbed her purse and took Gina by the arm. On their way out the door, Regina handed Segun a folded sheet of paper. She had written down all of Nicole's conditions.

He smiled. *Regina always assures my success.* He thought about his mother. *Nafisa, if you were here, you would be fond of Regina. She is like you in so many ways. I miss you, my mother.*

Segun returned to his office and telephoned his brother. When Segun read him the list of conditions, Sotonye thought they were hilarious.

"Face reality, Segun. When it comes to Nicole, you have met your match."

"I don't think so, Sotonye. I think I've met *your* match."

"What are you saying?"

"You know precisely what I am saying."

Sotonye smiled without comment. "I have a great deal to do in a short time. I've cleared my schedule for the rest of the day. Why don't you do the same? Let's really prepare a surprise for them tonight."

"If I left at this time of day, everyone at the office and factory would be in a state of shock." Segun paused. "I'll do it."

***

At 7:20 p.m., Sotonye and Segun Bada pulled up to the entrance of the hotel in Sotonye's custom-designed royal blue convertible Avanti. He handed the keys to the doorman as the parking attendants gathered around the car. They had only seen the Avanti in magazines, and Sotonye's convertible had been custom made by Avanti and was one of a kind. The attendants all vied to park the car.

They rode the elevator to Nicole and Regina's floor, each holding a corsage box.

"I wonder which door is Nicole's," Segun said, "and which is Regina's."

Sotonye walked to Nicole's suite. "This is Nicole's door."

"How do you know this?"

"Segun, are you saying you've never come to visit?"

Refusing to look over at his snickering brother, Segun knocked on Regina's door.

"Segun, is that you?"

"Yes it is, Regina."

"The door is unlocked. Come in." Segun entered the suite. Regina called again from her bedroom, "We'll be out in a second." Segun stood for a few moments, then Regina and Nicole entered the room.

Regina wore a strapless black evening gown with a plunging open back. Her hair was swept up in a French roll adorned with baby's breath. The gown was perfectly accented by a pearl necklace, earrings, and bracelets. The classic style of her gown complemented Segun's tuxedo perfectly. Nicole was a vision in silver. Her fitted gown sparkled and shimmered, catching the light in the room. A beaded lace sleeve accented the garment. Her hair was styled in flowing African braids crowned with a fitted silver hat.

Segun was mesmerized. He thought about the corsage Sotonye had selected for Regina. *Sotonye must be clairvoyant.* The oval corsage was made up of a cluster of white roses lying in a bed of tiny African violets. Segun did not realize he had not said a word.

"Segun, where is Sotonye?"

Segun snapped back into reality. "I left him outside, knocking on your door, Nicole."

On cue, Sotonye walked into the room. "You both look beautiful!"

This time the reaction was reversed. Nicole's mouth fell open, but no words came out.

"Segun, look at your brother," Regina said.

"It's a miracle, isn't it?"

Sotonye was dressed in a deep navy blue tuxedo with matching cummerbund and bow tie. His starched white shirt was accented with gold cufflinks and studs.

Sotonye's corsage was designed with species of flowers Nicole had never seen. In the center, the flowers had petals of silver and white intertwined with a delicate thread of minute, regal blue flower buds.

Segun removed his corsage from its box and walked over to Regina. The corsages were art. Neither of the two women could believe how impeccably they enhanced their gowns.

"Would you two excuse us for a moment?" Regina asked. She took Nicole's hand and went back into the bedroom.

The instant they left, Segun whistled. "How could you have designed those flowers so perfectly? I was as much in awe as Regina and Nicole!"

"There is only one dress designer in this city who can create such elegant gowns."

"Do you mean mother's friend from France, Antoinette?"

"Exactly. First, I called the hotel manager. I knew one of them would ask for the best shop. I told him to recommend Lady Antoinette's. Then I called Antoinette. I asked if she would design corsages to perfectly match their gowns. She loved the idea. I told her to spare no expense, you were paying for everything."

"When it comes to my money, you become more like our mother with each passing day. On the other hand, you had a stroke of genius. With a deceptive mind like yours, you should be in business, not medicine."

***

In the bedroom, the women were standing at the mirror admiring their corsages.

"I can't believe how perfectly these flowers go with our dresses," Nicole said.

"I can. They had to know what our dresses looked like. Their mother is a designer. They must know every designer in the city."

"I'll bet you're right, Gina. Aren't you proud of them?"

"I am."

Nicole and Regina came out of the bedroom. Sotonye offered his arm to Nicole and Segun his to Regina. They escorted their dates to the main entrance. As the quartet strolled through the lobby, all heads turned in admiration.

"I feel like a princess on parade," Regina said to Segun.

Not looking in Regina's direction, Segun said proudly, "You are a princess."

Regina gave no reply. She simply curled her arm deeper in his.

Sotonye and Nicole walked a few steps behind them. "I've never been one for this kind of attention," Sotonye said.

Nicole surveyed the crowd of admirers. All voices and sounds were muffled. This scene was alarmingly familiar. The vision of that horrible dream she had had several months ago after her bus ride home— her mother in chains, the attacking Bertrand Lwanga, and the letters *SOS* smoking in burning flesh exploded in her mind's eye.

Sotonye felt Nicole's arm tremble. "Nicole, what is wrong?"

The urgent inflection in Sotonye's voice pulled Nicole from her reverie. "Nothing's wrong, Sotonye. For some reason I was just haunted by a disturbing memory."

"Do you want to talk about it?"

"Another time. I won't let anything spoil this evening."

***

Sotonye stopped the Avanti for the valet at the Grand Palm Restaurant and Nightclub in Gaborone, the hottest place in town. The restaurant was on the top floor and looked out over the city. On the first floor, the elite danced and partied at the Grand Palm Nightclub. The Bada family had a lifetime membership.

A private elevator took them up to the club. When they entered the room, the crowd stood, giving the Badas a standing ovation. Dignitaries and corporate leaders shook Segun's hand and congratulated him on Q.P.S.'s unprecedented success in the international market. Some actually asked for his autograph.

"My brother and I," Segun finally said to all, "have come here tonight to honor the two young women directly responsible for the recent success of Q.P.S. I am privileged to introduce to you the marketing and advertising partners of Fresh, Inc., Regina Bovine and Nicole Johnson."

Nicole and Regina received a thunderous round of applause. The Badas had one of the few private tables in the club. Once Nicole and Regina had thanked everyone, Sotonye whisked them away from the crowd to their table with its excellent view of the skyline and the stage.

They dined on gourmet viands and sipped Perrier Jouët champagne. Then, as the flames flickered out on their soufflé au Grand

Marnier, the house lights dimmed and the spotlight bounced against an opening curtain on a half-moon-shaped stage. Hugh Ngwato stood in front of his orchestra at his ebony grand piano.

"Today, I received a call from a pair of childhood friends, Segun and Sotonye Bada. Perhaps you've heard of them." The audience laughed. Hugh looked in the direction of the Bada table. "The brothers Bada told me they were planning a special celebration tonight for two very talented women. Well, Nicole Johnson and Regina Bovine, if two men as remarkable as Sotonye and Segun think you are gifted, you certainly must be. I have a personal stake in this too. Sotonye has told me your favorite singer and pianist is the incomparable late Nat King Cole, who happens to be my idol." Hugh cued the lights. "Dr. Sotonye Bada and Miss Nicole Johnson, please follow the light to the center of the dance floor."

Sotonye stood up and offered his hand to Nicole.

Hugh sat down at the piano and nodded to his musicians. "Nicole, this Nat King Cole classic, 'Mona Lisa,' is dedicated to you."

Sotonye and Nicole glided across the floor to the melodic rhythm of the classic ballad.

"My parents used to dance to Nat King Cole in our living room when I was a little girl. How did you know he was my favorite?"

"The truth is I didn't know. He happens to be my favorite singer." Sotonye pulled Nicole closer and whispered in her ear. "Nothing in my life has moved me as much as when I first saw you at the airport." Nicole laid her head softly on his chest. When the music ended, the audience applauded. The spotlight followed Nicole and Sotonye back to the table.

"Regina and Segun," Hugh called out from the stage. "Please follow the spotlight. I know you won't let your younger brother out-dance you, Segun."

Segun took Regina's hand. "Let us show them how it's done." Segun and Regina stepped into the spotlight. Segun called to his friend. "Hugh, let's see if the spotlight can follow us." Hugh cued the musicians and they began to play "Unforgettable."

Palm to palm with arms extended, Regina and Segun did a hesitation side step to the center of the floor. Segun twirled Regina around with one hand and then scooped her by the waist with the other. Hugh started to sing, and they flowed like poetry in motion.

"Where in the world did you learn to step like this, Segun?"

"When I studied in the US, I would drive up the coast to New York and drop in on the oldie clubs. I studied the Soul Brothers' step, then returned to my dorm and practiced. I must confess, until now, I've never danced in public."

"Well, this won't be your last time. You're the best dance partner I've ever had."

"Honestly, Regina?"

"Honestly, Segun!"

When their dance ended, even Hugh applauded. Regina and Segun returned to the table.

Hugh was so inspired, he stayed in Nat Cole's voice. "Segun and Sotonye, I dedicate this last song to you. You must never forget the lesson in these lyrics." Hugh lifted his glass. Saluting in return, the brothers lifted their glasses. The horns began the haunting melody of "Nature Boy."

Nicole reached across the table and took Regina's hand. "This is our father's favorite song, Gina."

"I do not understand. You two have the same father?"

"Nicole's father adopted me."

"Did you grow up together?" Sotonye asked.

"No, I never met my adopted father."

"I am completely lost. What about you, Sotonye?"

"We are traveling in the same cloud, my brother."

"It's rather difficult to explain," Nicole said.

"One day, Nicole and I will tell you the whole story."

"I'd like that very much," Segun said.

Sotonye tapped his spoon against his glass. "I have an announcement to make. After watching the three of your outstanding performances over the first half of this business year, I, as a member of the Board of Directors of Q.P.S., have decided you are all due a vacation. Starting tomorrow, Dr. Sotonye Bada is officially on one month's leave. He intends to spend his time with the three of you. Segun Bada, you have never taken a day's vacation in your entire life. I see no reason why you cannot begin vacation tomorrow. You are totally prepared for your trip to the United States next month. Would you deprive Regina and Nicole these few short days of relaxation and rejuvenation?"

Segun paused for a moment. "I have never refused our mother or you, but I must have at least one day to meet with my team. I tell you, Sotonye, you'd better make sure we have a good time."

All at the table bubbled with excitement. Without thinking, Regina leaned over and gave Segun a kiss on the cheek. An enormous smile swept across his face. Sotonye placed his cheek playfully next to Nicole.

"See what you started, Gina?" Nicole kissed Sotonye.

"He's been that way since we were babies. Whatever I get, he gets too." They all laughed.

The Grand Palm Nightclub was rocking.

"Since this is a night of spontaneity, let's continue with the dancing," Segun said.

In no time, Regina and Segun were the stars of the club. The crowd recognized the industrial hero and cameras began to flash. Sotonye took Nicole's hand and shied away from the limelight. Regina asked Segun why Sotonye had left the floor.

"Sotonye has never liked to take pictures."

"Why not? He is a very handsome man."

"He has always been self-conscious about his looks. I know that sounds ridiculous. You see, my mother and I have the same skin tone. Even though Sotonye is lighter, he and Mother actually look more like one another in physical features. But he had more than a few fights about his light color in his childhood."

"It's unfortunate. People used to hassle my mother because of her light complexion. It always bothered her. My tone is as light as hers, but people didn't bother me as much. It is still an issue, though."

Nicole and Sotonye stood near the exit. "You look like you could use some air," Nicole said.

"That's a great idea. I don't think Gina and Segun will miss us."

They slipped out the back door and stood in a dark passageway. Sotonye faced Nicole and held her hand.

"Nicole, I know men say things to women that are not true. But this is from my heart. I believe you and I were created to be together."

"Unlike so many women I have known, I have never been hurt by a man, Sotonye, because I've never let a man that deep into my heart. But when I first met you, I said to myself, oh no, not me. This is no time for a schoolgirl crush. Sotonye, I can't believe how deeply I feel about you."

Both were about to speak. Instead, they locked into an embrace and a deep, lingering kiss. The kiss ended, only to bring on another and another. Suddenly, voices came out of the darkness that unlocked their embrace. Four ragged, desperate, and hungry-looking young men stood before them.

"The rich lovers go where they please, do what they want, while others suffer. Should we teach them what pain is?"

Sotonye stepped in front of Nicole. "Do not be mistaken. I do not fear you. I will give you money for food. If you try for more, you will pay a price you do not want to pay."

"Who do you think you are?" another said.

"I know who I am and I know who you are. We are the same."

Nicole looked on in alarm as two of them rushed toward Sotonye. Without thinking, she stepped in front of him.

"No!"

The night reverberated with her power, just as it had when the young mother mistreated her child on the bus and again when she stopped Lwanga at her thirtieth birthday party. The young men stumbled backwards and toppled over one another to the ground.

The unexpected power of the young, beautiful woman only made them more aggressive. With little to lose, they grappled to their feet, ready for battle.

Sotonye did a double take at Nicole before agilely maneuvering two of the young men apart while repelling the other two with strong, even punches.

Nicole was once again taken aback by her own powers, but was forced to focus on Sotonye and his prowess in protecting her. She could tell he wasn't trying to hurt the young men as much as to deter them. His doctor's fists hit their solar plexes with just enough force to knock the wind out of each of them.

When they ended up on the ground again, Sotonye took his wallet from his pocket, removed his money, and placed it on the ground where the young men lay. One kicked the money away and spit at Sotonye. On their feet once again, all four stepped back.

In the next moment, they all charged Sotonye with daggers and blades. Nicole was enraged and once again ready to use whatever powers she had when, with a powerful circular move, Sotonye swung his arms above his head, and an enormous sword appeared. As he twirled the sword over his head, the young men came to an abrupt halt to stay out of Sotonye's way, but Sotonye swiftly stepped toward them, slashing and jabbing the sword at his attackers.

With a clean stroke, he could have decapitated them all. Instead, with one rapid motion, Sotonye cut into the trunk of a tree, slicing through it. The tree fell directly onto the four. Sotonye swept the sword over the four and brought it down full force. The young men hollered out in terror.

Nicole ran up to stop Sotonye only to discover that the sword was thrust into the tree's trunk. Using the handle of the sword, Sotonye lifted the trunk from the young men.

"Have you shamed yourselves enough tonight? Have you shamed your parents enough? I have given you a chance to live your lives. I could have taken all of you. Leave here and shame yourselves and your families no more."

The trembling four got to their feet, apologized, and ran into the night. Sotonye raised the sword above his head and it disappeared from sight.

"Thank you, my mother." He turned to the stunned Nicole. "You thought I was going to hurt them?"

"Yes, I did, Sotonye."

"Nicole, I'm a doctor. I have dedicated my life to saving lives. I had to protect you. And the only way to save those boys was to frighten them almost to death."

Nicole calmed herself. "I've seen that sword, in a horrible nightmare the day before my birthday. The sword protected me from a demon. That was just a dream, but this was real. Can you explain this to me?"

"It would take more time than we have right now for us both to talk about our unusual powers, isn't that right?"

Nicole nodded, wondering how she could explain the power she had which she didn't understand herself.

Sotonye took her arm. "I am sure Segun and Gina are wondering where we are."

"Sotonye, this cannot wait. I want you to come back to my suite later tonight."

"I have never used the sword before, Nicole. Other than me, no one knows about it except Mother, and now you. Segun doesn't even know. You must swear to me you will tell no one, not even Regina."

"I promise. But we must talk tonight. Thank you for saving my life, Sotonye."

He kissed her. "You're welcome."

***

Regina and Segun were coming off the dance floor when they returned.

"It appears you two have been having a great time," Sotonye said.

Segun was wearing a smile brighter than any of them had ever seen. "We certainly have been. Gina is the best partner in the world. I can't remember enjoying myself more."

"Segun, do you realize you just called me Gina?"

"Ask my brother. He will tell you I am on vacation!"

Regina laughed. Then Segun looked at his brother. "Sotonye, there is something odd about your face. Are you feeling all right?"

Regina took a tissue and wiped the lipstick from Sotonye's mouth. "It looks like they were having their own party while we were dancing."

Segun's eyes widened. "Ohhh!"

Nicole snatched the tissue from Regina. "Give me that."

Segun and Regina walked away, laughing. Sotonye looked after them.

"I've never seen my brother with his guard down around anyone other than my mother and myself. If the two of them share friendship, it is a friendship I hope my brother never loses."

***

"You orchestrated a marvelous evening," Segun said to Sotonye as they drove home.

"Tonight was priceless."

"It was for me too." Sotonye parked the Avanti at the front steps.

"Sotonye, are you leaving your precious automobile out tonight?"

"No. I need to go to the hospital before I start my vacation tomorrow."

Segun got out of the car. "Spoken like a true Bada. You're as bad as I am."

Sotonye stopped by the Princess Marina Hospital to ensure coverage while he was absent. Then he drove to the Hotel Peermont Sun. At 3:00 a.m., Sotonye tapped lightly on Nicole's door. She eased the door open and put her finger over his lips. Once Sotonye was in, Nicole locked the adjoining door to Regina's suite and led Sotonye to her bedroom.

"I do not know if this is a good idea," Sotonye said.

"I'm sure it isn't, but we are here now." Nicole sat on the edge of the bed. "You might think I'm crazy for what I'm about to tell you, Sotonye. So you might as well grab a chair and make yourself comfortable."

Nicole explained the series of events that had begun the day before her birthday and ended with Alice Plunkett's death. She also confessed that she had no idea where her powers came from, only that the power seemed to come to her when she was protecting people close to her.

Sotonye held out his hand. "Let me see your right palm."

"My palm?"

Sotonye inspected her skin. "There's nothing here."

Nicole's eyes flashed. "I don't see your sword either."

Sotonye laughed. "You have a point."

"I know it sounds ridiculous," Nicole said. "Regina and I saw it one minute, and then it disappeared right after Alice's funeral, when we visited my father's grave and saw a message on his tombstone."

Sotonye interrupted her. "Was the message 'Children, Beware of BLUE'?"

"That's exactly what it read! How did you know?"

"Before my mother went into the Mayo Clinic, she asked me to drive her to a burned-out village in the far north. Many years ago, this village was destroyed in a terrible conflagration. Baba was the only known survivor. He would tell people that the Traveler Blue with mystical powers burned the village down. No one believed him except for my mother and me.

"Since the village's destruction all those years ago, the ground has looked charred, as if by a recent fire. I had never seen my mother afraid. But once at the site, she refused to leave the car.

"Ultimately, she told me she had heard of the village fire before meeting Baba. You can image my surprise. Mother was born thousands of miles away in Nigeria. She refused to discuss it further and gave me a medallion that I had to promise never to take off. It had the powers of the Elders and would protect me and those I loved.

"With this sword, she told me, I might be forced to fight a painful battle. She made me promise that I would love Segun no matter what and under no circumstances was I to tell Segun about this medallion. She said it might be the only chance for Segun's and my survival. Again she refused to elaborate."

He unbuttoned his shirt and displayed the sword medallion that hung from his neck.

Nicole leaned over to inspect it. "Sotonye, your medallion matches the design of the shield that Aunt Melinda gave to Regina. They had to be a set at one time. This is not a coincidence. But what does it all mean? Who is Blue?"

"I think we all must go to the village where no life grows. Perhaps we will be sent a message there. Nicole, there is something all four of us are destined to do. Keep in mind only good has come since the four of us have come together. We have faced no apocalypse. We might not be able to forecast the future, but whatever comes to us, we will defeat."

Nicole absorbed this. "Gina and I have never been happier."

"This is also true for Segun and me, but the instant anything goes awry, despite what my mother has said, we must tell them."

Nicole's eyelids grew heavy. She leaned over and laid her head in Sotonye's lap. "I feel so safe here."

Sotonye placed his hand gently on her head. "I will never let harm come to you, never."

Nicole climbed into Sotonye's lap, and then they slept.

***

As always, Regina awoke early. It was 5:45 a.m. She walked over to the sliding doors to see if Nicole was awake. The door was locked. She knocked. There was no answer. She phoned Nicole's room and office. No answer. Her next call was Segun's direct line.

"I have been expecting your call," Segun said. "Hold on for one moment." Segun was off for a few seconds and then returned. "Gina, I know the reason for your call. Sotonye was not at home this morning. I called the hospital. He had left hours earlier. On my way to the office, I drove by your hotel. My brother's car was relatively easy to spot in the parking area. Would you like to talk?"

"I'd really appreciate that, Segun."

"I'll dispatch a car to your hotel. I'll be awaiting you with breakfast at my office. Pick up a copy of this morning's newspaper to read on the way over. I guarantee you it will bring a smile to your lips."

***

In the lobby, Regina purchased the city newspaper. She laughed out loud at the half-page picture of her and Segun dancing at the club. "Industry King is King of the Dance Floor at the Grand Palm Nightclub." The Rolls Royce limo was waiting outside the door. By 7:00 a.m., Regina was walking into Segun's office. Everyone had seen the newspaper and seemed happy that Segun had enjoyed himself. Some employees smiled. Others applauded, while others created their own dance moves, all in good fun.

When Regina entered his office, her smile faded. Segun could tell she was worried. "Regina, I have come to a major life decision. I am going to sell Q.P.S. and become a professional dancer."

"Don't make me laugh, Segun."

Segun took her hand and led her to the table he had set up. "Let me feed you while we talk." Segun pulled back Regina's chair. She sat and Segun took the seat across from her. Segun reached over to pour her tea as she reached to pour his coffee.

"Are you bothered about Nicole and Sotonye being together?"

"I don't know for sure. I am so used to looking out for Nicole. In the world of business, few, if any, are Nicole's equals. In the world of romance, she is a babe in the woods. I can't think of a nicer man than Sotonye. But if a nice man breaks your heart, it's hard to recover."

"When Sotonye told me about the woman he had met at the airport, he acted like a schoolboy. I told him I'd never seen him act that way about a woman. Over the last three months, I have learned what an extraordinary person Nicole is. Yet I was concerned for Sotonye. He

291

seemed more passionate about her than she was about him. I was worried that it was he who was destined for heartbreak."

"We sound ridiculous, don't we?"

Segun smiled. "Amongst the four of us, I do not believe there is one year's difference in our ages. Yet you and I speak as if we were their parents."

"You and I were born old."

"For some reason, we think those two aren't smart enough to know how to fall in love."

"And if they did fall in love, it had to be approved by us."

"That's the crux of it, Regina. They did not ask our permission. What gall!"

Regina sipped her tea. "Do you know what I'd like to do?"

"What?"

"I'd like to take a walk in this morning air with my good friend, Segun Bada."

"I think that is a marvelous idea." Segun began to stand and grimaced softly.

"Are you okay?"

"Lately, I've been having some discomfort in my back." Regina told Segun to sit back down. She massaged his shoulders, and then she rubbed between his shoulder blades. Segun released a moan. "That is the spot, Regina. Your rubbing is relieving the ache."

"Segun, you've been feeling more than a little discomfort. Your muscles have knotted up. I can feel two lumps. Sotonye might need to examine them."

"If you tell Sotonye, he will have me in that hospital taking a million tests."

"Okay, I won't mention it, but I am going to check again in a week or so. If the inflammation does not subside, you have to tell him."

"If you keep rubbing, I'm positive the lumps will go away."

Regina laughed. "No way. Nicole's shown me not to rub on a Bada man too long."

Chapter 39

Regina and Nicole were wrapping Sotonye and Segun's gifts in Regina's hotel suite. Segun and Sotonye were planning a special Christmas Eve celebration. They were all spending the holidays at the Bada home.

Although Sotonye and Segun had traveled the world, they had never celebrated Christmas in the American tradition. Using pictures in a storybook from their childhood, they tried to recreate the American Christmas setting with a Christmas tree, ornaments, lights, and gifts. A wreath was hanging on the door. The stockings hung on the Christmas tree for lack of a fireplace or mantle.

This was the first year the Bada brothers would spend the holiday without their mother. Earlier in the day, they had called the Mayo Clinic. The nurse held the telephone to Nafisa's ear while they sang a song she used to sing to them as children. Although Nafisa was quiet, they were hopeful she heard them.

Regina and Nicole arrived at the Bada mansion around 9:00 p.m. and noticed the wreath on the door.

"Nicole, they're at it again."

"It's still working for me."

The men met the ladies at the door and walked them into the grand-room.

"This is like a storybook Christmas," Regina said. Sotonye and Segun laughed.

Nicole looked around. The way the house was decorated struck a too-familiar chord. Sotonye, Regina, and Segun all noticed Nicole's reaction.

"Is something wrong, Nicole?" Sotonye asked.

"This is the Christmas scene from the children's storybook *Donna and Modupe.*"

Segun and Sotonye stared at her, disbelieving.

"How do you know about *Donna and Modupe*?" Segun asked.

"My mother wrote the story when she was pregnant with me, and my father illustrated the book, finishing the etchings the day before I was born. It was my day-of-birth gift and it became a tradition to read it in our family every Christmas. *Donna and Modupe* was never published. How in the world do you two know the story?"

"Because we have the book," Sotonye said.

"That is impossible. I have the only copy of *Donna and Modupe*."

"Excuse me, I'll be back in a moment." Sotonye returned with the worn manuscript Joseph had given to Nafisa. The book was open to the Christmas scene.

"You two have almost duplicated the room," Regina said, looking at the book over Nicole's shoulder. "The only difference is that there is no fireplace."

"Our mother read it to us. It's the first book I remember," Segun said.

Nicole studied the cover page on typing paper. The title read *Donna and Modupe*. Under the title were the words "Seeds from the Same Tree." At the bottom of the page was typed "Written by Marion Johnson, Illustrated by Joseph Johnson." They all gathered around Nicole. She pointed to her parents' names.

"In a way," Regina said, "you three have known each other all of your lives. Do any of you know how this book came to the Bada home?"

"I only know it's my mother's," Segun said.

"Did your mother ever travel to the US?" Nicole asked.

"As far as I know, she never left Nigeria until I asked her to live in Botswana."

"Nicole, didn't your father travel overseas in the army?" Regina asked.

"Yes, but that was before my parents were married."

"Didn't you tell me your father remained in the Army Reserves for years? Wasn't he in some type of international division?"

"Yes, but he never left the country."

"Maybe he didn't have to leave. You've only mentioned three of your parents. We know for sure that Colonel Bada was involved in international affairs. Maybe he traveled to the United States for some type of military conference and met Joseph Johnson. He might have shared an evening at your home and heard Joseph or Marion reading the Christmas story to Nicole. It's possible the Johnsons gave him a manuscript, which he ultimately shared with his two sons when he returned to Nigeria."

"Everything you've said is plausible, Regina," Segun said.

"You'd realize the sense you're making, if you knew the story behind the story," Nicole said.

"All I know is I want someone to read the story to me!" Regina exclaimed.

They all sat on the sofa and Segun did the honors.

"Nicole's mother wrote a story within a story about the friendship that blossomed between a young African American girl, Donna, and an African boy, Modupe, after they heard a Christmas story read by Donna's father about a boy and girl their age who lived in the Motherland."

The boy and girl were talking under a tree near the beach when slave traders came to their village. The boy hid his girlfriend in the branches of a mighty tree. Then he showed himself to the slave traders so the traders would chase him. He was caught and transported to a slave ship, leaving his girlfriend and his homeland forever.

On the voyage, the boy found seeds stuck to his body from the tree where he had hidden his girlfriend. When he reached the shores of America, the boy planted the seeds.

As the years passed, the boy became a man and often snuck away from the plantation to visit the tree. There he reminded himself that it did not matter where he was planted. His girlfriend would always be a part of his heart, and he would always be a seed from the Motherland.

Donna and Modupe were so taken with the story that they promised each other that they would never forget that they too were seeds from the same tree.

Segun closed the book. "Well, Gina, what do you think of Donna and Modupe?"

"It's a wonderful story—ahead of its time."

"I haven't heard it for so long that it gave me chills," Nicole said.

"Hearing it as an adult gives it even greater significance. It's as if we were all destined to come together," Sotonye said.

"Everyone but me," interjected Regina.

"I am not so sure of that, Regina." Segun opened the book and asked Nicole and Sotonye to look at one of the drawings of the character Donna. "Look. Who is the first person who comes to mind?"

Nicole and Sotonye stared at the drawing. "Gina, Donna looks just like you did in the photo on Momma Emma's mantle!" Nicole said.

Regina glanced at the drawing. She didn't want to admit there was an uncanny resemblance.

"Now I know why I couldn't stop staring at you at our first meeting in my office. I kept saying to myself, how do I know this face?" Segun reflected.

"Are you saying we got this contract because of a character in a children's book?"

"I am not sure, Regina. It could have been a factor." All three focused on Regina.

She stood and straightened her dress. "I can live with that. I'm starving. Let's eat!"

They all laughed and headed for the dining room. After hours of good food and good company, they decided to turn in.

"You'd better get to sleep," Segun said as he and Sotonye showed Nicole and Regina to their rooms. "I am waking everyone up before sunrise. I saw a gift with my name on it. I can't wait eight hours to open it."

At 5:00 a.m., Segun was pounding on every door. "Merry Christmas! Wake up!"

Within half an hour, they were all assembled in the grand-room, exchanging gifts and sharing the wondrous day.

Chapter 40

Regina, Sotonye, Segun, and Nicole spent the three days after Christmas together driving through the different regions of Botswana. It was awe inspiring to view the wildlife in their natural habitat, but it was disconcerting to see the level of poverty and the prevalence of AIDS in the village where Sotonye provided free medical care for the poor.

Botswana was much better off than many of the countries in the Motherland. Segun was adamant that Q.P.S. remain in Africa and be controlled by Africans to prevent further poverty. In Segun's home office, there were blueprints for hospitals, schools, and industrial complexes. He had plans for Africa far into the twenty-first century. Sotonye was his staunchest supporter.

For the next ten years, forty percent of Q.P.S. profits had been earmarked to develop these projects. Out of the Bada brothers' personal earnings, they had already funded and built ten clinics and ten village schools. The people loved and honored them.

Nearly all Q.P.S. employees were from the villages. Schooled at the plant, they were taught their jobs and partook in continuous education as part of their terms of employment. In every nine-hour day of work, two hours were spent in the classroom. The Bada brothers never sought or accepted credit for this philanthropy. They viewed it, as Nafisa Bada had taught them, as their responsibility and privilege.

On the final day of their travels, the quartet drove far north to the place known as the Village of No Life, where Sotonye had brought Nafisa. Segun parked close to the Okavango River. For miles, they could see nothing but the charred, ashy remains of a great conflagration.

Regina sniffed the air. "Was this fire recent?"

"No. This village burned to the ground more than fifty years ago," Segun said.

"You can't be serious. The earth has not renewed itself at all. Time should have disintegrated these burnt wood chips. Am I the only one who smells the strong odor?"

"I smell it, Gina," Sotonye said. "That is what is so mysterious about this land. Nothing will return to the earth. People in neighboring villages tell the story of a demon setting the land on fire. They say nothing will grow here until the Blessed Children reclaim it."

Regina turned to Nicole. "Isn't this amazing?" But Regina found herself speaking to the wind. No one noticed that Nicole had wandered off into the rubble. They spotted her in the distance, picking up something off the ground.

Sotonye called out. "Nicole."

Without answering, Nicole continued her journey further into this raped and ravaged land. Unbeknownst to Nicole, she had begun walking in the footsteps of Kabaka and Hatshepsut.

Sotonye, Regina, and Segun all called out to Nicole. Still no answer. Without warning, Nicole broke into a rapid dash. She was running at breakneck speed. First Sotonye then Regina and Segun charged after her. All of Nicole's athleticism surged forth. Her distance and her pumping adrenalin had the others at a disadvantage. Sotonye ran like the wind, but it was not enough. Segun soon caught up with Sotonye and saw the panic on his face.

"Do not worry, my brother." Then, with an almost inhuman burst of speed, Segun shot like a missile through the desolate land. In a minute, he was running alongside Nicole. "What is wrong? Where are you going, Nicole?"

With fear in her eyes, she looked at Segun.

He called out to her. "*Nicole!* It's Segun! I will not harm you."

In a small clearing, Nicole came to a sudden halt and dropped to her knees to catch her breath. She cried hysterically as Segun knelt with her and placed his hand on her shoulder.

Rage swept across Nicole. She punched Segun with power she had never known, yet Segun was able to endure her force effortlessly.

"How could you do this? What kind of creature are you?"

Segun dodged the blows while he kept repeating, "It is I, Segun! Nicole, please! It's Segun!" Stammering and stuttering, Segun finally blurted out, "I could never harm you. I am… I am… your brother!"

With those words, Nicole's veil was lifted only to see Segun's painful expression. "Oh, Segun, I am so sorry!"

Segun released a sigh of relief. "All that matters is that you are all right."

They both collected themselves. Nicole noticed a small swatch of cloth on the ground, picked it up, and put it in her pocket.

In a few moments, Sotonye and Regina stood next to them. Nicole sprang to her feet and into Sotonye's arms. Sotonye held her tightly. "Whatever it was, you are safe now."

Segun rose to his feet.

"Thank you, Segun," Sotonye said.

Segun just smiled.

Regina finally caught her breath. "What just happened, Nicole?"

"Gina, the instant my foot touched this ground, the feverish beat of a drum pounded in my ears and horrible visions flashed before my eyes. I heard a baby crying. I saw a woman lying on the ground in a pool of blood with the baby in her arms. A winged man with a sword stood over the baby. I looked down at the infant and it had Sotonye's face. The winged man turned to me, and it was Segun. He handed the sword to me and said, 'Kill him.' I actually raised the sword.

"Suddenly, I realized I was running. I saw Segun running next to me, and I was afraid to look at him! My hallucination returned. There was a great fire blazing around a tree where a boy sat afraid on a branch. I tried to help the boy, but I couldn't get through the flames. The boy clung to a drum, covering it with his arms. Then the limb broke from the tree, sending the boy falling into a towering wall of fire. As he fell, he called out a word. He called out—"

"Kabaka!" Sotonye said.

"That's right! That is exactly the name he called out. How did you know that?"

Sotonye rubbed his forehead. "There were two names that old man Baba would say to me in private when I came to visit and we were alone. One was Kabaka, the other Hatshepsut. Sometimes, he would tell me, 'The demon thought he took the chosen infant after he killed Kabaka and Hatshepsut. But instead he took you.' I would tell Baba I was not born when the fire occurred. He would reply, 'You were there.'"

"Are you talking about the old man who died a few months ago?"

"Yes, I am, Gina."

"Hatshepsut was the name he called Nicole. Don't you remember, Nicole?"

"Yes. He called me Hatshepsut. And when he forced me to take the drum, he kept repeating the name Kabaka."

As the other three spoke, Segun stepped back a few paces. Regina noticed he was no longer next to her and glanced over her shoulder. Regina's heart dropped. Segun's head was bowed. "Segun, what is wrong?"

"There is nothing wrong. I am just winded from the run."

Regina placed her hands on each side of Segun's face, forcing him to look directly into her eyes. "Segun, for the first time since I have known you, you are not telling the truth. We are your family. With us, you are free to say what is on your mind and in your heart. Now, tell me what is troubling you."

"It hurts me to think I could be seen as someone so vicious and brutal. I knew nothing of the couple that died, the infant, the boy in the tree, or the old man and his drum. Yet what troubles me is I was not surprised that Nicole saw me as a demon. All of my life I have felt as if I have fought a demon inside me. I would only speak of this to my mother. I truly believe her love and kindness saved me."

Nicole put her arm through Segun's. "I've had doubts about myself too. About a darker side. But today, your words of love and kindness saved me from this nightmare. You came to rescue me, your sister. You brought me back to my senses. Segun, you must realize you are probably the most powerful man any of us has ever known. Yet in your life, you have used your power and vast knowledge to build, not to destroy. I could not be blessed with a finer brother than you."

Sotonye faced his brother, wondering about his mother's cautioning words about Segun. Should he fear his own brother because his brother feared himself? Sotonye thought not. In his heart, he could not believe it.

"I didn't know you felt that way, Segun. Why didn't you tell me? Maybe I could have helped."

"I didn't want you to worry."

Sotonye embraced Segun with a brother's love, wishing Segun to know he trusted him and would always be there for him.

Regina took Segun's hand. Nicole held Segun's arm and took Sotonye's hand, and they all walked out of the Village of No Life. They were the cement of humankind, a family.

***

The moment they drove away, life began again. In the spot where the children had embraced, grass forged upward through the charred earth.

In Nicole's hotel suite, under the table where her portrait sat, the skin of the drum began to expand and contract. The sound of its joyous beat echoed in the hallway. The spirits of Kabaka, Hatshepsut, Amin, the Elder, and the others of the village were finally free to leave their ashes.

Chapter 41

It was the morning of December 31. Segun was scheduled to return from Zimbabwe at 11:00 p.m., just in time to celebrate New Year's Eve at the Bada mansion.

Sotonye accompanied Nicole and Regina to the colorful marketplace for the afternoon. A little girl skipped up the road toward them.

"What a beautiful child," Nicole said.

The child held a lovely flower with petals of violet and gold in her hand.

"What can we do for you, pretty little one?" Sotonye asked.

The child with the angelic smile handed the flower to Regina.

"Down in the meadow, near the soft-shouldered road
There are people without shadows, eyes can't behold.
Soon, she'll walk among them and whisper kind words
And though you won't hear or see her, love still occurs,
As flowers for the young to smell in early May,
Dew drops that fall and cool the break of day.
She's been a love of yours a long time, you know.
She's been a love of yours, but it's her time to go.
Sunshine glows and dries your tears
She's happy where she goes, but will always be near.
She's been a love of yours a long time, you know.
She's been a love of yours, but it's her time to go."

Regina stooped down. The child placed her hands on Regina's face. Emotion bolted through Regina and tears fell from her eyes.

"Don't cry, sweetheart," the child told Regina. "Have you ever seen a happier child than I?" The child wrapped her arms around Regina and hugged her with all of her heart's warmth. "Regina, it is time for you to go home. You must pay your last respects. The gift now belongs to you. The gift was always intended for you!" The little girl skipped away, singing.

"Little girl, what is your name?" Regina called out.

"Regina Bovine, you know my name."

Then the child disappeared into the crowd.

Regina crossed her arms across her chest. "Goodbye, sweet Melinda." She released a sigh. "I must leave on the first plane out of here. My Aunt Melinda just left this earthly life."

They rushed back to the hotel. Regina telephoned New Orleans.

"Lucinda, don't explain. I already know Aunt Melinda has passed. Just write down the time my flight will arrive. When my mother returns, tell her I'm on my way."

As soon as Regina hung up the phone, Nicole told her she was going too. Sotonye secured a nonstop flight to New Orleans. Within twenty minutes of takeoff, Sotonye got them to the airport and rushed them through customs. Regina handed Sotonye a list of names and telephone numbers.

"Please tell Segun what has happened," Regina said, "and that I—"

"Don't worry, Gina. Segun will know the moment he returns."

Regina said goodbye and walked to the entrance gate.

"Take care of her," Sotonye said. "As soon as I contact Segun and the hospital, I will meet you in New Orleans. I think it's time for you to tell Regina about my sword. I want her to know her family here will be there to support her."

Nicole hugged Sotonye. "That's wonderful. It will mean so much to her. I love you."

"I love you too. I'll see you very soon." Nicole hurried to the jet.

***

At the airport, Segun walked toward his brother. "Where are Regina and Nicole?"

"Regina's Aunt Melinda died today. They flew to the States this afternoon."

"Regina spoke of her aunt with great affection. How badly has this affected her?"

"She wears her suit of armor. Inside, she is filled with sorrow."

303

"I must go to her."

"I knew you would feel that way. I have arranged a flight for us tomorrow evening."

On the way home, Segun asked Sotonye how Regina had learned of Melinda's death. Sotonye told Segun about the little girl.

"Sotonye, do you believe spirits can come to you?"

"I have witnessed birth and death. At birth, life's energy comes to your body. At death, life's energy or spirit leaves the body. I can only surmise if the spirit can enter and leave the physical body, it is boundless. What happened to Nicole in the Village of No Life and what happened to Regina at the marketplace were mystifying. There are no logical reasons for either to occur, but it's possible we are affected by these spirits."

Segun thought about this. "If that is our fate, it will be determined by our spirits. We are but the vessels they navigate."

***

Regina slept for nearly half the trip. Nicole nodded in and out, her thoughts on Regina's wellbeing. It was midnight when Regina's eyes opened. Slowly she rose to a sitting position and looked at her watch. "I can't believe I slept over ten hours."

"We both needed our rest before facing the New Year."

The pilot's voice came over the public address system. "Ladies and gentlemen, it is now midnight. I wish to extend to you all the hope of a happy, healthy, and prosperous New Year."

Regina and Nicole hugged. "Well, Gina, I always said, the way you start your New Year sets the tone for the entire year. Since we are above the clouds, I guess for us it means this year will be pretty much up in the air."

Less than ten hours later, the plane landed. No one was there to meet them. Regina assumed Lucinda had somehow botched the message. They went to claim their luggage, took their bags outside, and had the skycap flag down a taxi.

As they rode in from the airport, Regina looked perplexed. "What pyramid? What do you mean?"

"I didn't say anything, Gina."

"Sure you did. You just said, 'In the pyramid.' So, I'm asking, what's in the pyramid? And what pyramid are you talking about?"

304

"I swear, I did not say a word. I did not say anything about a pyramid."

Regina sounded rather agitated. "Nicole, I know your voice better than my own."

Nicole realized she was probably riding on an emotional rollercoaster. She held Regina's hand and they rode on in silence.

Twenty minutes later, the cab pulled in front of the house on Basin Street. Cars lined the block. There was absolutely nowhere to park. The cab driver asked if they knew Madam Bovine. Regina told him Melinda had been her great-aunt. He gave his deepest condolences and refused payment for the cab ride.

"Your aunt was one of the patron saints of Bourbon Street. The entire parish grieves her passing. Thank God Miss Emma came back home. Otherwise Madam Bovine's business would have become history. That surely would have been a crime and a shame."

"Emma is my mother."

The cab driver took off his cap. "Well, miss, I am proud to know you. I am sure you and your momma won't let Madam Bovine's life work falter." The cab driver carried their bags to the front door and then departed.

It looked like half of New Orleans was in the house. All had brought food, drink, and money. From the mayor to the cashier at the newspaper stand, everyone had been touched by Melinda and had a Melinda story. She had helped mothers with daycare money, teachers with extra money for student excursions. Melinda had even loaned the mortician the money to finish mortician's school. She had attended his graduation and forgiven his loan as a graduation gift. He refused to take one penny for Melinda's funeral. He had made all of the arrangements. He considered it an honor.

Emma was so busy trying to be the gracious hostess that she had not had a moment to grieve. Regina and Nicole tunneled their way to the kitchen. As expected, Lorraine and Lucinda were sitting idly at the table, drinking coffee and looking pitiful.

"Momma, we're here!"

Regina's voice startled Emma so she dropped the pan she was holding. "My baby! My baby!" Emma wrapped Regina in her arms with all of her might. "How did you get here? I called and left messages at your hotel. I was told you were on a trip. They didn't know when you would return."

Regina glared over her mother's shoulder at Lucinda, who turned her head in the other direction to avoid eye contact.

"You couldn't reach me because we were on our way here. I apologize if I worried you, Momma. I wasn't thinking. I should have called."

"That's all right, baby. I'm just glad you're here now. You said 'we'... did—"

At that moment, Nicole stepped up behind Emma. "I came too, Momma Emma. I'm so sorry."

"My baby, Nicole," Emma cried, holding Nicole in her arms. "You don't know how happy this makes me." Emma put her arms around both of their waists and announced to everyone in the room. "These are my daughters, Regina and Nicole." All in the room gave warm greetings.

As Regina walked over to the table to greet her cousins Lorraine and Lucinda, she overheard one of the guests talking to them. "Emma's daughters are gorgeous. They look like two movie stars."

"Gina is her real daughter," Lucinda said. "I don't know who that darker girl is."

The guest looked at Lucinda oddly.

Regina smiled at Lucinda and bent over and whispered in her ear. "With all due respect for your age, cousin, I am willing to forget how selfish, small minded, and self-centered you are. You are already on my shit list. If you cause any confusion or create any problems for my mother, you'll answer to me—and you'll be one sorry old broad." Regina stood back with a bright smile on her face.

"Lord, Regina, when you smile like that, you are the spitting image of Auntie. Lucinda, doesn't Gina remind you of Melinda?" Lorraine said.

Lucinda cautiously nodded her head. Regina thanked Lorraine for the compliment. Then she pointed at Lucinda, smiled, and walked back to Emma and Nicole. They all headed into the front room, picked up the luggage, and went upstairs.

"You girls will have to share a room. Lucinda and Lorraine are staying over tonight. I'm going to view the body in a few hours. If you feel up to it, I hope you two will come with me."

"Of course we will, Momma," Regina said. "We'll just unpack quickly. Then we'll be down. As a matter of fact, why don't you just have a seat and relax. We'll handle the guests."

"Thanks, darlin', but I know all of these folks. I've got to take care of all of Auntie's children now. Plus, I feel better when I keep busy."

Emma left the two in their room. She was halfway down the stairs when the front door flung open. Standing there blocking the sunlight was Big El.

"Oh, Elbert, Elbert, our momma is gone!" She raced down the stairs and into his arms.

Emma had shown no emotion and had not shed a tear. At the sight of El, all her pain burst forth. El held her safe and secure and surveyed the crowd.

"Good friends, we loved our Miss Melinda. I know, 'cause I am in a state of shock and confusion. But please, good people, her family needs this time for peace and quiet reflection."

The chief of police stood up. "El is right, folks. We are being thoughtless. Let's respect Miss Melinda's memory, her family, and her house. We can pay our proper respects tomorrow."

The people all agreed and filed out of the house in a quiet, orderly fashion. The police chief was the last to leave. He shook El's hand.

"I'm going to post an officer outside. He'll collect any gifts from well-wishers. Emma, I'm sorry. I just wasn't thinking."

Emma kissed the police chief on the cheek. "Simon, you didn't come here today as the police chief. You were the ten-year-old boy who could climb to the highest branch on the tree in Auntie's backyard."

"That's the pure truth, Emma. Time has really passed. Bye, y'all."

"Goodnight, Simon."

Regina and Nicole noticed the sudden quiet and came out of the bedroom. "Uncle Elbert!"

El looked up at Regina. "Come on down here, Sugarplum."

Emma released El and stood by his side as Regina wrapped her arms around El's neck. He lifted her off the ground the way he had since she was a little girl.

"Sugarplum, when did you get here?"

"Only a short time ago."

"You forgot. I could have come and got you. We've got to stick together. Miss Melinda would want it that way."

Nicole came down the stairs.

"Nicole, come here child," Emma said. "I want to introduce you to your Uncle Elbert."

El smiled. "I am so happy to finally meet you. I hear you are a firecracker of a businesswoman, and Emma was right, you are a beauty."

"You're very kind, Mr. Hunt. I really love your music."

"Why, thank you, darlin'. But you can forget that Mr. Hunt stuff. Call me El. Hell, you're part of the family. Call me Uncle Elbert."

"You know he likes you, Nicole. He isn't lying. Only family can call him Elbert," Emma said.

El laughed. "And that's just this family, my true family. My blood kinfolks call me Mr. Hunt."

Emma slapped El's arm. "Don't be bad, Elbert." El grinned and Emma continued. "I'll bet you all are starving. Come on into the kitchen. I'll cook up a late breakfast."

"No, you won't. Nicole and I will cook. You and Uncle Elbert sit in the living room and talk."

"Yes, ma'am. Come on, Emma, your daughter has spoken."

***

Emma sat next to El on the couch in the living room and laid her head on his chest. It was a matter of minutes before she fell asleep. El glanced up at the ceiling.

"Don't worry, Miss Melinda. Emma will never suffer another day in her life. You know I'd never lie to you, sweet Melinda."

Nicole was bringing out coffee and she overheard El's prayer. She took the coffee back into the kitchen quietly. She didn't want to disturb his private moment. Several minutes later, El walked through the kitchen door.

"I carried Emma up to her room and put her in her bed. She was out like a light. Sugarplum, do you know what she had planned for the rest of the day?"

"Momma wanted to view the body in a few hours."

"Well, we should let her sleep until then. She needs rest more than food right now."

***

The funeral director escorted Emma, El, Regina, and Nicole to Melinda and then left them alone. Melinda was beautiful, ageless and regal. She hardly appeared to be ninety-one years old.

Emma leaned over the casket and kissed her Auntie. Then she felt El trembling and guided him out the back door, where they sat on the back steps with arms around each other. Suddenly, El sprang to his feet, balled up his fists, and swung punches in the air.

"I never could pay her back. Never!"

"Elbert," Emma said from the steps, "I know what you are really fighting. Come to me."

El buried his face in Emma's lap and began wailing like a lost child.

Emma rubbed his head. "That's right, honey, let it out. Emma's going to take care of you."

Inside the funeral parlor, Regina and Nicole stood in front of Melinda. Regina reached into her blouse and pulled out the shield medallion. She held it in her left hand and placed her right hand on Melinda's chest. A halo of golden light ensconced both of their bodies. Regina released the medallion and grabbed Nicole's hand. Now the golden light engulfed all three. The light rose above them and gathered into a golden sphere. Its globe rose over Melinda's body and hovered. Then the golden ball of light levitated over Regina's head and rested there for a moment before it was gone.

"The power is yours now, Regina. Just as the little girl in the marketplace said it would be. There's something else I must tell you, even though I promised Sotonye I wouldn't. When the light came over me, it told me I must," Nicole said.

"What is it, Nicole?"

"Sotonye has a medallion in the shape of a sword. I am sure it is the mate to your medallion. His mother gave it to him. Now I am sure you and he have been selected. Together you have a mission. I believe it draws near."

***

They all returned to Melinda's house. El told Emma he had to take care of a few things at home. By 11:00 p.m., all were in bed except Regina. She sat on the sofa, trying to read a magazine. It was difficult to concentrate. She began to pace the floor. She spotted her mother's keys on the dresser and picked them up. A drive in the night air just might relax her.

It was around midnight when Regina pulled off in the van. She decided to go to the French Quarter. Two huge banners of purple and black were draped across Bourbon Street. Big El's pearl Cadillac was parked on the sidewalk in front of Melinda's shop. Regina unlocked the door and walked in. She noticed the light coming from under the door in Melinda's fortune-reading room. She walked toward the door and called out.

"Uncle Elbert, is that you?"

"Is that you, Sugarplum?"

"Yes, it is. Is it okay for me to come in?"

"Why sure, darlin'."

Regina opened the door, and there was El sitting in Melinda's chair. There was a fifth of Kentucky whiskey and a shot glass on the table.

"I'm glad to see you, Sugarplum. I went home, but I couldn't sleep."

"The same here, Uncle Elbert."

El poured himself another shot. "Miss Melinda gave me keys to the place when I was a teenager. She knew there was trouble in my house. She said, 'There might be some nights you'll need a place to come when you can't sleep.'" El swallowed the whiskey. "Believe me, Sugarplum, there were many such nights. My daddy spent his life blaming the world for his failures and mostly he blamed other races. He pulled my mother from the hills when she was just thirteen. When I was a baby, he hit her so badly she could bear no more children. Her life was such a nightmare. She died when I was seventeen. I often wonder why she was put on this earth."

"To give birth to the man who has impacted millions of lives through his music and kindness. Without her, there would be no Big El Hunt, and there would have been no one to watch over the Bovine family!"

"Thanks, Gina. You just reminded me to be grateful for how the Lord has blessed me. I sure wouldn't have had a chance to travel this earth without those two."

"At least you knew both of your parents. My mother was as good as, if not better than, two parents. But still I wonder what it would be like to have a father. I... never mind."

"Talk to me, don't be shy, Sugarplum."

"Well, Uncle Elbert, I used to pretend you were my real father. To tell the truth, I actually thought you were. I didn't believe the story about my mother and the soldier and the one-night stand. It doesn't sound like her. At this point in my life, I just want to know the truth. Who was my father? What really happened?"

El poured another shot, raised his glass as if he were about to make a silent toast, and then gulped down the liquor.

"You know, Sugarplum, always be careful for what you pray for. I asked to be given the chance to pay back a debt today, and now it's here." Big El cleared his throat, looking like he was trying to find the right words. "Before Melinda died, she made your mother promise to tell you the truth. Your mother felt she had waited too long and it had become too complicated. She asked me to tell you if you asked." He looked up. "Okay, Miss Melinda, help me do this right."

Big El got up and pulled his chair over next to Regina's. "Gina, let me start by saying when I first laid eyes on you, my love for you was automatic. To have a daughter like you would have been the privilege of my life."

"Then you're not my real father."

"No darlin', I'm not. Your father never knew your mother was pregnant. She fell in love with a decent man, a chivalrous man. I'm the one who pushed them together."

Big El explained about the disturbance in this very store so many years ago, his suggestion that the soldier accompany Emma to his Fourth of July concert, and what took place thereafter. "I know you might wonder how it was possible for them to fall in love in just two days, but in life, we have hundreds of rather meaningless days and can recall single days that have changed our lives. I hope I've made some kind of sense to you, Gina. You are the flower of two good seeds."

"You told the story beautifully, Uncle El, and I really do understand how it all happened. For the first time, I'm at peace, except for one thing. Who was he?"

El rubbed his face redder than it already was as he explained about the war, the soldier's life as a prisoner, and the woman he had been engaged to whom he had left behind and who thought he was dead. "Melinda had a vision that this woman was in grave danger and only he could save her. Miss Melinda told your father where to find his lost love. Although he loved your mother, he had to go." El delayed no more. "Your father's name was Joseph Johnson."

"Did you say Joseph Johnson?" Regina jumped up from her chair, shaking her head. "No! No! It's not true."

"Yes, Regina, it is true. Nicole's father is your father. I'm not sure if Nicole is Joseph's blood daughter. I never knew Nicole's mother. All I know is you actually favor Joseph Johnson. I don't see him anywhere in Nicole's face."

Regina flashed on the character Donna in *Donna and Modupe,* and she started feeling woozy. She flopped back down in her seat. Recollections began to piece together like chips in a mosaic design. Regina's reflection spiraled further back. *The tombstone sent a warning message to Joseph's children.*

El watched Regina as she struggled through this emotional quagmire.

Suddenly, Regina cupped her hands over her mouth and nose. "I am the daughter of his body, not Nicole! Oh my God! Nicole is the daughter of his choice!"

"I warned you, Sugarplum. Sometimes revealing the hidden truth doesn't resolve anything, but it always causes other truths to unfold. Will you tell Nicole?"

"How can I? What purpose would it serve? Who is her father?"

"I don't have those answers."

"Uncle Elbert, you answered the questions that have haunted me. I am proud to be Joseph Johnson's daughter. But Nicole is also his daughter. It would have to be a matter of life or death before she'd hear otherwise from me. Promise me this will remain our secret."

"You have my word, Sugarplum." El stood and extended his hand to Regina. "Come on, it's time for us to go. This day is over."

They switched off the lights, locked the doors, and left their secret within the walls of Madam Bovine's House of Mystery.

Chapter 42

The next morning, a traditional New Orleans funeral procession paraded down Bourbon Street. Tambourines jingled and people danced to celebrate the new life of Madam Bovine. The hearse finally led the seemingly endless train of cars into the cemetery.

The crowd of mourners gathered in front of Emma, and she recited a poem of farewell to her dear aunt. With her final words, Big El wiped his eyes and lifted his trumpet to play his favorite composition, "My Sweet Melinda." Nicole put her arm around Regina. They closed their eyes and swayed to the beautiful notes resonating in the air.

Regina felt gentle kisses on both sides of her face. When she opened her eyes, Segun and Sotonye stood before her. "You came all the way here just for me? You two are so wonderful!"

"We'll always be here for you," Segun said.

The four stood arm in arm, listening to El's song.

Lucinda poked Lorraine's arm. "Look at Gina hanging on that man. It's disgraceful."

Lorraine glared at her sister. "Lucinda, for years I've been trying to figure out which one was the bigger damn fool, you or our mother." Lorraine left her sister to comfort and be comforted by Emma. "I'm your sister now. The foolishness ends today."

Emma hugged Lorraine, then softly rocked from side to side with the music.

***

Emma, Lorraine, and El stood at the gravesite until the last moment. Finally, they walked through the assembly. Regina hugged her mother, and Nicole guided Segun and Sotonye to meet them.

"Segun, Sotonye, this is my mother, Emma Bovine."

"It is an honor to meet you," Segun said. "Please accept my sincerest condolences."

"Thank you, Segun. Tell me, young man, are you the genius Gina claims you to be?"

"Miss Bovine, my brother had to help dress me this morning. You be the judge."

"I understand. This morning, Nicole and Regina had to dress me too!"

Sotonye and Segun escorted Emma to the limousine. Regina and Nicole were left to follow.

"How did Momma end up with our men?" Regina asked.

"When you got it, you got it," Nicole replied.

***

The Bovine home was full of friends and family. The moment Emma walked through the door, she was surrounded by well-wishers.

"Regina," Nicole said, "let's introduce Segun and Sotonye to your uncle."

Nicole led them to Big El's table.

"Sotonye and Segun Bada, I'd like you to meet Regina's Uncle El."

El stood to shake Sotonye's hand.

Segun stood by staring intently at Big El. "You are Regina's uncle?"

"Yes, I am."

Segun enthusiastically shook El's hand with both of his. "Mr. Hunt, I am one of your biggest fans. Not only do I have every one of your albums, I brought a copy of your first album, *Bourbon Street,* with me. I attended your concerts for African Relief in New York and in Ethiopia. When I heard you play at the service, I thought it was very giving of you to salute a friend. I cannot believe Gina did not tell me her uncle was Big El Hunt. I am so excited to meet you."

Regina hugged El. "I didn't have a chance." She looked at Segun. "You continually surprise me, Segun."

Big El smiled. "I believe my niece is saying she might have underestimated you."

"As you wrote on the cover of your last album, 'All of God's children have a song to sing. And all God's children to this earth beauty bring.'"

"You really are a fan. Thank you, Segun."

314

By evening, all of the guests had left, and Nicole, Segun, Sotonye, and Regina sat around the dining room table discussing their plans. Regina was going to stay a few more days in New Orleans to help Emma tie up any loose ends. Segun was headed for Chicago to reschedule the Golden Guard presentation for later in the month. Nicole told Segun to stay at her house and gave him the keys. Sotonye was on his way to the Mayo Clinic to check the results of new tests he had run on his mother. Nicole decided to accompany him. They would all meet in Chicago at Nicole's on January 7th.

Emma came in from the front porch. "Segun, Sotonye, if you don't have a hotel room, you might as well stay here tonight. We've got plenty of room."

The brothers agreed to stay. Everyone decided to retire early. El wished them all a safe trip and said goodnight. Emma walked El to the door.

At 5:30 a.m., Regina was in the kitchen preparing breakfast. The aroma floated up the stairs. In minutes, Segun, Emma, Sotonye, and Nicole filed into the kitchen. By 6:00 a.m. they were all eating. After breakfast, Segun and Regina spent a last few moments on the porch.

"Regina, can you come to Chicago a few days before Sotonye and Nicole so we can spend some time alone together?"

"I wondered if you would ever ask. I'll call you at Nicole's Sunday morning to let you know when my flight will arrive."

Sotonye passed by. "Segun, why do you have that ridiculous smile on your face?"

"Do you think you are the only Bada who can be happy?" Regina said.

She walked them to the car, and Emma joined them. She handed Segun one of Big El's original albums. "Elbert told me to give this to you before you left."

On the cover El had written a note. *To Segun. What you've done for my Sugarplum has made Big El Hunt one of your biggest fans. You're a special man. Your friend, El.*

"I will treasure this album. Please thank him for me." Segun climbed into the back seat. Nicole and Sotonye sat up front. Emma and Regina waved as they drove off.

"What do you think of the Bada brothers, Momma?"

315

"They are everything you said they were and more. You know, Gina," Emma replied as they walked back to the house, "Sotonye reminds me of someone. The way he tilts his head, his eyes, and his smile are so familiar."

Regina did not respond to her mother's observation. She was distracted by a voice in her head. *In the pyramid, in the pyramid.*

"What pyramid?" Regina said out loud.

"What did you say?"

"Nothing, Momma. I was talking to myself."

***

Regina joined all of her family around the dining table, where Melinda's lawyer was sitting at the table's head. She glanced at Emma, Lorraine, Lucinda, and Elbert. They were all waiting for the reading of Melinda's last will and testament. Before the lawyer officially opened the proceedings, he asked the family members if they wished to make any statements.

Regina noticed her mother's surprise when Lorraine slowly rose out of her chair. Emma squeezed her hand as if to say, *I have no idea what she's going to say, but don't be offended.*

"I am now the oldest living Bovine," Lorraine began. "I've never acted the role of the oldest. I am really ashamed of that. I'm sure none of you even know how we got the name Bovine. This name we hold onto so dearly is symbolic of our ancestry. Bovine are cows, bulls, and steers. We were bred like human cattle! Too African to be white and too white to be African."

Regina had never heard anyone in her family talk this way, especially her mother. *Cattle!* She thought irritably. *What is she talking about?*

"Nine months after the Emancipation Proclamation," Lorraine continued, "Master's last bovine was born, Grandpa Russell. He retained the Bovine name as a reminder to us to always fight for our freedom. He insisted we keep our spirit free, even though he knew an evil master would challenge us every day."

Regina squeezed her mother's hand at the end of that sentence, surprised that her Aunt Lorraine knew anything about Blue.

"There was this folklore about great-aunts of the Elders of the Motherland. They foretold that Blessed Children would one day help us

316

destroy that evil master once and for all. Until that day, we might think we were free, but we would not be. Only when our spirit prevails would we truly understand freedom, and then, Grandpa Russell said, we must cast aside the Bovine name forever."

Emma responded in kind, shocked that Lorraine was privy to the identity of the Ancient Oracles.

"He didn't realize," Lorraine continued, "that being called Bovine was like wearing a yoke around our necks. Our ancestors had fought for their freedom. Why should they as free people be called a slave metaphor every day of their lives? They should have been rejoicing and embrace a new life of freedom and calling themselves anything but Bovine, no matter what the folklore foretold."

"Lorraine, I never knew that you felt that way," Lucinda said with tears in her eyes.

"I didn't either," Emma said emotionally. "I thought…"

"I'm sorry I've been so unkind to you, Emma!" Lucinda said, hugging her. "I've always been insecure, and I've always covered it up with arrogance."

Regina was amazed by these admissions and surprised Lorraine knew anything of the Twin Oracles and the Demon Blue. She watched her mother embrace her aunts. They had been through a history which had paved a way for her to be free of some of their pain. She felt closer to her aunts than she ever had and eagerly joined in, happy to see her mother so happy she was finally appreciated.

El sat and watched the mending of the spirit of the Bovine family.

He closed his eyes and nodded his head. *My sweet Melinda.*

***

An hour later, Regina took her mother aside and held her hand in a quiet moment.

"Momma, since this is a day for our family to heal," Regina said, "I want you to know that I understand why you never said anything about Joseph Johnson."

Emma had tears in her eyes. "Thank you, my daughter."

Regina held her mother. "Since Nicole and I met, you have known who she was and you have treated her with a mother's love. Oh Momma! What a life you have had! You left your world to allow Big El

317

to pursue his dreams and your world was left by the man of your dreams."

Emma regained her composure. "I have so much to share with you now. After your presentation in Chicago, I want you and Nicole to visit me here, and we will talk about everything. Just promise me you will choose the right time to tell Nicole about you being sisters."

"I promise, Momma. You think of everything."

Chapter 43

Segun met with Futrob's board of directors in Chicago to discuss details for the debut of the Golden Guard in the United States. Nicole and Regina had already begun the marketing campaign, but there were materials that needed to be transported and organized. They had to break down and calculate wind and temperature variations. Exact measurements were required for the exhibition. They still needed the rest of their staff.

On the night of January 31, the Sears Tower, the tallest building in the world, would be locked behind the Golden Guard. It would be one of the most spectacular demonstrations ever seen. Isaac Embel would supervise the production. Q.P.S. would be responsible for all installations, calibrations, and controls. Segun spent weeks designing for the minutest detail. The margin for minor error was .00002%. The Q.P.S. team would arrive on January 20th to begin construction.

Futrob would be responsible for media, transportation, and living accommodations for Q.P.S. staff. After five grueling hours, the meeting ended. All assignment completion dates were nonnegotiable.

***

An hour later, Segun drove the rented van up to Nicole's house. Once inside, he took himself on a short tour.

We have very similar tastes. She has an eye for detail.

At the stairs, he stopped before the Horus Crystal and leaned over to examine it closer. When he saw his reflection in the globe, his skin appeared to have a tinge of blue.

Must be the lighting. Segun chuckled. *Leave it to Nicole to have something unique.*

His calls were forwarded to Nicole's home number. The airport had telephoned to inform Segun that his crate had arrived. He decided he had better go get it. Before Gina arrived, he wanted to get some work done.

***

When Segun returned from the airport early Saturday morning, he called Isaac Embel's home in Botswana. Isaac answered, happy to hear Segun's voice. Everything was set. Segun updated Isaac on the project. Both men were pleased.

Segun examined Nicole's photos on the mantle. *What handsome parents you have, Nicole. You and your mother could be twins. And your father looks so familiar to me.*

Thoughts of his own mother came to his mind, and he recalled the only time he had gone against Nafisa's wishes. He had been twenty-three and had his sights set on MIT and IIT to get his PhD in engineering. Segun had never seen his mother so vehemently opposed to his ideas. Finally, they came to an understanding that he would interview at a variety of schools.

His first interview was in Chicago, July 13, 1983. The chancellor of the University of Chicago had read about the young genius from Nigeria. Segun attended his interview, and afterwards, the chancellor invited Segun to an awards dinner to be held in honor of the most prominent African American businessmen and women in the city. The chancellor felt the university's association with this group would help sway Segun's decision.

The dinner was being held at the Merchandise Mart. Segun was impressed with the collaboration between African American businesses. In Europe and in Africa, he had been led to expect otherwise. The chancellor introduced him to business giants, publishers, politicians, media moguls, professional athletes, and movie stars.

Ultimately, Segun needed a break and escaped to the balcony. His thoughts had wandered back home to his mother when a voice interrupted his musing.

"The stars are really brilliant tonight. I haven't seen such a light show for many years. Tonight is no ordinary night." One of the businessmen Segun had met before dinner walked over to the railing. "What do you think of our little group?"

"To be honest, sir, I was equally inspired and astonished. Most of my life I have been led to believe Blacks in America lacked education, refinement, self-direction, and motivation. They were a people freed from slavery, but still shackled in their own minds. I'm happy I reserved my opinions until I had proof."

"Believe me, son, those lies were intentional and designed to keep us separated as a people. It's called racism. One of the main reasons my wife and I formed this group of African American business people is to dispel many of the lies created by racism. It's a well-calculated plan designed to divide people which leads people to distrust each other and to create self-doubt. Ultimately, self-hatred kicks in, and people turn it into a self-imposed slavery."

"My mother always says, 'Anyone can be enslaved. Freedom has to be earned and defended.'"

"You are very wise for your age. Your mother must be very proud of you." The man paused. "But I see something else is on your mind."

Segun turned back to the starry sky. His expression saddened. "It's funny you should say that. I was thinking of my mother. That's why I'm out here."

"Is your mother ill?"

"No. She and I had a disagreement before I left for the United States. I have never gone contrary to her wishes. But this time I made commitments without her blessings."

"Would you like some free advice from a man who is also an overprotective parent with a child about your age?"

"That might be helpful."

"Believe me, what you're going through is not unusual. The rest of the world may see you as a young man with a brilliant future. Yet, although you may be a strong and powerful man, in your mother's eyes and heart, you are the baby she carried, loved, and protected." The man placed his hand on Segun's arm and pointed to the sky. "Son, you are as limitless as this great expanse before you. Look around. Everything God did not create was a vision, an idea in someone's mind. They took that vision and formed it into a reality. With a mind like yours, who knows what you will do to improve the world. Reach out and capture the sun's rays. Build a fortress of light that shines for all to see."

Segun felt great comfort and inspiration from the man's words. "Your children are fortunate to have a father such as you. I thank you. I feel so much better now."

"You're more than welcome. When I was your age, I went after my dreams. Even during the worst of times, I never gave up. I give thanks every day to the people who traveled the road before me. Once you start doing what you were put on this earth to do, everything and everyone you need will come to you. By the way, what is your name?"

"Segun Bada," the young man said. "And yours?"

Segun watched as the man tried to find his voice. "I am Joseph Johnson. It's very nice to meet you, Segun. Are you an only child?"

"My brother, Sotonye, sometimes accuses me of that!" he laughed. "He thinks I get away with murder."

"Is your mother an artist?"

"Why yes! Nafisa Bada. Do you know her work?"

Joseph choked, and Segun rushed to find him a glass of water while Joseph steadied himself at the railing.

***

My God, Joseph thought as he sipped the water Segun had brought to him. *This is the baby boy that Nafisa took with her those many years ago!*

"Are you better, Mr. Johnson?"

Segun showed such concern that Joseph forgot about himself for the moment and concentrated on the young man.

"I'm just fine, Segun. Now, where were we? Oh yes. Bada is a name I would not forget. Yes, I know of your mother's art. She is very talented."

Segun began talking about his mother's work, but Joseph was lost in thought. What had Nafisa said as they departed? "These children cannot be raised together. It is far too dangerous. Take your daughter back across the ocean. The boy will remain here. I will be his mother." Joseph cautioned himself. He was very taken with Segun, but he had to be careful. Not only for Segun, but also for his beautiful Nicole.

Joseph guided Segun back into the ballroom. A member of the staff sought out Segun to let him know that the chancellor had looked everywhere for him and had just left, thinking Segun had already returned to his apartment.

"I feel responsible," Joseph said. "Let me drive you back to the campus. I insist. It's no trouble."

Joseph introduced Segun to Marion and explained the situation.

322

"Of course you must drive him, Joseph. I will be fine until you return. It is very nice to meet you, Segun. Are you in Chicago for long?"

"I haven't yet decided, Mrs. Johnson."

"Joseph will give you our phone number. You must come to dinner."

"Thank you for the invitation, Mrs. Johnson."

A few minutes later, Joseph and Segun were driving toward the campus. Segun talked about his plans for the future, after he received his PhD.

"Segun, I'm going to ask you a question I was asked when I first started my business. Maybe it will put everything in perspective. What is the only reason to go into business?"

"That's easy. Success, of course."

"That's not the answer."

Segun made several attempts. None were correct. "I can't think of another thing."

"The reason for having a business is the continuance of that business. When you start your business, plan it and develop it to have a self-perpetuating life. All your goals only come to fruition if your business continues to thrive."

Segun looked at him. "I'll never forget what you just taught me."

They pulled in front of the campus apartments. As Segun was opening the door, Joseph reached into his pocket for a business card. "Here. If you decide to come back to Chicago, call me. But there is a professor at MIT who teaches advanced courses in quantum engineering. He is the best in the world. His name is Charles Bachar. I put his name on the back of the card. I was one of his assistants when I was in the army. He has the information you need." Joseph smiled. "You are gifted. You are free to go where your dreams take you. You made the free choice to come here. But when you get up to your apartment, pick up the phone, call your mother, and tell her you love her."

"I will do just that, sir. How can I thank you?"

"Tell your mother I was so happy to meet her son. Will you do that for me?"

Something in Joseph's voice caught his attention. "Of course I will, sir. I'll quote you."

Joseph noticed Segun's curious look and wondered if Segun sensed the importance of the message he wanted conveyed to Nafisa. "Now get out of here," he said playfully. "My wife and I have a plane to catch. We are going to surprise our daughter, Nicole. Tomorrow is her birthday!"

***

Segun snapped out of his daydream. He reached into his pocket and took out his wallet. The card was still in it. *Johnson's Construction Company, Owner and President, Joseph Johnson.* Segun turned over the card. *Charles Bachar, MIT.* Segun stared at the picture of Joseph and Nicole again. Nicole was his daughter!

Joseph Johnson, it was you! You changed my life. My God, you're Nicole's father. That's where my favorite quote came from, and Regina's, too. A sudden thought changed his mood. He wondered if Joseph knew that Charles tried to influence him to focus on military contracts and weaponry with his inventions. He doubted it. Joseph was a man for humanity, not destruction.

The events and revelations of the last five days finally took their toll on Segun. He fell sound asleep on Nicole's sofa, holding the picture of Joseph Johnson in his hand.

***

It was nearly 5:00 p.m. when Sotonye's and Nicole's flight landed in Rochester, Minnesota. They rented a car and headed straight to the Mayo Clinic.

"Sotonye, for some reason, I believe your mother is aware of what's going on around her. "

"I feel the same way. There is no neurological explanation for her condition. I have a team of leading psychiatrists working on a diagnosis, too. I think I've lost all objectivity. All I can see is my vibrant mother lying lifelessly in a bed. I can barely handle it. Poor Segun cannot accept it at all. That is why I try not to pressure him too much about visiting her. But I feel pressured. Segun believes with his heart and soul that I will find the solution, but it's been ten months and I don't have the answer. Why?"

"Don't do this to yourself. The answer will come."

Nicole followed Sotonye into Nafisa's hospital room. He placed his hand on Nafisa's shoulder and kissed her forehead. "How are you this day, my mother?" Sotonye studied the chart. "I see no change. You must have really been tired to sleep so long, Mother. I brought someone with me to visit you. Her name is Nicole."

Sotonye reached out his hand.

Nicole came up beside him and stared at Nafisa's face. She was slightly taken aback. Nafisa was like a tiny flower. Her face was endearing with character. Nicole could only think of her own mother, Marion, when she gazed upon Nafisa Bada.

"Hello, Mother Nafisa. I am Nicole. You are so beautiful. I must tell you the truth, I love your son, Sotonye. I hope you approve. You have raised two of the finest men I have ever known. I can imagine how proud you must be of them."

Sotonye put his arm around Nicole. "Mother, I love Nicole. I know you will love her too."

Nafisa lay motionless. Sotonye pulled her quilt up to cover her shoulders.

"This is the most magnificent quilt I have ever seen," Nicole said.

"My mother has had it all of her life. Sometimes, I think it is what has kept her alive."

Nicole noticed that a triangular swatch was missing from the center of the quilt.

"Sotonye, the day we went to the Village of No Life, I noticed a triangular piece of fabric on the ground. I thought it was odd because everything else was completely scorched, so I picked it up. I was going to sew it into my next quilt. But I swear it looks as if it would fit perfectly into that blank space in the center of your mother's quilt. I think I have it in my travel sewing kit at your apartment. I'll bring it here tomorrow."

As soon as they returned to the apartment, Sotonye took off his coat, walked into the bedroom, flopped across the bed, and fell into a deep sleep. Nicole took off his shoes and covered him up.

She went in search of her sewing bag and found the triangular piece of cloth from the Village of No Life. She took a blanket into the living room and sat on the sofa. She held up the small piece of cloth and examined it closely. It would fit perfectly into Nafisa's quilt.

Nicole fell asleep clutching the fabric in her hand. She dreamed she was lying on her back watching trees whisk by. A man was carrying her bloody body and running at a furious pace while she held the perfect baby daughter of the Motherland in a quilt. The glowing aura of the baby and her goodness and loving strength touched her heart.

Suddenly Nicole heard herself calling out. "Kabaka, stop!"

With those words, Nicole's dream transported her to a thatched hut. A faceless man with no shirt was lying on a cot of straw, writhing in pain. His back was turned towards her revealing a hideous *SOS* brand. When he finally rolled over, she gasped.

"Daddy, Daddy!" she screamed. Still she was unable to move.

A woman wrapped in Nafisa's quilt walked toward the cot where her father lay. She opened the quilt and lay on top of her father. Nicole could see the impression of their two bodies cocooned in the quilt. A hand reached out from under the quilt, pulling the blanket back and away. Completely nude, Sotonye emerged wearing the sword medallion. Nicole then realized she was also naked. Sotonye pulled Nicole to him and the quilt wrapped itself around them.

Abruptly her dream changed course and she and Sotonye stood on a snowcapped mountain. An icy wind pierced the air. Sotonye stepped away from Nicole. The quilt remained around her shoulders. Sotonye thrust his arm forward and, with an open hand, presented the vast world below to Nicole.

"Behold your Motherland, every tribe, every nation, every child born and every child waiting for birth beseeches you. What destiny have you selected? Be you the future Daughter of Blue or be you Daughter of The Freedom Code?"

Suddenly, Nicole stood alone. Over the ridge, four tiny silhouettes approached her. At a distance, they appeared to be holding hands, but as they drew closer, Nicole realized they were toddlers shackled together. The children were of Asian, Middle Eastern, European, and African descent. If one stumbled, the others would help. They had walked to the edge of the frozen cliff. They stood there, not knowing which way to walk.

Nicole fell to her knees to look into their worn faces, only to discover they were blind.

The first child spoke. "You must make the decision."

The second child spoke. "Will you break the chain that enslaves us all?"

The third child spoke. "Soon we will all fall crashing to our doom."

The fourth child spoke. "The decision is yours. Will you lead us from our darkness?"

In unison, they spoke. "We are the children! *What shall be our future?*"

The sounds of their voices created a vibrating echo, and the ground beneath them began to tremble. The tiny parcel of earth between Nicole and the children began to crack and separate. If one child lost footing, the chain that bound them would drag them all over the side. If Nicole reached out to them, her life could be in peril.

"What am I going to do?" Nicole cried out.

Nicole closed her eyes, bowed her head, and clamped her hands over her temples. Then the moment of her revivification came. She raised her head, opened her eyes, flung her arms and her hands to the sky.

"I am daughter of The Freedom Code!"

But the children had vanished.

Gradually her vision cleared, and she found herself on the sofa in Sotonye's apartment. Although disoriented, she sat up straight. An uncomfortable electric tingling was pricking her hand. Slowly, she opened her clenched fist, discovering the triangular cloth. She put the cloth back into the kit and into her purse. Tomorrow she would have to deal with this.

She got into bed, laid her head on Sotonye's chest, and fell asleep.

***

The next day, Sotonye and Nicole returned to the Mayo Clinic. Sotonye was meeting with the specialist working on his mother's case. Nicole sat next to Nafisa's bed. Softly she hummed spirituals that Marion used to sing to her as a child.

Nicole felt comfortable sitting with Nafisa. Somehow it made it easier for her to reexamine last night's dream, which she would not discuss with Sotonye until she had made sense of it.

Nicole took the triangular cloth out of the sewing kit, leaned over Nafisa's bed, and laid the triangle in the vacant spot. The triangle fit perfectly into the space. She threaded her quilter's needle, stood over Nafisa, and gently lifted the center of the quilt to reattach the triangle.

To Nicole's amazement, the point of her needle could not penetrate the fiber of the quilt. After several attempts, she reached over to remove the triangle. When she tried to lift it, the quilt raised up. The triangle had mended itself back into the quilt. The seams connecting the triangular swatch were exact and binding.

How did this happen?

Nicole walked to the foot of the bed to view the quilt from a different perspective. At that moment, Sotonye entered the room.

"What are you staring at, Nicole?"

"I placed the piece of cloth I found into the empty spot in your mother's quilt. Before I could sew it, it mended itself. Come, take a look at it."

"All of my life I have seen this quilt," Sotonye said, brushing the fabric with his hand, "but with that triangle in the middle now, I actually see a picture."

"What do you see?"

"The center now appears to be a pyramid. It sits on a green circle with specks of colors dancing through it. That means the pyramid is not in an arid desert. It stands on an oasis. The arrows that lead from the oasis appear to be roads. Each road sprouts into several new roads. On the sides of every road there are pictures and symbols of the history of those that traveled these roads. Nicole, the quilt is a map! This quilt is more ancient than I ever imagined. The map depicts the earliest travels of our people. A journey that began from a pyramid. This concept is a complete paradox. The inscription below the pyramid translates to 'The Blessed Children chose freedom.'"

"What do you mean?"

"A pyramid is a tomb!"

"Sotonye, pyramids were houses of new life. Could it be possible that Blue is using a pyramid for his new world order?"

"At this moment, a thousand questions race through my mind. The pieces of a puzzle are coming together, and I am frightened by the picture that is forming."

"What is going on in your mind, Sotonye? Tell me!"

Sotonye grabbed Nicole, bending her backwards and off balance. "Why are you here? What brought you here? Who are you? Who was your father? What does he have to do with my family?"

"Sotonye, you're scaring me!"

"Have you told me everything, Nicole? I must be prepared for whatever is to come. I can protect no one if I do not understand what or whom I'm about to face."

"I told you everything our first night together in my hotel room. That's the truth. Please stop looking at me as if I am some kind of monster. I could never do anything to harm you or your family. Sotonye, Sotonye, I love you. You must believe that. You must!"

Sotonye stared deeply into Nicole's eyes. Slowly his angry fervor dissipated. He released her arms. "It is clear to me that the reason you and Gina are here has very little to do with Q.P.S.," Sotonye said. "We were brought together for reasons that I don't understand."

Nicole hesitated. "I had a dream last night I feel compelled to tell you."

After Nicole had told her dream, Sotonye looked dazed and disoriented.

"I don't know who our father is," Sotonye blurted out. "With all of my resources, I have never found a history of Colonel Segun Bada, Senior—not a picture, not a trace. Segun and I hardly resemble each other. Years ago, I ran a DNA test on Segun and me. I told Segun the tests were a part of his routine checkup. Nafisa is my mother, but not Segun's. We don't have the same father, either.

"I love my mother and brother far too much to ever let them know what I know. I would never allow them to lose dignity or feel ashamed. They didn't tell me for a reason. Nicole, you do not seem to understand what this could mean as far as you and I are concerned."

"I'm sorry, Sotonye, I don't see a connection between you and me."

"Remember Christmas Eve?" Sotonye asked, "And the theory Regina created of why we had the Christmas book? I went along, but I knew it was wrong. Your parents owned one of my mother's earliest sculptures. How did they get it? My mother just started exporting to the US fifteen years ago. My father never existed. This means that one or both of your parents knew my mother. Somehow, there is a relationship between my mother and your mother or there is a relationship between my mother and your father. The one human being alive who can tell us the truth lies before us in a coma. Unless your dream was not a dream and your mother is alive"

Nicole wasn't listening to him. Segments of the dream she had just told Sotonye flashed in her mind. "Oh my God, what have we done? The woman who lay down with my father was your mother, Sotonye! They disappeared and you appeared."

Sotonye unlocked a cabinet against the wall. He removed a swab and airtight container and took a sample of Nicole's saliva for DNA. He also took a sample of her blood. All the material was sent to the lab on a rush.

Sotonye and Nicole sat in silence waiting for the blood test results. The DNA would take a week.

Nicole looked over at Nafisa, and suddenly she was on her feet, staring again at the quilt.

"Sotonye, look!"

Sotonye looked at the quilt where Nicole was pointing. "That's an ancient script that my mother taught me. It's as though it's writing itself over the pyramid!"

"Can you read it?"

"The Blessed Children will face the children of Blue to determine the fate of all of African descents. The Blessed Children are two, but the choice can make them four." Sotonye stared at Nicole.

A nurse interrupted them and handed the results to Sotonye, then left. He carefully studied the findings.

"Your blood type is AB negative, the rarest blood type in the world. 'Blood of the gods.' I have only tested one other person with it."

"Do you remember who it was?"

"I certainly do. The person whose blood matches yours exactly is our brother, Segun!"

***

Brrring, brrring, brrring, brrring, brrring, brrring.

By the sixth ring, Segun awakened and answered the telephone. "Hello."

"Hello back to you. From the sound of that voice, I just woke someone up."

"Regina, is that you?"

"I knew all this traveling would catch up with you."

"Correct as usual. I hear noises in the background. Where are you calling from?"

"I'm at the airport in New Orleans. My flight to Chicago has been delayed. A storm is blowing over. It might be several hours. I don't know what time it will take off. "

"If the weather does not improve, Gina, I don't want you to fly at all."

Regina laughed. "Segun, I didn't know you cared."

Segun did not change the seriousness of his tone. "Oh yes, you do."

"I promise I won't fly if there is any danger."

"Thank you."

"If I have to schedule another flight, I'll call you from here in about four hours. All right?"

"That's perfect. I will wait for your call."

Segun was revitalized after his long slumber. Using some of the contents from the crate, he prepared a surprise for Regina's arrival. At 10:00 p.m., Regina called from a Yellow cab on her cell phone as she was leaving Chicago's O'Hare Airport. Segun asked if she was hungry. Regina told him she was famished. As soon as they hung up, Segun called Soul Queen and ordered dinner.

***

The cab driver carried Regina's bags to the front door. She gave him a generous tip. When he drove away, she rang the doorbell. There was no answer. She turned the knob and the door opened. When she entered, the foyer was pitch black. She assumed Segun had gone for food.

I'm going to have to remind Segun he isn't at home. He can't leave doors unlocked.

Then the lights popped on and Regina jumped. Segun stood at the top of the staircase.

"Regina Bovine, welcome. I have prepared a special greeting party for you. Please be seated on the throne that awaits you at the bottom of these stairs."

"You scared me to death!" Regina laughed. "What are you up to?"

Segun laughed as well. "I can't divulge that information. Please take your throne."

331

Regina found one of Nicole's armed dining room chairs sitting by the stairs. Attached to the arms, legs, and back of the chair were looped straps, the type used to hoist cargo. "I don't know what you've got in mind here, Mr. Bada. If something happens to Nicole's chair, I'm blaming you."

"Just sit down, will you?"

Regina sat. In the next moment, a flock of white terns came flying over Segun's shoulders. The bantam seagulls, with their whitened plumes and ebony crests, glided down the stairway. At first, they circled over Regina. Then, they slowly descended to the floor on all sides of her chair. How had Segun trained these birds? The terns perched on the four handles of each strap and locked their claws around the handles, then began flapping their wings. In seconds, the birds were in flight, lifting the chair into the air.

"How can these little birds lift me like this, Segun?"

"Bring her to me, my friends. I think you'd better hold on, Regina!"

Regina closed her eyes as the birds lifted the chair higher and sailed her up and over the staircase, finally hovering on the top step, suspending Regina six feet in the air.

"Segun Bada, tell these birds to put me down before they drop me."

"Regina, I believe you've hurt their feelings."

Regina looked at the birds. "I'm sorry. I really enjoyed the ride. Now, let me down."

Segun gestured to the birds to descend by lowering his hand. When the chair was at chest high, he lifted Regina out and into his arms. The birds allowed the chair to rest on the landing. Regina put her arms around Segun's neck.

"Now, this is much better," Regina said.

Their lips met and exploded into a deep, passionate kiss. Neither realized how the other had hungered for this moment. Segun sat in the chair with Regina on his lap. Every kiss, each touch inflamed the fire for the next. Regina felt as if she were spinning. She opened her eyes to find she and Segun were suspended twenty feet in the air, nearly touching the vaulted ceiling of the foyer. The excitement of floating heightened their sensations. Regina fell limp and abandoned all inhibitions. Segun kissed her under her chin and along her arched neck.

"Downward," he commanded.

The birds gently lowered them to the floor. Regina stood up and reached out to Segun. He lifted her in his arms once again, and she tilted back his head and locked her mouth against his as they made their way to the bedroom.

***

Around 4:30 in the morning, Regina awoke to the sound of Segun's heartbeat. Nuzzling closer onto his chest, she raised her head and stared at his face. He slumbered peacefully. His expression was boyish—relaxed. Regina had never seen him so at ease. She felt serene.

When you awaken, will the dream have ended or just begun? You men are confused by passion and frightened by love. Will you tell lies you think I want to hear? Will you try to apologize and act as if it did not happen? Oh well.

Regina softly kissed Segun's chest. She eased out of the bed, trying not to wake him.

Out the window, she saw the thick fluffy snowflakes falling from the sky and a blanket of snow covering the trees and ground. Regina was so enthralled by nature's artistry that she didn't realize Segun was awake. Covering himself with the blanket, he walked up behind Regina and put his hand on her shoulder.

Regina braced for Segun's words. "What a beautiful picture. I was twenty-three when I saw my first snowfall. It still amazes me. Regina, I want you to make a promise to me. It's a little embarrassing."

Regina wondered where this was leading. "What is it, Segun?"

"I know it is a lot to ask, but I want you to teach me how to ice skate."

Regina turned around. "Did you just ask me to teach you how to ice skate?"

"Oh yes. I remember when you told me that you would return soda bottles as a child to earn money to go ice skating. It will be something grand we can do together. But we cannot tell Sotonye. I want him to look ridiculous when we skate together!"

Regina shook her head and laughed. "What made me think you would respond to anything like the average man? Are you hungry?"

At 5:00 a.m., Segun and Regina sat at the kitchen table eating the dinner they had not eaten the night before.

"How in the world did you train those birds to do all those things, Segun? As a matter of fact, how did you train all of the animals at Q.P.S. and at your house? They're all so gentle."

"The truth is I did not train any of the animals. I programmed them."

"Are you telling me all of those animals are robots?"

"Let me get my laptop. It'll be easier to explain." Segun retrieved his computer and pulled his chair over next to Regina's. "This is not an ordinary computer. I designed it and developed it at the factory. It has all the functions of a computer, but it also serves as a command station." Segun took a small microphone from the base and instructed Regina to say, "Horace—three—Regina—Bovine—of sky and water—of water and sky."

After Regina recorded this message, Segun placed a set of headphones over her ears. Segun pressed Enter, which created a suctioning vacuum that temporarily locked the headphones to Regina's ears. Segun pressed Exit and released the vacuum. Then, he had Regina type backwards her name, her mother's name, and the phrase *open the doors and let in the light*. Segun wrote on a piece of paper: *Say, "come here, my friends."*

"Come here, my friends."

All of a sudden, the flock of terns flew into the kitchen and landed at Regina's feet.

"They are also programmed to respond to your hand signals and computer commands."

Regina opened her hand, pointed to one of the birds, and then pointed to her open palm with her other hand. The tern jumped from the floor into Regina's hand. Regina's mouth fell open. She rubbed her finger along the back of the bird. "This bird is real. I can feel its warmth. It's breathing. Its little chest is going in and out."

"Friend, repeat Regina's text," Segun said.

The bird turned to Regina. "Segun-this-bird-is-real. I-can-feel-the-warmth-of-its-body. It's breathing. Its—" the bird said in Regina's exact voice.

"Okay, enough. You can return to wherever you were." The bird went silent at her command. The other Terns went into formation and flew from the room.

"Segun, does this mean every animal I thought was real is a robot?"

"Not just the animals. The grass, trees, and flowers all are computerized. I prefer to call them faunadroids and floradroids. If they got into the wrong hands, my inventions could be used in destructive ways. I know Futrob is interested in my secrets."

Segun rubbed his chin and spiraled into deep concentration. "There is only one other computer in the world like this one. And there are only three people in the world who know the code that disengages the security system. You are one."

"Segun, Futrob worries me!"

"I've got it under control. I learned a heavy lesson." They looked each other in the eyes. "Gina, do you like surprises?"

"You're trying to distract me."

Segun laughed. "How am I doing?"

"I'll let you know. What is the secret?"

"It's not exactly a secret."

"Yes?"

"Did you know I knew Nicole's father?"

Gina was immediately distracted from her worries as she focused on Segun's amazing story about his chance meeting with Joseph Johnson. When he finished, she wanted to tell him that Joseph was really her father, but decided against it. This moment was for them.

"What a coincidence, Segun!" She told Segun about her unusual encounter with Joseph when she had heard him speak at the Palmer House.

"That's right, Joseph told me that theory." Segun laughed. "Sotonye and I have Joseph and Marion's Christmas story, and now I find out Joseph was my inspiration and guide in one of the most important decisions I made in my life."

"You would not believe the coincidences between Nicole and me." Regina wondered whether she should say something about Joseph after all.

"What is it, Regina?"

"Hello, hello, is anyone here?"

A familiar voice called from one of the front rooms. Regina and Segun rose from the table. They walked to the front of the house to discover Nicole standing in the foyer, looking at the straps attached to her dining room chair.

"Nicole," Regina called out as she and Segun turned the corner.

Entering the foyer, Nicole raised her head from the chair to the much more interesting picture of Regina wearing one of her robes and Segun in just his pants. Nicole looked at them and then back at the chair. She dusted the snow from her sleeves.

"I was going to ask about the chair, but after seeing you two, I don't think I really want to know."

Segun and Regina burst into laughter.

"Now I know I don't want to know."

Segun took Nicole's coat and hung it up. "Where is Sotonye?"

"He decided to stay a few more days and observe your mother."

"I am afraid I will miss him. I must return to Botswana on a morning flight. By the way, I met your father years ago."

"What!" Nicole said in surprised. "You just say that to me causally?"

Segun broke into a smile. "He changed my life."

Regina joined in, unable to do anything else for the moment. "Wait until you hear about it! You won't believe it!"

Part VII

Blue and Joseph

1983, Kilimanjaro, Sudan, Chicago

Chapter 44

It was 1983. Blue had been imprisoned in the bowels of the volcano for twenty-three years. As Nafisa had predicted, he had not perished. He lay dormant, regenerating. Slowly, he regained his telekinetic powers. Liquid orbs without pupils or irises now filled his empty eye sockets. Even the beginnings of a neck and spinal cord were forming. After this, asexual reproduction of his central nervous system and all other physical systems would follow. For the first time in years, he could send thought waves to the outside world and hear higher-frequency sound waves. But he was limited.

He needed a host who had been channeled. The only human on Earth who had been stripped of all human identity, void of any human influence, and totally channeled was sealed in a hidden pyramid. Since the day of her birth, she had been his slave. The inner sanctum of the pyramid was the only world she had ever known. On this day, after forty-seven years of internment, the woman would enter the world. Her master needed her physical body to settle an old score and destroy his opposition.

Slightly before the midnight hour on July 12, 1983, a buzzing sound pierced Blue's inner ear. His head rotated from side to side within the walls of the metal box that held his cranium captive. As a distant jet gained an altitude that exceeded the height of the volcano's precipice, the signal became clear. Blue heard a voice coming from the aircraft, a voice only he could hear. It was the voice of the man-child he had created with Zinzi. The jet was taking him across the great sea to a land where Blue's daughter and his greatest enemy resided.

If Blue followed his son, he might be led to one or all of them. Blue needed eyes and a body, so he sent a signal to his only receptor. "Mongrel, I have a task for you."

Zinzi lay sleeping on the pyramid floor. She had not heard the voice of her iniquitous dominator for decades. The words transmitted into her mind's ear horrified her. Shocked from her sleep, her eyes raced around the chamber, searching for Blue. The voice in her head spoke again.

"Do not search for me, sub-creature. Listen carefully. You will do as I command."

Soon, Zinzi was in a deep hypnotic trance. Blue's thoughts governed her mind, using it as a vehicle for his evil will. Blue began to experiment with her. He levitated her body, sending her soaring to the top of the pyramid. He forced her body to spin and flip in the air. His powers delighted him. The more she screamed, the more hungry his sadistic appetite became. He sent her into freefalls from the pyramid's heights and caught her seconds before she crashed to the stone floor. She was out of her mind, screaming then panting and finally fainting, only to be revive again for another round.

When he tired of the game, he made her stumble over to the great stone that sealed the entrance. He transferred his energy into her arms to push the barrier open to the outside world.

For the first time in her life, Zinzi entered the world of her kind, but even in her rightful world, she was ruled by her master's will. Zinzi spread her arms as a bird does its wings and ascended into the night. She followed the course of Segun's jet until it landed in Chicago. Hiding in the shadows, she stalked her target, hoping he would lead her to her prey.

On the night of July 14, 1983, Zinzi stood on the window ledge above the balcony where Segun, the future college student, and Joseph talked. Blue was outraged that Segun enjoyed Joseph's company.

Through Zinzi, Blue followed Segun and Joseph until Segun was dropped off. Once Joseph was alone on the highway again, Zinzi, possessed by Blue, was able to grab Joseph's steering wheel and jam her foot down on the gas pedal. The second before the truck crashed into Joseph's car, spinning him into the concrete wall, Joseph heard an insidious laugh from the volcanic depth of Kilimanjaro.

Joseph watched the concrete wall rocketing toward him and yelled out, "Blue!"

Zinzi found Marion outside the Wells Street East entrance of the Merchandise Mart, waiting impatiently for Joseph to take her to the airport.

"Stop where you are! Don't come any closer," Marion commanded, sensing danger from the woman in the flowing garments.

Zinzi opened her hands and extended her arms with a wicked smile. "Have you missed me, Marion? I told you I would return for you. The creed of my race does not allow me to destroy the mother of my child, so you shall have the privilege of dedicating your lower life to serving me. This is your reward."

Marion cried out, "What have you done with my husband?"

The woman took flight with Marion trapped in her embrace. Blue's voice resounded in the night air. "The Son of Slaves lives no more."

***

When she left the ballroom, Marion's friends thought Joseph had picked her up. Everyone assumed Marion had also perished in the accident. Instead, Marion was taken to the pyramid. Blue instructed Zinzi to chain and shackle Marion and guard her. Since that day, Marion remained Blue's prisoner.

Part VIII

The Choice Is Yours

1991, Chicago, Botswana, Rochester, New Orleans, Sudan, Kilimanjaro

By noon, Nicole and Regina were sleeping soundly. Segun sat at the dining table entering data into his computer. His mind wandered back to the conversation he and Regina had had before Nicole's arrival. His musing was interrupted by a ringing telephone. He hurried to answer it.

"Hello?"

"Segun, is that you? It is so good to hear your voice."

Segun recognized the heavy Bostonian accent. "Charles Bachar? I don't believe it. How long has it been?"

"Nearly six years, my friend."

"Tell me, Charles, how did you know you could contact me at this number?"

"I followed in the footsteps of my famous student, Segun Bada. The corporate world has embraced me with open arms. I've just completed a project for Futrob. Officially, I have been promoted to Vice President of Engineering. We're together again."

Charles Bachar was the one scientist and engineer in the world who possessed acumen comparable to Segun's. Segun had studied under Charles while working on his PhD at MIT. It was not long into their relationship before teacher became student and vice versa. Charles had the reputation of being the world's foremost authority on quantum engineering and nuclear fission. He would often joke with Segun—"In a few years, people will say the name Bachar and someone will correct them and say the name is pronounced Bada!"

"Are you serious, Charles?"

"I'm sitting in the President's office at this very moment. I was so excited. I couldn't wait to call you. I talked Mr. Byron into giving me your number."

"Charles, we need to meet today. I'm returning to Botswana tomorrow."

"Mr. Byron would like to join us. He's also leaving tomorrow. Is four p.m. good?"

So they brought you in to soften me up. "I'll see you both then," Segun said.

Futrob Chicago Headquarters utilized the top five floors of the Sears Tower. When the elevator door opened, Charles Bachar was standing there. The two men embraced.

"I knew you would be early. Segun, you look great."

"So do you, Charles."

"Thanks for making time for this old man. You know, I'll be fifty-nine this year. Another year and I'll officially be a geezer."

"You're ageless, Charles."

"Byron is waiting for us in his office."

"I've never met Byron."

"Are you serious? I find that difficult to believe. He has talked about the great Segun Bada so often I thought you two were golf partners."

Charles led Segun down several hallways before they reached Byron's secluded office. Charles had to use a special code to enter the outer sanctum. He spoke to Byron over the intercom, and the double doors swung open. Byron came from behind his nouveau chic desk and walked briskly toward the two men.

"Well, it's about time we finally meet face to face." Byron shook Segun's hand. "I'm one of your biggest fans, Mr. Bada. I feel like I know you. Old Charles here tells me you're even better than your press. Very few people in this world can make that claim."

"That is very generous of you, Mr. Byron. I know of no one who is truly the person the media projects them to be."

Byron looked to Charles. "You said he was a genius. You didn't tell me he was wise too." Byron escorted Segun to a chair and began the meeting by singing the praises of the Golden Guard. "Indicators are that within two years Golden Guard will exceed a billion dollars in US sales. The launch ceremony will be all-important. I had full confidence in the Q.P.S. team, but I must confess, I did not have the same confidence in Futrob's team until Charles was placed in charge."

Segun agreed.

The three spent an hour and a half deliberating. All parties were clear on their roles.

It was nearly 6:00 p.m. when Byron looked at his watch. "Gentlemen, I am very sorry, but I have a flight in less than two hours."

"That business in the Middle East?" Charles said.

"It disheartens me to say it. I'm afraid we are on the verge of war," Byron said.

"Take my word as a veteran of three wars. This one is inevitable," Charles said.

"The UN has asked Futrob to play a major role in the further development of laser weaponry technology."

"Well, the man you need to talk to is sitting in front of you."

"Come again, Charles?"

"The Golden Guard is a project Segun Bada probably completed his first month at MIT. Even then, he was designing defense mechanisms light-years ahead of any current technology."

Byron looked at Segun. "I was unaware until our research determined it that Q.P.S. had inventions far exceeding our current portfolio, but I had no idea these inventions were related to warfare. If what Charles says is true, you could corner the world's defense market with Africans as full players in the global economy. I can see the headlines—'Segun Bada, the Man Who Won the War.' Every person of African descent would be full of pride."

Segun raised his open hand, signaling Byron to halt. "To clarify, Charles and I hold each other in such high esteem, we each might exaggerate the other's prowess. I am in the process of developing a peace-enhancing protection system. It is hardly operational. Secondly, my company is already part of the global economy. The Golden Guard has been marketed successfully everywhere in the world, with the exception of the United States. Most importantly, I did not found Q.P.S. to seek fame, infinite wealth, and undue power. We have given away what is ours and have let outsiders determine what we deserve. Success found overnight is usually lost in the next few days. I have designed my business to continue, therefore the natural evolution is inherent."

Segun knew he could revolutionize the espionage business with his floradroids and the faunadroids, but he would never allow Futrob, Charles, or anyone else to use his inventions for destructive purposes.

"Charles," Segun said, baiting his old mentor. "You have changed. All these years, you denounced instruments of war, destruction, and death. War is a sad reality born of oppression. In the year of my birth, fifteen African nations gained independence. Cultural and economic bridges were extended, linking Africa with all of its children around the world, particularly stolen children here in the United States of America. My company's participation in this war would create the type of acclaim I shun. Q.P.S. will maintain its focus on growth, protection, and development. I choose not to participate. I have a greater goal."

Byron looked at Segun and shook his hand. "Well, that is unfortunate for us, but I respect and support your decision. I must get going. I will see you both back here later this month." Byron departed.

Charles gathered the notes he had taken during the meeting. "I'm sorry. I was so wrapped up in the moment that I spoke out of turn. I have become too accustomed to the world of research and academia, which takes one on those speculative tangents allowable in the classroom but not in the boardroom."

Segun put his arm around his old professor. "No harm done."

***

As Segun drove back to Nicole's house, he analyzed the meeting arranged to create a perception of trust. Had they really thought he would relax? All of the specs for the marketing project had been thoroughly covered. It was only necessary for him to meet with Charles.

Byron had no hands-on participation in the project. What a charade. Byron sold products and pipe dreams. His exiting act did not fool Segun one iota. Since the day he had opened for business, Segun had known Futrob's industrial spies had Q.P.S. under surveillance. For the most part, their espionage had been an exercise in futility. After all of their covert activities, the best they could do was to speculate on Q.P.S.'s top-secret projects.

Only Segun knew the entire equations to any of his creations. Only Isaac came close to his level of knowledge. Segun knew what Byron wanted, but Byron could never fathom what Segun had already created. It was too bad his old professor had betrayed him.

***

Nicole awoke a few hours after Segun had left. Regina was still sleeping peacefully. Nicole found Segun's note and read it as she walked into the kitchen. She was still trying to come to grips with the probability that Segun was her half-brother. She filled the tea kettle and put it on the stove.

"No, Nicole! Don't do it!" Regina screamed from upstairs. "Don't do it!"

Nicole rushed from the kitchen. Regina was sitting straight up in the bed, still asleep.

"Gina, Gina!" Nicole said, putting her arms around her. "Wake up, sweetheart! You are having a bad dream. Come on, Gina. It's me, Nicole."

Regina's eyes snapped open and she broke from Nicole's embrace. "Get away from me!"

"Gina, you had a nightmare. My goodness, I must have done something horrible! Sweetheart, you know I would never hurt you. I love you, Gina."

Regina cleared her eyes. Looked at the innocent Nicole, she reached out for her. "Oh my God, Nicole! It was so awful, so real and so hideous! You were a demon and you cut out Sotonye's eyes with a sword. Then you came after me!"

"I've got some water boiling for tea. Let's talk about this downstairs."

Still trembling, Regina followed Nicole down to the kitchen.

Nicole watched Regina sip her tea. "Are you feeling any better?"

"Actually, I am."

"Then tell me everything about your dream."

"I was inside of a pyramid, walking along the wall, staring at these beautiful hieroglyphics. Then the drawings changed. They didn't seem ancient at all. The wall of pictures told the story of a great battle between a Segunor and a monstrous blue creature with enormous white wings. The later pictures showed a woman kneeling and crying over a skinless body.

"Then I heard a baby crying and the dream completely changed. I was downtown, right here in Chicago, in the middle of some type of catastrophe. A mob was running, tripping over each other, covering their heads. I saw Segun running toward a building. I called him, but he did not look back. Suddenly, I was on top of a snowy mountain. That's when..." Regina paused and sipped her tea.

"That's when... what, Regina?"

"That's when you murdered Sotonye, carved out his eyes, smashed them with the butt of a sword, and came after me. You were like a possessed fiend. I can't even describe how sinister you were."

"Regina, you've had nightmares before..."

"Nicole, I don't know how to handle this."

"I'm having the same problem."

Nicole filled Regina in on Rochester—her dream, Nafisa's quilt, the triangle and the nonexistent Colonel Bada. She went on to tell Regina how Sotonye's sword medallion had magically transformed into the sword that he used against the robbers in the alley behind the nightclub. Nicole told her why Sotonye returned to her suite that night.

After hearing all of this, Nicole wondered if she should tell Regina that she and Segun shared the same rare blood type and probably the same father. She and Sotonye still were waiting for the DNA results. Nicole decided to wait.

"Gina, do you remember the man in my first dream?"

"Bertrand Lwanga? How could I forget him?"

"Sotonye believes Lwanga may really exist. He's visiting his mother at the Mayo Clinic. The hospital has a far-reaching network and the staff is letting him use their facility to try to track down Lwanga's medical records."

"Nafisa would probably know, right? Are they any nearer to discovering why she's in a coma?"

"No."

"Nicole, we both have had dreams about Blue. Your father told us to 'Beware of Blue.' So did Baba..."

"There is one thing I do know. Blue wants us to fail so he can own us. We have to do our best work for Segun. We have to make sure he succeeds. We will have time to figure this out later."

"I agree, Nicole," Regina said wearily. "I think I'm going to rest a little more."

***

Upstairs, Regina sat on the bed and picked up the medallion from the nightstand. As she examined it, a startling thought came to her. Sotonye also had a medallion. If Nafisa and Joseph had conceived a child together, that child had to be Sotonye. *We're lighter. Our skin is the same shade. That would mean Sotonye is my brother!*

Regina put the medallion back around her neck. She bowed her head and prayed. "I don't know what to think of all this. Lord, please help us. We are like lost children. We don't know if our fears are real or imaginary. Like a child, I cannot help but fear there is something or someone out there in the darkness waiting to destroy us all."

"Amen," said Nicole, who was standing in the doorway with folded hands.

Regina looked over at Nicole and repeated, "Amen."

The telephone rang. Nicole picked up the receiver. It was Sotonye.

"Nicole, I have found Lwanga."

"How?"

"Bertrand Lwanga's early medical records show he was born in Kenya. He ultimately moved to Ethiopia and earned a living as a diamond cutter. His wife was killed in 1936, and Lwanga disappeared shortly afterwards. Akim Dessalgn was Bertrand Lwanga's brother-in-law. He is seventy years old and presently in a hospital in Nairobi, Kenya.

"I am leaving on a flight to Nairobi tomorrow morning. Tell Segun I had medical business in Kenya. I will meet him in Botswana before the weekend and see you back in America. I've got to hurry now. I love you, Nicole."

"I love you too, Sotonye. I don't want you to go!" Nicole held tightly to the telephone with a look of panic. "Bertrand Lwanga is a dangerous man. He may harm you. I couldn't live with that."

"I must do this," Sotonye said. "It's better to find your enemy before your enemy finds you. If I meet Lwanga, it will be on my terms, not his." Sotonye paused. "Is Gina close to you? If she is, put her on the telephone."

Nicole handed the phone to Regina. "Hello, Sotonye."

Sotonye told Regina where he was going. "Did Nicole tell you what happened here?"

"Yes."

"Then you know how important this trip is."

"Yes, I do."

"Gina, you can't tell Segun what I'm doing. Tell him I am on medical business. I want him to focus on his presentation."

"I promise, Sotonye."

"Thanks. May I speak to Nicole again?" Regina gave the phone back to Nicole. "I'll call you later tonight. I might have further news."

When Segun returned to the house, Regina gave him Sotonye's message.

"I wonder who is ill in Kenya? My brother is always trying to save the world."

"Sotonye says the same about you with your new inventions," Regina said, guiding him upstairs. "You need some rest before your trip. I'll wake you."

"I think you're right," Segun said as he lay across the bed and instantly fell fast asleep.

Chapter 46

Sotonye stopped by the Mayo Clinic before his flight to Nairobi. He had to see Nafisa before he left.

"Mother, please awaken. I know a storm approaches. You are a child of nature. You can tell me which way the wind is blowing and when the storm will arrive. I know you can."

Nafisa lay motionless in her bed. He did not notice her right eye beginning to twitch. The nurse had come in with the results of Nicole's DNA test, and they occupied his attention.

He sat down and stared at the results for many minutes before he picked up his mother's hospital telephone and called Nicole.

"Nicole, we are not brother and sister!" Sotonye said simply. He heard a relieved sigh from Nicole. "Segun is definitely your brother."

"Segun and I! Is my father his father?"

"Before I answer any more questions, please let me visit Akim Dessalgn." He heard her sigh. "Don't worry, Nicole. You will know where I am and what I am doing every day. You have a lot of work yourself. Your marketing extravaganza is a few weeks away, and I expect this to be your finest work."

"It will be. I guarantee it," Nicole said, getting focused.

"That sounds more like you. I love you, Nicole. I will call you after I speak to Akim. We will sort all of this out. I promise."

He hung up the phone, kissed his mother, and departed, unaware of the tear falling down Nafisa's check.

***

Sotonye arrived in Nairobi the following evening and took a taxi directly to the hospital. Fortunately, Sotonye was known at the Nairobi Hospital and had no difficulty gaining access to Akim Dessalgn's room. Sotonye found Akim resting. Sotonye moved a chair to the side of his bed and sat there quietly. Several minutes later, the elderly man finally sensed Sotonye's presence and opened his eyes.

"Do I know you?"

"No sir, you do not. I am Dr. Sotonye Bada. I have traveled a long way to ask you about Bertrand Lwanga."

The old man stared at Sotonye. "How do you know Bertrand Lwanga?"

"Sir, you may think that I am not in my right mind, but I will tell you the truth. I am in love with a woman who met Bertrand Lwanga in her dream. From her description, he has special powers and could be dangerous."

Akim said angrily, "You wish to talk unkindly of a brother-in-law I loved who disappeared over sixty years ago!"

"Sir, please, I have not come here to cause you discomfort. I have come because the woman I love, my brother, and my friends may be in imminent danger. In some way, Bertrand Lwanga is at the core of many abnormal and even mystical occurrences." Sotonye paused for a moment. "Sir, there is something else. The woman I spoke of inherited a wealth of diamonds from her mother. I know Bertrand Lwanga was a diamond cutter. I'm wondering if he is linked to her somehow."

"Tell me about the diamonds."

"I have never seen them. I was told they are flawless. They range in size. I believe there are twenty or more."

"Tell me, in what manner of package were these diamonds kept?"

"I was told the diamonds are kept in a brown pouch made of animal hide. At the opening there is a drawstring, also of hide."

Akim spoke in almost a whisper. "That is Bertrand's pouch. My sister Eleni made it for him to carry his jewels." Akim looked away from Sotonye and stared upward.

Sotonye gazed into Akim's face and stood up. "Please sir, tell me the secrets you are holding inside. I need to know what you know of Bertrand Lwanga."

Akim signaled with his trembling hand for Sotonye to return to his seat. Sotonye sat and Akim told him the story of his amazing sister and brother-in-law and their stolen daughter.

When he finished his story, Akim reached over and grabbed Sotonye's hand. He could barely breathe or speak. "If Blue prevails, my life is not the only life that will soon end. Blue has sired children to destroy The Freedom Code. If the children support their father, they will be too powerful to defeat."

"Who are these children?" Sotonye asked, almost afraid to know.

"My sister's baby girl, Zinzi, would be fifty years old," Akim said breathlessly. "One of the children is hers. There's supposed to be a girl and boy. Watch out for them, Sotonye. Help them to resist their father."

"How?"

"Teach them about The Freedom Code and that they must see that its prophecy is fulfilled! May the gods be with you, Sotonye Bada."

Akim's grip grew limp and his hand fell to the side of the bed. The heart monitor flatlined. Sotonye sprang to his feet and tried to revive Akim, but he had left this earthly life.

***

It was January 19, 1984, when Blue returned to a dormant state. The woman who'd captured Marion was finally freed from mind control. Marion had been confined to less than forty square feet of space for more than six months. Her chains permitted her only enough distance to walk from the stone table where she ate to where she slept. Once her captor was released from Blue's spell, her true personality resurfaced. She removed Marion's chains and shackles, and Marion was free to roam her prison.

Zinzi followed Marion everywhere, but never spoke a word. Marion did not realize that Zinzi had never seen another woman or that Zinzi had no recollection of kidnapping her.

Walking through the pyramid, she found several chambers filled with ancient writings, vegetable gardens, and fountains of pure spring water. What stopped Marion, however, were the drawings on the walls of a modern-day pictorial history of Blue, uniquely sculpted. It told a modern story of imprisonment, torture, and enslavement. It depicted the atrocities her prisonmate had suffered at the hands of Blue. Marion was horrified. She looked at the sad, heart-stricken Zinzi, then back to her story on the wall. As Marion traveled down the storyline, she came to a profoundly different series of pictures. This montage depicted a fierce battle between a Segunor and Blue. And then it happened.

Zinzi tugged at Marion and pointed to the picture of the Segunor. She swallowed several times. Finally, Zinzi used her strained vocal cords and emitted the word "Bertrand." Then she pointed to herself and back to the picture and choked out, "My father, Bertrand. I, Zinzi."

Marion was shocked. Reexamining the drawings, she discovered the Segunor was Bertrand Lwanga.

As time passed, Marion taught Zinzi to speak, read, and write, and about her true kind, humankind. In exchange, Marion learned about the real Bertrand Lwanga and his great valor.

Marion and Zinzi became sisters in spirit. Marion never gave up hope of escape. They filled many of their hours sharing their lives. Zinzi told Marion of the birth of her son, whom she had cared for in this pyramid until Blue brought a girl child too, and she breastfed them both. Zinzi expressed the grief she had felt the day Blue left with her child and the other infant, never to return them.

Marion told Zinzi the story of the battle Joseph and Nafisa had waged against Blue. She assured Zinzi that both children were rescued and taken to safety. Zinzi was unable to recall her life when Blue held her in his hypnotic trance. She did not remember flying across the ocean, capturing Marion, or creating the collision that led to Joseph's death. It was better she did not know she had killed the man who saved her infant son and inspired that same child as an adult. And on that July evening in 1983, when she stood on the window ledge over the balcony, Zinzi did not know she looked down upon the grandson of the real Bertrand Lwanga, her son, known to the world as Segun Bada.

Chapter 47

When Segun arrived in Botswana, he knew time was of the essence. They had less than a week. Segun was determined that everything run smoothly. At Q.P.S., he met Isaac and recapped the meeting he had had with Byron and Bachar.

"It appears, from what you have told me," Isaac said, "that your professor was an equal partner in this ruse. His so-called accidental disclosure of your inventions opened the door for Byron. Byron knew he could not discuss inventions he supposedly did not know existed. Segun, I am afraid your old friend is of greater concern to me than Byron. If you cannot digest this possibility, do not worry, I will be your clear eyes."

"If I was blind when I walked into this office, once again, you have made me see."

***

Byron and Bachar sat in the same office they had the day before, but this time without Segun Bada. Byron had had no flight last night. It was all part of the gambit.

"Bachar, I am disappointed. You led me to believe that you and Bada had deep ties."

"We do."

"Then why am I sitting here with nothing? You were supposed to unlock the doors to the nuclear treasures hidden at Q.P.S."

"I'll need more time."

"Unfortunately, Charles, we don't have more time. It's time to change our strategy."

"Segun Bada is different. He has no vices. He's never done anything immoral, unethical, or illegal. If you expect a glitch or a fault in his work, you'll find even greater disappointment. I have never known any other scientist to consistently reach so close to hundred percent accuracy."

Byron sat back in his chair, rubbing his chin. "I agree with the old adage, 'You can't cheat an honest man.' I can't cheat Segun Bada or compete with his technical genius. I can't even steal from him that which I can't get to. But, since Segun has what I want, I will destroy him, and you, Bachar, will assist in the annihilation. Once Bada is out of the picture, his inventions will become your inventions, and again you will sit on the throne you abdicated."

***

Nicole left early that morning to meet with the photographers and video crew. She wanted to be sure there were aerial shots to use for the advertising campaign. Word had already hit the public relations hotline that Nicole and Regina were in charge. The telephones rang off the hook. Nicole had transferred the office line to her house, and Regina decided to stay home and man the phone.

Between noon and 1:00 p.m., there was a lull. Regina went into the living room and took one of the photo albums from the shelf. She thumbed through an album filled with pictures of Nicole and her parents. Every picture reflected how much they had loved and meant to each other. There was a photograph of Nicole's mother feeding her as an infant. Regina looked at it and turned the page. Then something odd about the picture registered. Regina flipped back. In the picture, the top button of the nightgown Marion had on was unbuttoned. The opened gown exposed a necklace. On closer examination, Regina was sure that Marion was wearing the sword medallion.

The telephone rang. Regina put down the photo album and answered it.

"Sotonye? Nicole is working."

Sotonye told Regina of his visit with Akim Dessalgn and the story of Bertrand Lwanga. When he got to the part about Bertrand's journey to the pyramid, Regina described the dream she had had of the pyramid oasis.

"It ties in with my mother's quilt," Sotonye said. "I'll tell you more about it when I see you. Akim has no living relations. Right now, I have to take care of his funeral."

"The poor man," Regina said. "It seems like he was holding on to life just long enough to tell the right person all he knew. And you were the right person."

"I certainly hope so," Sotonye said thoughtfully. "In the morning, I'm going to his apartment to get clothes for him to wear for his burial. I am hoping to find something in his personal effects which might help us as well."

"I'll tell Nicole when she comes home," Regina said and then paused. "Sotonye, what is the probability that Nicole and your father share the same blood type?"

"You know the answer to that question."

"What would you say if I told you Joseph Johnson was not Nicole's biological father?"

"What are you talking about, Gina?" Sotonye asked. "How do you know that?"

"After Aunt Melinda died, Big El told me Joseph Johnson was my real father. I just looked in a photo album. Nicole's mother was wearing the same sword medallion that is now around your neck. That means your mother did not have possession of the sword medallion until after Nicole was born. Segun is older than Nicole. Both were born before Joseph Johnson traveled to Africa."

There was a lengthy quiet. "Regina, I want you to take a DNA test."

"I'll do it right away. Sotonye, I haven't told Nicole yet that Joseph is my father. I hate keeping it from her. I really don't know why I told you."

"Don't worry about it, Regina. I'll be there in another week. Wait to tell Nicole until I return."

***

The following day, at Akim Dessalgn's funeral, Sotonye assured himself he had made the right decision not to tell Regina about Nicole's and Segun's DNA tests. It would be best for everyone to learn all the findings once all the tests were completed.

After the simple ceremony, he had Akim's body flown to Ethiopia to be buried next to his parents and sister, Eleni. Sotonye went to Akim's house and had all of Akim's worldly possessions put into storage. The only thing Sotonye took was a sealed box with the names Eleni and Bertrand Lwanga written on top. He took the box back to his hotel room and examined the contents. The carton was filled with mementos, from photos of Bertrand as a boy to Eleni's blueprints for

359

the multi-terrain solar automobile. Under the blueprints, he found Akim's diary. In it, Akim had detailed the information that his sister had dictated to him. He had even made drawings of the pyramid and written the story of Blue, including details about The Freedom Code.

Chapter 48

T he following two weeks were tumultuous. Everyone was feeling the pressure. Isaac made several adjustments to the original traveling plans and schedules. He tripled the workforce traveling to the United States. When the Futrob trucks arrived to ship the crates of equipment, a Q.P.S. employee accompanied each crate, swearing to stay with it throughout the trip. No Q.P.S. crate was to be opened unless Isaac or Segun were present. Isaac changed all flight and hotel arrangements made by Futrob. He leased an apartment building through a friend that lived in Chicago. The building was swept for wiretaps, cameras, and any other surveillance. All Q.P.S. employees would reside at the house during their stay. They were sworn to secrecy.

Segun, feeling totally confident that Isaac could handle all of the details on the home front, returned to Chicago at the end of the week.

On the same day, Sotonye returned to Botswana. After reading Lwanga's diary, a new universe had been unveiled to him. If Lwanga's writings were not the ramblings of a disturbed mind, his people would soon face an abominable transformation. Sotonye prayed constantly for Nafisa's return to consciousness. The truth was with her.

***

Blue had used Zinzi as his surrogate for years, but where Nafisa was concerned, he wanted to take vengeance on her personally.

Once Nafisa had given Sotonye the sword medallion, she became vulnerable. Blue had used his advanced telepathy to create Nafisa's paralysis.

Viewing her travels from one hospital to another gave Blue some satisfaction. He would never forget that she pretended to be his sister and helped the SOS Joseph take his children away from him. Once he was out in the world, he would personally show her his wrath.

Until then, those doctor friends of Sotonye's would spin their wheels, never finding out what was wrong with her.

By Segun's thirtieth birthday, Blue's cognitive powers had returned and his physical regeneration had begun. He was still unable to penetrate the barrier he had created. He could not pass through to the children who wore the shield and the sword. Once his development was completed, he would find a way.

***

Sotonye went to the hospital not long after his return and sat down to a huge backlog. He worked around the clock, but that only added to his anxiety until Regina kept her word and took the DNA test. Seven days later, he compared the results to Nicole's, Segun's, and his own tests. He picked up the phone.

"Regina, you are my sister! But you are not Nicole's. You must tell Nicole the truth about your father."

***

Regina sat Nicole down in the middle of their frantic schedule and told her about Sotonye's findings.

Nicole was stunned. "You and Sotonye are brother and sister and Segun and I are brother and sister. But Joseph is not my blood father? Then who is my... Segun's and my father?"

"I don't know," Regina said honestly. "I love you, Nicole. I am so sorry all of this is happening!"

Nicole hugged Regina. Her world was crashing in on her. She was the daughter chosen! *Stop it!* she told herself. Joseph was not her father, but Marion was her mother. She felt secure in the knowledge that Joseph had loved her as a daughter and she had loved him as her father. She held back her tears. What it all meant would have to wait until after the Golden Guard presentation.

***

To their surprise, Futrob's public relations division was being fully cooperative, even overly cooperative. Futrob was maintaining a very low profile. This was in direct contrast to every other campaign. Futrob had previously fought to give the appearance that they had played an integral role in the development of the Golden Guard.

Segun, Isaac, and Charles met daily. Charles tried on several occasions to endear himself to Isaac. His efforts were futile. Twenty-

362

four-hour guards from Q.P.S. watched over the Sears Tower's rooftop, and Isaac checked the walls of the Tower's roof on a daily basis.

What the guards didn't see were three dark figures on the side of the building a floor below the roof after midnight two days before the exhibition. Bachar gained access to the exterior wall of the building from a top-floor suite. Using a laser to drill tiny holes into the exterior wall, he injected a chemical he had developed which would weaken the roof's support. It took time for the chemicals to react, so Isaac wouldn't know Segun was being sabotaged.

The day prior to the exhibition, during Isaac's inspection, Charles Bachar arrived at the entrance to the roof. When he was not permitted access, he demanded to speak with Isaac. Isaac met him at the entrance.

"Your guard won't let me through. Surely that was an oversight?"

"Surely it was not."

"What is the problem? We are on the same team. Do you realize who I am?"

"There is no limit to my loyalty to Segun Bada," Isaac said, staring directly into Bachar's eyes. "Your presence here is suspect. Who you are is the exact reason you are not allowed access to this roof. Tell me, Bachar, what is the current market value of a soul? I can guarantee you, you won't be paid the agreed amount."

Bachar was livid. He stormed off, cursing Isaac.

***

The day of the Q.P.S. Grand Exhibition finally arrived. Everyone was prepared. The exhibition was scheduled for 8:00 p.m. The Chicago winds were increasing and the temperature had dropped with each passing hour, but Segun had accounted for all of these possible variables. They would have no significant effect on the operations of the Golden Guard.

At 6:00 p.m., crowds of reporters, cameramen, and curious spectators began to form behind the roped area surrounding the Sears Tower. At 7:30 p.m., Segun, Nicole, Regina, and Sotonye took their places on the stage. The mayor, several corporate officers, and local VIPs accompanied them. The only notable guest not present was the President of Futrob, Mr. Byron.

Out of the crowd, a familiar figure appeared. It was Ray Oliver. He walked to the side of the stage and passed a note to Nicole. As the mayor gave his welcoming speech, Nicole read Ray's note. It said Byron had been delayed and to proceed without him. Oliver added a postscript. "Good luck. I knew you two were winners the moment I laid eyes on you." Nicole smiled at Ray. He, in turn, flipped two thumbs up.

At exactly 7:55, Segun walked to the podium to address the shivering crowd.

"Today, Q.P.S. brings our light to shine in these United States of America. Today, Africa will open the Golden Guard for you. It is our profound hope that the Golden Guard will ensure confidence, trust, and belief in our security technology. Let today mark the beginning of this mutual respect." With those words, Segun opened his computer and signaled Isaac on the roof. Segun began his countdown. "Five—four—three—"

The entire crowd accompanied him. "Two—one!"

"Let there be light," Segun commanded.

At that instant, the magnificent Golden Guard appeared, completely engulfing the 108-story Sears edifice. Its brilliance illuminated the entire metropolitan area. Segun escorted the mayor and other dignitaries to the golden wall of bars. The spectators were in awe. There had never been such an extraordinary display. Cameras were flashing, videotapes rolling, and anchormen reporting live from the scene. Segun handed sledgehammers to the mayor and other officials. They repeatedly delivered blows having absolutely no effect on the golden bars. They were all amazed; praises soon filled the air.

Segun invited the dignitaries to return with him to the stage. On the roof, Isaac paid no attention to the show below. He was constantly patrolling the walls of the roof, making sure all units were secure. The light units were ten times the size of ordinary commercial units. These units weighed as much as the average industrial flagpole. Isaac had left nothing to chance. In five minutes, the demonstration would end. Every minute was a lifetime for Isaac.

Three minutes before deactivation, a fierce wind swept across the roof. Isaac thought he heard a cracking sound at the front wall. He threw off his hat and ear warmers and rushed over to the sound. He placed his computer on the rooftop and knelt with his ear next to the wall.

In the next instant, he shouted, "Get over here. This wall is about to cave!" Isaac reached over the wall and grabbed the light unit. Holding it secure, he yelled, "Pick up my computer, enter 'g-g' and hit Escape." The crew scrambled over to the computer and did as ordered.

The light bars went out and the audience applauded. Segun looked at his watch. Deactivation was a minute early; something was wrong. Segun stared up.

On the roof lit with strobe lights, Isaac leaned over the cement wall surrounding the circumference of the roof, straining to hold onto the loosened light unit which was the brain of Golden Guard. His crew raced towards him.

"Stay back! It isn't safe!" he yelled out to them.

But some leaned over the wall to help him with the unit while others held fast to his legs. Without warning, the wall completely crumbled.

"Isaac, let go of it!" the crew all screamed. "Let go of it!"

The men trying to help hold the unit let go, but Isaac would not. The others in the team were losing their grip on his legs. All were sliding closer to the roof's edge.

Another burst of wind shifted the weight of the unit. Remnants of the wall crashed to the earth.

Isaac looked down. The frightened crowd panicked and started dispersing in every direction. He held onto the unit with all his might, but his ankles slipped from the crews' grips and it happened. Everyone watched in horror as he and the unit spiraled downward.

***

Segun jumped from the stage, landing on the sidewalk at the very moment Isaac's body and the Golden Guard operational system collided with the pavement.

"No!" Segun yelled, dropping to his knees. He lifted Isaac's lifeless body in his arms. Tears drenched his face. "Isaac, Isaac, Isaac…"

Having seen someone fall, Sotonye forced his way through the screaming crowd. Nicole and Regina followed, getting bumped and

365

shoved along the way by a hysterical stampede. At last they saw Segun. Holding Isaac.

Sotonye dropped down on his knees beside his brother, trying to convince Segun to release Isaac.

"Please, Segun, let me look at him. I can help!"

Nicole and Regina hid their emotions, but tears snuck through their reserve and rolled down their cheeks anyway.

Sirens were heard growing closer, yet Segun refused to let go of Isaac. Only when the attendants rolled up the gurney did Segun turn his tragic face to Sotonye.

"You have to let go, Segun. We have to get Isaac to the hospital!"

Stone-faced, Segun, let go and watched as Sotonye and the paramedics raced back to the ambulance.

Regina and Nicole turned to comfort Segun, but he had already walked away.

"Segun, where are you going? Come back," Regina called out.

Segun gave no reply and disappeared into the crowd which was again gathering around the scene.

***

Moments later, Segun leaned against the loading-dock wall around the corner. Panting, he tried to catch his breath.

A limousine pulled up and Charles Bachar exited the building. The driver opened the limousine door for Bachar. Segun could see another passenger inside. It was Byron. Segun felt dizzy and sick to his stomach as a maniacal expression captured his face.

While watching the limo drive away, he thought, *You shall pay dearly.*

Then a voice came to him. "Come to me, my son. I will show you the way to destroy the infidels. Reign will you. Reign Blue!"

***

As the limousine headed back to Futrob Headquarters, Byron looked over to Bachar. "I understand there was an unfortunate accident at tonight's exhibition." Bachar gave no reply. "It seems our friend, Segun Bada, is rather incompetent. It never fails. You try to help and elevate the third-world businesses, and they inevitably fail. They lack the sophistication to become true players in the business world."

"None of what you're saying is true. For God's sake, a good, dedicated man just died."

"Come now, Bachar. You are an old soldier. He was just a casualty of corporate war. If you don't believe what I am saying is true, read tomorrow morning's edition of the newspaper. Who knows, you might read the same story I just told."

***

The following morning, the national newspapers and television media depicted Segun as a heartless demagogue. The people in his employ were little more than slaves. He was an egotistical power monger who proclaimed himself ruler of Africa's economic destiny.

According to a statement from Futrob: "Our company disassociated itself from any dealings with Q.P.S. when we were made aware of its inhuman business practices. Futrob was only trying to develop a struggling third-world business. Helping others is part of our corporate mission. Unfortunately, this company did not have the skill or technical know-how to enter the global economy, and a precious life was lost. We deeply regret the unfortunate death of Isaac Embel. Futrob wishes to extend its deepest condolences to the Embel family."

Chapter 49

T he media bashing did not end in the United States. Once UPI got ahold of the story, reporters flocked to the front gates of Q.P.S. They shoved microphones into employees' faces as they left the building. When the employees refused to make comments, the media reported the employees were in fear of repercussions from the infamous Segun Bada.

Regina knew Segun would not return to Nicole's house after the tragedy at the Tower. When she opened the front door to Nicole's house, the flock of terns flew out into the sky.

Sotonye, Regina, and Nicole made all of the arrangements for the Q.P.S. crew and the transport of Isaac's body. They submitted a press release denying the charges against Q.P.S. and Segun, but it was not printed or aired.

Two days later, they were all on a flight back to Botswana. The entire Q.P.S. staff mourned the loss of Isaac Embel. There was no one whose life he had not touched. Isaac's wife had made all of the funeral arrangements for the day after their return. Sotonye, Nicole, and Regina all went to the Bada estate from the airport

The servants told Sotonye that Segun had returned in the middle of the night, packed a bag, collected things from his lab, and left. The rest of the management team was holding operations together. They had never been without Segun and Isaac.

The following day, the cemetery was filled to capacity with all of Isaac's friends and family. Segun had not appeared for the ceremonies. As Isaac's casket was lowered into the ground, a flock of doves appeared out of nowhere. They swooped down over the casket, dropped flowers from their beaks, and then propelled straight up into the clouds.

Regina looked over in the direction from which the birds had entered and spotted Segun standing on top of the twenty-foot concrete cemetery wall. His open arms were stretched to the sky as the birds ascended to the heavens. Regina took Sotonye's arm and whispered into his ear. He reached into his pocket and handed Regina the keys to his car.

Regina drove Sotonye's Avanti to the one place she might find Segun. The Q.P.S. complex was wide open. The Golden Guards had been disengaged. Regina hastily parked the car, dashed into the building, and pushed the button to Segun's floor.

He was sitting behind the desk in his darkened office entering data into his laptop computer. He had not slept. His complexion had grayish tones and there were prominent lines and circles under his eyes. He was talking to himself and responding to a voice.

"The time has come, my son. I will help you destroy your enemies. Come take your place next to your father. We will destroy them all."

Regina burst into the office. Segun stood up. "Leave here at once."

Regina walked closer. "Segun, it's me. I've come to help."

Segun had his letter opener in his hand. When Regina was within arm's length, Segun grabbed her shoulders and pushed her to her knees.

The terrified Regina looked up. "Segun, what have I done?"

"For your crimes protecting The Freedom Code, you are sentenced to die by the sword."

"Segun, it's me, Gina! What are you talking about? Segun, look at me! You're acting just like a demon in one of my nightmares. I love you! Don't do this!"

Segun shook his head and dropped the letter opener to the floor. Regina reached out to him, but he pushed her away.

"Don't come near me, Regina." He stormed past her and out of the door.

Regina ran outside to Sotonye's Avanti. Segun had disappeared.

Suddenly, the earth began to tremble. A golden light glared overhead. Regina watched the beam of light fan out over the buildings. She raced the Avanti off the grounds. In the rear-view mirror, she watched a golden dome cover the entire Q.P.S. complex.

Trying to catch her breath, Regina watched images of an oasis suddenly flash before her eyes. A pyramid glowed in the middle of her panoramic vision. Inside the massive structure, she saw two women.

"We are here and alive," one woman called out to her. "If you can hear my voice, we are prisoners in this pyramid! My name is Marion Johnson and my friend is Zinzi Lwanga!"

When the vision faded, Regina held onto the steering wheel, trying not to shake. No longer hidden in dreams, Melinda's power was now Regina's. She had to get to Nicole and Sotonye and tell them about Segun and this vision. She collected her wits and drove to the Bada estate.

Nicole and Sotonye met Regina at the door. She was trembling uncontrollably and blurted out everything before she sat down.

"My brother is having a nervous breakdown," Sotonye said. "I must find him."

"I'm not a doctor, but I think there is more to Segun's condition than that. It is like someone is controlling his mind, and there is more…"

"What is it, Gina?" Nicole asked.

Regina spoke slowly. "Nicole, it's about your mother… I believe she is still alive."

"What? What are you saying? You know my mother died in a car crash years ago."

"Did she?" Regina held her. "Have you forgotten? She burned the imprint of the key in your hand." She looked at Nicole with all the strength she could muster. "When I was fleeing from Q.P.S., I had a vision. This time I am positive it was real. Your mother is imprisoned with another woman inside a pyramid, the same pyramid I dreamed about at your home. Your mother is still alive," Gina said firmly. "She wants us to rescue her and Zinzi Lwanga."

"Are you sure? Is it possible your mind was playing tricks on you?"

"It was real, Nicole. I can describe it in detail. The power has come to me."

Sotonye opened Bertrand Lwanga's box and removed a book, drawings, and photos. "Is this the pyramid you saw?"

Regina gasped. "That's it exactly!"

"Sotonye, where did you get this book?" Nicole asked.

"All this belonged to Akim Dessalgn."

Sotonye handed Regina the book, open to a drawing of Lwanga Bertrand. "Gina, you said Zinzi Lwanga was also in the pyramid. Did she look like this man?"

"Yes, she did, but she was older."

Nicole looked at the picture and flashed back to the day in the bus when Lwanga appeared. "That's Bertrand Lwanga. I would recognize him at any age."

"I told you and Gina I wasn't too sure how much of Akim's story was true. His diary is either that of a madman or instructions for the soldiers of an apocalypse."

Regina looked at the diary in astonishment.

"This is insane. What are we to believe?"

"The truth," Nicole said, thinking for a moment. "We need to collect our facts. May I see that picture of Lwanga again?" Nicole stared at the photo. "Look for yourselves. It's uncanny how much Segun resembles Bertrand and Zinzi."

Regina and Sotonye glanced at each other and then to Nicole.

"Segun taught me a problem-solving vector. It is called 'elimination and association.' Believe me, Nicole, it works," Sotonye said, "but I have to have all the facts. You must tell me in detail every extraordinary event that has happened, starting with the day before your thirtieth birthday. Gina, if she misses anything, fill it in."

As stories unfolded, Sotonye wrote down every detail and the initials of every person mentioned. Sotonye was a taskmaster. Hours passed. He drew circles around each person and event and finally drew lines from one circle to others. He added Nafisa, Segun, and himself. Then he wrote down everything he had heard and read about Bertrand Lwanga.

Nicole finally looked at the circle-and-line diagrams on his paper. Emotions had run high and tempers were on edge. All were drained. She asked with hope, "Did you come up with anything, Sotonye?"

"Let's see. I'm going to walk backwards through this. Then I'll come forward. To begin, I can tell you Bertrand Lwanga is not Segun's or Nicole's father. According to Akim, Lwanga went to save his daughter, Zinzi. Gina saw the pictures of the battle between Blue and Lwanga in her dream. We know Lwanga lost the battle because in Gina's visions his daughter, Zinzi, was still imprisoned in the pyramid with Nicole's mother. According to Akim, Bertrand Lwanga was an exceptional person.

"From the pictures, we have seen the great likeness Segun shares with Lwanga. There a possibility Segun is Lwanga's grandson. But if Lwanga didn't survive the battle, there is no way he could be Nicole's father. I believe Bertrand Lwanga's daughter, Zinzi, is Segun's real mother. I don't know if what I am saying is the absolute truth. I'm just following the evidence and chain of events.

"A question. My mother went from rags to riches overnight. Moreover, she could read, write, and speak several languages, along with being a gifted artist with a head for business. What is the average literacy for a person with my mother's background? There is only one constant in my mother's life. That quilt. Everyone who comes in contact with it learns something. I don't know how, but it has powers. Nicole and I have been witness to some. Since there was no wealthy Colonel Bada, I think that my mother received money from the same person who gave her the sword medallion. I think it was Joseph Johnson."

"Where would my father get that kind of money?" Nicole asked.

"From your mother, when she sold the diamond. Alice Plunkett, from the bank, told you that your mother was nervous when she came for the safety deposit box. That meant there was some kind of emergency. Your mother needed a lot of money quickly—to finance Joseph Johnson's trip to Africa to rescue you. In Africa, Joseph and my mother connected.

"Nicole, in your birthday dream, Blue disguised himself as Lwanga. When he became angry, he called your father a Son of Slaves—SOS. In your second dream, you saw SOS branded on your father's back. Nicole, did you ever see your father without a shirt or tee shirt?"

"I don't think so."

"I think he really had the SOS branded on his back and kept it hidden from you. He and Blue must have fought. My mother used the powers of the quilt to help cure him. That's how I was conceived," Sotonye said bluntly. "I don't know how many times Joseph Johnson fought Blue, but with Nafisa's help, he won.

"Nicole, in your dream, Blue was repelled by the sword medallion. That is why Joseph gave Nafisa the medallion, to keep Blue away. Joseph returned home, knowing Ade had another medallion. Both Nafisa and Joseph felt safe, maybe because of the medallions and maybe because Joseph fought Blue with Nafisa's help and kept Blue from using his full strength for thirty years. Whatever it was, the Johnson family lived a happy and prosperous life, and so did the Bada family for years.

"Joseph might have traveled to Africa to fight Blue, but he was also trying to find someone. Marion stayed in Washington, DC. Where was their newborn daughter, Nicole? Nicole, your father was your guardian angel. He must have gone to Africa to rescue you. Joseph and Nafisa did rescue you and another child. The child Nafisa raised as her own son. Segun."

"And I learned that the Bovines were always there to protect The Freedom Code," Regina said. "One of the Ancient Oracles, twin sisters of my great-great-great-grandmother, descendants of one of the Elders who formed The Freedom Code, was sold by Blue into slavery and brought the Horus Crystal to the United States. She knew that Horus would protect the future of our family and our people.

"Amazingly, generations later, Ade, Melinda, and Lula, descendants of the Twin Oracles, protected the child, Marion. Ade carried the medallions and the diamonds from Africa. Melinda and Ade became partners. That's how Melinda's business came about during the Depression. Afterwards, Melinda, Lula, and Ade, the three wise women, took the baby, Marion, to Lulu's friends Jesse and Bernie to keep her safe from Blue. It seems that Lula was Marion's–godmother and my grandmother. That would mean she was also your mother's godmother and Protector, Nicole.

"Ade gave the shield medallion to Melinda and the sword medallion to baby Marion. She also left Marion's diamonds with Jesse and Bernice," Regina concluded.

Sotonye looked at them thoughtfully. "And Baba knew your grandparents. Before the fire, they all lived in the Village of No Life. Baba gave you his drum, your inheritance from your ancestors."

Sotonye stared at Gina. "It is time, my sister. It is time."

Nicole had never seen Regina so distraught. Regina paced, her body literally tilting forward, responding to the pressure she felt. Nicole stopped her midstride and placed a hand on her shoulder.

"It's okay, Gina. I already know that Segun and I could be the spawn of Blue." Nicole pulled them both to her. "Can you ever forgive me? I robbed you both of your real father."

Regina looked at Nicole very seriously. "You robbed me of nothing. Our destinies were written long before we were born. I'm so happy you figured this out. I didn't know how to tell you. It doesn't change our course. We are supposed to be together. I know that in my heart, Nicole!"

"I think you know I feel the same," Sotonye said, kissing Nicole.

"Did we tell you that Segun met your father, Sotonye?"

"No."

They told Sotonye about the meeting and Segun's favorite quote.

"You're right, Regina. Our destinies were written long ago. We'd better figure out what it all means, and quickly. Let's take another look at this diagram, because it's clear that Blue has the power to get into minds.

"A healthy Nafisa went into a coma not long after she gave up the medallion. Nicole's mother appeared to Nicole. Blue got into Nicole's mind. From Regina's description, he's gotten into Segun's mind. But Nicole and Segun are human and don't show any of Blue's traits. I need to study this diagram more."

"We don't have the traits right now," Nicole said thoughtfully. "In the diary, it is written that there is a little more than three decades left to resolve The Freedom Code. *Free Restraints, Eliminate. End Domination of (the) Master.* Segun's thirty-first birthday is March Fourth. That means we have slightly more than three weeks before…"

"Nicole, despite the powers Blue wanted you to develop, you fought against him, without even realizing it. You love too deeply and care too much for humanity to submit to Blue. You already chose in your dream, remember? You rejected your father and embraced The Freedom Code," Sotonye said.

Nicole stopped to think. Suddenly her face lit up. "I did! But is that enough?"

Regina and Sotonye put their arms around Nicole. "It is!"

She looked at them thoughtfully before she spoke. "Thinking of myself as Blue's daughter—"

Regina interrupted. "Think of my momma as the daughter of a rapist. Your parents don't necessarily make you who you are. You overcame Blue years ago, Nicole. Never doubt it. Your real parents were Joseph and Marion and they loved you, and I love you, my sister."

The two women embraced.

"Thank you, Gina," Nicole said. Then she looked at Sotonye. "As you reminded me, the quilt said the choice was Segun's and mine. I made my choice. Has Segun made his?"

"Oh my God!" Regina blurted out. "I forgot. The morning after we all went out, Segun's back was aching. I rubbed it. He had two small lumps. I felt them again at Nicole's house. They had grown larger."

Sotonye hurried for the door. "We have to find him."

Chapter 50

Sotonye, Nicole, and Regina arrived at Q.P.S. knowing the key to Segun's whereabouts was probably inside his office.

"Unfortunately, this part of the complex is locked. Mr. Bada is the only one with the code combination."

Q.P.S.'s remaining management team was working at the annex to the main building, but when they heard Sotonye, Nicole, and Regina were at the complex, they rushed over. Everyone crowded into the main lobby conference room.

"I assure you," Sotonye said, surrounded by the eager faces, "if all contracts are fulfilled before Segun's return, all plant operations will be put on hiatus, but no employees will lose pay. We will give you further updates in a few weeks."

The telephone rang just as the meeting was ending.

"Mr. Bada," the security guard said, "there's a call coming in for Nicole Johnson and Regina Bovine."

Sotonye thanked the Q.P.S. staff for their time.

Once everyone had cleared out of the conference room, Sotonye protectively picked up the telephone. "Hello. May I help you?"

"This is Ray Oliver from Chicago. I am calling for Nicole or Regina."

Sotonye signaled for Nicole and Regina to both get on the line. "It's Ray Oliver."

Nicole took his phone, and Regina picked up an extension. "Hi, Ray," they chimed.

"I only have a few minutes, but I wanted to call you. I am under federal protection. I've agreed to be a key witness and testify against Futrob for the Feds. Please read tomorrow's headlines. Segun was set up. He will be vindicated."

"Ray," Nicole said, "this call means a lot."

"Let Segun know I would have told him, but I didn't know until after the fact. I've got to go."

Once Sotonye had heard about Futrob and the setup, he was fighting angry and wanted to get the news to Segun.

"This is great news. Now we just need to find Segun. Unfortunately, only two people know how to access the entrance through the computer. One of those people is dead and the other has disappeared," Sotonye said.

"Segun told me three people knew the code. I assumed the other was you, Sotonye," Regina said.

"I've never known the code."

"Gina, you're the third person. Segun gave you the code when he showed you how to access the birds. It was his way of saying *I trust you*. Do you remember how you got into the computer?" Nicole asked.

"I think I do, but we don't have the laptop."

"Isaac's wife has his laptop. I'll call her," Sotonye said.

Twenty minutes later, Sotonye's Avanti pulled up in front of Isaac's house. Mrs. Embel stood in front waiting for them.

The grieving widow gave Sotonye the computer. "Don't let anything happen to Segun," she said bravely.

Sotonye embraced her. "I'll bring him home, Mrs. Embel."

Sotonye and Regina drove back to the Q.P.S. complex. Sotonye opened the laptop and followed Regina's instructions, but the shield remained.

"What am I doing wrong?" Regina said.

Nicole looked at the golden dome. She noticed something she hadn't seen when they drove up. There was a flock of birds inside the dome trying to escape. Nicole asked, "Did anyone see those birds before?"

Regina quickly followed Nicole's gaze. It was the flock of terns from Nicole's home. "The computer is working, I've accessed the birds."

"There is a locked file with 'Horace' on it," Sotonye said. "Horace is an ancient god who took the form of a bird. We have to change 'Horace' to the right code word for this project. What did Segun say to you again?"

"Horace—three—Regina—Bovine—of sky and water—of water and sky."

"If he's my brother, he used your name, Regina, just like I would have used Sotonye's," Nicole exclaimed.

Sotonye keyed in "Regina," and the golden dome evanesced. They all rushed into the complex and up to Segun's office. His desk was covered with notes and drawings. On a sketch of a volcano was written, "My Father's Prison." On a notepad, three degrees south and thirty-seven degrees east was written over and over. Sotonye pulled the world atlas from Segun's bookshelf. He checked the longitude and latitude.

"Segun is on his way to Kilimanjaro. Nicole, those were the snowcapped mountains in your dream. Somehow, Joseph and Nafisa must have imprisoned Blue there, and Segun has gone to rescue him. I have to stop Segun. It's a two-week climb to the volcano. I must leave at once."

"Sotonye, have you ever climbed before?" Nicole asked.

"Many times, but never Kilimanjaro."

"We will go with you," Nicole said.

"No, you would only slow me down. I must go alone. I will leave tomorrow."

They left the complex and returned to the Bada estate.

That night, Regina made flight reservations for Sotonye. Nicole helped him pack his climbing gear. Sotonye sensed Nicole's fear.

"It will almost be Segun's birthday by the time I catch up with him. He already has a two-day lead, and he always was a better climber than I."

"I know you will find him. I am just worried about what will happen when you do."

"I've thought of that, Nicole. If the roles were reversed, he would come for me without hesitation. Segun would give his life for those he loves. If I must, I will give mine for his. If I don't do this, you will be lost, too."

***

Nicole kissed and held onto Sotonye tightly before he boarded the jet. Then Regina lifted the shield medallion over her head and placed it around Sotonye's neck.

"Wear the sword and the shield, Sotonye. Save our Segun."

"I promise you I will, my sister." With those words, he kissed Nicole one last time and boarded the jet.

***

Nicole and Regina drove to the Bada estate. They picked up their luggage, Bertrand Lwanga's box, and the papers from Segun's desk. They drove to their hotel to study in the office space they had created in their suites. The more they studied, the more concerned they became for Sotonye.

Nicole was restless. "He can't do this alone, Regina. We shouldn't have let him go. We have to find the pyramid where Segun's mother and my mother are inside. The mothers will know the answers. If only Nafisa could talk to us! Regina, let's call your mother. She might know what happened before we were born."

Emma was relieved to hear from them. Regina and Nicole told her how Sotonye had pieced all the facts together, including that they were not blood sisters but sisters of the heart, and that Nicole had made her choice.

"I am overwhelmed by your journey," Emma said sincerely, "and I love you, Nicole, as if you were my own." She paused for a moment to collect her thoughts. "Before Melinda passed, she told me about The Freedom Code," Emma said. "Blue wants to place our people back in chains. If Blue is still alive, Sotonye faces great danger. If Segun has made the transition, he won't even recognize Sotonye. Together, Segun and Blue will attack him."

Nicole began to think. "Joseph is dead, and Sotonye's mother is in a coma at Mayo. If my mother and Segun's are alive, they might know how to prevent this tragedy. They know Blue better than anyone. We don't have much time. Momma Emma. Can you visit Nafisa at the Mayo Clinic on your way here? Please. She must help us!"

"Momma," Regina told her, "Big El said we could use his plane any time. Ask him to help! Get here as quickly as you can!"

"And Momma Emma, my spare key is still on your ring, isn't it?" Nicole asked.

"Yes."

Nicole told Emma where to find the diamonds in the basement. "Bring them with you, Momma Emma."

379

Regina took the receiver from Nicole. "And Momma, bring the Horus Crystal. It's in Nicole's entry. When you see Nafisa, place her hands on it with your own. Please, Momma, just do what I say!" Regina explained the whole procedure, starting with placing Horus on the magical triangle that Nicole had found and that had sewn itself back into the quilt.

***

Big El was back in the States for a week before heading to Asia. Once he heard about Emma's emergency, he told her his jet would arrive in New Orleans within the hour. A limo would pick her up. She only needed to instruct the pilot where she wanted to go.

"If I could break my engagements, I would, Emma. "When I return, you and I will never be apart again."

This part of Emma's life was perfect. "I love you, El, forever."

***

El's limo arrived on Basin Street at 5:00 p.m. By 6:00, Emma was in the air on her way to Chicago. Before they landed, the pilot phoned ahead for a limo. Emma was unlocking the door to Nicole's house by 9:30. She collected the Horus Crystal Ball and the diamonds and returned to the airport, where the pilot had refueled and had the plane ready for takeoff.

"Where to, ma'am?" the pilot asked.

"Rochester, Minnesota. The Mayo Clinic."

Again the pilot radioed ahead for Emma's transportation. Emma used the cellular phone to call the hospital to inform the staff that she was flying in to visit Mrs. Bada per her son Dr. Sotonye Bada's wishes. Her time was limited, for she was flying to Botswana to meet Sotonye Bada. She hoped for quick access to Nafisa's records and a private visit.

True to their word, upon Emma's arrival, the nurses were expecting her and immediately showed her to Nafisa's room. Emma had the Horus Crystal in her bag. She quietly locked Nafisa's door for privacy.

"Nafisa," she said, standing beside the bed. "Our children are in danger. They need us. I am the mother of Joseph's daughter, Regina. I know you are the mother of his son, Sotonye. We must break the spell Blue has cast on you."

Emma was drawn to Nafisa's quilt, remembering Regina's instructions. She placed the Horus Crystal directly over the triangle. Climbing onto the bed, Emma knelt facing Nafisa, straddling her body. She placed Nafisa's hands on the Horus Crystal and placed her own on Nafisa's.

"Nafisa, your hands are on the Horus Crystal Ball. Concentrate on my words.

"Not Negroid, not Mongoloid, not Caucasoid.
It is Blue that must be destroyed."

Words began to form in the Horus Crystal. Emma read the message to Nafisa.

"One truth remains constant through all time. There
is no love greater than a mother's for her child.
Awaken now, sweet Nafisa. It is time to save your children."

In the next instant, the ball was clear. Nafisa's eyes remained closed. Emma bowed her head in frustration.

"Thank you, mother of Joseph's daughter."

Emma raised her head and looked into the wide-eyed, smiling face of Nafisa Bada.

Emma immediately got off the bed and stood beside Nafisa. "You're welcome! How are you feeling?"

"I know I am in a hospital. I know I've heard my son talking to me for months. I have even heard Nicole's voice. I so much wanted to speak! I could have helped them." She sat up, her eyes filled with tears.

Emma handed Nafisa a tissue. "You are at the Mayo Clinic in Rochester, Minnesota. Sotonye brought you here almost a year ago. You weren't in a coma, it was Blue."

"I knew he would come after me. And you saved me, mother of Joseph's daughter. May I ask your name?"

"I am Emma Bovine."

"Thank you again, Emma Bovine. You are correct. If a year has nearly passed, we have much to do and very little time to do it. Do you know my sons?"

"Yes, I have met both of them. They are wonderful men. You should be very proud."

"I am proud. I was blessed with two wonderful children."

"I believe my daughter Regina and your son Segun are in love."

Nafisa stared at Emma. "Segun has found love. The gods are good. I always knew Sotonye would find love. I thought I would be the only love Segun would hold for a woman. He has always guarded his heart."

"So has my Gina."

"Sotonye brought Nicole, the woman he loves here. She spoke to me. And the moment she touched my hand, I knew she was the infant girl Joseph had come to rescue. The vibration in a person's touch remains the same through life. A touch communicates what words cannot. Just as your touch freed me from my spell, it was your unselfish love for my children that gave me the strength to fight the demon again."

Nafisa sat up and took Emma's hand and placed it on her cheek. "I knew the courageous love of your daughter's father. Now I know the love in her mother. Your Regina must be a magnificent child."

"That she is. That she is."

Nafisa asked Emma to help her to her feet. They walked around the Mayo Clinic room for Nafisa to regain her bearings, but it didn't take long.

"How is it that I feel as if I have awakened from a wonderful sleep instead of Blue's exiled void? Emma, I commend you and the Horus Crystal."

"I'm not sure whether its magic that helped you walk or simply your mother's will. Either way, I am grateful. We have got to sneak you out of here quickly!"

Nafisa reached for Emma's hand. "One moment. As you have seen, my quilt has magical powers. I learned of you through it. For years I have waited to meet you. Not I as Sotonye's mother, not you as Regina's mother, but the two of us as cousins—direct descendants of the Ancient Oracles and now the Mothers of the Blessed Children. It is so nice to meet you at last."

Nafisa took Emma in her arms and the women held onto each other.

"Thank you for taking that moment," Nafisa said.

"No, thank you, Nafisa."

Emma had brought an extra set of clothes in the same bag she used to carry the Horus Crystal. Nafisa had never dealt with this type of winter weather. Emma helped her into a winter coat and hat. She put the folded quilt under her arm. Emma checked outside of the room to see if anyone was in the hallway. It was very late, and the smaller night crew was on duty. Emma and Nafisa made it to the elevator undetected. In a few minutes, they were out of the door and into the limo on their way to the airport.

Nafisa and Emma spent the time on the flight learning as much as they could about each other. Nafisa told Emma about Blue. Emma told Nafisa how the children had come together and what had caused Segun to disappear. Emma also described Regina's vision of the pyramid where Marion and Zinzi were imprisoned. Nafisa confirmed the validity of Regina's vision. Nafisa told Emma that Blue could not take the lives of the mothers of his children.

The mothers decided to call Regina and Nicole on the plane. "Girls," Emma said in a clear voice, "I want to introduce you to Nafisa Bada, Sotonye's and Segun's mother."

Regina and Nicole high-fived. Emma and Nafisa told them everything they had discussed.

"Nafisa, you are the only person on Earth who can speak Blue's language, aren't you?" Nicole asked.

"Yes, Nicole, you are right, although it could become your second language, if you chose not to live for humanity," Nafisa said bluntly.

"I know," Nicole said quietly, "but I have already chosen." She paused again, then continued. "And you are the only person who can call upon this pyramid. You are also the only person who knows exactly what Joseph did with Blue." Nicole paused and released a stressed sigh.

"Yes, I can help with all of that," Nafisa said bluntly. "Joseph climbed to the top of Uhuru Peak and threw Blue's head into Kibo, the volcano at Kilimanjaro, where he had to remain for thirty years. Blue is ready to resurface."

Emma heard gasps. "Are you all right, girls?"

383

"When Regina and I researched Botswana, I came across an article about Uhuru Peak. It is an inactive volcano with gas vapors. As a symbol of gaining their freedom in 1961, the Tanzanians named the peak Uhuru Peak. It's Swahili and means 'Freedom.'"

"And now Blue's ready to reemerge as we are about to fight for all of our freedom," Emma said.

"Yes, Momma," Regina said.

"This is the dilemma," Nafisa said. "If we save Sotonye and Segun first, Marion and Zinzi will perish. If we save the mothers first, Segun and Blue will kill Sotonye."

Nicole spoke over the phone. "We have one choice. No human life shall be sacrificed. We will save them all." She told the mothers what she and Regina had planned.

When they hung up the telephone, Nafisa smiled. "My sons are in good hands."

***

Sotonye dug his pick into the stone face of Kilimanjaro. He planted stakes to grip where there was no footing. The harsh wind gusted, sending him slipping as he inched around the narrow cliff edges.

***

Nicole was able to drive Sotonye's Avanti onto the airfield. When the stairs were rolled up to the jet and the hatch swung open, Regina and Nicole ran up the stairs to embrace Emma and Nafisa.

Nafisa hugged Nicole and Regina. Now they understood what Segun and Sotonye had told them about the spirit of joy Nafisa created. Her mere presence gave them a feeling of hope.

Nafisa looked at the girls admiringly. "Regina and Nicole, you are such beautiful young women. Nicole, did you visit me with Sotonye?"

"Yes! He and Segun have been so worried!"

"And now we're worried about them," Regina said.

"Yes, we must hurry," Nicole said. "There's a lot to do."

Emma handed the luggage to Regina and Nicole and gave instructions to the pilot to be on call early tomorrow.

***

When Nafisa got out of the Avanti in front of the Bada mansion, every one of the house staff surrounded her. Their eyes filled with joy.

"The mother has returned home!" echoed across the estate.

That evening, the four women stood around the dining room table. Nafisa had spread the quilt over the table and showed the other three the route they would travel through the desert. Emma called the pilot to arrange for a helicopter to meet them at their destination. Nafisa informed them of the possible dangers.

"The pyramid is Blue's last fortress. It's designed to repel enemies. Things that appear to be real might not be. When we reach the forest, you must follow my every command. You can only step and speak as I instruct. Nicole, you must be behind me at all times. Blue will not let anything happen to you."

That night, Nafisa provided them with desert wear. Before sunrise, they were in flight. Five hours later, they landed at twenty-three degrees north and ten degrees east, the Sahara Desert, but there was no helicopter waiting for them at the airstrip. All available helicopters had been sent to the Middle East to support the war effort. The same was true of most of the desert vehicles.

The best transportation they could find was an older model army jeep with no overhead covering. They leased the jeep at an extraordinarily inflated cost. By this time, the sun was at its highest point. Nafisa told them the heat would be too extreme for them to venture out at this time of day. They drove back to the jet and waited for the sun to lower.

***

Whenever Sotonye lost his balance, it almost seemed as if a hand would support him and push him back safely onto the thin ledges. He was filled with the fear of what was to come, but he refused to give in and let it turn him around. He would conquer the mountain, as his father had before him.

***

The mothers and daughters sat in the aircraft. Nicole was quiet. Her mind wandered back to the beginning of this epic. From a simple bus ride home seven months ago, she had traveled a global journey. All she had held to be absolutely true had either been altered or refuted. Her true father was Blue, not Joseph.

385

Nafisa sensed Nicole's discontent. "Nicole, you appear to be contemplating the Elephant's Dilemma."

"What is that?"

Nafisa put her arm around Nicole. "For centuries, the elephants traveled in herds, coexisting peacefully. They kept their young close and taught them the customs of the elephant. Then their world was invaded. The invaders put tight metal yokes around their necks and chains to their legs. Whenever the elephants tried to free themselves or walk beyond the limits of the chains, the yokes would cut off their life-sustaining air. After a time, the elephants no longer ventured out for freedom. Once the stake was removed from the ground, the elephants would only travel as far as the invisible chain would let them.

"You, my dear Nicole, have traveled beyond the boundaries of your chains. The truth has shocked you. What was true is false. Whom you have been you will never be again. And what is the question plaguing you the most? You wonder whether you are part of this herd at all?"

"You're right. How do I know when I wake up tomorrow he won't have possessed me?"

"I've already told you! By your own admission, you chose humanity," Regina said. "Besides, I know you, Nicole. I know!"

"He can try to kill my body. He can try to shut off my mind, but my spirit will prevail. It's time for me to venture out," Nicole said with conviction. "I need to find my truth and save the man I love, the brother I've just found, and the mother taken away from me before I was ready."

Nafisa, Regina, and Emma embraced her.

***

They boarded the jeep with a map from the past, water, fuel, faith, and the indestructible power of their combined spirits. The hot sun bore down upon them until it set. The night brought the blowing sands, too mighty for them to drive forward. Instead, they huddled together beneath the ancient quilt. Their bond grew closer as the quilt protected them against the desert's wrath.

In the morning, the winds subsided as the sun rose. They had passed through the night's storm unharmed, and they continued their journey. By the next day at noon, they had reached the desert's core.

386

BLUE

Nafisa placed the quilt around her shoulders and stood at the center of the golden triangle represented on the fabric. "Nicole, you should stand right behind me," she commanded. "Everyone else line up in a single file behind Nicole. From this point forward, no one should speak unless I give you permission. Do not question any path I take, even in your mind. Put your faith in me and follow my exact footsteps."

In the language of Blue, Nafisa intoned:

"Of sky and water, of water and sky
Mother of the mother of the ancient daughter
The new world order shall bring them to slaughter
Reign once more, will you
Reign once more, Blue
Come forth, house of the last
Open the door to the child of the past."

Suddenly, a beautiful tropical oasis appeared. Tiny pools of water were laden with colorful flowers. Palm trees with enormous, supple leaves shaded thick-flowing grass. A path of perfectly laid, brilliantly colored stone led directly to the open entrance of the pyramid in the center of the island. Nafisa did not step onto this path. She stepped onto the flowers floating in the pools of water. With each step, the flowers turned to circles of stone. Nicole and the women followed Nafisa's exact path.

When they had all gathered at the pyramid's doorway, Nafisa looked back over her shoulder. They all repeated her motion. When they looked back, they saw a split in the earth where the stone path had been. The path was now a bottomless ravine.

Nafisa did not try to enter the pyramid. Once again, she spoke in the language of Blue. *"I know my house. This is not it. Let my house reveal itself to me."*

The pyramid disappeared, and Nafisa found herself standing on the bank of a wide, raging river. Its waters were rushing, rough, deep, and impossible to swim. She saw the real pyramid across the raging water. Nafisa was baffled. She searched her mind. She knew not of this river. She turned her head. Nicole and the women were gone. She stood alone.

Chapter 51

A voice bellowed out over the land. "This time you will drown in the river. Plague me no more. Meet your doom!"

The earth began to quake. Nafisa felt the icy water rushing over her feet. Within seconds, the river had risen to her waist. The undertow of the blue water surged to yank her beneath. Her body weakened and she started to succumb, but in a moment of supreme resolve, Nafisa raised her hands to the sky.

"You are no greater than I!"

She tore the quilt from her shoulders and cast it into the furious river. The water stilled instantly. The floating quilt transformed itself into a bridge, binding the two sides of the river. Nafisa looked over her shoulder. Nicole, Emma, and Regina stood behind her. Nafisa led the way across the bridge to the pyramid.

Outside the pyramid, Nafisa placed her hands on the wall. "This is Blue's lair. You all may speak and walk freely now." Nafisa paused, settling her thoughts. "I knew not of the river we had to cross."

"What river?" they all asked.

Nafisa spun around. Sand separated the oasis and the pyramid. There was no river.

It was an illusion, Nafisa said to herself. *Blue tried to make me drown in my own fear. I had to face my own past.*

Nicole hugged Nafisa. "You did well, but where is your quilt?"

"I had to release my blanket of security in order to move forward. I have covered myself with it all of my life. Now I must feel secure within myself to face the future." She held onto Nicole and told the others to move back. "You must call upon the massive stone to clear the entrance. Say, 'In the name of my ancestors, open and allow my entrance.'"

Nafisa stepped back and Nicole stepped forward.

"In the name of my ancestors,
open and allow my entrance."

The stone started to roll to the side with a loud rumble. When it had moved enough for a body to pass through, Nicole rushed into the pyramid. Marion and Zinzi stood a few feet from the entrance. At first sight of Nicole, Marion clutched her heart.

"Am I dreaming? Is that you, Nicole?"

"Yes, Momma, it's me!" Nicole exclaimed, wrapping her arms around her mother. "It's me. You're free now. You are coming with us."

"Talk later," Nafisa said behind them. "We must leave at once."

The walls of the pyramid began to shake and crack.

"Follow me, everyone!" Nafisa said as she rushed to the doorway.

Pieces of stones shattered on the floor. Zinzi stood frozen.

"You must come with us, Zinzi! Your father wanted you to be free," Marion said, grabbing Zinzi's hand.

Shattered stone hit the walls and floor, ricocheting around their feet. Nicole hurriedly led her mother and Zinzi out of the pyramid as the walls began to crumble and cave in.

"Run! It's going to sink!" Nafisa yelled.

Marion stumbled out into the open air. Nicole and Zinzi put their arms around her waist and carried her forward, afraid to look back toward the terrible sounds of the crumbling ancient structure.

Once all were in the jeep, they looked back. The pyramid was leveled. The last stone rolled down and the desert floor parted. The remains of the pyramid sank into an abyss. The pyramid's grave was covered in a sea of sand.

"We are finally free," Marion said. "Zinzi and I thank you. Oh, thank you!"

Tears flowed from Marion's eyes. Nicole held her mother closely.

"Momma, I want you to meet—"

Marion pulled Nafisa and Emma into her embrace. "I know who you two are. Joseph and I had no secrets."

"How did you know it was them, Momma?"

"This is not the first time these two wonderful women have saved my life. I may have never seen them before this day, but I have thanked them in my heart for so many years for how they protected you."

"Marion, I want you to meet my daughter, Regina," Emma said.

Marion turned around and gently brushed Regina's cheek. "This I did not know." She looked back over her shoulder at Emma.

"Neither did he," Emma replied.

"She is my best friend," Nicole exclaimed. "I have so much to tell you, Momma!"

Marion held her daughter as she again looked at Regina. "Your father would have been so proud of you. You have his eyes. I can see his face so clearly in yours."

Regina was speechless. Emma held her close.

"Momma," Nicole said, "Daddy Joseph also had a son. Nafisa is his mother."

Marion paused, then nobly kissed her daughter. "I am looking forward to meeting him," she said without missing a beat. She reached out for Zinzi's hand. "Everyone, this is Zinzi. She is Segun's mother and—"

"Her father was Bertrand Lwanga," Regina said.

Marion and Zinzi were amazed. Zinzi did not speak, but a faint smile came to her lips and then she looked around her. The smile turned to awe.

The women watched her spin around, looking at everything in sight. What was this world she had walked out into, painted in blue skies and sands of gold? The women brushed away their tears of empathy and understanding, allowing her a few minutes to enjoy that which she had never seen.

"We have much to talk about, but now we must go," Nicole said.

Zinzi followed them into the vehicle. "What is this called?"

"It's a jeep," Marion explained. "It will carry us across the sands."

Marion knew if she was accepting of this strange vehicle, then Zinzi would be, too.

Regina got behind the wheel, put the key in the ignition and turned it. There was no sound from the motor. It had frozen.

Zinzi pointed to the jeep. "This brought you here?"

"Yes, it did," Emma answered.

Zinzi looked at Marion. "My—my father, Ber—trand... came here," she said, straining to speak.

Marion had seen the articulate Zinzi stammer before, whenever her father's name had been mentioned. Marion had to calm her down before Zinzi had a panic attack.

"It's all right, Zinzi," Marion said.

Frustrated, Zinzi spoke to Nicole. "Bertrand came here."

At first, Nicole just stared at Zinzi, a slight frown creasing her forehead. Then suddenly the frown vanished and she sprang to her feet. "Just as we drove here, so did Bertrand. But he did not leave. Where is the car Eleni built? Akim's journal said it was run by solar power! Nafisa, how often is this part of the desert traveled?"

"No one may have passed through here for many decades."

"That means Eleni's car may be hidden close by. He must have camouflaged it," Nicole said, scanning the desert. "If we were traveling to Kenya, in which direction would we go?"

Nafisa pointed southeast. Nicole and Regina searched for a tall sand drift or an unusual mound of sand. They found none.

"Nicole, I think our perception of this car is all wrong. We are looking for what we know as a conventional automobile. I saw something kind of odd much closer to where we were parked," Regina said.

There was a five-by-ten-foot area where the sand was slightly sunken. Regina and Nicole started digging with their hands. About a foot and a half down, they came to sand-colored canvas cloth. They called out to the others. In no time, they had uncovered a rectangular canvas cover stretched across lightweight metal bars. It looked like a trampoline.

The women stood on each side of the canvas. They were surprised to see how easy it was to raise, but once it was waist high, it would move no more. Regina looked under the canvas while the others held it up.

"I don't believe this!" she called out.

The others heard locking and clamping sounds beneath the canvas.

"Gina, what are you doing?" Emma asked.

"You can let go now and see for yourselves."

The women released the canvas and bent over to see what was underneath. They had been holding the collapsible top to Eleni's desert transport. The interior was very similar to a luxury motorboat. Regina was sitting behind the steering wheel examining the controls on the panel. The key was in the ignition. She turned it and felt a vibration but heard no motor.

She put the vehicle in gear and told the group to stand back. A red arrow light began to flash, pointing to a button. Regina pushed it. The vehicle began to elevate. The car had a hydraulic lift system that allowed the wheels to retract into the hollowed bottom of the vehicle. When the wheels were retracted and the top was collapsed, the transport was less than three feet high and easy to hide.

Nicole walked to the back of the transport and examined it.

"There is a grid attached with a prism under it. This is amazing. This car is definitely solar powered, and sixty years ahead of its time. Zinzi, your mother was brilliant!"

Zinzi smiled broadly.

Nicole jumped in next to Regina. The girls took it for a test ride. The vehicle traversed the desert like a speedboat on a calm lake. The prism magnified solar power and created five times the acceleration capacity of an average solar car. The tank-like treads on the tires minimized lag and friction.

They all boarded the transport. There was a briefcase on the floor, leaning against the rear seat. Marion picked it up. When Zinzi sat next to her, she placed it on her lap.

"This is yours, dear Zinzi. It must have belonged to your father. You might want to open it before we leave."

Zinzi handed the case back to Marion. "I cannot do this. Please open it, Marion. I don't need to look. Just tell me what you see."

Marion skimmed through files of legal documents. "Zinzi, you are an extremely wealthy woman."

Marion handed Zinzi the file, which held a copy of the deed to a diamond mine in Botswana. As Zinzi took it, the papers slipped out.

There were two photographs attached to the inside of the rear cover. The first was of Eleni and Bertrand standing in front of St. George's Cathedral on their wedding day. The second showed the pregnant Eleni leaning back into her loving husband's embrace. Zinzi stared at the pictures in amazement.

All at once, she raised her head and opened her mouth. Marion could see the movements of her vocal cords, but heard no sound. Then a loud, resonant, high-pitched scream of anguish filled the air.

They all wanted to comfort her, but Zinzi leaped from the auto onto the desert sand with the pictures still in her hand. Nicole and Regina started to follow her, but Marion stopped them. She alone knew how to ease Zinzi's pain.

Again, Zinzi stared at the photos. She put her arms on top of her head and started turning in circles, then fell to her knees. Only then did Marion rush to her sweet Zinzi, who cried like a wounded child in her arms.

Zinzi's whole life, she had been tormented. Often, Blue had donned her father's skin, pretending to be him to gain her confidence long enough to confuse, torture, and berate her. But just as her father's flesh aged but did not disintegrate, neither did his spirit. Often, when Blue slept, Lwanga's flesh would engulf Blue's body. Although he could not speak, he would go to Zinzi, lift her onto his lap, and comfort her. Before he would leave her, he'd point to himself, clutch his heart and point to her. Her father loved her and she loved him.

"My father was Bertrand Lwanga. I loved him. He loved me. He loved me!" She shook her fists. "My father was Bertrand Lwanga. I loved him and he loved me. The demon was not Bertrand Lwanga, my father was, and my father was good!"

Nafisa and Marion now stood on either side of Zinzi. "We have all been enslaved by him," Marion said.

"It is time to free our children," Nafisa added, "and fulfill the prophecies of the Twin Oracles."

***

"You're already back," the pilot said in surprise.

The women had driven up to the airfield in Elena's automobile.

"This vehicle got us here in half the time," Regina said.

"Where did you get it?" the pilot asked, looking at it in amazement.

"Long story," Regina said as all the women smiled. "Can it be transported in the plane?"

"I've carried sound equipment that was larger and heavier."

He lowered the cargo plank, collapsed the top, and pushed the car on board with ease.

As the jet soared south to the peaks of Kilimanjaro, the anticipation of where they were going and whom they would face was foremost in all of their minds. Time grew short. The first of March had arrived. Blue had cast a shadow over all of their lives. Emma, Zinzi, Marion, and Nafisa would all rather face the most violent deaths than allow this cursed demon to plague another generation.

***

Zinzi was now free in a world she did not know. The power of her father's spirit and memory inspired her to think back over the years of teaching at her father's hand. Her knowledge helped to lead them all safely from the desert's unyielding clutches. Zinzi had faced Blue more than any other human. She knew deep in her bones why Blue had to be destroyed, and with every step out of the desert, she founded renewed determination and courage.

***

Marion closed her eyes and pretended to sleep. She was in excruciating pain. Only Zinzi knew how she was suffering. The others thought Zinzi needed the security of being near Marion. Quite the opposite was true.

Blue had been infuriated that she had forced him to reveal his true nature by altering the illusion he designed for Nicole's thirtieth birthday. When Blue transported Marion back to the pyramid, he had tortured her near to death, stopping only when she would have died.

Marion had seen Nicole's rage in the gold ballroom on her thirtieth birthday when Blue was disguised as Bertrand Lwanga and had threatened her. Nicole must not become one with her father to protect her mother.

***

No one could sleep. Everyone suddenly turned to the other. They all wanted to talk.

"We only have two days to reach them. How will we do it?" Regina asked. "I have Segun's computer. Maybe it will have some answers."

Regina removed the Horus Crystal from the overhead rack. "I don't know if that computer can help. But if there is a chance for an answer, I'm holding it now."

The women sat in a circle and placed Horus in the center. They all laid their hands on the crystal, and its golden light shone. A message quickly formed:

Friends will help. The Blessed Child is about to join the son of Blue. Hurry on. Hurry on.

In the next instant, the words disappeared, as did the light. They all stared at each other. Calling on the ball again did not help. There was no light or message.

"My sons are known throughout the Motherland. They have made many friends," Nafisa said.

"We must have faith. Rest for tomorrow," Nicole said.

***

Within an hour, all were sleeping except for Regina. She stared out the window, thinking about Segun and their time together. She rested her right hand on Segun's laptop computer as if she were touching him, and her left arm cradled the Horus Crystal. When she turned her head, her eyes fell on Nicole. Segun and Nicole were sister and brother! She loved them so. She would not rest until they were both safe.

***

The next morning, after landing, the pilot successfully procured a helicopter while Nicole and Regina purchased climbing gear. By noon, the helicopter was loaded with their luggage, the priceless pouch of diamonds, and the Horus Crystal.

They took off at 1:00 p.m. The wind started to pick up and made it difficult to maneuver the helicopter. The pilot was forced to set down on a plateau below their destination.

"It's dangerous. You ladies shouldn't do this!"

"We cannot wait another day. Leave us here. We must prepare to climb!" Nicole called out to the pilot.

Nicole and Regina unpacked the gear and a huge basket from the chopper.

"You're making a mistake!" the pilot yelled as everyone disembarked. "I don't feel right about this!"

"Pick us up tomorrow!" Regina yelled. "We'll be fine. I promise you!"

They gave him a thumbs up. Reluctantly, he took off.

"It will take us more than a day to make it to the ridge above us," Emma said.

"I've called for friends," Regina said. "They will come. Have faith."

Chapter 52

It was nearly 11:00 p.m. when Sotonye made it to the top of the Kibo Crater. He forged forward and saw a silhouette at the summit of the volcano.

"Segun, Segun, is that you?"

"It is I, Sotonye. I have been waiting for you."

Sotonye was overjoyed by the sound of his brother's voice. He scaled the volcano's wall in seconds and stood before Segun. He was not prepared for what his eyes beheld.

Segun stood shirtless in the icy cold winds. His skin was blotched with huge patches of pale blue. His face and body were equally brown and blue. His eyes were cruel. Miniature wings sprouted from his back, uneven and malformed.

"Son of Slaves, you are out of your chains." Segun balled his fist and hit Sotonye with a pulverizing blow. The force sent Sotonye tumbling down the hill. When Sotonye looked up, Segun was standing over him.

"Fight, you worthless sub-creature!" Segun demanded.

"You're my brother. I came to save you from Blue! He's captured your mind."

"Blue is my father. You are not my brother. I know who I am, and I will enslave you as you should be!"

Segun grabbed him by the throat, lifted Sotonye over his head, and threw him down to the edge of the precipice, where he crashed into a head of ice.

Sotonye felt the protection of the sword and shield medallions and saw that Segun was amazed that he had rebounded so quickly. "Segun, please. I don't want to fight."

Segun returned to the volcano's mouth and reached into the hole. When he raised his arms from the chasm, he held a blue shield and sword in his hands. Suddenly he was again upon Sotonye, drawing back his sword to strike.

Sotonye thrust his arm over his head. The blade of Segun's sword came down and the golden shield appeared in Sotonye's hand. The shield repelled Segun's sword. Sotonye threw his other hand into the air. The golden sword appeared.

"Well, you have decided to fight. I will enjoy beating you before you are shackled."

"Segun, I would rather see us both dead than allow the demon to usurp your soul!"

Sotonye fought to disarm and protect. Segun fought to dominate and master. The swords clashed in midair. With blow after mighty blow and lunge after lunge, the Segunors fought from the edge of the plateau back up to the volcano's peak. Both of their spirits were irrepressible.

"Segun," Sotonye pleaded, "you are the best of humankind. Look into your heart!"

Segun cursed Sotonye's words. Everything Sotonye said increased his rage. Segun backed Sotonye down the side of the volcano. When Sotonye stumbled, Segun cut into his arm. Sotonye's arm went momentarily limp and he dropped his sword. Segun knocked the shield from Sotonye's other hand before kicking him hard down the hill.

A flock of terns flew above the crest of the plateau, clutching the cables of a helibasket in their claws. Regina, Nicole, Marion, Nafisa, and Zinzi stood inside. Before the basket hit the plateau, Regina jumped out and ran toward Segun, but Nicole overtook her.

"This is between Segun and me! Stay back, Regina!"

Regina rushed to Sotonye's side and dropped to her knees to aid him while Nicole ran to Segun.

"Segun! I am your sister! Don't do this!" Nicole yelled.

"You are my sister? You must stay with me."

Segun grabbed Nicole with one hand while carrying his sword and shield in his other. Nicole tried to resist.

"Let go of me!"

Nothing happened. Segun forced her effortlessly down the hill. *I've lost Blue's powers,* she thought. Still she struggled against Segun's grip as he dragged her along like a rag doll. Only when they came to a stop standing over Sotonye and Regina did Segun release her.

"They are the Children of Slaves," Segun declared, pointing at Sotonye and Regina. "They are our property! We own them!"

This time Nicole pushed Segun away before stepping right back up to him on her own terms.

"No, Segun, we don't! True slavery only exists through acceptance. The master has achieved his goal when it becomes more difficult for the slave to accept freedom than for the free man to accept slavery. You have a choice, Segun. You love me and Sotonye and Regina. Join us as the extraordinary man you are. Don't let him destroy all you are and will be!"

Regina looked up into Segun's eyes. His breathing was heavy. "You told me you would never hurt me." She rose to her feet. "I believed that then and I believe it now!"

Sotonye stood up. "I believe it as well."

"As do I," Nicole said.

Segun's eyes roamed from Regina to Nicole and then to Sotonye. His expression grew more and more bewildered.

Then, from the depths of the volcano, a voice commanded him. "Hear my voice! You are their master! Dominate them, then bring my daughter to me! *Do as I bid!*"

"Hear my voice!" another voice bellowed. "Do not harm them! You do as *I* say!"

Zinzi stepped forward. She put her hands on Segun's chest and he froze. "I am your mother. You can feel my touch in your heart. Blue took you from me so he could live. He has enslaved me all of my life. Will you obey Blue when he made your mother his slave? Will you obey Blue when he wants to destroy the people you love and all that you cherish?"

Segun felt her hands, the hands of love he had not felt for years, the hands of love he had never forgotten. Regina, Sotonye, and Nicole gathered close around him with Nafisa and Emma as he drew Zinzi close.

"Blue helped them sabotage your exhibition," Sotonye said. "You've been exonerated. It's all over the papers. He tried to kill your spirit and turn you against us and our people. He insisted on being the master. Just as your mother says, Blue wanted us to be his slaves. He killed your grandfather and imprisoned your mother. He killed Joseph, my father and Regina's father and the man who you say is your inspiration. Blue has destroyed so many of our people. People who could have made such a difference in our lives. Segun, you are my brother. Look at those who love you. You are a part of us, not him. The choice is yours. We are your choice!"

Closing his eyes, he released an anguished cry. He dropped the sword and shield and proclaimed, "I am a Blessed Child!"

In that instant, his true color returned. The wings on his back shriveled and fell to the ground. His complexion transformed from grey to a rich brown as he once again was a true son of Africa. With radiant eyes, he stared at his mother.

"I have never forgotten your touch. Thank you! Thank you!"

Segun had chosen, and with that choice, all that he had damaged healed. Sotonye's arm stopped bleeding and his wound closed. Nicole went to him.

Segun enclosed Regina in his arms.

"You'll never stop amazing me, will you, Segun?"

"Never, I promise you."

Nafisa joined them. "You had us worried for a moment, my son."

"You are awake! Mother, I was so worried! Sotonye, look! Mother is here!"

Nicole and Sotonye laughed, but Segun's eyes were now on Nicole anew.

"You are sister of my blood."

"Yes, Segun."

Segun turned her around and felt her back. "You did not succumb—you have no wings—no malice—no revenge?"

"You fought him for my freedom. I am safe. You fought for all of us!"

"Sotonye?" Segun hugged him. "I'm sorry, my brother."

They all came forward and stood together.

"The children have been freed," Segun proclaimed. "Blue shall be no more."

As the words echoed on the mountain, the earth began to tremble. They all turned to the erupting volcano to see flashes of blue light break from the volcano's mouth. Blue emerged, spreading his enormous wings, and flew into the light. Then he lowered himself to the volcano's summit, laughing as he slowly walked towards them.

"I shall reign forever. The children I have created shall be mine. The destiny for the rest of you is servitude. Bow down to me, sub-creatures."

Sotonye charged toward his shield and sword. "Segun, we will defeat him together!"

Segun picked up his sword and shield and raced to join Sotonye, who was now within grasp of his weaponry. With brutal force, Blue flapped his wings, creating a violent wind. Segun and Sotonye were knocked backwards and helplessly rolled and slid in opposite directions.

"The Horus Crystal, Nicole!" Regina yelled. They ran to their gear and pulled out the diamond pouch and the Horus Crystal Ball.

Blue stopped the motion of his wings and walked toward Sotonye's shield and sword. He bent over to pick them up. Regina collected all of her strength, ran forward, took aim, and sent the Horus Crystal catapulting at Blue's head. When he felt the blow, Blue's rage blazed. He palmed the Horus Crystal and flung it upward with all of his strength. The orb rocketed into the sky. The force was so powerful that the Horus Crystal jarred the heavens, creating a blinding bolt of lightning followed by a deafening clap of thunder.

"Nicole, Regina!" Marion screamed. "Come to me." They ran to her. "He has done it for us! Give me the blue diamond, Nicole!"

Marion held the diamond above her. A blur of golden light shot over her head and swept the diamond away. In a split second, the golden sword and shield were gone.

Everyone saw Blue's disbelief as Joseph Johnson suddenly appeared midair in front of him in a gown of black and gold, with golden wings. He held the shield in his left hand and the sword in his right. The blue diamond was again affixed to the sword's handle.

"You have been destroyed, SOS!" Blue declared. "You have lost your battle, son of slaves!"

"I bow to no man, nor do the Blessed Children. You only destroyed my earthly body. Never my spirit. Free restraints eliminate, end the domination of the master! Is that The Freedom Code you think you are destroying?"

"I am the master!"

"The ancient oracles wanted you to believe you were the master, but you never were. They hid the true history of our people in The Freedom Code, knowing if you found it, the Blessed Children would never be safe.

F   Our people were FREE, and built a great
    empire, and you didn't want us to know that
    we had once been great!

R   Our ancestors were RESPECTED until you
    destroyed their world.

E   You ENSLAVED them.

E   They struggled to regain EQUALITY

D   and although DETERMINED

O   they needed help to return ORDER

M   and MAJESTY to our mankind.

C   So Blessed CHILDREN were to be born and
    taught our essence, and your two children

O   chose not to continue the OPPRESSION
    you wielded to try to perpetuate the myth
    of degradation, inferiority, and dominance.

D   The four Blessed Children rose up to follow
    their DESTINY without your influence,

E   and they are and will continue to return the
    state of EXCELLENCE to our people and
    our world by their example.

Now you and I will decide the outcome of my children's freedom."

Blue rose to Joseph. "Your children! Nicole and Segun are *my* children!"

Joseph and Blue elevated higher into the sky. The earth shook as their swords collided. Avalanches plummeted down every mountain. The sky filled with flashes of blue and golden light. Blue's rage escalated each time his sword was deflected by Joseph's shield.

Joseph's sword cut into Blue's flesh. Blood gushed from Blue's body. His hatred couldn't even heal him.

"Gaze upon the children of the future. They'll never be Blue."

With those words, Joseph thrust his sword into Blue's heart, sliced the shield and sword from Blue's hands, and watched Blue spiral down and collapse onto the frozen tundra.

Joseph laid Blue's body on the golden shield and carried it to the volcano and spoke.

"You are the father of self-hatred, the Spirit of Slavery, the destruction of Africans and their descendants. Today you are no longer. The true Freedom Code lives, and our history shines bright as a beacon for us to return to the greatness that was ours."

Joseph dropped Blue's remains forever into the molten lava, which erupted in a blazing, thunderous explosion, illuminating the sky and deafening all on Earth. When finally the sky calmed and a brilliant light shone through, Joseph turned to his family.

Nicole sat in the snow with Marion's head in her lap. The others knelt around them. Marion had used the last of her strength.

"Oh, Momma, please don't leave me again!"

Nicole cried.

Joseph's spirit landed next to Marion. Gazing into her eyes, he held out his hand, "Arise and be healed, my beloved, it is not your time to leave this earth. You have given up too much. Spend time with your daughter. I will be waiting for you when it's your time."

Marion took her husband's hand and came to her feet. Everyone watched her realizing at last that she was free. Free to love her daughter. Free to share with her friends. Free! The pain she had suffered for years vanished. Her spirit healed. Her face took on the most beautiful hue as she smiled at her husband and placed her hands across her heart.

Joseph mirrored her gesture. Marion turned and extended her arms to Emma, Nafisa, and Zinzi. The three women stood together facing him.

"Zinzi, you have returned by your courage and bravery from the dark side into the light. You are hope, you are the best that humankind has to offer. Marion, who has my heart for eternity, Emma, who by loving me for a day brought a daughter of joy to life, and Nafisa, who by saving my life gave life to our child, *you* are the true heroines. Look at the children you have selflessly raised and given your lives to. I thank you with my deepest love and respect."

Joseph gathered Segun, Regina, Nicole, and Sotonye at the crater's rim. Their mothers stood behind them. To Regina and Sotonye, he spoke from the depth of his soul.

"I did not know you or watch you grow up into the handsome young man and beautiful young woman you are, but I am here now and my heart is yours." Joseph stared into Regina's eyes. "Regina, you are a descendant of the Elder and the Ancient Twin Oracles, and a Blessed Child. My daughter, the world needs your compassion. You are the heart of this quartet. Promise me you won't let them depart from their mission of humanity."

"I promise, Father," Regina replied with tears in her eyes.

Joseph turned to Sotonye. "My son, you are a descendant of Mpho and Aliko and the Ancient Twin Oracles, and a Blessed Child. When I look at you, I see a better man than I. You are a healer of bodies and minds. You bring balance to this family, as you will to the world. I could not ask for a finer son."

Sotonye released a profound sigh. "To see your face, to hear your words, is something I've dreamed of my entire life. Thank you, Father. I am so proud to be your son."

Joseph pulled the two into a deep embrace. "I couldn't be more proud to be your father."

After all these years, Sotonye and Regina finally felt the love and protection of their father's embrace and understood why he had not been able to share their lives. Arm in arm, they smiled at each other, feeling a sense of relief and peace.

Joseph stepped in front of Nicole and Segun and took their hands. "Segun and Nicole, you must understand your brilliance and greatness are from your human ancestors, both descendants of tribal royalty. Now there is only human within you." Joseph gazed deeply into Segun's eyes. "Segun, you have lived a thousand years since we last spoke."

Segun smiled. "It's good to see you again. You changed my life. I never had a chance to thank you."

"Descendant of your grandparents Bertrand Lwanga, Son of the Mountains, and Eleni Lwanga, Daughter of the Valleys, and son of Zinzi, you are now a Blessed Child. I am the one who should thank you. Heavy is your responsibility. Future leaders of nations and industry will use you as their model. You are free. By your example, you will teach all the significance of your freedom so they will also make it theirs. Stay strong and pure of heart and listen to the counsel of your family, especially your beloved, Nicole."

"I will. I promise you, I will," Segun answered.

Finally, Joseph turned to Nicole. Her head was bowed. Joseph lifted her chin and smiled at the daughter *chosen*. "Baby girl, why do I see tears in your eyes?"

"Oh Daddy, you gave up everything for me!"

"To the contrary, I traveled halfway around the world to find you, for you are the reason we are all here. Without you, Blue would have lived and we would have been no more. Despite your father, you always were pure of spirit, Nicole." He smiled at Marion. "You are, after all, your mother's daughter, and the granddaughter of Hatshepsut, Daughter of the Valley, and Kabaka, Son of the Mountains, and now a Blessed Child." He held her close. "I must pass my responsibilities on to you. You are the shepherd of this family. Protect and care for the future mothers, brothers, sisters, and the children, and inspire them to follow their destinies."

Joseph reached out for Segun to join them. For the first time, Nicole and Segun felt what it was like to be free from all that had encumbered their people. Together as sister and brother, they would bridge the worlds of the past with the present so all would feel as they—free to pursue their futures.

Joseph studied them all. "Daughters and sons, I love you all and I will always watch over you. You must stand together in a binding love. There will be no more crystal balls, magic shields, and swords to aid you in life's battles. No mystical quilt of knowledge will cover you. Those who have been enslaved in mind and spirit should fear no more. From this day forward, you will forge your own futures.

"Take your place in society. For centuries, your chairs at the table have been waiting for you. Raise your heads. Hold them high.

Shed the *mental* chains that have bound you. You are free! Walk free, my children, walk free!"

Joseph stepped off the precipice into the air.

As he ascended, a ray of light emanated from him to Nicole. Before he vanished, he called out, "Remember, my children, this is the beginning. The future is yours."

***

The sun's golden fringe on the horizon divided the morning sky and the billowing snow. A new day was summoned. The mothers and children prepared for their departure. They had spent hours sharing stories of their lives and rejoicing in their reunion. Before their journey, the four children stood again at the mountain's edge, their mothers nearby.

Nicole slowly turned her head from side to side, viewing her beautiful family. "Joseph sent me this message as he left.

"We are the light, but we have to continue the work to shine. Although Blue is defeated, he will never be gone. Never believe the struggle is over. We have to fight for our freedom—it is not given. Our people's destiny must be cloaked with self-love. It will defend and protect them in life's battles and keep all of us free. Are we ready?"

They all nodded.

The Day after Tomorrow begins. The Freedom Code reigns supreme.